HUNTING PREDATORS

By

Anthony Karrier

COPYRIGHT

All rights reserved. No part of this book may be reproduced or transmitted in any form or by any means, graphic, electronic, or mechanical, including photocopying, recording, typing, or by any information storage retrieval system, without the written permission of the author /publisher, except in the case of brief excerpts in critical reviews and articles.

Exclusive publication /distribution by Andrew Porter

Copyright © 2025 Andrew Porter

FIRST EDITION

The scanning, uploading and distribution of this book via the Internet or via any other means without the permission of the publisher is illegal and punishable by law.

Your support for the author's rights is appreciated.

DEDICATION

For Jimmy Cluckie.

A man who saw the fire in others long before they ever felt its warmth. When he saw it in you, there were only two choices: rise to meet it or cut ties with him— because he'd never let you snuff it out.

If death came easy, it was the only thing in his life that did.

Thank you for always believing in me.

ACKNOWLEDGEMENTS

Firstly, to the usual suspects—Marleah Stout, my incredible agent. Once again, your guidance and unwavering commitment have kept me on the right path. Thank you for always believing in me and for helping shape my career with such care.

To my most trusted beta reader, Greta Dearing. For several years now, you've been there with invaluable questions and advice, ensuring my ideas resonate with readers. Your input has been a guiding light in making my stories clearer and more engaging.

To the most unlikely ally, Kara McCaughen. Once again, you've amazed me with your ability to take a lump of senseless coal and polish it into a diamond. I am endlessly grateful for the time, energy, and brilliance you've invested in bringing my characters and stories to life.

To my wife, Mitch—since day one, you've been my biggest supporter. Your love, encouragement, and belief in me have carried me through the toughest moments. I wouldn't be here without you.

HUNTING PREDATORS

To my friend and fellow author, Ross Davies—thank you so much for helping me navigate this confusing world. Your insights and support mean the world to me.

To Ralph MacIsaac—a brother Ironworker in every positive sense of the word. Your opinions, advice, and guidance—not just on both novels but in life—are appreciated more than you know. Thank you for always being there and for helping me stay grounded.

And finally, to R. Bryam Rumble (yes, that's his real name), my former Brazilian jiu-jitsu professor. Thank you for your time, advice, and for helping me articulate grappling in a way that even those without experience can grasp. You are a man I hold in the highest regard, and I deeply appreciate every minute you've devoted to making this story better.

To all of you, thank you for helping me breathe life into these characters and stories. I couldn't have done it without you.

-AK

Chapter 1

Friday May 12th, 2023. 7:00 am.

A chilly grey sky looming overhead showed the promise of incoming rain that would last throughout the day. The air was damp and cold as a group of west-coast Indigenous people began setting up a small blockade along

Highway 19 on Vancouver Island. The protest was being set up in response to another oil company's attempt to run a pipeline to the coast of the island through the small native community of Lantzville. The protestors had set up early. Most people in the area were aware of the plan to block the highway. The small community had posted flyers, consulted with the local RCMP detachment, and had even run a radio ad to give commuters proper warning.

The group was mostly made up of elders, a few young mothers, and a handful of men ranging from their early twenties to late sixties. A local coffee chain had supplied the group with coffee and muffins. The protestors had planned a peaceful action, more an information session, and invited residents of other small local communities to come and speak openly and honestly about their concerns. This was one of several protests about oil companies running pipelines through indigenous territories that had happened in recent years.

Jacob Woods, a young resident of Lantzville, was standing near the highway when he saw a large black 1980s Ford pickup truck in the distance, rumbling down the road towards them.

HUNTING PREDATORS

This isn't good, he thought to himself. The truck was big and loud, with belching black smoke pluming out of the exhaust. As the truck neared, Jacob could hear loud music blaring. He saw two people in the cab of the truck and two more standing in the back holding onto the white rollbar with added aftermarket halogen lights. The truck blew through the blockade, the driver stomping on the gas and releasing a large cloud of black smoke into the group as he did "rolling coal." The two in the back were hooting and hollering as they threw various pieces of trash at the protestors.

Jacob watched as the truck drove on about fifty yards and came to a stop. It turned around and aimed itself directly at the folding table with the coffee and muffins on top. The driver stomped on the gas, releasing another large cloud of black smoke. The back tires screeched in a protest of their own as the truck lurched forward and started coming back towards the group.

Jacob looked and noticed an elderly woman refusing to move. The truck made its approach, coming in much too fast. Jacob looked back and forth between the elderly lady and the truck. He knew that the truck was playing a game of chicken, and the elderly woman wasn't playing at all. At ten yards away, Jacob realized that even if the elderly woman wanted to move, she wouldn't be fast enough to get out of the way safely. Jacob dove into action. He tackled the elderly woman out of the way, using his own body to cushion her fall just as the truck flew by, smashing the table and sending its contents flying in its wake. The big black truck with a Confederate flag in the back window and a set of bull testicles hanging off the trailer hitch sped off.

7:30 pm

Kevin Marin drove his blue 2019 Chevy Silverado to a Walmart parking lot in Nanaimo, BC. He had been texting on a burner phone with a young girl named Ashley. He first saw her videos on TikTok almost seven months ago and then began following her on other social media platforms. He began cautiously chatting with her a few months later. First, he'd give the occasional compliment and cautionary warning about speaking to strangers online. Later he started giving her suggestive messages, coaxing her along, grooming her for their eventual meeting.

Kevin was forty-four years old. He stood at six foot one and weighed in at about one hundred and ninety-five pounds. His brown hair matched his eyes and was a shade or two lighter than his dark goatee. He dressed well and had a clean look, though a closer inspection showed the remnants of some scarring on his face. It didn't come up often, but when it did, Kevin claimed he got banged up playing hockey. The truth was, Kevin had a big mouth and got himself beaten up a lot when he was younger.

Over the course of the past few months of grooming, he had bought Ashley clothing and a cell phone that she hid from her parents so they could stay in contact. On this particular night, Kevin made the drive from Victoria to Nanaimo after convincing Ashley to lie to her parents and claim she was staying at a friend's. She had done as she was told and even had a friend's older sister pick her up at home and drop her off at Walmart.

Ashley had just turned fifteen years old a week before on May 8th. Kevin knew this. He knew she was underage, but it didn't stop him. As he pulled into the lot, he texted Ashley. *"Are you there?"* He waited a few seconds before the reply came. *"Yes."* He drove around the lot, staying vigilant, looking for any signs that there were police nearby. He saw none.

He stopped in a dark area of the parking lot and texted her again. *"Walk across the street to Dairy Queen; I'll be right there."* He waited. A few seconds passed, and his phone dinged, *"OK."* Kevin stayed put, leaning back in his truck seat in the dark parking lot. He watched as the young girl made her way to the intersection. She stopped at the light, looked in all directions, waited for the crosswalk sign, and made her way across the street. There were no cars or people that followed. He waited a few more minutes, and his phone dinged, *"Here."* He kept looking around. No movement. He put the truck in gear and drove across the street. Ashley was standing out front in bright pink running shoes, light blue faded jeans, and a maroon bomber jacket. A purple backpack was slung over her shoulder.

Ashley had dark skin that was clear of blemishes and long, straight hair that was naturally jet black, but showed light brown from where she'd dyed it before. Even though she had just turned fifteen, her very small frame meant she could still be mistaken for an eleven- or twelve-year-old. She looked out of place standing out in front of a fast-food restaurant by herself. To anybody seeing her for the first time, she looked like a child waiting for a parent. Kevin pulled up in front and waved. Ashley walked to the passenger door and jumped in.

Chapter 2

Saturday May 13th, 2023, 11:00 am.

The waves crashed down on Sasha, chilling the top of her head. The wetsuit she was wearing kept her warm except for the icy cold water coming in at her neck that trickled down her back. After three months in Tofino, BC, and two months of weekend trips to the beach, she was starting to get the hang of surfing. She positioned herself in the water, saw her wave, and started paddling. This was it. This was the one she was going to catch. Eight weeks of hard work was finally going to pay off.

As the wave rose under her board, she popped up onto her feet and started to stand. She was doing it! She struggled for balance as her weight shifted slightly, and she pitched left and fell, the waves bouncing her around. Her board, though tied to her ankle, somehow bounced back and hit her in the mouth. Salt water went up her nose and down the back of her throat. She stood up in the now knee-high water, coughing, hacking, and gagging, spitting out saltwater, wiping her mouth, checking to see if her teeth were still there and if her mouth was bleeding.

"Fuck, that hurt!" she cursed.

"You okay?" her boyfriend yelled from the beach.

She gave a thumbs up and paddled back out to try again. She positioned herself like her neighbours had showed her, saw her wave, and started paddling. The board rose on the wave. She popped up. She was really doing it this time! As she tried to straighten herself upright, she fell again. This time the board bounced back and hit her in the ribs on her right side, knocking the wind out of her. "That's it," she said as she stood up again in the same spot, with the water around knee level. She picked up the big, bulky surfboard and trudged her way up the beach.

She made her way back to her group. It included her boyfriend Mike, with whom she'd relocated to BC from Southern Ontario; their next-door neighbours, Raye and Vicky, who were a gay couple that Mike and Sasha had instantly hit it off with; and their collective three dogs.

The dog pack included Sasha's mean little black-and-white French Bulldog/Boston Terrier named Domino, Vicky and Raye's scruffy mutt named Dingus, and Oscar, Mike's big grey-and-white American Bulldog/Mastiff mix that they rescued from a trash stop on the Trans-Canada highway. Someone had abandoned the big dog in the middle of winter. Mike noticed him at the side of the highway, shivering and emaciated. He and Sasha spent two hours at the trash stop trying to lure the poor thing over with food.

Mike wrapped him in a blanket, both to warm him up and prevent the big, scared dog from biting. They loaded him into their silver camper van and drove to the closest emergency vet in Dryden, Ontario. After spending three days and $3,900, the dog was released and has since then lived his life at Mike's side. Everywhere Mike went, Oscar the Trash Dog was prancing beside him, staring up with admiration.

Sasha dropped her board and plopped down in the sand. "Surfboard two, Sasha zero."

"Saw ya out there. You almost had it." Vicky encouraged optimistically. Vicky was in her late twenties and was very pretty with a bright smile and square glasses that accented her round face. She was femme and had an infectious laugh and a positive attitude. Her hair was purple this week, worn long on top with the sides shaved. She was still sitting in her wetsuit sipping on a hard root beer.

"Almost. I'll get it," Sasha vowed. Vicky had been trying to teach Sasha to surf for a few weeks. Sasha reached into the cooler, grabbed a beer, and asked if anyone else wanted one. Both Raye and Mike put their hands up. Sasha tossed two cans, cracked one open for herself, and sat in the sand.

Their Saturdays at Long Beach, a public spot about twenty minutes southeast of Tofino, were becoming a welcome tradition. Every Saturday Mike and Sasha would wake up and pack up a cooler with beer and various other drinks. Raye and Vicky would pack lunch, and the four of them would head to the beach. Weather permitting, they brought the dogs. Today it was foggy, with the sun trying its hardest to burn off the mist and managing to peek through occasionally.

Where Vicky had stepped in to teach Sasha how to surf, Mike had started teaching Raye how to box. The same age as Vicky, Raye was masc, a little shorter than Vicky, with round glasses and short brown hair usually worn in a messy style. Raye's wardrobe varied, but they were often found sporting a loud Hawaiian shirt. Mike and Raye had clicked immediately, partially due to their shared dark sense of humor. Mike felt Raye had a healing presence about them. Raye enjoyed Mike's companionship because, despite his large, brutish appearance, he was very welcoming and open-minded. The two often shared beers on the front porch and pointed out the girls jogging by, and in the short few months they'd known each other, they had developed a number of crude inside jokes. The four of them all became friends naturally.

Mike was leaning back on the beach. Oscar demanded his dad play with him by continuing to nudge Mike with his snout while holding a large rope, trying to instigate a game of tug. Mike opted to play ball instead, throwing a tennis ball towards the water. Oscar would bring it back, nudge Mike with it, and refuse to drop it. *No take, only throw.* Each return becoming a two-minute-long argument between Mike and Oscar to get the ball back. Every morning, Mike would feed the big fellow before they would go for a run together. Mike had made a point of weighing him daily. This morning when Mike held him and stepped on the scale, Oscar the Trash Dog weighed a healthy 94 pounds.

Sasha, Raye, and Vicky returned to the water. Sasha continued trying to surf, wiping out, getting up, asking what she did wrong, then trying again. Dingus and Domino were basking in the warm sunlight that had finally broken through the mist. Oscar was running and playing but keeping a close eye on his dad. Mike watched his girlfriend and their new friends in the water as they laughed and hollered. He couldn't help but smile to himself. His life had found some sense of peace and contentment; a big difference for the man who had hidden in shadows and acted as judge, jury, and executioner at his own discretion a few short months ago.

HUNTING PREDATORS

Around 2:00 pm, the four of them called it a day. They worked as a team, strapping the four boards to the rack on Raye's little red Ford Ranger pickup. Sasha ran to the far end of the parking lot to use the public bathroom. Mike, having already stripped his wetsuit off at the beach, tossed it into the back of the van. He opened the side door and loaded the three dogs in one after another, making sure each one got kisses and scratches as they were lifted in.

Raye and Vicky began removing their wetsuits at the back of the van with the doors open. Mike was still at the side getting the three pups situated when a large black Ford pickup with a confederate flag on the back window and a set of truck nuts hanging off the trailer hitch pulled up beside them. Three guys in their mid-twenties jumped out, the first one ogling Vicky.

"Can I help you?" Vicky asked rhetorically. He just sneered at her.

"Take a walk, pal." Raye advised. The three guys shared a joke between them. Raye went back to putting their wetsuits away while Vicky threw on jean shorts and a dark blue T-shirt over her black one-piece bathing suit. "Assholes," Raye muttered, loud enough to be heard.

"Shut up, Dyke," spat the one who had been checking out Vicky.

"The fuck did you just say?" Mike asked, stepping out between the van and Raye's truck. Mike was a large man, standing at six-foot-five and coming in at 260 lbs. He was wearing grey surf shorts and worn Converse running shoes.

HUNTING PREDATORS

The three guys were caught off guard, first by the fact that Mike was there and second by the sheer size of him. He was big, not jacked with muscle, but the type of big that showed years of manual labour fused with a couple of days a week at the gym hitting a heavy bag. He was an intimidating sight to behold, even to a group of self-proclaimed tough guys. Both arms from elbow to shoulder showed various bright, colourful tattoos. His body also showed a multitude of tattoos and visible scars, telling the history of a life filled with obvious violence.

The guy with the mouth hesitated for a second before putting on a false bravado. Puffing out his chest, raising his chin, and adding a strut to his step, he was clearly trying to make himself seem like a badass. *Empty drums make the most noise*, Mike's grandfather used to say. He walked toward the younger guy. "You owe my friend an apology," Mike demanded.

"Or wha-" His sentence was cut short when Mike threw a four-punch combination. The first three landed perfectly clean and on target. The fourth grazed the top of his head as he was falling to the asphalt.

Mike immediately switched his attention to the next closest of the three. The guy looked down at his friend, then, as his eyes came back up, mouth agape, Mike hit him with a tooth-shattering uppercut. The guy's legs went limp as his head snapped back violently, and he crumpled. The faint sound of teeth hitting the ground around him was followed by the echoing clunk of his head hitting the ground.

Mike focused on the third guy from the truck, who had grabbed a two-foot-long piece of two-inch pipe out of the back of the truck.

HUNTING PREDATORS

"You're holding it wrong," Mike chastised. As the guy chanced a look at it, there was a loud *thunk* with a slight metallic ring. The guy fell, dropping the pipe and holding the back of his head. His pipe clanged as it rolled away. Sasha was standing behind him, her wetsuit rolled down to the waist. She was wearing her blue bikini top, showing two half-sleeves of ink and a large sugar skull tattoo in the centre of her chest with pink spider webs spreading out towards her shoulders, accented with cherry skulls on the ends. She was holding a similar pipe that she had also grabbed out of the back of the large black Ford on her way by.

"Who was holding it wrong, me or him?" she asked.

Mike smiled at her and replied, "He was." He looked at the three guys on the ground, then at Raye and Vicky. "We should probably go now," he suggested in an overly calm tone. Vicky and Raye stood frozen with their mouths open in shock at how fast it started and how it was over just as quickly. They jumped into their vehicles and left.

That evening Sasha had a shift working at a local bar, which meant it was Mike's turn to get dinner ready. There was a barbeque owned by Raye and Vicky on the front porch that extended across the front of their adjoining duplex. Mike and Sasha bought the propane in exchange for usage of the barbeque, and everyone was happy. Mike was sitting on the porch making dinner when Raye came out.

Raye leaned against the doorframe. The building was painted dark burgundy with white trim, reminiscent of Mike's previous home. It consisted of two small units that mirrored each other. Mike and Sasha's unit opened into the living room, with the stairs immediately on the right. Through the living room was the kitchen, and a small two-piece bathroom off to the right side. The upstairs had a small hallway with two bedrooms and a bathroom. The units were small but comfortable, ideal for a couple that had an occasional overnight guest.

"Hey, neighbor." Mike greeted with a quick nod. Raye handed him a beer and sat down, a look of concern on their face. Mike knew what was coming. "What's on your mind?"

"What the hell was that?" Raye asked.

"Which part?" Mike raised an eyebrow, knowing Raye was talking about the parking lot incident.

"All of it!"

Mike flipped the chicken over and smeared BBQ sauce on it. He closed the lid and dropped the heat a touch. H opened his beer and replied, "Had to be done."

"Did it though?" Raye asked, skeptically.

Mike sighed. "Look, where I come from, we don't stand around and talk about it. We don't draw lines in the sand and dare people to step over them. I know it sounds juvenile, but they started it. They had no issues harassing a gay couple until they saw me. They were bullies."

"Okay, but you just hit that guy without warning," Raye continued, a little exasperated.

"Well, yeah. If I'd warned him, he'd have known it was coming." Mike laughed. "There were three of them. I needed the element of surprise."

"They were really hurt." Concern clouded Raye's eyes.

Mike sat down on the chair next to Raye. "Not sure what you want me to say here. They were itching for a fight. I just happened to be better at it than they were. How do you think that would have gone if I hadn't been there?"

"I've been called names before," Raye explained.

"I'm aware, and you've been assaulted by people like that before too. I find it's always best to err on the side of caution." Mike smiled sympathetically.

"Yeah, but how do you know they were going to do anything?" Raye continued, still not sure that they were okay with the day's violent outcome. "Maybe they just had big mouths."

"I don't," Mike replied. "But I've also been on the receiving end of more than one swarming by multiple people. As far as those guys were concerned, when I stepped out, it was three against one. Guys like that love those odds. They're tough when they think they'll win."

Raye, having seen the scars on him, understood he wasn't lying or exaggerating. "But how can you turn it on and off so..." Raye paused, looking for the word. "Easily?"

"It's a gift," Mike explained with a grin, "or a curse. Not sure which."

Raye nodded. Mike flipped the chicken again and sat back down.

"Sasha brained that guy with a pipe," Raye observed, staring at nothing in particular across the street.

HUNTING PREDATORS

Mike sometimes forgot that his reactions to what he perceived to be a threat could be seen as traumatizing or horrific to people who didn't live the same life he had. He looked over at Raye, hoping they could understand one another.

"Well, in fairness, he was going to hit me with one." Mike defended. "What lengths would you go to, to protect Vicky?"

Raye nodded, understanding Mike's point as he continued.

"I'm sorry if I upset you. But once the line is crossed, it becomes about self-preservation; it's not about hurting others. I reacted because I felt they were going to attack me. The third guy pulled the pipe before I swung. In their minds, they were always going to jump me."

They sat quietly for a few seconds. "We good?" Mike asked.

"Yeah, we good," Raye said, raising their beer can. Mike clinked it with his own, and they sat on the porch watching the people of their small town pass by. "Look at that one," Raye nodded at a pretty blond girl in her late twenties as she jogged by wearing tight black shorts and a black sports bra.

"Yup," Mike said with a smile. "Disgusting."

Chapter 3

Sunday May 14th, 2023, 10 am.

Mike woke up to soft light filtering in between the blinds. Sasha had worked until a little after 2:00 am the night before. On the nights she worked, Mike would walk Domino, the mean little bulldog, and Oscar the Trash Dog down to the bar so the four of them could all walk home together. Sasha had mentioned on the walk home that the guy she had hit with the pipe was at the bar.

"He came in around 9:00 pm," she explained. "Looked around, like he was looking for you, then left."

Mike didn't pay it much attention. The guy hadn't seen her, so she was safe. But he did make a mental note: if these jackasses were local, then the parking lot wasn't the end of it.

He got up, made breakfast, fed the dogs, and took Oscar for his daily run. When he got back, he checked his phone. He had a message from his friend Claude.

Mike had worked for Claude when he was seventeen, cleaning and rebuilding chimneys. Claude, now in his late sixties, rented out a room in the house Mike's uncle had left him when he passed in 2012. By 'renting a room,' it meant Claude occasionally paid for the utilities and kept an eye on the property in exchange for full use of the house. He made sure the snow was shovelled, the lawn was mowed, the fridge was stocked with beer, and the pool and hot tub were just right in the summer. It was hard work, but Claude didn't mind. Mike called him back.

"Hey ole' timer," Mike greeted Claude as he answered on the third ring.

"Hey Mike. How's things?" Claude asked.

"Not bad. Nice, relaxing Sunday. Supposed to rain all day."

"Hey, listen," Claude interjected, cutting through the small talk. "I got a guy interested in your bike."

Mike owned a 2015 Harley Davidson Street Glide that was currently sitting in the garage of the house in Windsor. He initially looked into the cost of shipping it out, then at the cost of flying back to Southern Ontario and riding out. Eventually he decided it was his best option to sell it and buy a new one in BC. "What's he offering?" Mike asked.

"$21,000," Claude replied.

"Is the guy legit?" Mike was a little concerned. Claude was showing his age, and Mike worried someone may try and take advantage of him.

"Yeah. He's a friend of Chris and Tammy." Claude answered, referring to the couple across the street that helped Claude with yard work.

Mike thought for a few seconds. The bike was just collecting dust, and money wasn't really a concern.

"I want $19,000." Mike instructed, "Anything above and beyond you can pocket."

"Guy said he has the money right now. He's just waiting for me to call him back. I can deposit it into your account tomorrow morning."

"Sounds good." Mike agreed and rung off. It was closing in on the middle of May. Riding season was starting, and he was looking forward to getting back on a bike.

Sasha awoke shortly after the phone call. She came into the living room wearing one of Mike's white tank tops and black underwear. "Who was that?" she asked, yawning.

"Claude. Bikes sold. Wanna go shopping?" he asked.

Sasha's face lit up. Shopping meant they would pack up for a couple of days, drive to Victoria, and visit her older brother. "Just let me wake up, and I'll start packing."

Since settling in Tofino, Mike had picked up part-time work with an older welder named Tim. Tim had a small fab shop where he fabricated and installed various metal works in the area: marinas, boat docks, and decorative pieces. Tim kept himself busy, and business was steady, but he hated doing the installations, especially as he got older. The two met at the bar. Where Sasha worked part-time with Hailey, Tim's fiancé, and over the course of a few meetings and conversations, Tim asked Mike if he was interested in working for him. Mike would do the installs, which allowed Tim to stay in the shop. The two worked out a deal where Mike was paid in cash. The hours were flexible, and Mike didn't mind the work. It kept him busy. He phoned Tim, who answered on the second ring.

"Hello."

"Hey Tim, how's this week looking? I'm thinking of running to Victoria," Mike advised.

"Could really use you Wednesday and Thursday if you can be back by then," Tim replied.

"Shouldn't be an issue. I'll call you Tuesday if I can't make it.?"

"Sounds good," Tim said and rung off.

Mike packed up a few things and messaged Sasha's brother. *"Coming to town today, Dinner?"* two minutes later the reply came in.

"Hell yes, how long are you staying?"

Mike typed back, "Tuesday. Shopping. See you soon."

They loaded up the van with the two dogs and a few days clothing, and by 11:30 am, they were on the highway heading to Victoria.

The drive was steady and quiet, the rain coming down lightly most of the day with the sun occasionally breaking through the clouds. Just before 4:00 pm they pulled up at a large blue and grey house in a new development: Sasha's brother's house.

Her brother Adem, spelled differently but pronounced "Adam", was a large guy, not quite as tall as Mike, maybe an inch shorter, but carrying a large muscular build. He sported a shaved head, but the family resemblance to Sasha with the light blue eyes and large welcoming smile was definitely there. He and Mike were the same age and got along well. Mike figured Adem was mostly just happy that his sister was close by, but he appreciated that Adem always went out of his way to make Mike feel included.

HUNTING PREDATORS

As the silver van pulled up, Adem was standing in the doorway, front door wide open, welcoming their arrival. In the last three months, Mike and Sasha had made the trip a few times for various reasons: shopping, picking Sasha's younger brother up at the airport when he flew out to see them, and occasionally just to visit. Adem was married, and while he and Mike forged a friendship, Sasha and his wife Melissa had built their own as well.

Once offloaded after the long trip, the two dogs burst through the door of Adem's house, chased his dog Joe around, and subsequently knocked over everything that wasn't nailed down in the process. Mike and Sasha left the big silver van and joined Adem and Melissa in Adem's SUV and set out for dinner at a small local beachfront tavern.

Once they had all eaten, they occupied the table for another two hours, having drinks and catching up. They had done this routine a few times. Every time the bill came, Mike and Adem would both insist on paying. After several deadlocks, Melissa had suggested that the two men flip a coin and save the argument. Mike called heads; it was tails. Adem paid.

The following morning, both Mike and Sasha were up early. Mike fed the dogs and took Oscar for his daily run. When he got back, Adem and Melissa had already left for work. He and Sasha sat together on the couch discussing the day's plans. They had breakfast and decided that while their camper van was comfortable to travel in, it wasn't very practical for day-to-day driving. They opted to find either a truck or an SUV.

They were sitting at the island separating the kitchen from the living room in the big, modern, open-concept house, looking at used vehicles online while a morning news show played in the background.

"RCMP in Nanaimo are asking for the public's help in locating fifteen-year-old Ashley Brock. Brock was last seen Friday night at the Walmart Plaza on Island Highway North when she was dropped off by a family friend…" The voice trailed on while a picture of a young girl who looked not more than eleven or twelve flashed onto the screen. Mike had to do a double take and verify the age at fifteen compared to the young-looking picture.

Sasha's focus was on the T.V. "Poor thing. Hope she's okay."

Mike agreed. He went to shower, and they started their day.

They stopped for lunch at a small deli. They ordered sandwiches and dessert and took their time eating. Sasha had found a black 2013 Range Rover with a roof rack: a private sale. Mike usually wouldn't have wanted a luxury car, but Adem worked with cars, and after giving his opinion and assuring them replacement parts and labour wouldn't be terrible through his connections, Mike agreed to look at it. Plus, with it being a private sale, an envelope full of hundreds wouldn't send up any red flags.

At 1:30 pm they looked at the Range Rover. Sasha loved it. The mileage was low. They test drove it. Everything seemed to be in working order, so they bought it on the spot. Next, they went to a kiosk to register and plate the vehicle, a task that proved to be a little more difficult. Both Mike and Sasha still had their driver's licenses registered in Ontario. Sasha made a phone call to

Adem, who offered to put the Range Rover in his name until they got things sorted.

At 4:00 pm they returned to Adem's in both vehicles. They barbequed burgers and had dinner together on the back deck of the postage-stamp yard. Afterwards, Mike brought Oscar the Trash Dog out for an evening stroll along the beach. Coming back up the street as the night's darkness started to set in, he noticed Adem waiting at the corner under a streetlight.

"You lost?" Mike joked.

Adem looked slightly uncomfortable. "Can we talk?"

"Yeah, what's up?" Mike was curious.

Adem took a breath and began, "Okay, I need to know what's up with you and my sister."

"In what regard?" Mike asked.

Adem, still seemingly uncomfortable, continued. "You guys just show up one day, no warning, then head down to Tofino and set up shop. That's not a cheap place to live. You're buying expensive cars. She's working in a bar. You weld a couple of days a week. There's no way you can afford to stay there based on that. I don't like getting into other people's business, but she's my sister, and she's had a hard life. I don't want her getting into any trouble." Adem finished his sentence and, whether deliberately or unknowingly, straightened up and puffed his chest out. Mike caught the small act of aggression, but he understood where Adem was coming from. Though he didn't know her whole story, Mike knew Sasha had been to hell and fought her way out. It seemed only natural that her big brother would want to be protective.

"Relax," Mike reassured calmly. "I'm not going to hurt her."

Adem relaxed his posture a bit, realizing he was tense.

Mike continued, "The van was my uncle's. It sat in his driveway for a few years before we drove out here. It's comfortable but not practical for day-to-day use. I sold my truck before I left and my motorcycle yesterday. That's why it looks like we're splurging. We're just replacing what I left behind."

Adem seemed to understand, but he had more questions. "How are you able to afford Tofino? Are you selling drugs?"

Mike barked out a sharp laugh, then apologized right away. "No, no, I'm not. If you knew me a little better, you'd understand why that's so funny."

Adem held his stare. "Well?"

"Okay," Mike conceded, knowing Adem wouldn't stop until he had answers. "You know it's not polite to ask people about money, but since you're not just being nosy and you're legitimately worried about your sister, I'll tell you."

Mike leaned back on the waist-high chain-link fence. "I travelled a lot for work over the years. Nick and I, we worked a lot of money jobs, three or four weeks in camp, one week out. We both lived simply, or so I thought. Both our trucks were used; he had the same one the entire time I lived with him. When he died, I got everything.

Truck, bike, the van, his pension, savings, insurance, and his houses," Mike said, accentuating the plural on "houses". Adem seemed to relax a little more.

Mike continued, "Nick lived in a small wartime house. He inherited my grandfather's house when Gramps died, and he owned two small rentals in Windsor as well. When he died, I became the proud owner of four properties. We sold Gramps' place. I gave half the money to my sister. I still have the other three. They're paid off, and I rent them out. Between the three rental incomes, I'm semi-retired."

Adem held Mike's stare for a few more seconds then seemed to relax completely.

"Why Tofino, though?"

"You've been there; why not?" Mike replied. "It's beautiful. Truth be told, we don't know how long we're staying. Another month, 10 years. Who knows? I know Sasha had a rough life. Mine wasn't a walk in the tulips either. We have nowhere to be and nobody to answer to. If we get tired of Tofino, we'll move on. The only thing I can tell you is I'm not going anywhere without her. If anything happens to me, she'll be taken care of."

Adem nodded. "I'm sorry if I came off like an asshole there. I worry about her."

Mike clapped Adem on the back of the neck and shook his big frame as they started walking up the street. "Understandable." Mike paused and then promised, "I'll take care of her, although I don't think she needs it."

Chapter 4

Friday April 25th, 2003. 4:30 pm.

A thirteen-year-old Mike walked up the back steps of a modest brick house in Windsor's west end after jumping back the fence, droplets of blood trailing him. A frail kid, tall, just shy of six feet, but rail thin. He wore black warm-up pants with the Slater Street Boxing Club logo in yellow down the right leg. His once-white t-shirt was balled up, covering his nose and mouth, soaking up the bleeding, which was starting to subside. His bony knuckles rapped on the glass storm door. A few seconds later the curtain moved. A moment later the door opened, showing a young girl of the same age.

She had blond, straw-like hair, a tattered Detroit Tigers t-shirt, and red cut-off jean shorts, and was a tomboy in every sense of the word. Her name was Angela, and the two had been friends since they were six years old. They met on their first day of grade one. Angela had given Mike his first fat lip when he told her, "Girls can't play with G.I. Joes." The two had been friends ever since.

Angela opened the door and looked at Mike. She stepped to the side without saying a word and let him in. Mike walked past her, straight through the mudroom, into the kitchen, and over to the sink. He moved the bloodied shirt, leaned over, and spat blood out, letting the tap water wash it down. Like a well-rehearsed dance, Angela went to the freezer, grabbed an ice pack, set it in front of him, walked back to the living room, and flopped back on the couch. She heard him spit out the blood a few more times, along with his slight gasps as he touched his face, the swelling and bruising already starting. Five minutes later, he walked into the living room and sat on the couch beside her.

The TV was tuned in to Much Music; the song "All the Things She Said" by T.A.T.U. seemed to be on a continuous loop lately.

"They play this song a lot." Mike commented, sounding stuffed up.

"Shhhh," Angela hushed him, enthralled with the music.

This dance was happening more often. Mike's dad Ed, a retired cop and boxing coach, was drinking more and becoming more abusive. Ed was an equal opportunity ass-kicker too. Wife, son, daughter—it didn't matter. When Ed was angry, someone got hurt, and Mike, at thirteen, had taken to subtly provoking the angry man. He figured it was better than Ed turning his rage on Mike's mom or sister.

Angela's house had become Mike's safe haven. After Ed beat him, Mike would go to Angela's until Ed calmed down. At first, she showed concern, freaking out the way only a young preteen girl can, but after a while it became normal.

Angela was raised by a single father, named Bill, or "Big Bill" around the community. He was a large man with a big muscular frame, short, cropped hair, and a neatly trimmed beard. He was in his late forties but was still constantly receiving attention from women of all ages. Although he was large and intimidating to look at, he was friendly and very comical. Most of the kids in the neighbourhood knew Big Bill and liked him. He worked for the rail yards as a conductor and spent his weekends fronting a blues/rock band. He had two daughters, Angela and her older sister, Sarah. No matter how busy his work schedule was or how busy his band was, the girls always came first.

One day in Mike's absence, Angela had sat at their dining room table and explained to her dad and older sister what life was like for Mike at home. Big Bill and Sarah never mentioned it to Mike, but they always made him feel welcome. On the occasions that Ed's rage happened later in the evenings, Mike never questioned why Big Bill had placed a small step ladder next to the house that allowed Mike to climb on top of the roof of the mudroom to knock on Angela's second-floor window. Mike never questioned why the ladder was always folded back up and placed back in its spot in the morning. And Mike never stopped to wonder why Big Bill never said anything about the scrawny neighbourhood kid sleeping on the floor of his youngest daughter's bedroom when he checked on his girls before leaving for work early in the mornings.

Although Mike and Angela made an unlikely duo, they became fast friends at six years old and spent most of their free time together. On Mike's eleventh birthday, Angela kissed him. Not knowing how to react, Mike punched her in the face. She hit him back, and the two started scrapping in her backyard until Big Bill pulled them apart. When Bill asked what started it, Angela punched Mike again and stormed off.

Two years later, having both forgotten about the kiss, they decided the best way to forget about how Mike had shown up bloodied again was to build a ramp for their bikes. Both kids ransacked her father's garage in search of tools and building material. After finding an eight-foot-long, two-foot-wide piece of plywood left over from Big Bill's tool shed and several pieces of three-foot-long two-by-fours, the kids worked together to build a large ramp. Angela was already showing a natural gift for building and engineering.

Partway through the ramp's construction, the familiar scrape and thump of someone jumping over the back fence. Mike looked up and saw Wallace, the third musketeer.

Wallace was a year older than Mike and Angela. He and Mike both trained under Ed at the Slater Street Boxing Club.

The trio struggled to get the ramp out of Angela's backyard, dragged the cumbersome ramp down to the local park, and placed it at the bottom of a small hill. Taking turns, they each tried to build up as much speed as possible and hit the ramp, to lacklustre results. Unwilling to give up on their endeavour, Mike had the brilliant idea to place the ramp at the top of the hill. After careful planning and a few small adjustments, the ramp was positioned, and Angela was ready.

"Tell me how high I get?" she yelled.

"K," Mike yelled back, now standing at the bottom of the small hill. Angela started to pedal as fast as her legs would take her. She built up a good deal of speed and hit the ramp.

Mike later recalled the incident and swore that time went in slow motion like it did in the movies. He vividly remembered staring upwards in awe as Angela sailed over the top of him, unaware that her back tire was

7 feet in the air. What followed next would years later still be referred to as the crash of the century by Mike and Angela. Angela's back tire hit the ground and folded in half as her feet slipped off the pedals. Her torso was thrown forward as her sternum collided with the handlebars. Mike remembered seeing a lot of rolling with a small person and a red bike tangled together. He stood in shock, looking at his friend, who was not moving.

Mike and Wallace ran to her as she sat up gasping for air, her skin white as paper, blood trickling out her nose as she fought for words. "Can't breathe!" She let out a gasp and fell over.

Mike and Wallace were young, scared, and panicking. Mike didn't know what to do, so he did what any kid would in that situation: he ran away and left her for someone else to find. The next morning, he went to check on her. Thankfully she was still alive and had made at least a partial recovery.

At age seventeen, Angela joined the army reserves and later the regular forces. She fought and clawed her way through her career, carving out a respectable name for herself and a chest full of medals and awards to prove it. She served in Afghanistan, saw combat, but still used "the ramp incident" as her benchmark for whether she was just hurt or *really fuckin hurt*.

Chapter 5

Wednesday May 17th, 2023. 8:05 am.

Mike pulled the silver van into the parking lot at Tim's shop. Tim had a respectable-sized pre-engineered "butler building" on his property. A small yellow-sided house where Tim lived with his fiancée, Hailey, sat nearby on the lot. Mike wasn't sure how long Tim and Hailey had been together, but their engagement was only a few months old.

Mike walked in through the large overhead door. There were a few guys running MIG welders on pieces of steel in various states of fabrication. Mike made his way into the room next to Tim's office. Inside, each worker had a cubby where Tim would leave the daily work assignments. As Mike got closer to his cubby, he noticed it was empty. *That's odd,* he thought as he walked back out. He looked over at Tim's office. Tim was standing in the window, a serious look on his face, motioning with one finger for Mike to join him.

Tim was a short block of a man in his early fifties with a year-round dark suntan, a shaved head, and a grey goatee. He was friendly enough but had a hard vibe about him and was well known around town as a man that could take care of himself. He dressed in the same black T-shirt and blue jeans every day. His only adornment was a gold chain around his neck with a diamond-shaped gold medallion showing a simple "1%.".

Tim was a biker with one of the larger 1% motorcycle clubs. The 1% aspect didn't affect Mike one way or the other. After years of working in trades, he knew dozens, if not hundreds, of guys from almost every club out there. He didn't believe the nonsense the media tried to spin, that "bikers were running organized crime." The notion was laughable, not because they couldn't do it, but because every 1% biker Mike had ever known was too busy working ridiculous hours, either in trades or their own business, to be able to get involved in that mess.

Nobody running millions of dollars of hard drugs was also waking up at 5:00 am and working in minus 50-degree weather in the winter because they had to keep up a front. Sure, there were people affiliated with bike clubs, even members, that were involved in shady dealings, but Mike would bet anything that for every biker that broke the law, you could find a dozen cops doing a lot worse.

The majority of 1% bikers Mike knew followed a very simple philosophy: give respect, get respect. It wasn't hard to figure out, and Mike found their values generally paralleled his own. Theirs was a code of honour and loyalty, a code many felt should never have been forgotten but had been abandoned by society long ago.

Bikers called each other "brothers" and acted as such. They knew each other's wives and children. They supported each other's businesses, be it roofing, welding, mechanic shops, or whatever. If a brother had a family member die, it was always the club brothers that called or would show up first. They'd close ranks quickly to protect their own.

Each club chapter also generated thousands of dollars annually for local charities like toy drives, food banks, and women's shelters. Unfortunately, these actions never got written about in the newspapers or appeared as segments on TV news.

There have been people obsessed with the "biker gang" lifestyle for as long as it has existed; those who would do anything to be a part of it. But the ones that don't understand loyalty, respect, or honour are generally weeded out and have had it explained in no uncertain terms that they are not welcome.

Mike sat in the guest chair in Tim's office. "What's up?"

Tim seemed more concerned than angry, but there was definite tension in his face. "You involved in a fight over the weekend?"

Mike held his gaze, calmly, "Where?"

Not expecting a question as a reply, Tim was taken aback. He paused before answering, "Long Beach." After a few seconds he added, "three kids."

"Yup," Mike admitted without hesitation.

Tim's face dropped. "Fuck, Mike. That's not good, man. That was one of my brother's nephews."

"Well, your brother's nephew is a fucking moron." Mike said evenly, still holding eye contact.

"He said you jumped him," Tim elaborated.

"Nobody *jumped* anybody. There were three of them. They were mouthing off, and one grabbed a pipe, so I defended myself." Mike explained.

Tim's eye went wide. "Walk me through it."

HUNTING PREDATORS

Mike ran Tim through the events, taking very small liberties. He explained the harassing comments towards Raye and Vicky. Tim knew them both; they were regulars at the bar, and Tim and Raye had often joked with each other. Mike explained how he stepped in, and the three men approached him. He mentioned seeing one of them grab a pipe out of the back of the truck.

"When I saw that, I figured game on. I hit the one closest to me. Once he was down, I took out the second guy. The third had the pipe and tried to hit me with it." Mike finished his explanation with a small lie, leaving Sasha out of the equation. "I took it away from him and gave him a rap on the head with it. It ended there."

Tim sat staring at Mike, then finally spoke. "The story they're giving is that you and two other guys had words with them, and then you guys jumped them."

"It was me, Sasha, and my neighbors. Same group at Long Beach every Saturday. I only know three other guys in Tofino, Tim, and you're two of them." Mike smiled slightly.

Tim sat staring at the wall above the door for a few seconds. "Okay, I might be able to help you. Give me a few minutes."

Mike left the office as Tim picked up the phone and dialed a number. Mike milled around the shop. The song Vicarious by TOOL echoed over the speakers. A few minutes later Tim opened the door to his office and motioned Mike in again.

"Okay, here's the deal," Tim began. "My brother, the kid's uncle, wants to talk to you face to face. He wants to hear your side of the story."

"Which one is his nephew?" Mike asked. Tim held his stare, and Mike clarified, "One got hit three or four times, another lost some teeth, and one got clugged on the head. Which one was his nephew?"

"Well, from what you described, the one that got hit a few times. I didn't hear anything about a pipe to the head or broken teeth. I did hear his eyes are swollen shut, though."

Mike nodded. "When's this meeting happening?"

"Noon, today."

"Am I walking into a hornet's nest here?" Mike asked.

Tim, again holding his stare, sat quietly.

"Where?" Mike sighed as he asked.

"Restaurant where the girls work." Tim replied, referring to the bar Sasha and Hailey worked at part-time.

"Until then?" Mike asked. Tim answered with a shrug, and Mike saw himself out.

Mike was at the bar at 11:45 am. A fun, open-concept pub made to look like a beachfront bar on the main strip, it seemed a little out of place but was usually packed with tourists. He pulled up a stool at the bar and waited.

At 11:59 am a large man walked in with three other men close behind. The large man was in his mid-fifties and carried the same hard look Tim had. He was around six-foot-two, pushing 250 lbs., which he carried mostly around his chest and shoulders. His face and knuckles were battle-scarred, showing a roadmap of boxing rings, barroom brawls, and prison yard fights. The man looked dangerous. Even in his fifties, he looked like the type of man that loves nothing more than a good ol' fashioned knockdown dragout.

    Mike took a quick inventory of the other 3 men: various sizes, all gym rats, with large muscles aided by anabolic steroids. One showed similar battle scars to the man who had walked in ahead of them, although he was twenty-five years younger. The other two men were still pretty; they were there for intimidation purposes, or maybe to administer a beating if they were asked to. Mike hedged his bets that one-on-one he could beat each of them, the oldest likely being the most dangerous of the group. But four-on-one? He didn't have much of a chance. He'd been in worse situations, though it didn't make this one any better.

    "You Mike?" the older guy asked, walking up. The other three men hung back.

    "I am." Mike stood up and reached out a hand.

    The older guy shook it reluctantly. "What happened?" he demanded.

    OK, No small talk, no niceties, Mike thought to himself. He motioned for the guy to sit and asked, "What are you drinking?" The guy seemed like a no-nonsense type. He wasn't angry or agitated; he seemed like he genuinely wanted to know what happened. He ordered an IPA from Millstream Brewing Company and sat.

    "You want the full play-by-play or the cliff notes version?" Mike asked the man as he took a pull off his beer.

"I want to know why my nephew has a broken orbital bone." The older guy snapped, foam sticking to his upper lip. "The only reason I'm talking to you and not beating your head in is because Tim asked me to hear your side. You're running on borrowed time right now, sonny, so quit being cute and tell me what the fuck happened."

Mike's back tensed up. The four of them may take him out in a mad rush, but not before he landed a few of his own. This was a no-win situation for everyone involved if things got violent.

Taking a breath, Mike relaxed a bit and began. "Okay, we were leaving the beach the other day..."

"WHO?!" The older guy interrupted loudly, a little spit flying out of the corner of his mouth.

"Myself, my girlfriend, and my two neighbours."

"Were those the other two guys?" the older man demanded.

"This will go a lot smoother if you let me talk," Mike said calmly. "I mean you no disrespect; I'll tell you everything you want to know. But let me speak."

The guy was starting to get agitated now. He shifted in his seat, positioning himself to throw a punch if he felt the need. Mike adjusted also, ready to move if he had to. "Go ahead," the older man permitted, picking up on Mike's movements.

Mike said, "Myself, my girlfriend, and our neighbours, Raye and Vicky. They're women."

"What, like dykes?" the old guy asked innocently enough, maybe not realizing that wasn't the ideal term.

HUNTING PREDATORS

Mike sighed a bit. "No, not 'like dykes.' But yes, they're a gay couple."

"Fine," the older guy said impatiently. "Then what?"

"We were packing up to leave. A big black truck pulled in, and three guys jumped out. They didn't see me. They were acting like assholes to the girls. I stepped out. The first one, I'm assuming that was your nephew, started mouthing off to me. I stepped between him and the girls. One of his buddies grabbed a pipe. I understand one of them was your nephew, but three on one, and one had a weapon. I wasn't waiting around to find out if they just had big mouths."

"So, who helped you?" the older guy asked.

"Helped me? In the fight? No one." Mike admitted.

"The way I heard it, you guys had words in the parking lot, and you and your buddies jumped them." The old guy contradicted.

Mike snorted a small laugh. "No, no, sir. Just me against the three of them while my two neighbours watched on. My girlfriend wasn't even there. She ran to the bathroom, and the entire altercation happened before she got back. Your nephew and his friends had no problem harassing two girls. When I stepped in, they had no issues coming after me, three against one. I did what I needed to do."

The older guy sat quietly for a second and took another sip of his beer. "He's still my family."

"I respect that. But honestly, the kid has a bad attitude. If you go around and thump everyone that punches that kid out, all you'd ever do is drive around thumping people. And all I did was defend myself. You'd do the same."

The two sat in silence, letting the words hang in the air. The TV on the wall was showing the lunchtime news when the anchorwoman said, *"New development coming from the attempted vehicle assault during last Friday's Pipeline protest in Lantzville."*

The screen cut to a cellphone video taken inside the cab of the big black pickup. It showed the driver, a dark-haired boy in his mid-twenties wearing a camouflage John Deere hat. It was the same guy that Mike rapped on the head with a pipe. The passenger was filming and encouraging the driver to ram the blockade. A loud thump could be heard as the driver and passenger started cheering and laughing. The passenger turned the camera to his own face and yelled, "*BEEP* you, wagon burners!" and continued laughing. The screen cut to a second view, showing a stocky First Nations boy diving and tackling an elderly woman out of the way as the truck narrowly missed her.

Mike looked over at the older guy, who now had his head tilted down. This man came to the bar to discuss what happened to his nephew, only to see that same nephew's face laughing as he encouraged a friend to ram a peaceful protest. Mike stayed silent, knowing this was not a *told-ya-so* moment.

After a few seconds the older guy sighed and muttered, "Jesus, fucking Christ. What an idiot." He looked at Mike and said, "You may have actually done me a favor." He pulled a twenty out of his pocket, placed it on the bar, then added, "Thanks for your time," and started walking away.

Mike called after him. "We good?"

The older guy stopped, turned, and nodded. "Yeah, we're good."

"That driver came in here later that night looking for me." Mike advised. "My business with them is done; I left it in the parking lot. If any of them come at me again, I'll still defend myself." He didn't say it as a threat; he was explaining to the large man in terms he could appreciate.

"I'll have a chat with him. You have nothing to worry about." The man stepped out into the street, his three friends following behind.

Chapter 6

Thursday May 18th, 2023. 1:38 am.

Ashley Brock woke up shivering cold on top of a dingey maroon floral bedspread in a dirty motel room. The air smelled damp and moldy. Her head was throbbing. Nausea hit her with every breath; she needed to throw up, but her head hurt too much to do it. Every inch of her body ached. A blurry figure came into her vision.

"Here, take this," the figure gruffly offered, a hand coming out towards her. The room was spinning violently. Ashley pushed the hand away. The thought of even drinking water made her stomach turn. She saw a faint movement, and suddenly it was as if a stick of dynamite went off in her head as the sound of a slap echoed through the room. With the dynamite came a bright white flash that was gone in an instant, but the feeling of having her head ripped apart from the inside lingered much longer. Her eyes welled up with tears. The blurry hand grabbed her throat and started squeezing. She gagged, needing to vomit, but the force of the hand prevented it.

"I said take this!" The voice barked, the noise feeling like someone driving ice picks into her ears. She bucked, the hand let go, and she rolled onto her side and vomited on the floor. Her stomach was contracting hard; the pain was unbearable.

"Oh, for Christ's sake," the voice yelled. Ashley could hear another man in the room laughing at her. "Someone clean this bitch up." She wanted to cry. This felt like a terrible dream, but she couldn't wake up. She felt someone reach under her arms and try to lift her.

"Come on, honey, let's get up." This time it was a woman's voice. Ashley resisted only slightly; she had no fight in her, but she willed herself to stay put. The woman's voice instantly turned from calm and soothing to fierce and hateful. "You stupid little cunt," she growled.

A hand grabbed the back of Ashley's head as she was wrenched off the bed and dragged to the bathroom. She was shoved forward, unable to see. The edge of the bathtub hit her shins as she fell forward and felt her face slam into the cold white tiled wall. As she crumpled down inside the bathtub, she could hear the two male voices in the room laughing at her again. Cold water blasted her body. She started sobbing and was slapped again, not as hard as the first time, but the pain in her head hurt just as badly.

"Bitch," she heard the woman snarl as several more slaps rained down on her and she tried to cover her face. The water felt horrible; she was already freezing, and this was making it worse. A hand forcefully shoved something in her mouth, the woman's nails scratching her gums in the process. The taste of salt and dirt from the woman's unwashed fingers was followed by the bitter taste of a pill. "Swallow it!" the woman's voice demanded, followed by another white flash-inducing slap. "Swallow it!" Ashley choked the pill down as the ice-cold water blasted against her body. She continued crying and drifted out of consciousness again.

HUNTING PREDATORS

Mike woke up at 6:30 am. Sasha stirred as he crept out of the room. He fed Domino and Oscar the Trash Dog, went for the morning run, and weighed Oscar: 99 lbs. He was still packing on weight. Mike started wondering how much bigger the pup could get. He'd see American Masti-Bulls get up over 100 lbs. The vet determined Oscar was coming up on eighteen months old when he was rescued. At not even two years old, he was large and muscular. He had a gentle temperament; he was protective over his family but cuddly and loved nothing more than flopping on the couch with Dad getting pets.

Mike showered, kissed Sasha as she slept, and went to Tim's shop. When he walked in, Tim was sitting in his office reading over some drawings. Mike rapped on the door.

"Morning," Mike greeted, popping his head in.

Tim looked almost surprised to see him. He did a quick once-over but didn't see any visible marks. "How'd it go?"

"Well, I think I was marked for at least a mild ass-kicking. Then the 12 o'clock news showed a video of his nephew cheering as his buddy rammed a native blockade." Mike explained.

Tim sat motionless, looking at Mike, who waited for a reply. Finally, Mike widened his eyes in a look that said, *Well?*

"I'm fucking speechless," Tim admitted with a smile, then added, "Yeah, I guess that's not a hill he wanted to die on." He paused as he rifled through a mess of papers on his desk. "Clarke is a good man; he's solid," he offered as an explanation. He pulled a page out of the pile and offered it to Mike. "Steel's loaded onto the service truck. Feel like an install?"

"I've still got a job? Has this been put to bed?" Mike was genuinely surprised.

Tim's smile never left his face. "If you're here, we're good. What did he say to you yesterday?"

"Asked for my side. Saw the news footage and said I might have done him a favour after all. When he was leaving, I asked him if we were good. He said yes."

"Then you're good. If there was an issue, he'd have dealt with it then." Tim advised.

Mike nodded and took the page from Tim. "What's this one paying?"

"$850 for the install, cash in hand at the end of the day. Bring me back $600 when you're done. Rest is yours."

"See ya later then." Mike walked out of the office, grabbed the keys for the service truck, and drove away.

Sasha Woke up around 8:30 am, let the dogs out, made a coffee, sat down at the table, and read the newspaper. The front page showing a still shot of a blue Chevy Silverado with giant block letters asking, *"HAVE YOU SEEN ME?"* A missing person's picture of Ashley Brock was printed under the photo of the blue truck.

Sasha read on. The photo of the truck was a still shot from a traffic camera. Several people had come forward saying they witnessed a young-looking girl fitting Ashley's description get into a blue Chevy pickup on Friday at the local Dairy Queen. The pink shoes and purple backpack were what made them sure. Traffic cameras had picked up the same blue Chevy running a yellow light shortly after Ashley was last seen, but when the camera snapped a picture, the license plate was unreadable. It was suspected the driver covered the plate with clear reflective spray paint or reflective tape.

The still frame showed a blurred image of the driver, who was sitting back in his seat. It seemed like he was sitting just outside of the camera's abilities.

Sasha folded the newspaper and put it away. She stared at the wall for a few minutes. A tear welled in her eye, and she blinked it away.

Kevin Marin read the morning newspaper. A picture of his blue truck on the front page and in giant block letters, *"HAVE YOU SEEN ME?"*

"FUCK!" he yelled. This wasn't good. They had his truck. He read the article. Thankfully they didn't have the plate number or a clear photo of the driver. That was good, but still, there couldn't be too many North Sky Blue Chevy Silverados on the island. A couple, half a dozen maybe? It wouldn't be long before someone came knocking on his door. He paced around his living room for a few minutes trying to think of his next move when his phone rang. No name, just a number.

"Hello?" Kevin answered.

"You see the paper?" the voice on the other line asked with the slightest hint of a West Indies accent.

"Yeah. Fuck." Kevin could feel the sweat gathering on his brow.

"Eh, relax." The voice soothed. "They don't know it's you. It wouldn't be in the paper if they knew."

"Well, it's not going to take long for them to put two and two together." Kevin wiped his forehead, his anxiety climbing. "Fuck, what should I do here?"

"You keep your mouth shut! That's what you do. Don't say nothing to nobody about anything. Cops come by; you shut the fuck up and ask for a lawyer."

Kevin indicated he understood and rung off.

He decided this would be the best time to wash his truck. He peeled the reflective tape off the plates and sprayed them with WD-40 to break down the adhesive. He then washed the exterior, wrapped up the hose when he finished, and put away the bucket. As Kevin went inside to grab the vacuum for the interior, he saw an unmarked Victoria Police car pull to a stop in front of his driveway. It sat parked for what felt like an eternity.

A large First Nations man finally got out. He was dressed in a dark grey suit with a white button-up shirt and blue tie. His badge peeked through at his right hip as he walked up the driveway. Kevin watched through the window as the cop got to the front door. There was a loud knock, and Kevin opened the door.

"Morning," Kevin greeted, focusing on remaining calm, despite his adrenaline spiking through the roof.

"Good morning," the cop replied without any cheer in his tone. "Mr. Marin?"

"That's me." Kevin wondered if he looked nervous.

"I'm Detective Grant with the Victoria Police. We're looking at north sky blue Chevy Silverados in connection with a case. Would you mind if I looked at your truck? We're hoping to eliminate as many suspects as possible."

"Yeah, go ahead," Kevin was sweating again. He did his best to hide how badly he was panicking. "Need to look inside?" he offered, then immediately regretted it.

"If you don't mind, sure.".

Fuck! He thought again, but it was too late to rescind the offer.

He reached for the keys on the wall and noticed his hands were shaking. Pressing the fob, he said, "Help yourself. I need to get ready for work."

The detective thanked him, and Kevin calmly closed the door. He sprinted up the stairs to the guest bedroom that overlooked the driveway and peeked out from beside the blinds. His heart was slamming in his chest. He chewed ferociously on his thumbnail, feeling a pinch and drawing a little bit of blood.

The cop was kneeling at the back of the truck. Kevin could only see the top of his head. Kevin watched as he stood, looking like he was rubbing his thumb and finger together, like there was oil or something on it. He walked around to the passenger side and opened both the front and rear doors. His upper body disappeared inside. Kevin could see his outline but not what he was looking at. The detective finished what he was doing, shut the doors, looked back at the house, then walked back to his car.

"Okay," Kevin exhaled for what felt like the first time since the cop arrived. "He's leaving." He relaxed a little as he watched the large man get back in his car. His anxiety climbed again when it didn't pull away. It just sat there, blocking the driveway. Kevin looked at the time: 9:06 am. He kept watching. At 9:14 am, his heart sank when he saw two more police cruisers pulling onto his street.

The cars pulled up. Three more cops got out. Two went around to the backyard, and the other one walked up the driveway with the detective to the front door and knocked. Kevin was frantic. He called the number again.

"Yeah," the voice answered.

"The cops are at my house, man. They searched my truck!" Kevin was frantic.

"Delete your call log! And don't say anything without a lawyer." The line clicked off.

Kevin walked downstairs and opened the door. Without further formalities or explanation, the detective said, "Mr. Marin, we're going to need you to come with us, please."

Kevin looked past them at his truck, wondering what they found inside it. His eyes locked onto a small white sticker in the bottom corner of the windshield: a parking permit sticker. The same sticker was clearly visible on the still frame.

He wasn't handcuffed but was placed in the back of a cruiser and taken to the Victoria Police headquarters. Built in 1996, the large, multi-structure glass buildings took up an entire city block. The police shared the building with the headquarters for the Victoria Fire Department as well as several other municipal branches. Kevin was escorted in and sat in a small windowless room.

The police said nothing, barely even made eye contact. It felt like days passed. Kevin had no idea how long he'd been there. Nobody came by at all; nobody talked to him. He didn't even hear people in the hallway. The minutes crawled by. At 4:55 pm, almost seven hours later, he heard the door open, and a middle-aged woman with shoulder-length auburn hair walked in.

She was wearing a dark blue jacket over a pink blouse with black dress pants, her gold RCMP badge showing on her hip. She placed a manila folder on the table.

"Mr. Marin, I'm Detective Sergeant Robson," she began in a dry tone.

"I need to piss." Kevin replied.

"We'll get to that. I'm going to talk, and you can listen. You don't need to speak." She placed a small recorder on the table and hit the red button. "It's Thursday, May 18th, 2023, the time is 4:55 pm," she said, checking her watch. "This is Detective Sergeant Gale Robson with the RCMP Major Crimes Unit. I'm speaking to Kevin Marin of 11236 Nanticoke Crest, Victoria BC."

She paused and opened the folder. "Mr. Marin, today you permitted Detective Grant of the Victoria Police to perform an inspection on your vehicle. Detective Grant noted a sticker in the lower driver's side windshield of your vehicle, similar to one shown in the photo of a matching vehicle suspected to be involved in the abduction of a minor. Detective Grant noted what he described as an oily residue on both your front and rear license plates. A subsequent search of your trash bin uncovered used clear reflective tape, which we suspect the same vehicle had placed over the plates to prevent traffic cameras from positively identifying the license plates."

HUNTING PREDATORS

She paused and looked at him, her dark brown eyes hardened by years of dealing with the lowest society had to offer. "With your permission, Detective Grant performed a search on the interior of your vehicle, where he discovered several long strands of dark hair with blonde tips. They were found both on the seat and headrest. These hairs are being checked as we speak to see if they match Ashley Brock."

She stopped and looked at Kevin. He sat silently for a few seconds before speaking. "I, I think I need to see a lawyer."

Robson nodded sternly and left the room. The gravity of the situation weighed him down. The hair was going to match, and he was in deep shit now.

At 8:30 pm, Kevin Marin's lawyer, a short man in his late fifties with male pattern baldness and a close-cropped beard, reeking of pipe tobacco, sat at a table with Kevin. At the suggestion of his lawyer, Kevin agreed to speak to Detective Sgt. Robson. Kevin stated he didn't know Ashley, but he did pick up a young hitchhiker at the Dairy Queen in Nanaimo last Friday that could have been her. He said he dropped her off in Victoria at an intersection he didn't remember, and that the last he saw of her, she was walking toward a young teenage boy.

When asked why he, a full-grown adult man, gave what clearly looked like a child a ride almost two hours away from home, he stated she approached him and asked, "For a ride home to Victoria." He stated he had hitchhiked across Canada many times when he was younger and simply wanted to make sure the young girl made it to her destination safely.

"Where is she now?" Sgt. Robson demanded.

"Okay, we're done here," his lawyer interjected. "My client has cooperated and answered your questions truthfully." He stood up and motioned for Kevin to follow him. The interview room door was opened, and they walked out.

"Did they take anything from you? Wallet, keys, cell phone?" his lawyer asked as he walked fast down the hall. The lawyer was shorter but walked and spoke very quickly and with purpose.

"No, not as far as I know. I left everything at home." Kevin scurried to keep up.

"Good. Follow me out of the building. Don't say anything to anybody. Do you understand me?" It was clearly more of a demand than a question. Kevin nodded. The lawyer stopped and looked at him. "Did you hear what I just said?" he asked sternly.

"Yes," Kevin said solemnly.

"Good." His lawyer turned and resumed walking at the same pace. "Not a word!"

The way the lawyer was talking, Kevin expected news cameras and microphones to be shoved in his face, but when they stepped outside, no one was there. The streets looked empty. His lawyer continued walking towards the sidewalk.

"Hey, how am I getting home?" Kevin asked.

"Uber," his lawyer replied and kept walking without looking back.

HUNTING PREDATORS

Kevin stood in front of the police station and looked around. It was pushing 9:00 pm. He had no phone, no wallet, no cash. He figured he'd need to walk home. It would be at least an hour, but after the day he'd had cooped up in the small room, he could use it.

He started walking down Caledonia Ave when he heard a vehicle approach. A large blue Jeep drove slowly past. The driver looked at Kevin; they knew each other. The driver pointed, telling Kevin to turn right on Quadra St. He did and saw the Jeep's taillights pull into a church parking lot.

He walked up to the Jeep, opened the door, and jumped in.

"How'd it go?" The driver had the slightest touch of a West Indies or Jamaican accent, worn down over years in Canada. He didn't exaggerate it or fight to keep it.

"They asked what I knew. I said I picked up a hitchhiker who needed a ride home from Nanaimo to Victoria." Kevin explained.

The driver nodded. He was a big man in his mid-thirties, dark-skinned, standing around six-foot and weighing two hundred and twenty pounds. Today he was wearing light brown pants, brown loafers, and a purple silk shirt unbuttoned mid-way with his sculpted muscles showing underneath. His look was accented by a lot of gold: rings, bracelets, and more than one chain around his thick neck. He wasn't exactly subtle.

He had a very hard look about him: flattened nose, heavy scarring around the eyes, cauliflowering on the left ear. He usually wore stylish sunglasses, mainly because direct sunlight gave him headaches. Kevin was grateful for the sunglasses. The odd time he had seen the man without his shades on, the stare he gave off chilled Kevin to his core. Not much was known about the man. It was suspected he was born somewhere like Jamaica or Trinidad, but nobody seemed to know for sure. He went by the name Lumpz. Nobody knew his real name. Kevin met Lumpz in prison in 2012 when he and his brother were arrested for smuggling cocaine into Canada.

They thought they'd discovered a foolproof plan. Kevin stayed in Canada; his brother Jesse picked up the product in the US. They met around eight kilometres east of Abbotsford, BC, and Sumas, Washington, at 3:30 am. Jesse hurled several bricks of cocaine across the boundary road, a two-lane highway separating Canada and the US. Kevin caught the packages and disappeared seconds later on an ATV. The first two times it was a success. Unfortunately, the third time they attempted it, Kevin was arrested by Canadian authorities who had been watching nearby. Jesse was arrested by the Americans. Kevin was given two years in a Canadian prison. Jesse was sentenced to twenty five years and was still serving time in the US.

During this stint in prison, Kevin met Lumpz. Lumpz was serving a sentence for several violent crimes, all committed over a weekend when he'd kidnapped a man that owed him money. He held the man hostage while he forced the man's girlfriend to prostitute herself until the debt was paid off.

Kevin also witnessed firsthand how ferocious Lumpz could be during an argument over a card game in prison. Kevin watched as Lumpz not only beat another man to the ground, he then picked up a forty five pound metal weightlifting plate and dropped it on the man's head

HUNTING PREDATORS

while he lay unconscious. When Kevin was released and returned to Victoria, he was relieved to be away from everyone, especially Lumpz.

Kevin's relief was short-lived. Nine months later, Kevin answered a knock at his door and saw Lumpz standing there. Eight years later, Kevin was still terrified of the man. He tried to keep him at arm's length and sever ties, but Lumpz kept getting back in.

Lumpz didn't directly threaten Kevin into doing anything. He'd ask, but in ways that Kevin was terrified of the consequences if he said no. Lumpz would ask him to transport some drugs but would be practicing his swing with a golf club or baseball bat when he asked. He would ask Kevin to pick up another young girl but would pick up a picture of Kevin and his then-girlfriend or of Kevin's mother from the mantle. It wasn't *what* Lumpz asked for; it was *how* he asked that scared Kevin.

"So, you're good then?" Lumpz asked.

"Yeah, as far as I know. They let me go. I told them I can't help 'em" Kevin, still anxious, was cautiously optimistic.

Lumpz sat quietly staring ahead for a few seconds. "You hungry?" he asked.

"Starving," Kevin admitted.

"There's a little Jamaican place around the corner." Lumpz put the jeep in reverse.

Lumpz had built several small cash businesses in and around Victoria. He was the sole owner of a tattoo parlour and part owner of two more. He also owned three laundromats. He conducted most of his business out of a small autobody shop on the west side of the city in Esquimalt. The lot was always empty, as were the paint booths, but on paper the small shop did very well.

Friday May 19th, 2023

Ashley woke up again. She thought she was in the same room; she didn't remember moving, but the bedspread was green now.

Did they change the blanket? Was it always green? No. It was red before. Am I somewhere else? Her head hurt badly. Like that time, she and her sister were playing tag at the local park. Ashley was running away, looking back at her sister. She saw a bright flash and suddenly was lying on the ground. She had run into the post holding the basketball nets and knocked herself out. That's what she felt like now: a bad headache with the throw-up feeling she had before. She opened her eyes, but the light in the room made her head hurt more.

"Okay honey, c'mon in," Ashley heard a woman's voice. The air got colder, and she heard the door shut. She felt someone sit on the bed; a cold, clammy hand touched her thigh.

"She's just a baby, this one," Ashley heard a man's voice, a deep one. "Is she okay?"

"Yes, honey. We partied a little earlier. She had a bit too much, but she'll come around," the woman assured.

"Looks a little beat up. What happened?"

"You know these young ones can't hold their liquor. Poor doll fell into the bathtub yesterday," the woman explained with a casual wave.

Ashley felt the hand on her leg move up higher. She tried to move it off, but it squeezed tighter.

"The marks on her neck?" the man inquired.

"That's nothing, baby. You want to play or not?"

She felt a hand tracing her neck, then down lower on her body.

"You staying? Or going?" the man's voice asked.

"Whatever you want, baby," the woman purred.

"Stay," he invited. "I like an audience."

Ashley was trying to figure out what was going on when she felt the man's weight suddenly on top of her. She drifted out of consciousness again.

Chapter 7

Saturday May 20th, 2023, 10:00 am.

Mike, Sasha, the neighbours, and the dogs made their trek to Long Beach for their usual Saturday routine. It was a cool morning, hovering around 10 degrees Celsius, but the wetsuits helped keep the chill at bay. The four people and three dogs set up at their usual spot on the beach. Sasha wasted no time and immediately hit the water. Today was the day she was going to ride a wave. All the way to Long Beach, she made sure everyone in the group understood they weren't leaving until she did it. Mike had started playing fetch with Oscar the Trash Dog, who was still acting like a pup and had a lot of energy to burn off.

The cool weather didn't stop people from visiting the beach. It was unseasonably cold, but the large parking lot was already three-quarters full by 10:00 am, and more people were showing up steadily. After a solid hour of trying, Sasha came trudging up the beach, her bulky green surfboard under her arm.

"Tag you in?" she asked, rooting around in the cooler for a drink.

"Yeah, sure," Mike obliged. Sasha sat with the dog while Mike joined the neighbours in the water. Surfing was coming a little faster to Mike than it did to Sasha, but he didn't gloat about it. He swam out and waited with the neighbours, each catching waves in turn, sometimes riding them. After another 30 minutes, they made their way back to the beach for lunch.

Mike noticed a man and a woman sitting on a blanket close to their spot. They seemed to be engaged in small talk with Sasha. Both had the telltale signs of current military service: close-cropped hair, muscular builds, and seemingly effortless alertness. The man was tall, around six foot two. The female was more compact and wore her dyed blonde hair in a fauxhawk; not a common style, but fitting considering she appeared to be military.

"Hey, babe," Sasha called out as Mike got closer. The blond girl looked over her shoulder at him to say a polite hello. Instead, her jaw dropped.

"Mike?" The woman's voice cracked in disbelief. "Mikey!" She jumped up, started walking slowly, not believing her own eyes, then ran to him. Sasha and the other man stared after her, confused.

Mike was frozen stiff, not able to process what he was seeing. On a beach in Tofino, BC, 3000 miles from home, Mike saw Angela, his childhood friend, running towards him.

She collided with him, and the two hugged fiercely. "What the fuck are you doing here?" He squeezed her so tightly he had to release her a little before she could answer.

"I'm stationed in Victoria! What are you doing here?" she grinned, wiping away tears. "How long have you been here?" Without waiting for answers, she backed up and looked at him. "I thought you were dead! You asshole!" She punched him in the chest, then hugged him again. By now Sasha and the taller soldier were standing up. Mike looked over and saw the confusion on both their faces.

"This is Angela. We grew up together."

Angela looked at the taller soldier. "Rick, this is Mike. I told you about him. He's the guy I built *'the ramp'* with," adding the inflection on the word ramp.

"The ramp! The one that almost killed you?" Rick said in a thick British accent.

"That ramp," she confirmed with a big smile. She turned back to Mike again. "I haven't seen you since..." she paused for a few seconds, thinking.

Mike gave a smile tinged with sadness. "2008. Your 18th birthday. You left the next day." He felt a lump in his throat thinking about that day.

Mike had been in a bad motorcycle accident a few months before that day. He'd suffered multiple broken ribs, a severe concussion, a broken wrist, a broken ankle, and a shopping cart full of internal injuries. But his greatest pain came from losing his girlfriend in the accident.

He had limped his way through the snow to Angela's party, avoiding Ed's house in the process. He knocked on the door. Big Bill invited him in, but Mike opted to stay on the front porch. Angela came outside to meet him. The two stood in silence looking at each other, tears in both their eyes.

As happy as Mike was that Angela was going to make her dreams come true, part of him resented her for leaving. She was his safety net. As the two grew into their teen years, they had drifted apart slightly. They went to different schools and had different friends. Mike became consumed with boxing while Angela, even at a young age, knew she was going to be a soldier. But at seventeen he was still knocking on the back door. Still spitting blood down her sink. She was still handing him ice packs, and he was still waking up on the floor in her bedroom, or had been until a few months prior when Mike moved into his uncle's to escape his dad's abuse.

They stood in silence, neither child knowing what to say or how to articulate the hurt they were feeling about leaving each other. Angela hugged Mike. When they let go, Mike looked her in the eyes. "Please be careful."

He turned to leave. Angela grabbed his hand pleadingly.

"Mikey, take care of yourself, please. Nobody else will." Tears streamed down her face.

Mike smiled, trying not to break down. He limped off the front steps and down the street. At the last moment he looked back and saw her standing on the porch, freezing, arms wrapped around herself, watching him leave.

Mike and Angela finished introductions with everyone else. The group of six, plus three dogs, spent the afternoon on the beach. Angela and Mike played catch-up. She told him about her time in the army, how she'd risen to the rank of Warrant Officer and was a combat engineer. She had served in Afghanistan and was injured on two occasions. He asked about her sister Sarah, who was now happily married, and Big Bill, who was happily retired. Mike filled her in about travelling with Nick and living an almost nomadic lifestyle since his passing until meeting Sasha.

"I heard about Nick," Angela sympathized. "That's the last anybody from home heard about you. Rumour was, you packed up and left Windsor the day after his funeral."

"No, not quite. I had a bit of a run-in with Windsor Police," Mike confessed. "Got into a scuffle. Beat it in court. Decided it was best to leave. There was nothing there for me anymore anyway."

As he spoke, Angela took a running inventory of him. His hands looked battered and broken too many times to count. His face still had the telltale signs of a fighter: flattened nose, scarring around the eyes and cheeks. Angela was wise enough to know not all of it came from the ring. Mike also had an assortment of tattoos placed seemingly at random all over his torso and legs. The more she looked, the more Angela realized many had no real meaning and were there to cover the scars from various altercations: cuts from what she guessed were knives or broken glass, a scar from what appeared to be having the claw end of a crowbar or hammer stuck in his bicep, and an offset from where his collarbone had been broken and never reset properly. His hair was cut short, and several scars on his head were also visible, most notably a large one looking like a road map on the back of his head that clearly came from being hit with a beer or liquor bottle. Her smile faded a bit as she remembered those same words said of her front porch: *Mikey, take care of yourself, please." No one else will.*

"Jesus, Mike, what happened to you?" She interrupted.

Mike was caught off guard. "What do you mean?"

HUNTING PREDATORS

Her face was a mixture of sadness, pain, and guilt. Her eyes scanned his various battle wounds. "You look like you got stuck in a gear box."

"Oh," he paused for a second, looking at the same spots on himself. "Yeah," he added but didn't continue.

The group left the beach later than usual. Mike and Angela exchanged contact info and made plans to meet in Victoria soon. They hugged in the parking lot again. "I thought you were dead," Angela murmured. She squeezed him one last time, and they left in separate directions.

Angela was sitting in the passenger seat of her big black Dodge pickup. Rick was driving. "So, that's the guy, is it?" he inquired with his thick accent.

"That's him," she confirmed, staring out the window.

"Out with it then." Rick probed gently, knowing his wife was upset.

"See the scars on him?" she asked.

"I've seen worse on others," Rick replied cautiously. He understood his wife was concerned, but he worried for her. It wouldn't be the first time she'd slipped into another one of her bouts of depression, usually brought on by feelings of guilt.

"Yeah, me too." She looked wistfully out the window before taking Rick's hand on the centre console. "It's just," she paused, looking for the right words. "In the field it's different, you know? A bomb goes off; there are going to be wounds. Mike is four days older than me. Did you see how bad it was? He's thirty-three years old. Those scars are in varying states of healing too. Looks like he never went more than a couple weeks without getting fucked up."

"He's had a hard go. Seems okay now," Rick offered.

"Yeah, but..." She trailed off as she stared.

"You think it's your fault." Rick finished her thought.

Angela looked at him with pleading eyes, wanting him to understand. "Hon, he had nobody. His dad was a monster. His mom got as far away as she could. His uncle was infantry and a lawn dart," she explained, referring to Mike's uncle Nick. Nick was an army vet and infantry airborne. "He was a bachelor, and he was really just a big kid himself. I was all he had. And I left him." She looked at her husband, her face crumbling with remorse.

"Oh, love. You can't save everybody. He's seen some shit, but he's still standing." Rick gently pointed out. "You've reconnected. He's alive and looks happy."

Angela smiled and squeezed Rick's hand again.

"So, he's the one who ran when you crashed, is he?" Rick asked again. Angela barked out a laugh.

"Yeah, but he came back after." She smiled at the memory. "He redeemed himself later on too, when we were fifteen. Aaron Taylor, my first boyfriend, cheated on me with that slut Tammy Buchanan. When Mike saw me crying, he walked right up to Aaron's front porch and knocked on the screen door. Aaron opened the big door, and Mike punched him, right through the screen, pulled him outside, and beat the shit out of him on his own front porch." She laughed softly, staring out the window, remembering the event.

HUNTING PREDATORS

"Did you guys date or something?" Rick asked.

"No, never. We were friends. Started kindergarten together, and until the day I left for basic, he was always there. He had a terrible home life. I was his escape. I was a tomboy; kids would try to pick on me. Mike would beat them up for it. We were more like brother and sister than friends. Just always had each other's backs." She looked at Rick and teasingly added, "Do I detect a hint of jealousy?"

"No, love. He looks like a bulldog now." Rick said honestly.

Angela smiled and held his hand as they drove.

Mike and Sasha drove back to town. Sasha worked on Saturday nights and would usually try to catch a quick nap during the drive, but today was the first time she had ever seen Mike's face light up like that. And stay lit up. She was too curious to snooze.

"So, I get that you guys knew each other as kids, but tell me about her," Sasha probed as they drove down the winding highway.

Mike stared out the windshield. "She shared a backyard with my next-door neighbour growing up. We started kindergarten together. Same bus stop in the mornings. Things were pretty shitty with my old man. I used to hide at her place."

"You guys date? Or..." Sasha asked, genuinely curious, not threatened.

"No, nothing like that. We were homies. She knew what it was like for me at home. I trusted her. Her dad would lie for me if Ed came looking. She never threw it in my face the way others did. Kids can be cruel, ya know."

Sasha, having grown up poor, knew firsthand what little assholes kids could be.

"If he was really bad and I had to get away from him, I'd hide at her place," Mike elaborated. "We were just buddies. She was a tomboy. We played baseball, GI Joes, shit like that. Built ramps for our bikes." Mike grinned, remembering the crash of the century. "We just... lost touch. She joined the army. I left Windsor. But as kids we did everything together. There was no tension, even in our teenage years when we both started dating other people. We always had each other, at least until she moved. Things were harder with her gone. It was really good to see her again."

Sasha smiled in understanding, happy to see Mike looking so content. Then, despite her best efforts, she started to nod off as Mike continued down the highway, lost in fond memories.

Chapter 8

Saturday May 18th, 2023, 5:30 pm.

Kevin woke up early. He showered, paced the house, and decided to go grab some groceries. When he stepped outside, the next-door neighbour glared at him. He lived in a relatively new area with semidetached homes, although he couldn't figure out why they called them that. They were completely attached. He didn't have a job per se; he made money off Lumpz, which landed him in a strange position. He couldn't own a home, as he had no income on paper, but he made enough off one score a few years ago to walk onto a car lot and pay $65,000 cash for a new truck.

After putting his groceries away, Kevin sat on the couch. The anxiety was killing him. He kept staring out the windows wondering if the police were coming back. At 5:30 pm he sat down on his couch and had just cracked open a beer when his phone dinged. He opened it to a Facebook message from his ex-girlfriend. It was a link to a news article. He opened it and coughed out his beer; it was a picture of him walking out of the police station. *"Police release suspect, not enough evidence"*

"What the fuck!" Kevin yelled. This was bad. They didn't say police questioned a man and cleared him. They thought he did it. Again, it's not what is said; it's what isn't said that matters sometimes. He read the article, seething with anger. His phone dinged again. Then again. Everyone he knew was seeing this!

HUNTING PREDATORS

He decided he needed to get away for a couple of days. The whole thing would blow over by the end of the weekend. Honestly, how long would they look for a missing native girl, he rationalized? A couple of days tops, then something else would happen and he'd be fine. He loaded up his truck and set off for Tofino. If he started packing now, he'd be there by 11:00 pm. It was a long weekend. He'd blend in.

Sasha was working her usual Saturday night shift. Tonight, the place was packed. It was Victoria Day weekend, named after Queen Victoria, a monarch born May 24th, 1819, who took the throne on June 20th, 1837. She remained there until her death on January 22nd, 1901. An act of Canadian parliament riding off the popularity of another dead queen established that from then on, the third Monday in May was a holiday in honour of Queen Victoria, the longest-serving monarch in British history. The record was held until her great-granddaughter, Queen Elizabeth II, surpassed that title in 2015. Over 120 years after Queen Victoria's death, most Canadians gave less than a shit about either of the queens or the monarchy as a whole. But almost everyone in Canada looked forward to the long weekend; the weekend signified the start of summer.

Unofficially, most people dropped the name "Victoria Day," drifting away from the queen's birthday. As most beer companies in Canada sold cases in bottles of twenty-four, a "two-four" was the official slang term for a case of beer. Consequently, Victoria Day weekend was unofficially redubbed "Two-Four weekend." And on every two-four weekend in Canada, bars, campsites, and beaches were packed with Canadians looking to shake off the winter blues.

HUNTING PREDATORS

Sasha was slammed all night with orders. Part-time waitressing suited her. She was short and muscular and navigated around a packed bar with an efficiency rarely seen. She had a big, genuine smile that lit up her crystal blue eyes and had quickly developed a reputation with the regulars as funny and pleasant. She was welcoming and friendly, but she had very clear boundaries that she stood by and defended.

Mike would visit her on occasion and often met her after work to walk her home, but a stranger seeing them in the bar at the same time would never suspect they were together. She worked mostly for tips, and having a large, battle-scarred boyfriend watching over her would hinder her cause.

On this particular Saturday, Mike, Raye, and Vicky had a few drinks at home in the evening. As the night wore on, Raye decided they should walk down and visit Sasha at work. They made their way in and found a table in the far corner. A few minutes later they were joined by Mike's boss, Tim, whose fiancé, Hailey, was working the bar while Sasha hustled with the tray.

The four of them were engaged in their usual banter when they heard several glasses break and Sasha yell. Mike sprang up from his seat and saw Sasha punching a man that was trying to cover up. Onlookers stood there shocked. Mike rushed in and grabbed her around the waist, hoisted her up, and rushed out the door with her.

"What happened?" He inquired as he set her down gently in the gravel parking lot.

"That fucking piece of shit!" she replied with fire in her eyes.

"Did he touch you?" Mike had never seen Sasha so angry. Sounds drifted outside, indicating whatever had started in the bar wasn't finished.

"No!" She snapped.

"Okay babe, what happened?" Mike's concern for Sasha had him so focused, he didn't hear the sounds coming from inside the bar. A loud scream broke his concentration.

"Shit! Tim!" Mike exclaimed and ran back inside. Tim was old school. Mike knew if one of the girls had a problem with a customer being inappropriate, that customer would be fighting Tim whether they wanted to or not. Mike rushed back in and saw the same guy Sasha had been punching trying to hide under a table.

Tim flipped the table over trying to get to him. The patrons who were tourists were in shock. The regulars knew better than to get in his way. "Stop! Hey, stop!" Mike yelled, stepping in front of his friend and holding his ground. Tim didn't want to take on Mike, so he begrudgingly backed off. The man on the ground scurried out the door, a trail of blood behind him.

Tim's teeth were showing. The short, squat, olive-skinned man who usually had a big friendly smile was panting and snarling. He resembled a feral dog looking for a fight. The two men said nothing to each other; both knew better than to open their mouths and say something stupid around this many people.

After a few breaths, Mike looked at Tim. "Back door, check on Sasha, please," knowing the only thing more important to Tim than hurting this guy right now would be making sure the girls were okay. Tim's eyes flickered to Mike. Still seething with rage, he walked out the back.

Mike could hear the crowd. The murmurs of "What was that all about?" He looked at Hailey behind the bar, the look on his face asking, "*What happened?*" Hailey shrugged as if to say, "*I don't know.*" Mike shifted his attention out the door. He watched as the bloodied man ran across the street and jumped into a late-model blue Chevy pickup.

Raye and Vicky started cleaning up the mess, Raye resetting the tables and stools and Vicky cleaning up the broken glass. Hailey came from behind the bar with a mop and bucket. Within minutes the place was back to normal; the people seemed to have already forgotten about the incident.

Mike made his way back outside; Tim was smoking, and Sasha was still furious.

"Okay, you have to tell me what happened." Mike needed answers.

Sasha looked at Tim. "Can you give us a minute?"

Tim nodded. He reached over and squeezed Sasha's hand. "You good, hon?"

She nodded and thanked him. He gave Mike a pat on the shoulder and walked back inside.

Mike held her stare. She took a deep breath. "That's him."

"Him, who?" Mike was puzzled.

"That's the fucking guy that took that little girl on the news." Sasha insisted.

Mike didn't say anything. Not *"Are you sure?"* Or *"How do you know?"* He just held her stare. "So, what happened?" he asked again calmly.

"I just saw him, and" she paused. "That stupid smug look on his face. Sitting in the bar, ogling women when that poor girl is..." Her voice cracked.

"We don't know for sure that it's him." Mike countered calmly.

"It's him!" she said sternly but not yelling. "His stupid face is seared into my brain. I'm certain."

"Okay, but you don't know if he did anything." Mike added. She was still worked up, but not angry. There was something off about her. "Talk to me," he pleaded.

"That poor girl. She's gotta be in hell right now." A fresh tear slid down Sasha's cheek.

Mike pondered what she'd said. Not *"lying in a ditch somewhere."* Sasha was talking like she was certain the young girl was still alive.

Vicky popped her head outside. "Everything okay?"

"Yeah. I'm taking her home. Can you fill in for the rest of tonight?" Mike asked.

"Sure, I'll split the tips." Vicky offered.

"No need, doll, you keep 'em." Mike said as he and Sasha started walking.

They walked home in silence. Mike let the dogs out. Sasha took a shower, then joined him on the couch. Mike pulled her in so she was leaning against him. "It's pretty clear there's something you want to tell me."

"I want you to help me kill him." Sasha announced very matter-of-factly. "I'm not stupid. We were driving across the country, but I saw the newspapers at every stop. And I heard the radio, Mike. I saw you the next morning. I know it was you."

Mike looked into her bright crystal blue eyes and noticed they had a different look in them. "What was me?"

"That fucking massacre in the Falls," she said, somewhat exasperated, referring to five dead bodies scattered around the Niagara Falls area the day before they left to drive out west.

Sasha elaborated when Mike didn't say anything. "That cop, the one who threatened me. I read that someone attacked him and held him hostage. Suddenly there are five guys lying dead, and the cop turns up fine. Then we just left. That's not a coincidence! You killed them. I saw you when you got home the next morning; you were covered head to toe in blood. The first thing you said to me was, 'It's not mine.'"

Mike didn't say anything. He just looked at her. Sasha continued. "We have a deal, Mike. I'll follow you into hell, but don't lie to me."

"Will you marry me?" Mike asked, catching her off guard.

"What?" Sasha was taken aback.

"Will you marry me?" he asked again.

"What the fuck are you talking about? Quit fucking around."

"I'm not fucking around, Sasha. I'm asking you. Right now. And I'm dead serious. Will you marry me? I'll tell you everything. Right after we get married."

"Why? What's going on?" Sasha looked at him wearily.

"Two things: one, spousal immunity. If we're married, you can be asked, but you're not compelled to testify against me. Two, I'm rather fond of you. So," he paused, "will you marry me? I was going to ask you anyway. This isn't exactly what I had in mind. But what the hell."

She stared at him in disbelief. "You're serious, aren't you?"

"Yes. I'm serious."

She paused for a few seconds. She'd seen him come home the morning after the massacre. She wasn't exaggerating; he looked like he was soaked in blood. She saw that he had over two million dollars in cash. She'd heard that James, the guy that had threatened her senior citizen landlord, had turned up dead. She had watched this large man go from calm and collected to releasing unbridled violence in the blink of an eye, before going right back to calm and collected again. Watching Mike manage his moods was like watching someone flip a light switch on then off quickly. Part of her wondered how he could do that so seamlessly. She knew it should scare her.

But Sasha had also seen how much this man loved her. He wouldn't think twice about hitting someone else, but he would never hurt her. For the first time in her life since losing her father, she felt safe, protected. It was the same feeling her dad gave her. *"They'll have to kill me before I ever let them hurt you."*.

"Yes," she replied. "Yes. I'll marry you."

"Is it only because you want to kill someone?" Mike grinned at her.

"No, asshole. Even without premeditated murder on the menu, I'd have said yes if you asked me." She shoved him. "When?"

"Who do you want there?" Mike asked.

"No one."

"Okay, soon then. We'll get it done. Tell everyone after," he promised.

"So. You'll help me?" she asked.

"No. You'll help me," he corrected.

Chapter 9

Saturday May 20th, 2023, 11 pm.

Kevin got to Tofino just as the nightlife was getting into full swing. He knew from years past that Two-Four weekend was a busy one. He drove up Campbell Street looking for a place to park. A white Jeep Cherokee pulled out of a spot directly across the street from a bar.

"My lucky day," he said out loud to himself as he pulled in right behind it. He hopped out of his truck and made his way across the street.

The place was packed. He wormed his way through the crowd, found a small table that another couple had recently abandoned, and sat down. It was a nice place. The bartender was a short, curvy girl with long black hair. She was cute; her eyes sparkled as she laughed with the customers. The waitress was a little powerhouse of a woman. She wore light blue jeans and a black t-shirt with the sleeves cut off. Kevin liked the ink on her biceps, and after giving her a thorough once-over, concluded she was hot. She came walking by quickly with a tray full of pints.

"Excuse me," he interjected.

"Just a sec, hon," she threw back as she scooted by. She returned less than a minute later, her tray full of empties. "What can I get ya?"

"What do you have on tap?" he asked, smiling up at her. If he played his cards right, he was going to see all the tattoos she had on her. Their eyes met. He thought she had a beautiful smile. Without warning, the smile dropped from her face. Pure disgust crossed it. Her crystal blue eyes went from friendly and welcoming to furious and full of hatred. She used the tray like she was trying to nail someone with a pie, only there were glasses on it instead of whipped cream. He saw it coming and put his hand up, knocking most of the glasses off, save for one that hit him on the side of the head. She used the tray and smacked him on the head with it twice, then started punching him.

"You fucking piece of shit!" she screamed, landing blow after blow. Kevin couldn't understand what had happened. This girl he'd never seen before was attacking him! As fast as it started, it ended. He chanced a look up and saw a big guy carrying her away. Suddenly he was hit again. A bright flash. He blinked and was on the floor. A kick hit him on his side. There was a man attacking him now.

What the fuck, he thought, but this guy wasn't stopping, so he scurried under a table trying to protect his head. There was a crash as the table was flipped. A foot stomped on his back.

"I didn't do anything!" he yelled. Another stomp and Kevin went into survival mode. No sense trying to figure out why it was happening; it was happening just the same. Best to try and survive and figure it out later.

The commotion around him stopped. He chanced looking up again. The same big guy that grabbed the girl had stopped the man. Kevin didn't wait to ask questions. He saw a second to move, and he took it. He crawled off the floor and ran out to his truck, jumping over the waist-high fence on the patio on his way. Fumbling with his keys, he managed to get in his truck. He got it started and stomped on the gas, not looking to see if anyone was in front or behind him.

He drove around the block and floored it out of town. A few minutes later he pulled into a local gas station. The sky was dark, but the green and red neon sign with the white halogen lights looked like a beacon in the woods. He went in and saw a heavy-set middle-aged woman behind the till. She had grey hair in a ponytail and thick Buddy Holly glasses.

"Sir, are you okay?" she asked, panic in her voice.

"Some people just attacked me. Can I use your bathroom?"

"It's around the outside," she pointed. "Want me to call the police?" she offered.

"Already did," he said. "They're on their way." He lied; the last thing he wanted to do was talk to the police again.

Kevin went around to the bathroom and let himself in. The bathroom was small with white walls and tiled floors. He looked in the mirror: his face was a mess. His nose was bleeding, his mouth and chin were covered in blood, and he had a small cut on the side of his head. The swelling on his cheeks and forehead was starting to show.

He washed his face in the sink. It seemed like there was an endless supply of blood for a few minutes. Eventually the water returned to clear. He used a paper towel to dry his face off and looked in the mirror again. He had some red marks and some spots that would bruise. His side and back were throbbing, but most of the damage seemed minor. He left the once clean bathroom a bloody mess. Jumping back in his truck, he drove away from town towards the line of resorts and hotels.

Kevin pulled up at a secluded resort made up of small hut-shaped stand-alone units that faced the water. He went to the front office; it was closed up and dark, but there was a doorbell. He pressed it and waited but got no response. He pressed it again and waited. A woman's voice came over the intercom.

"Can I help you?"

"Do you have any vacancies?"

There was a long pause, then finally, "I'll be right there."

About five minutes later, a young woman appeared in the parking lot. She was pretty, mid-twenties with long blonde hair worn up. She had on plaid pajama pants, slippers, and a bulky sweatshirt. She unlocked the office door and let him in.

"Sorry about the time. Was planning on getting here a lot sooner, but my flight was delayed," he lied.

"That's okay. Did you have a reservation?"

"No. I stayed here a few years ago. Just pulled in."

She typed away at the keyboard. "Okay," she paused. "We have one single. It's $560 for tonight or $990 for two nights."

Kevin felt like he'd been punched again. "I'm sorry, what?"

"Long weekend," she shrugged.

He was tired and sore. "Fine. Two nights, please." He handed her a Visa with someone else's name on it.

Fifteen minutes later, he unlocked the door to his hut. It was a quaint little dome shape. Red cedar horizontal slats lined the inside. No TV. Just a bed, living area, and small kitchen. The smell of the cedar wood and coffee from the previous occupant filled his nose; Kevin liked this place. He'd been here a few years before with his then-girlfriend, Lisa. It was the only weekend trip they took that didn't end up in a drunken fight.

He showered and examined himself in the mirror, the bruising on his back and left side more obvious now. The red swelling on his face was starting to bruise too. "What the fuck was all that about?" he asked himself aloud. That girl attacked him for no reason. Then some fucking guy jumped on him. He'd never seen either of them before. Thank Christ for that bouncer, he thought.

At 12:28 am he stripped back the blankets, crawled into bed, and started to doze off. He wasn't sure how long he had been out or, given what happened at the bar, if he had slept at all, when he heard pounding on the door. He jumped out of bed. More pounding.

"Sir?" Pounding. "Sir! Do you own a blue pickup?" More pounding.

"Why?" he asked through the door. He looked at the clock. 2:17 am.

"There's black smoke coming out from under the hood. Is that your truck?" replied a woman's voice. It sounded like the girl from the front desk. He opened the door, ready to run to the truck in his underwear, when what looked like a tree stood in front of him. There was a bright white flash, and it felt like his nose exploded. He was knocked back into the hut, his vision blurred. The pressure behind his eyes was numb at first, then the pain became excruciating. "What the fuck?" he groaned.

"Hey," Kevin heard a man's voice. "Hey, look at me."

"HEL—" Kevin tried to yell for help, but the sole of a boot stepped on his throat. What came out was a split-second yelp.

"Close the door," he heard the voice say. "Look through the side of the curtains, see if any lights come on or anyone comes out." The voice was calm, calm enough that it scared Kevin to his core.

Thirty seconds passed. The male spoke again. "Good?"

"Nothing," a female voice replied.

It was dark in the room, the only light coming from the night sky through the large sliding glass door with the curtains half open.

"Cinch the curtains tight," the man directed the woman before turning his attention back to Kevin. "Hey." The boot jolted down. "You hear me?"

Kevin tried to answer, but the pressure was on his windpipe.

"Listen closely," the man instructed. There was an audible click, the distinctive sound of the hammer of a revolver being cocked. Then the barrel pressed to his forehead. "I'm going to take my foot off your throat. If you make any noise. Even gasp for air too loudly, I'll kill you where you lay, do you understand me? Tap the floor if you do."

Kevin's right hand tapped the floor. "Good," the man kept the pressure on but shifted his focus to the woman in the room. "Point your gun at his head; if he tries anything when I move my foot, shoot him. And be ready to get the hell out of here."

Kevin couldn't help but think this was not only terrifying but strange. It was like a school lesson on home invasion. The foot moved as the man ordered, "Get up."

Kevin slowly got up. The man in the room was huge; the female was small. Both were wearing dark browns and greens; both had on camouflage ski masks. The man was holding a black revolver; the girl had what looked like a matte black plastic automatic pistol. She was looking out the window. She hadn't budged.

The man tied Kevin's hands behind his back with industrial zip ties. The girl at the window looked at him, crystal blue eyes behind the mask. *The waitress*, he thought. He heard duct tape tearing; it was placed over his mouth. Next, a black bag went over his head and everything went dark. He was effortlessly hoisted over the big guy's shoulder and carried outside. The air was damp and cold. He was thrown roughly into the back seat of his own truck. He then heard the man say, "Follow me."

He felt like they pulled onto the highway and turned right. Left would bring him back to Tofino. He wanted to ask why they were doing this. He didn't know these people. Had they seen him in the paper? That must be it. He had no idea how long they drove; the big guy left the radio off.

Kevin wanted to sit up, to do something. You don't realize how much you use your arms for balance until you can't use them anymore, and you don't realize how slow time drags when you have nothing to gauge it, no music, no conversation. The first minute can feel like an hour, and the second hour can feel like a minute. Kevin must have dosed off; he didn't remember stopping but heard the truck door slam.

The rear door opened. Two large hands grabbed him by the head and yanked him right out and let him fall to the ground like a rolled-up rug. Twigs, sticks, and rocks dug into his body. The ground was cold and soggy.

"Get up," the man barked.

Kevin tried to say, "I can't," but was restricted by the tape on his mouth.

A kick to his sternum. "Get up!" The voice was a little more forceful this time. Kevin rolled to his stomach, onto his knees, and started getting up. He was helped to his feet.

"Let's go." The man started leading him. Kevin couldn't see anything. He was cold, the ground was rough, and every step hurt. He wasn't sure how long they walked, at least 10 minutes. Kevin repeatedly tripped over roots, rocks, and mounds of dirt. His feet were stabbed and punctured by who knows what.

"Wait," the voice commanded. "If he tries anything, shoot him." The voice was still so calm, it was terrifying. One zip tie was cut free. Kevin's back was slammed against a tree, and his wrists were retied around it. He felt a hand grab whatever was over his head and pause there. Kevin overheard the man tell his partner, "If you want out, we do it now. Otherwise, there's no turning back."

"Do it," the female instructed, and in an instant the cover on his head was ripped off. His eyes adjusted. It had to be around 4:00 am. It was still dark, but the sky was starting to lighten. He focused in. There were two of them. Large man, small woman. The man reached out and ripped the tape off his mouth.

"OW!" Kevin hollered. "What the hell is going on here?" His question was met with silence. "If this is about the bar earlier, I didn't touch her," he explained to the large man, then looked at the woman.

"Where is Ashley Brock?" the woman asked.

"Who?" Kevin didn't recognize the name. The woman stepped forward and smashed the butt of her pistol into his nose, resulting in a white-hot explosion of pain. "Jesus! Why are you doing this?" he cried.

"Easy," the big man cautioned.

"Thank you," Kevin whimpered. The big man stepped forward and punched Kevin in the stomach, hard. Kevin tried to buckle from the pain but couldn't move. He threw up on himself.

"Shut up, asshole. That wasn't for your benefit." Then to his partner, the big guy advised, "Don't hit the face or head too much. It's not like the movies. If you knock him out, you'll scramble his brain. He'll be useless for a couple of hours. Won't tell you anything worth knowing."

"Okay." The woman nodded. Turning back to Kevin, she repeated, "Where is Ashley Brock?"

"I don't know who that is!"

The big guy continued ignoring Kevin, addressing his partner instead. "Even though we're in the middle of nowhere, keep him from yelling. Worst-case scenario, some tree-hugging hippie is out for a stroll, and then we'll need to deal with them too."

His attention returning to Kevin, the big guy advised, "Raise your voice again, and I'll staple your tongue to your chin. After that it'll be 'blink once for yes and twice for no' type questions. Got it?" Kevin looked down and realized the guy was in fact holding a staple gun.

Then the big guy turned back to the woman. "You've asked him twice. Ask him a third time. If he's still playing dumb, hurt him. Don't knock him out, though. If it were me, I'd tape his mouth shut so he can't scream, then I dunno, grab that bat and smash his knee in."

Kevin was panicking now. Who the fuck were these two? They weren't cops, that was for sure.

"Where is Ashley Brock?" the woman asked for the third time.

"I swear I don't know anything." Kevin pleaded. The guy let out a sigh, reached behind where Kevin was tied, and produced a wooden baseball bat.

"You want to do it? Or want me to?" the guy asked his partner.

"I will." The woman took the bat in her gloved hand. She took a step towards Kevin.

"Okay, wait, wait, wait," Kevin pleaded again. "I'll tell you what I know."

"Too late," the big guy said, stuffing a small rag into Kevin's mouth, then adding more tape.

Kevin tried screaming, but he was gagged and muffled. The woman, a lefty, wound up and swung, smashing Kevin's left knee. The sound was a dull *thonk*, and Kevin wailed from behind the gag. The pain was intense. He wanted to fall over but couldn't. He wanted to slide down the tree, but it was too wide. His stomach wretched, and he tried to throw up, but he was gagged. Seeing this, the big guy stepped in and ripped the tape off. Kevin threw up again, heaving between sobs. The tape was reapplied. His breathing was shallow. He wanted to faint.

"Listen to me," the big guy tilted Kevin's chin up so he could look him in the eye. "How you're feeling right now, that's the best you're going to feel for a very long time. But believe me, it can get a whole lot worse; we haven't even scratched the surface of what you can live through. Now we're going to ask you again. If you play dumb, or if I don't believe your answer, I'm going to tape you back up, and she's going to smash that same knee two more times. Blink once if you understand me."

Kevin blinked hard but looked like he was going to faint. The big guy grabbed the tape and paused. "Remember, if I don't believe you, she's swinging again." He yanked the tape off.

"Where is Ashley Brock?"

Kevin took a deep breath. He was in so much pain it was hard to think.

"Okay," the big guy sighed, reaching to put the tape back on. "Hit him again." His partner wound up.

"Wait, wait, wait," Kevin was desperate. "I dropped her off in Victoria."

"The more we have to ask, the more we have to hit," the big guy advised. "Last chance. You tell us everything. Or Barry Bonds here is going to smash a couple of dingers out of the park."

The woman positioned herself and wound up again. "Where is Ashley Brock?"

"I picked her up in Nanaimo and brought her to my friend's in Victoria. We hung out. Partied. She left there with one of them. I haven't seen her since."

"Did she leave on her own, or did you guys drug her?" The woman hadn't loosened her grip on the bat.

"On her own," Kevin answered.

She nodded. The tape was put back on, and she smashed his knee a second and third time. Both hits were loud and dull. She was putting everything she had into it. Kevin was screaming from behind the gag. His left knee was destroyed; each hit felt like nothing he'd ever experienced. A few minutes passed. He quieted down, and the tape was removed.

The woman tried again. "She was drugged, wasn't she?"

Kevin was panting, barely able to stand being alive right now. "Yes."

"And whoever took her, they're getting her hooked on dope and pimping her out, aren't they?" Her question was more of a statement.

"Yes."

"You've done this before for them, haven't you?" The woman looked at him with such hatred and disgust. In his painful delirium, Kevin thought it was ironic how such icy blue eyes could have such fire in them.

"Yes," Kevin sobbed.

She nodded, satisfied. The tape went back on. She stood facing him and swung back and forth from left to right 5 times "You. Fucking. Piece. Of. Shit." hitting his ribs on both sides with each word.

Kevin tried to bring his left knee up to shield his body, but it was so mangled, he could do nothing to cover up. He thought those blows killed him; it was just a matter of time before his body realized it.

"Anger," the big guy cautioned. "Keep your emotions in check."

The girl took a step back and a deep breath. The tape came off. Kevin coughed and spat out dark blood. He sobbed and coughed up more blood. "Please stop," he whimpered. His crying seemed to anger the woman.

"Who took her?" she asked.

"If I tell you, they'll kill me," he whispered.

"Maybe," the big guy conceded. "But you'll have a chance to run. You could be bandaged up and gone before they even realize the cops are on to them. But as sure as the sun will rise and set today, if you don't tell us. I'll kill you and leave you tied to this tree."

"Who took her?" The woman asked more firmly.

"I swear I don't know his real name. They call him Lumpz, like with a Z," Kevin replied, recognizing that telling the truth was his only way out alive. "Black, mid-thirties, slight Jamaican accent. I met him in prison. He's got his hands in everything: dope, pimping, and setting up robberies. The guy is bad news. I don't know where he lives, but he drives a blue Jeep."

"Light blue, dark blue?" The big guy wanted specifics.

"Dark, like a navy blue metallic. Leaves the top off. Has a black ragtop. No bumper stickers or anything I can remember. But there's a set of small boxing gloves hanging off the mirror; one has a Canadian flag, and the other I think is Jamaican, maybe? Black, yellow, and green."

"Anything else we should know?" the big guy asked.

"No," Kevin replied honestly. Then everything went dark.

Chapter 10

Sunday May 21st, 2023, 3:55 am.

The sound of the gunshot was deafening, and it made Sasha jump. She was outside, six feet away, and it didn't stop her ears from ringing. The sound was so loud she felt it in her core, like an unexpected lightning strike that you can feel. It dawned on her that she wasn't even aware that Mike had drawn his gun. He had dropped the staple gun and pulled the revolver out of his waistline so quickly she didn't see it.

"Why'd you do that?" Sasha asked, confused.

"He knew who you were." Mike advised.

"How?"

"Your eyes. I'm guessing." Mike mused, wiping down his gun. "Earlier, he'd said, *'If this is about the bar, I didn't touch her.'* He said it to me, about you. You have very distinctive eyes. He knew it was you."

Sasha nodded. "You weren't going to let him go regardless, were you?"

"Nope," Mike confirmed. "He's an animal."

Initially Sasha had been feeling weird about the whole situation. She'd just taken part in a cold-blooded murder. She reminded herself the guy kidnapped and sold children. She didn't so much have a moral problem with what she and Mike had done. It was the fact that she wasn't bothered that seemed unsettling.

"Now what?" Sasha had no idea where to go from here.

"Nothing. I picked this place because there's wolves and bears. We're deep enough in the woods that nobody will stumble across him. By tonight the critters will be eating him." After a minute Mike added, "Are you okay?"

"Kind of..." Sasha paused for a few seconds. "Numb?" she replied, more as a question than a statement.

"Okay, we need to burn these clothes. Blood, brains, puke, sweat. This guy is all over them. We'll stash his truck too."

"Why don't we burn it?" Sasha was looking to keep things simple.

"Well, for one thing, it could start a forest fire," Mike replied. "For another, if the truck is found burned, the cops will start looking for him. As far as they're concerned now, he's on the run."

"So that's it?" Sasha looked from the body on the tree back to Mike. "We're done?"

Mike looked back at the guy's dead body. He walked over and cut the zip ties free. The body crumpled in a twisted, bloody heap. "With him, yes."

"What about that Lumpz guy? Are we going after him?"

"In time. We need to figure things out. There's a process here; we don't run in guns blazing. This guy was a schlub, a foot soldier at best. As we work our way up the chain of command, they get harder to reach," Mike explained. "We need to be smart about this. Go running in without knowing who we're dealing with, we could both end up dead."

"We have to get her out of there," Sasha pleaded.

Mike was walking back toward the vehicle and stopped. "I understand you're upset over her, but why is this particular missing girl so important to you?"

Sasha stared at him. "She just is," she said dismissively.

"No, there's more to it than that. If we're doing this, I need to know why." Mike gestured toward the corpse on the ground. "Babe, few things say I love you more than killing a pedophile together. You can trust me."

Sasha took another deep breath, stared at the wall of trees surrounding the small clearing, and started to speak.

Friday, October 21st, 2011.

A shy eighteen-year-old, Sasha, was working at a small coffee shop in Hamilton. It had been almost 3 months since her dad had died, and she was struggling to get by. Her older sister left for Europe to study abroad. Her older brother, Adem, had also left town recently. They had buried both parents in a little under thirteen months, and at 20 years old he felt he'd had enough of reality and needed to get away. Her younger brother was barely out of diapers and was with his biological dad, Sasha's stepdad. She was young, short, chubby in her own eyes, and felt lost. Her siblings were gone or too young. Both parents were gone, and her stepdad was an asshole on a good day.

HUNTING PREDATORS

She had initially moved into a small three-bedroom apartment with two friends from high school. They helped tear through her small inheritance in a couple of months. Once the money dried up, so did their friendship. They quickly turned from kind and supportive to cold and callous when Sasha couldn't fund the weekend parties.

When a new girl named Kimmy started at the coffee shop, she mentioned her roommate had recently moved out. Sasha jumped at the chance to take over the other half of the lease. Kimmy seemed nice. She was in her late twenties, pretty but a little weathered looking. Kimmy was taller than Sasha, around five foot nine, and curvy. She had dark, tanned skin and long, black hair. They partied a lot, and for an eighteen-year-old in mourning hoping to escape her own reality, partying seemed perfect. Eventually Kimmy's work started to suffer. Sasha always made it in, but Kimmy didn't, and she was eventually let go. Kimmy didn't look for another job. Sasha still paid rent weekly, and Kimmy never asked her for any other money, so Sasha didn't pay it any mind. One Friday morning after a night shift, Kimmy met Sasha in the parking lot driving a brand-new silver Chrysler 300.

"Like my ride?" Kimmy flaunted.

Sasha, young and impressionable, couldn't help but gawk. "Yes, where'd you get it?"

"C'mon. We're going to Montreal today." Kimmy skirted around the question and opened the door for Sasha.

"I just worked all night," Sasha hesitated.

"Sleep in the car!" Kimmy suggested.

"But I need clothes."

"We'll get new ones there!" Kimmy grinned, flashing a wad of cash. "C'mon, Momma got paid today!" Sasha's face lit up with excitement, her resolve melting as she hopped into the car. They made the drive from Hamilton to Montreal, stopping to pick up two of Kimmy's friends in Toronto. They were two men, both in their thirties. One was of East Indian descent and went by the name Beeb; the other was a white guy named Darren.

Kimmy picked them up at a small grey apartment building complex that smelled like weed and hot garbage. Darren climbed in the back with Sasha. She instantly got a creepy vibe from him. Next Kimmy stopped at a liquor store. Once back in the car, the drinking started. Sasha relaxed a little bit after a few drinks, and the drive continued. Darren kept inching closer to Sasha, to the point where she was so pressed up against the door, she worried it would open and she'd fall out on the highway.

A few hours later they made it to Montreal. They found a motel on Westmore Street, a seedy little place on the edge of the city, and booked a small room with two beds. To an eighteen-year-old who had never left her hometown, the whole ordeal was exciting. They smoked a joint, had a drink, and were feeling really good when Kimmy leaned into Sasha. "Come on, we're going shopping."

They made the twenty-five-minute drive to Marche Central. Sasha, still feeling buzzed, was in awe as the big city landscape of Montreal passed by the window. They parked the car, and Kimmy sparked another joint. This time the smoke almost stung Sasha's nose.

"That smells funny," Sasha observed innocently.

Kimmy puffed on it, taking in a deep lungful. Still holding it in, she replied, "Paper's wrapped with oil," then sputtered and coughed long and hard. She handed the joint to Sasha, who took a small puff.

Kimmy laughed. "C'mon, hit it!" Sasha took a couple of big puffs and held it. Her chest felt like it was burning, and she coughed as hard as Kimmy did a few seconds before.

They made their way into the mall, checking out a few stores. Sasha was high, as high as she'd ever been. She and Kimmy laughed at nothing in particular. She didn't know why, but she couldn't stop laughing.

Kimmy kept handing Sasha clothing she wouldn't normally wear: short shorts, low-cut shirts, fishnets, and vinyl miniskirts. Sasha was feeling the effects of the day's partying, and though usually modest, she was having a good laugh and felt lucky to be getting spoiled. Kimmy continuously complimented her, telling her how hot she was and how she was driving all the boys they knew crazy.

After buying several of the new outfits Sasha had tried on, they went back to the motel room. Kimmy and the guys started feeding Sasha more drinks, more weed, and a couple pills. They convinced her to try on and model her new clothing. They were all laughing and whistling, showing the young drunk girl the only positive attention she'd received in a very long time. She would go into the bathroom, get changed, and with each new outfit came cheers and encouragement to show a little more. They took photos and made her feel like a rock star. Sasha was feeling weird but euphoric. The high was like nothing she ever experienced.

"Show them the little black skirt with the red top," Kimmy directed, laughing and cheering her on.

Sasha stumbled into the bathroom. Removing her current outfit, she fell over. Steadying herself, she managed to get changed and came back into the room. She was surprised to see only Darren was still there. Kimmy and Beeb had left.

"Where did they go?" she slurred.

"They'll be right back. Just went to get some more whiskey. A creepy smile crossed Darren's face. "You look good, baby doll. Come sit with me." He patted the bed beside him.

Sasha felt dizzy. The room was spinning. She didn't know what to do. She didn't like this man. But she was too scared to do anything.

"Come here," he coaxed again, getting up. He took her hand and led her back. She felt sick. Scared. The room was spinning faster. "Are you okay, baby doll?" His voice sounded hollow and distorted.

"I," she slurred. "I need to sit down for a minute." She tried to walk to the other bed, then everything went black.

When she woke up the next morning, she didn't know where she was at first. She felt sick. Not hungover, but sick. Her head hurt, the room was spinning, and she felt nauseated. She ran to the bathroom and threw up in the toilet. It wasn't until afterward she realized that she was naked.

She washed her face in the sink, trying to clear her head. Next, she used the toilet, but when she wiped, she noticed blood on the toilet paper. She realized that she hurt down there. She tried remembering last night but couldn't.

She started to cry in the bathroom. After a few minutes she composed herself, wrapped herself in a towel, and went to find her clothes. Kimmy was sitting on the edge of the other bed, angry.

"What happened last night?" Sasha asked timidly.

"What happened?!" Kimmy scoffed. She jumped off the bed and slapped Sasha. "You fucked my man last night, you little whore."

Sasha was shocked, first by the slap, then by the words. "But. I didn't. I've never…"

Kimmy interrupted her stammering. "Yes, you did! I left to go to the store. I come back, and you're fucking my man right there!" she shouted, pointing at the bloody spot on the bed. "While you're on your rag too, you nasty little cunt."

"I'm a virgin," Sasha defended through tears. "I didn't…"

She was cut off by Kimmy slapping her again.

"Yeah, well, not anymore!" Kimmy yelled angrily. "And you owe me for yesterday too. I spent over $1,000 on clothes. The rental car was $500, and you owe me another $500 for being a little whore. So, where's my money?" she demanded.

Sasha didn't know what was going on. Was this a dream?

"Hey," Kimmy snapped her fingers in front of Sasha's face, then pulled her hand back, ready for another slap. "You owe me $2,000. So, you better give me my money."

"I don't have that much!" Sasha sobbed.

"You'd better find a way to earn it." Kimmy advised.

Sasha started trying to gather her clothes. Kimmy slapped her again.

"Please stop," Sasha squeaked out. "I didn't do anything."

Kimmy went from angry to animal. She grabbed Sasha by the hair and yanked her around, holding her head down; she punched her upward several times.

"You think I'm playing with you?" Kimmy snarled, spit flying out of her mouth. She threw Sasha on the ground and kicked at her. "You owe me money. And you're not going anywhere until I get it."

She kicked at Sasha again, connecting with her shoulder. "Tell me you understand!" Another kick, this time to Sasha's stomach. Sasha couldn't understand what was happening. The sound of Beeb and Darren's laughter cut in. At some point while Kimmy was beating her, they had come into the room.

"Okay," Sasha sobbed. "I understand. Please stop."

What followed was an eight-week-long tour from Montreal to Ottawa, Kingston, Belleville, Oshawa, Toronto, and London, then to Windsor, where in each city Kimmy and whatever guy she knew there would post ads online, forcing the young, scared 18-year-old girl to have sex with strangers for money. They would supply her with drugs, hard drugs that numbed the pain but kept her reliant on them. And with every hit they fed her, they tacked more on to her debt.

If she protested, she was beaten. If she cried, she was beaten. If she tried not to get high, she became violently ill, which meant she couldn't earn, which meant she was beaten. After eight weeks she found herself in Windsor at a hotel near a very busy street. It was almost like the highway was right outside. Kimmy had posted the ad online. The first John came in around 5:00 pm. He seemed nice at first, but partway through the interaction he turned violent.

Three more men that night also got rough with her. They hurt her in different ways. When the last one left, she made up her mind; tonight was the night she would make her escape. After the last john had left the room, Kimmy and an East Indian man who was keeping watch over Sasha were counting money. Sasha got up off the bed.

"Where are you going?" Kimmy snapped.

"I have to pee. It hurts." Sasha placed a hand over herself, acting like she was uncomfortable.

The man laughed. "Fucking dirty bitch."

Sasha walked towards the bathroom. At the last second, she used one hand to flip the deadbolt open and the other to flip the latch; she opened the door and took off running as fast as she could.

"Hey, bitch, get back here!" She heard Kimmy yell, but Sasha didn't slow down. She ran as fast as she could towards the stairwell, down two flights of stairs, and to the fire door. She collided with it hard as the alarm sounded, but she kept running through the wet parking lot in her socks and down a busy street. She saw a street sign that said 'Huron Church.' She kept running. The sky was clear, but there had been a mix of snow and rain falling earlier that evening.

She ran past the first set of traffic lights, seeing the red lights for the Ambassador Bridge ahead of her. Something told her to get off that road, so at the next side street she turned left and ran down a residential street called Dorchester. She ran one more block then stopped.

She looked around and had no idea where she was. It was the middle of the night in a strange city in December. The ground was covered in slush. She looked back at the way she came. A small gold car went through the intersection. Partway through, the brakes locked up. She could hear the scratching sound as the tires slid over wet asphalt. It was Kimmy.

Sasha looked at the house she was in front of and ran up the driveway, through the yard. She jumped the fence and waited. Peeking through the slats in the wood, she saw the gold car race by; she jumped back over the fence and ran back toward the front of the house. She looked down the street the way Kimmy went and didn't see anything.

She crossed the street, cut through the yard, and hid in the shadows for what felt like hours. She was feeling sick. She felt wave after wave of nausea, her bowels rolling. She was scared and cold.

As the sun started peeking up, she moved. Her whole body hurt, cramping from both the lack of toxins in her system and from having been curled up in a ball for most of the cold, damp night. She made her way back to the busy street. She looked up and down for Kimmy or the gold car, but she didn't see it. Cautiously, she crossed the busy road and headed towards a Tim Hortons.

"If I can get there, I can use the phone," she thought. Then she was hit by the sudden realization: she had no one to call. Sadness and fear overwhelmed her.

She quickly crossed the street, ignoring the few stares she got. Her guts were burning, and she desperately needed a toilet. She raced in. Thankfully, the bathroom was empty. Twenty minutes later she walked outside with no idea where she was or what she would do.

"Are you okay, honey?" Sasha turned and saw an older man in his forties. He seemed genuinely concerned for her. He was a shorter guy, five-foot-six, with a dad bod, heavyset, bald on top with a push-broom mustache. He wore thick, brown, plastic-rimmed glasses, navy blue work clothes, and a name tag that read "Ted" on the left breast. He looked like he had just got off a night shift.

Sasha caught a glimpse of herself in the window's reflection. She had on white socks stained with mud from running, green jean shorts that were filthy and torn, and a white t-shirt with nothing underneath. She was covered in mud and dirt, and there were small shrubbery leaves matted in with her messed-up shoulder-length brown hair. The dirt on her face was streaked from tears. She looked homeless. She was homeless.

"Some people were holding me. I had to run," was all she could get out.

"Where? When?" concerned, the man began looking around.

"Last night," she whispered, tears flowing again.

"Where do you live, hon?" he asked gently.

"I'm from Hamilton."

The man was still looking like he was worried her captors would pull up any second. "Come with me. Let's get you somewhere safe." He ushered her towards his black minivan.

Ted explained he was a machinist, divorced with two kids, and that he worked nights for an auto parts supplier. They drove for a few minutes and pulled up to his house.

Ted lived in a small white wartime house with blue trim and a steep-pitched roof. The house sat on top of a small hill. The yard was clean, but the house looked dated. He pulled up the driveway towards the garage at the back and led Sasha in through a small utility/laundry room, an add-on from sometime in the 1960s.

Sasha needed the bathroom again, badly. Her guts were burning, not only from the withdrawals but also from her nerves after fleeing her captors. Directly outside the utility room was a small three-piece bathroom on the left and a set of stairs on the right. Sasha used the bathroom. She could hear Ted walking around. There was a small rap on the door.

"There are some clothes and a towel on the floor outside the door." Ted explained.

Sasha's stomach was screaming with both diarrhea and vomiting as the withdrawals took over and became more intense. She cracked the door open, reached out, and found a pair of black sweatpants, a red t-shirt, and a well-worn but clean blue bath towel. She showered, turning on the hot water, almost ignoring the cold entirely. The heat blasted her, cancelling out the chill her bones felt from hiding in the cold all night. For a brief moment it felt like she was washing the last eight weeks of horrors off her body.

After her shower she was feeling a little better; she was coming up on twelve hours without any drugs. She remembered learning in high school that the peak for opiate withdrawals was around 36 hours. The worst was yet to come, but she was free from Kimmy.

She left the bathroom. There was a small, dark hallway about eight feet long. At the end on the left was the kitchen with dated dark wood cabinets and wood panelling walls, probably from the 1960s or 1970s, heavily tarred with years of cigarette smoke. On the right was another small hallway that led into the dining room/living room. Ted was standing at the kitchen counter stirring an orange drink.

"Here, drink this," he offered.

Sasha's stomach rolled at the thought. "What is it?" She reluctantly reached her hand out to take the glass.

"Metamucil," Ted replied. "It'll help settle your stomach." His bushy moustache lifted as he showed a friendly smile. Sasha sipped lightly. "Down in, hon, I know it seems gross, but slam it back. It'll soak up the water in your guts."

Sasha took a bigger sip. Then drank it down quickly. She was leery about taking drinks from strangers lately, but her stomach hurt so bad that she'd try anything to cure it. She initially felt some nausea. After a few minutes it passed. Ten minutes later she realized her bowls weren't nearly as bad. She still had to go, but it wasn't as horrible as before.

Ted led her upstairs and showed her one room with two beds.

"This is my kids' room," he explained. "They don't come back 'til next weekend. You can crash in here. I'm across the hall," he pointed at the open bedroom door on the other side. The bedrooms weren't small, but the steeply pitched roof caused them to forfeit a lot of headroom.

Sasha was exhausted. She was mentally, physically, and emotionally drained. She used the bed on the left-hand side of the room. The small alarm clock with red numbers showed 8:04 am. She fell onto the bed and felt like she was asleep before her head hit the pillow.

She wasn't sure at first how long she slept, but she was startled awake when she felt something on her ear. She woke up with a jolt. Ted was in her bed. He had crawled in behind her, his moustache scratching her, his hand down the front of her pants.

"No," she protested.

"Shh, shh, shhh," he soothed. "Just relax." He held her tighter.

"No. Please," she begged. This couldn't be happening. This man was supposed to help her.

"It's okay." His hot breath blasted at her ear as he pressed himself into her. She protested some more, trying to wiggle away, but she was pinned against the wall. He tried to pull down her jogging pants. She gripped the elastic waistband.

"No! Stop!" She was half pleading, half yelling.

His hand let go of her pants. He grabbed a handful of the hair at the back of her head and slammed her face into the wall. He held her head there. "Stop it," he yelled. "Just relax!"

He jarred her head, banging it one more time. Then in a vicious yank, he ripped the back of her pants down. He stuck himself inside her. She wasn't ready, and it hurt. He moved a few times, grunted, and she felt him climax inside her. He panted and lay still, then, without a word, he left the room.

She lay in the bed crying, but soon enough the burning in her stomach took over. She raced to the bathroom. When she finished, she cleaned herself off, opened the bathroom door, and heard Ted.

"Over here," he called out from the kitchen. She slowly walked towards him. "Good morning," he greeted as if nothing had happened. "How did you sleep?"

Sasha didn't know what to say. This man just raped her, and now he was making her breakfast.

"I need to go," was all she could get out.

HUNTING PREDATORS

She started down the dark hallway towards the back door, but before she could walk into the utility room, she was shoved hard from behind and fell face-first into the dryer. Ted was short and chubby, but he was fast, and she didn't even hear him coming. Her face collided with the dryer door. He grabbed her by her hair and dragged her back down the hallway.

"You're not going anywhere!" he snarled. "Get back upstairs. Stay there 'til I call you." She started to protest but was struck in the side of the head so hard it almost didn't hurt, just a purple flash, followed by a headache. He kicked at her, connecting with her left hip. "Move!"

Sasha was terrified and ran back up the stairs. The clock beside the bed said 4:36 pm. She tried to sleep again, but the fear of Ted coming back scared her, and sleep wouldn't come.

He had kids, so he couldn't keep her there forever, but what would he do when he was done with her? And until then? She shuddered thinking about it.

Shortly after 6:00 pm she heard from the bottom of the stairs, "Come eat!" It wasn't an invitation; it was an order. She made her way downstairs. Ted was sitting at the table reading the newspaper, a plate of food in front of him.

She pulled out a chair to sit. Without looking up, he pointed, "Yours is over there." She looked in the corner. On the floor were two bowls: one had a mash of food, and the other had water. She looked at him in shock. His eyes were cold and scary.

"Don't waste food," he chided with a chill in his voice. "Eat."

Sasha didn't know what to do at first, but the last eight weeks had taught her that not doing what she was ordered to do would result in a beating.

She got on her hands and knees and ate, compartmentalizing what she was doing in order to numb herself against the horror and indignity of it all. She wasn't hungry, especially not for food this way, but her survival instincts had taken over, so she did as she was told.

After dinner, Ted ordered her to do the dishes and went upstairs. Sasha could hear him walking around, going from room to room, and assumed he was getting ready for work. She cleaned the kitchen spotless. Ted called her into the living room. He was sitting on the couch, naked. He ordered her to do things. Forced her to strip down in the middle of the room and stand in various poses. She felt embarrassed, ashamed, and more alone than she had ever felt. After everything she had suffered through in the last two years, especially the last eight weeks, this was by far the worst. She had been beaten, abused, and was now being degraded. Ted taunted and mocked her, made fun of her body while he pleasured himself at her expense. Tears streamed down her face, but that only seemed to arouse him more.

He ejaculated on himself, ordered her to clean it up, then sent her back to her room. Naked, with her clothing bundled under her arm, she walked back up the stairs and froze in the doorway. The bed she had been sleeping on was covered in industrial black garbage bags. Lengths of rope were tied to the four bedposts. She spun around, and again, Ted was right there. He pushed her into the room, her stomach rolling from both the withdrawal and nerves again.

"Lay down," he commanded.

"No, please," she begged. He slapped her again.

"Do as you're told!" he barked.

The plastic crinkled and chilled her skin as she lay face down. Ted tied her hands and ankles.

"Please," she sobbed. "My stomach is upset. I need the bathroom." She was desperate for anything to get her out of this.

"You can clean it in the morning," he called out as he walked out of the room.

Sasha was able to see the clock. It said 7:28 pm. She lay there bound, her stomach turning in knots. She couldn't hold it anymore and released herself on the plastic. At 9:30 pm she heard him leave for work. She drifted in and out of a fitful sleep.

The worst of her withdrawals took effect around 3:30 am. She vomited on herself; she was filthy with diarrhea. This was hell. She sobbed, unable to comprehend how she ended up like this. Nobody cared about her. Nobody bothered to look for her. She woke up around 7:45 am when she heard Ted stomping up the stairs.

"Jesus Christ!" he exclaimed as he opened the door. "Bad dog!" He laughed to himself as he untied her feet, then her wrists. Her muscles were screaming. "Clean this mess up, then go shower." He opened a window to air out the room and left.

Sasha bundled up the plastic, gagging while she did it. She placed it all in another garbage bag and tied it tight. Next, she took a shower, washing the filth off her. She stood in the water and felt disgusting, worthless, used. Surprisingly, the worst of the physical problems had dissipated, but she felt like her soul was broken.

Over the next five days Ted used her at his will, even bringing two friends home one morning after work. The three of them abusing her, both individually and as a group.

On the sixth night, Ted had switched the rope out with cuffs and shackles. He bound her to the bed and left. Sasha drifted off to sleep and had a lucid dream. She was running around the playground at her grade school, playing tag with her friend Carly. The two started grade school together and graduated from high school at the same time.

Carly came from an affluent family that owned a large construction company in Hamilton. Carly and her mom Linda were the ones that sat with Sasha the night her mother passed away.

Sasha's eyes snapped open. Still lying in bed, the realization that she actually did have someone to call for help after all hit her. She lay awake for the rest of the night. At 7:45 am she heard Ted stomping up the stairs again.

"Make me something to eat," he demanded, uncuffing her.

Sasha got out of bed, made her way to the kitchen, and started rooting through the pots and pans. She had a plan, and she was getting out of there. Today. She decided on bacon and eggs and put on a small pot of water to boil. While that was cooking, she started a load of laundry, quietly unlocking the deadbolt while in the laundry room. She inched the door open and made sure the screen door was unlocked. Pressing the door closed again, she made sure it didn't latch. She saw his van keys on the hook.

"What are you doing back there?" she heard Ted yell.

She quickly opened and slammed the dryer door. "Finishing the laundry, sir," she replied obediently. She hurried to the kitchen. This was it; it was now or never.

"What's taking so long?" he complained from the dining room table. Sasha looked at the small pot of water, a rolling boil.

"Coming, sir."

She hurried over, bringing a plate stacked with three eggs, half a pound of bacon, and two pieces of brown toast. "I'll get you some ketchup," she offered as she hurried back into the kitchen. When she walked back into the dining room, he was looking down at the newspaper. He reached his hand out without looking up. Sasha waited; he wagged his hand as if to ask for the ketchup, then looked up at her.

Sasha had been standing across the table with a pot of recently boiling water. She threw the scalding water in his face. He let out a blood-curdling scream, and Sasha ran from the dining room, down the hallway, and into the back room. She grabbed his keys and ran out the door, still hearing the screams from the dining room.

Without looking back, Sasha jumped in his black van, threw it into gear, and spun gravel as she stomped on the gas. The front of the van felt like it had become airborne as she flew backwards down the small hill. She sped out of his driveway without looking and smashed into a parked car on the other side of the street in the process. She slammed the gear shift into drive, cranked the wheel, and floored it, driving away.

She was pulled over minutes later by a Windsor police SUV that noticed the back bumper dragging behind her as she drove. A female officer approached the van. When Sasha saw her, she broke down crying. She explained the hellish nightmare she had been through. The cop looked at the young, terrified girl in the driver's seat and immediately called for help.

At 9:01 am, Sasha was brought to Windsor Police headquarters, where she was interviewed by two female detectives. The younger detective was a pretty Middle Eastern woman with dark skin and eyes. She had light brown hair with blond highlights and was wearing a royal blue pantsuit with a baby blue silk shirt. She was calm and soothing. She didn't seem much older than thirty but had a maternal way about her.

The older of the two was in her mid- to late-forties but still very pretty. She had long reddish-brown hair and was wearing a similar suit, only in burgundy, paired with a white blouse. She seemed a little rougher around the edges. The two had a great system. The older one would ask the hard questions; the younger one would calmly and gently extract the details.

When they asked, "Is there someone we can call?" Sasha gave them Carly's parents' home number.

Hamilton was three hours away. Three hours and forty minutes later, Carly's mother, Linda, burst into the front doors at Windsor police headquarters. Linda was a short, curvy woman with dark brown, curly hair and a warm smile. She quickly hustled to the front desk. She was polite but demanded to see Sasha right away.

Less than five minutes later, the older detective met Linda in the hallway. As delicately as she could, she explained the horrors Sasha had been through in the last eight weeks. She explained how Sasha had escaped, first from Kimmy and then from Ted. Linda stood shocked, her right hand over her heart, horrified that the poor child had suffered through so much.

"We had no idea," was all Linda could muster.

"Of course not. Do you need a minute?" The detective knew it was a lot of information to process.

Linda initially nodded, then changed her response. She took a deep breath and said, "That little girls needs me more." The detective saw Linda's determination and promptly led her into the interview room.

Sasha saw Linda in the doorway and was instantly overcome with shame and guilt. She couldn't stand to look Linda in the eyes and suddenly didn't want to be seen. She felt like she had caused and deserved everything bad that happened to her and instantly regretted calling Linda. Sasha lowered her head and started sobbing. Linda rushed in, dropped to her knees, and hugged her.

"Oh, little lamb," Linda said. "You're safe now. You're safe."

That day Sasha moved into Carly's house. Oliver, Carly's dad, gave her a job with his company. It wasn't exactly her dream job, but it was steady, and it kept her close to their family. On her 25th birthday, Sasha moved into her own apartment owned by a coworker's mother, an older French woman named Sophie who had a triplex. Sasha moved into the upper unit.

Oliver and Linda helped her move in and get settled. When the last box was brought in, Linda placed it on the counter. She stood with her hands placed on the lid. Sasha could hear scratching coming from inside.

"Happy birthday, little lamb," Linda beamed.

Confused, Sasha opened the box; inside was a black-and-white, 6-week-old Boston Terrier/French Bulldog puppy. Sasha was overcome with love for the pup immediately.

"This little girl needs a new momma," Linda advised. "You guys can take care of each other."

Chapter 11

Sunday May 21th, 2023. 4:05 am.

Mike stood silent, looking at Sasha, trying to process her story.

"I hate when you do that." She nervously flashed him a smile, trying to break the tension. "When you just stare like that, I never know what you're thinking."

"It's a lot to unpack at once," Mike replied honestly. "But I get why you want to find her so badly."

Sasha had told Mike her story. Part of her was initially worried he would look at her differently, but when she saw the sympathy in his eyes, she knew he didn't. "If we're done with him, what do we do next?"

Mike thought for a minute. The sky was getting brighter by the second. He wanted to be out of here and back on the highway before traffic picked up. People have been known to remember weird details like a blue pickup with the driver wearing a ski mask and a Black Range Rover pulling onto the highway from an old, abandoned logging road.

"Let's go home," he suggested. "The dogs need us. We're going to Victoria tomorrow morning. We'll start then."

Sasha nodded, and they started walking back to the vehicles. "Gunshots are louder than I thought," she commented.

".357." Mike looked back at Sasha and raised an eyebrow. "Packs a hell of a wallop."

"Scared me," she admitted.

"He didn't like it either," Mike retorted, and Sasha barked out a cackle.

Monday, May 22nd, 2023, 2:04 am.

Ashley Brock was sitting on the bedspread in another dirty motel room. She felt strange, woozy. Her head was spinning. She felt sick and stoned at the same time.

"Take this baby." An older lady named Sadie handed Ashley two small white pills with *"80"* etched on them. "Chew them up. You'll feel better faster," she promised.

Ashley did what she was told and chewed the pills. They were chalky and bitter. She took a big gulp from a water bottle to wash the taste out of her mouth, and within minutes was feeling the effects. Shortly thereafter there was a knock on the door.

Sadie stood at the curtain and peeked out. She put on her best smile and opened the door. "Hey baby. How you doing?" Her voice was full of fake cheerfulness.

A large man in his early fifties walked in. His hair was grey, still showing some flecks of black. He had a black goatee with streaks of grey. He was barrel-chested, accentuated by his white and black patterned short-sleeve silk shirt paired with black dress pants. He spoke with a

French accent. "Hey, Sadie." He kissed her on the cheek. "How's the talent tonight?"

"Oh, she's good, baby. Just took her medicine. She's coming around nicely."

Ashley's head felt heavy. She smiled, one eye drooping.

The large man sat on the bed. "She's just a lil baby, this one, yeah?"

"She's older than she looks, Cher." Sadie replied. "And still fresh."

Ashley was confused. She felt happy and sick at the same time now. This guy made her feel weird, but it was like somehow the voice of reason in her head had a hand over its mouth. She thought back to an animated show where a coaxing devil popped up on a character's shoulder while the corresponding angel was stuck in traffic. She snickered a laugh. That's how she felt: like something was wrong, but no one was there to correct it.

Sadie looked at the man. "You want me to stay or go?"

"Leave," ordered the man.

Ashley was in her own world. She had a weird sensation like she was being yanked around but had no idea what was happening.

8:00 am

Mike and Sasha left the dogs with Raye and Vicky. They had packed up for Victoria and planned on staying for a few days, maybe a week. Sasha kissed Domino; Mike gave Oscar the trash dog some cuddles, then they switched pups.

At 8:05 am they pulled up at Tim's garage. Tim was standing out front talking to a client. Mike waited patiently. When the other man left, Tim walked over. "What's up, buddy?" he asked.

"I have an ask," Mike began. Tim's eyebrow raised. This wasn't a favor. A favour you could do for a friend, no problem. An *ask* was likely unethical.

"What do you need?"

"Wheels in Victoria. Nothing fancy. It's gotta have balls, but nothing flashy. Doesn't need to be super clean. If I get lit up. I ain't stopping." Mike requested.

Tim had been around the block a few times. It wasn't an unreasonable request; it wasn't even an uncommon one, but it was strange coming from Mike. He knew Mike wasn't a cop, that was for sure. It was clear Mike hated cops. But Tim had always figured Mike to be legit. Tim had never seen Mike break the law and had assumed he'd always stayed on the right side of it.

Part of Tim was intrigued. He was curious as to why Mike would need a getaway car, but he also knew better than to ask. In fact, the less he knew, the better. Tim looked at Mike and walked into his office. He emerged less than a minute later with a piece of paper containing a scribbled phone number.

"Last four digits," Tim instructed, getting Mike's attention. "One up, one down, one up, one down," meaning when Mike dialled the last four digits, if the paper showed 1313, Mike would dial 2222. It was a simple code, but it worked.

By 8:35 am they were on the highway, having opted not to tell Adem they were coming since they wouldn't be staying with him this time. As they drove, Mike explained to Sasha that they needed to do some research. He advised that they wouldn't get anywhere by driving down to the seedy parts of town and asking people questions. He also said there was almost never a good reason to question anyone in a strip club.

An hour out of Tofino, they pulled off the highway and drove up a logging road. The blue pickup was still there. They switch over to it, placing seat covers over the interior. Mike used a small utility knife blade and peeled the small sticker off the window. Mike told Sasha, "We'll have two days with this truck. That's all. After that we need to assume they know that shitbag is missing."

In Nanaimo they pulled over and bought two prepaid burner phones. Mike explained that until further notice, they had to be unremarkable and untraceable. All transactions were to be made with cash, tattoos covered by clothing, and ball caps with either no logos or local BC or Washington teams were to be worn.

"Keep your head down, with sunglasses on as much as possible. Wear a mask in busy places," Mike instructed. "Covid has been a blessing in that regard at least."

HUNTING PREDATORS

He explained that when the shit hit the fan, the police would cast a large net, and there was virtually nowhere in society anymore that you weren't always on camera. From the second you pulled up in a parking lot until you left whatever place you were at, you had to assume you were being filmed and thus had to protect your identity.

As they drove, Mike told Sasha about the time he spent at his uncle's farm in Ohio. Throughout his younger and teen years, Mike would stay there for weeks and sometimes months. His uncle was a bit of a sociopath and had taught Mike several tactical skills, like how to move silently at night without being seen, how to create diversions, and how to set up boobytraps or delayed fuses and detonators. He had taught Mike how to shoot and to fight with knives and clubs. He taught Mike how to kill and how to wound.

Sasha had put some of the puzzle pieces together since meeting Mike. He was different, that was for sure. Not long after they first met, Sasha's ex-boyfriend and his brother appeared at a bar where she and Mike had been visiting a friend. The ex and the brother tried to intimidate Mike, who in turn put them both away in what felt like the blink of an eye.

A few days before that, her old neighbour had threatened her elderly landlord, Sophie. Mike beat the man senseless in the front yard without a second thought. When the police arrived, he was calm and cooperative. Sasha received a message a few weeks later saying her old neighbour had been found dead after a failed attempt at autoerotic asphyxiation, but Sasha suspected Mike had killed him.

Then there was the massacre that was all over the news for a few weeks. An undercover cop had been kidnapped and taken hostage. Between 12:00 am and 6:00 am, five people were slaughtered, and the cop didn't remember anything. The official story released by the Ontario Provincial Police seemed too convenient. They claimed that the bad guys had realized they kidnapped an undercover cop and performed an internal cleansing, killing everyone involved so the big fish could get away. But Sasha saw Mike come home the next morning. Everything he was wearing looked saturated with blood. Still, he was calm. He assured her he was okay.

Twenty four hours after the massacre, when they were packing up to leave and head out west, Sasha saw Mike had over two million dollars in cash. They made several stops at various places on the trek to B.C. where Mike would stash money in safety deposit boxes or on friends' farms. Sasha always knew where it was. If they ever had to run, or if she was running on her own because something happened to him, it was there for her.

"What happened in the Falls?" she asked.

Mike looked at her through the side of his eye while driving. "Tell you after we're married."

She rolled her eyes.

As they were driving into Victoria, Mike began instructing Sasha on their next steps. "So, here's where we need to start. This is going to be unpleasant, but we're going to need to discuss your past. I don't have a lot of experience with any of what you went through."

Sasha took a deep breath. She had been expecting this. "Okay, what do you want to know?"

"How do they stop the girls from leaving?"

"Keep them high, threaten them, threaten their families," Sasha recounted, trying to answer without remembering the details.

"I mean, when they're with a client," Mike clarified. "Actually in the room?"

"They're not clients; they're tricks," Sasha corrected. "I know it sounds funny. But in my head, *'client'* sounds official. These men know they're raping young girls that don't want to be there." She paused. "But to answer your question, it depends on the layout of the room. Usually they pick a small drive-up-to-the-door style motel. At least, they did in my case. They would go outside right before he got there. If I tried to run, they were right there. If the bathroom window was big enough for me to fit through, one would be standing out back in case I tried to run."

Mike nodded. He didn't like thinking of her in that situation, but this wasn't about him. He didn't want to push too much and upset her, but this was her quest, and he needed to know the details if they were going to succeed. He reminded himself of the men they were dealing with and what they were doing.

"And if it was a hotel? One with multiple floors?" Mike asked.

"Same thing. They'd leave the room right before he got there. Usually there are adjoining rooms, or they're directly across the hall or hiding in the hallways. The pimps are never far," she explained before adding, "Bathrooms too."

"Bathrooms?"

"Yeah, sometimes the tricks would be there before the pimps had a chance to leave. If that happened, they would hide in the bathroom. If the trick asked to use it, I'd say the water didn't work."

"Regular occurrence?" Mike asked.

"Not uncommon," Sasha answered truthfully.

They stopped at a light, and Mike looked at her. "I'm sorry you went through that." He was sincere and added, "I'm also sorry to make you relive it. But this is information that can help us. I think I know how we're going to work this. It'll get ugly. We're going to hit first, hit fast, and hit hard."

"I'm ready." Sasha replied, determination set in her posture.

"Okay, you need to point me towards a motel where you think it might be happening."

She stared at him sympathetically. "Mike, my love. That's all of them."

It took them some searching, but eventually they found a seedy little motel with a Wendy's across the street that provided them with an unobstructed view of the parking lot. It was a small, yellow-brick, one-story building with a row of rooms. The sign was big and lit up at night. The only thing advertised on it said, "Weekly or hourly rates."

They parked, pushed their seats back so they couldn't be seen, and waited. It didn't take long at all. In less than ten minutes, two men walked out of a room and sat in a red Dodge Charger. Five minutes after that, a small black Japanese SUV pulled up in front of the room. A middle-aged man got out and knocked on the door. It opened, and he went in. Twenty-two minutes later he walked out, got in his SUV, and drove away. The two men exited the Charger and went back in the room.

Mike started the truck and put it in reverse.

"Aren't we going in there?" Sasha was confused.

"No, we're going after the trick." Mike advised.

"But there's a girl that needed help in there," Sasha protested.

"Babe, this will go a lot smoother if you trust me. I need information. And he'll have it." Mike explained.

He understood her position. She saw a chance to prevent someone from suffering through what she herself had endured. With this in mind, Mike added, "We can save one girl now or a whole lot more soon. But if we go smash our way in there, every other pimp in the city is going to hear about it, and they'll all be on guard. Please trust me."

Sasha understood and sat back. "So, what do we do?".

"Pull up your map," Mike instructed, referring to her burner phone. "Look for someplace secluded, like where we had our friend the other night. Off the highway. Logging roads are usually pretty good. We're doing this one in broad daylight. At least, that's when we're grabbing him. So, it'll be a two-man job. I'll get him in the truck. You'll keep your gun on him the whole time." Mike paused and then added, "Remind him about the accidental gunshot in Pulp Fiction, but keep your finger off the trigger.

I don't actually want an accidental gunshot like in Pulp Fiction."

Sasha scrolled through her browser, looking for a decent place to bring the trick while Mike tailed him. At a stoplight, Sasha noted the back of the small SUV had one of those obnoxious family stickers showing a mother, a father, a ballerina, and a baseball player. "Jesus, the guy's married with kids," Mike observed.

"Most of them are," Sasha murmured, staring out the window. "They're the worst ones. Sick father-daughter fantasies. Or they're abusive. I mean really abusive."

Mike didn't want to pressure any more information out of her, so he sat quietly. Unprompted, she added. "I dunno, it's like their wives are ball-busters and these assholes beat on the young girls to make up for it. Like they're taking their frustrations out."

"Don't the pimps or handlers step in?" Mike asked, still trying to understand. He genuinely thought that was the whole point of pimping. Sure, they rented the girls out, but he thought they offered some protection against aggressive johns.

"No, most of the appointments are set up via text. But it's the pimps posing as the girls that the john communicates with. Pimps post the ads too. That's where it'll say what can happen and what can't. There are code words. 'Girlfriend experience' means it's more intimate, for the john at least. Things like kissing. There are other codes too. Usually 'low restrictions' means just that: the john can do whatever he wants. When they're responding to an ad, the pimps will ask what they're looking for. That's when the 'I want to do a rape fantasy' or 'pretend you're my daughter' comes out. The pimps agree. The girls are given minimal information. These guys come in, beat up and rape teenage victims, then go home to the wife and kids." She concluded her explanation with a look of disgust and sorrow in her eyes.

Mike was trying to keep his emotions in check, but the more Sasha spoke, the more he wanted to literally pull the man in the SUV apart with his bare hands. He had to remind himself not to envision Sasha suffering through that hell and, more importantly, not to force her to relive it either.

"Okay," Mike began, forcing a topic change. "Game plan. We're going to grab this asshole first chance we get. We'll take him out to the middle of nowhere and get what we need out of him."

"I read torture doesn't always work," Sasha commented.

"Maybe not on soldiers or spies, but I've always had good luck with it," Mike retorted calmly. "Take a fat idiot from the suburbs and pull a few of his teeth out with a rusty pair of pliers; he'll tell you his mother's bra size. Everyday people aren't cut out for that type of pain."

Sasha laughed a little. She knew it was morbid and knew he wasn't kidding, but his delivery made her chuckle.

"There are people that will tell you anything because they're afraid, including lies, because they want you to stop. Or they'll tell you the truth because they want you to stop. It's important to know the difference. If someone legitimately doesn't have information, they'll tell you they were the second gunman on the grassy knoll if they think it'll stop the interrogation. But when they know, and they know *you* know, a couple of well-placed whacks to the knee with a baseball bat will get them to tell you everything.

"Usually, at first they'll deny," Mike continued. "Deny, deny, deny. You have to make it clear that you don't believe them and that there's a penalty for not believing them. That way you're taking away their incentive to lie. In fact, it's not about getting them to give you information. It's getting them to understand that it's *not* giving you the information that will result in extreme pain. You need to learn to watch them. It's a process, but it's pretty fail-safe. Ask them a question; they'll always lie at first. So, you hurt them. Ask them again and watch; if they lie, they'll flinch because they know there's pain coming. If they're telling the truth, they'll answer you and almost seem relieved."

Sasha was completely mesmerized by Mike at this point. Not staring like a teenager with a crush, she was staring at him, wondering how this man who would walk to the end of the earth to keep her happy could also pull someone's teeth out with pliers and not lose any sleep over it.

"How many times have you done things like this?" The question jumped out of her mouth before she realized it.

Mike glanced at her but didn't say anything.

A minute later the black SUV pulled into a shopping center. The man got out and walked into Starbucks.

Mike circled the parking lot. "Small change of plans."

He pulled in beside the SUV facing the opposite direction with the driver's side doors facing each other. He inched forward so the rear door of the truck was in line with the SUV's driver's door.

"What's the plan?" Sasha asked.

"Pull up where we're going on your GPS," Mike directed, then added, "You're driving," as he hopped over the seat into the back. He was big, but Sasha was surprised at how nimble he was for his size.

They waited a few minutes and saw the man return to his SUV. He was a short man, around five foot nine, with a fat build. His dark hair was combed to the side, meeting the wispy sideburns that led to a black beard. He wore rimless glasses with thick lenses, a white short-sleeved button-up shirt, navy blue cargo shorts, and black socks with brown sandals.

"He looks like a substitute math teacher," Sasha observed, trying to crack a joke. But the reality that this man might work with children made the events earlier even more repulsive.

The man was carrying a tray with two cups on it. He hit the unlock button on his fob and stepped between the two vehicles. Placing his keys on the tray between the cups, he reached for his door handle.

Mike had been watching him, barely breathing, when the man reached for the door. Using his own body weight, Mike flung the back door of the truck open, grabbed the man by his left shoulder with one hand, and around his throat with the other. In the blink of an eye, he yanked the man into the back of the truck and slammed the door shut. The whole ordeal took about three seconds.

"What the he—," the man tried to demand, but the barrel of a faded black .357 was rammed into his mouth and down his throat. The man gagged on it. The cylinder hit his teeth, cutting his lips. The taste of blood, gun oil and the faint bitter taste of spent gunpowder filled his mouth. His eyes went wide as he looked at the man holding him down. The audible *click* as the hammer was cocked could be heard in the truck.

The man was confused. They weren't robbing him. They weren't asking questions. Even if they did, he couldn't answer. The big man holding the gun looked over his shoulder and said, "Drive." The truck lurched forward.

Sasha put the truck in drive and made her way out of the parking lot, through the city, and headed west towards the small town of Sooke. After ten minutes of driving, they turned right. Now off the highway, they started up a logging road. The man almost had a heart attack when they hit a large bump and he thought the gun might go off. They drove deeper into the woods for what felt like an hour.

"Here's good," Sasha advised as she pulled off the logging road and stopped on an overgrown two-lane trail. She hopped out and opened the back door. Mike pulled the gun out of the guy's mouth and yanked him out of the truck.

"One of two things will happen here," Mike said to Sasha. "He'll comply with everything and do as he's told, or he'll try to run. If he decides to run, he may trip, try to throw a rock or handful of dirt, or come up swinging a stick. Anything. Be ready at all times. If he tries to run, shoot him. Aim centre mass and fire till you're empty."

Mike's voice was so calm it made the circumstances even more terrifying to the man.

"I won't run," the man squeaked out. Mike nodded at Sasha, who kicked the man in the nuts as hard as she could. He screamed and buckled. Mike stood on his head, pressing it into the mud.

"Don't say another fucking word unless we tell you!" Mike growled, then turned to Sasha. "Grab the bag."

Sasha reached onto the floor on the back seat and came out with a black knapsack with a small wooden baseball bat stuffed in, with the zippers done up to the handle. Mike reached down, grabbed a handful of the man's hair, and lifted him up. "Walk, asshole," he ordered, shoving him forward.

They walked in silence for another fifteen minutes, getting deeper into the forest. Finally, they came to a small clearing. Without warning, Mike threw the man against a tree.

"If he moves, shoot him," he instructed Sasha. He reached into the bag, pulled out more zip ties, and fastened the man's hands behind his back around a tree.

"Please," the man begged. "I didn't do anything."

Mike stepped back in front of him and landed a series of punches to the ribs on each side: left, right, left, right, left, right, taking his time to line up each hit. The man sobbed and wailed, raising his knee to try and block the punches, but it was a pointless gesture.

"Gag him," Mike directed. Sasha stuffed a small rag into the man's mouth, then placed a thick strip of duct tape over top. The man continued crying through the gag, eventually slowing down.

"We're going to ask you some questions. If you lie, we'll start breaking bones. If you yell for help, I'll kill you where you're standing and leave you tied to this tree. Blink once if you understand me." The man looked Mike in the eyes and blinked hard. Mike ripped the tape off, a small patch of the man's moustache coming with it.

"What do you want from me?" the man whimpered. Mike hit him in the stomach again. A deep guttural "ooof" came out of the man as he threw up on himself.

"What did I say?" Mike asked rhetorically. "Don't say a fucking word unless you're asked to."

Sasha began the interrogation. "How old was that girl?"

"What girl?" the man replied, faking confusion.

Sasha nodded, the tape went back on, and she kicked him in the balls again. He screamed from behind his gag, she took a step back, paused, then did it again, harder. They waited a minute.

Almost as if reciting a script, Mike repeated his instruction. "We're going to ask you again. If you play dumb, or if I don't believe your answer, I'm going to tape you back up." Mike was emptying out the man's pockets: cell phone, wallet, keys. "A couple kicks in the nuts will be the least of your problems then. Do you understand me?" The man nodded. Mike reached for the tape and added, "Remember, if I don't believe you, it's going to get a whole lot worse."

HUNTING PREDATORS

Mike ripped the tape off. Sasha, staring fiery daggers, asked a second time.

"How old was the girl you were just with?"

The man, sobbing and panting, wanted to fall to the ground and curl up in the fetal position. Being tied to the tree prevented him from being able to do anything but stand and face his accusers. "Eighteen," he replied with his rapidly decreasing resolve.

Mike was scrolling through the man's phone. He looked in the history and found the page with the escorts. After a brief search, he found the conversation about setting up the meeting. He turned the phone to face Sasha.

The ad contained several photos of the same girl, a thin black bar over the eyes. The girl was in various poses, some in lingerie, some nude. The girl couldn't have been any more than fifteen or sixteen. Sasha's blood began to boil.

"She looks eighteen to you?" Sasha demanded as she rammed the phone into his face.

Mike flipped through the man's wallet. The driver's license said his name was Orin Bondy. Mike searched more and found a business card that identified him as the vice principal of St. Paul's Private Elementary School in Victoria.

"You weren't far off," he observed, handing Sasha the card.

Sasha scrolled through the conversation and found that Orin had asked for a teacher/student fantasy. As he got into the details with what he thought was an escort, he went into graphic detail about how he wanted to force himself on *"the student."*

HUNTING PREDATORS

Mike picked up the black bag and began rooting through it. He came out with a pair of twelve-inch channel locks, heavy-duty pliers that plumbers use. He turned to Orin. "How often do you do this?"

"It was my first time, I swear!" the man pleaded.

Mike sighed. "Why do you guys always say that?"

In a flash he grabbed Orin by the face, forcing his mouth open. Shoving the channel locks in, Mike pinched the two front teeth and squeezed the handle. He didn't so much yank them out as he crushed and shattered them. He put the gag back in and the tape over top. "Let the little piggy squeal for a few minutes," he told Sasha.

Sasha continued scrolling through the messages. Her stomach was a pit of rage. She looked up at Orin, pure hatred and disgust crossing her face.

"We got the whole convo there?" Mike asked. Sasha nodded.

"Okay. We're done with this asshole. Let him live, or no?" Mike asked, toying with the man who started screaming under his gag. "Shut up, quiet down, and I'll take the tape off. Jesus Christ," Mike assured with annoyance.

The man settled. Mike ripped the tape off, and a mouthful of blood spilled out. Despite his lack of front teeth, Orin pleaded, "Please, I have a family."

"We're doing them a favor!" Sasha snapped, stepping forward. She raised a black .380 semi-automatic pistol and shot him twice in the head. He slumped down, the binding on his hands keeping him mostly upright. She paused, staring at him, then shot him twice more.

She felt like she had just reentered her own body. Like she just watched someone else that looked like her shoot a man. She looked back at Orin, then at Mike, then at the gun in her hand.

The silence was driving her crazy. She looked at Mike. He was quiet. "Say something, please."

Mike was watching her, surprised at how violent her reaction was. "You're okay," he soothed. "Easy. Finger off the trigger, please."

She stared at it for a second longer. Then handed it to him. She had just killed a man. She looked back. His dead body slumped down, arms stretched back, blood still pouring out of the crater that was once his head.

"I—" She paused. "I just…"

"It's okay," Mike said gently. "I get it."

They walked back to the truck in silence.

Chapter 12

Tuesday, May 23rd, 2023, 9:00 am.

Lumpz sat in the office of a small autobody shop in Esquimalt on the west side of Victoria. He had been trying since Sunday night to reach Kevin Marin. He knew Kevin was leaving town for a couple of days, but now he was starting to get nervous. His phone rang.

"Yeah," he answered.

"He ain't here." The voice advised. Lumpz had sent a man to check out Kevin's house. "Truck's gone. House is dark."

"Where the fuck he at?" Lumpz swore, disgruntled. "Keep looking." He rung off.

Kevin in the wind was bad. Kevin was a stooge, a loser. He'd sell his own mother out for money. Lumpz knew that about him, and it was why Lumpz used him. He was a piece of shit that wasn't above fucking young girls; Lumpz let Kevin try the young talent out and even gave him some money for bringing new girls in.

He usually had Kevin too scared to do anything but comply. Lumpz knew the cops were causing Kevin to panic; that's why he paid for Kevin's lawyer: to get the idiot out as soon as possible before he said anything. He followed up with the lawyer as well; Kevin hadn't said anything. Lumpz wondered if the cops got to him again or if he worked something out before the lawyer got there. Either way, Kevin not getting back to him wasn't good. He picked up the phone and dialled another number. The phone rang three times, and a male voice answered.

"Yeah?" A man sitting in a black Honda Accord answered. He was sitting outside Kevin's mother's house.

"You see him?" Lumpz asked.

"Naw man, been here since 7:00 am. He ain't been by."

Lumpz hung up without a word.

Ashley Brock was lying in an almost catatonic state in a small motel room. There had been at least eight men that came to see her that night. She had no idea what time it was. She thought they checked into this room yesterday evening around 7:00 pm. Since then, men would come, use her, and leave.

She tried to protest, but no one cared; she asked one man for help. He laughed at her. Some of them weren't bad. They would use her and leave within a few minutes; others were mean. They would degrade her, hit her, and make her do things she thought were disgusting or painful. If she protested, some of the clients hurt her more. If they complained about her resistance to Sadie, the lady that had been with her for the last few days, she was beaten.

Between customers, she would be forced to shower and take pills. One of the guys watching over her forced her to have sex with him while the other guy filmed it. Sadie interjected at first, giving Ashley a feeling that she was going to be saved. Then Sadie said, "If you're going to fuck her, do it quick. There's someone coming in 20 minutes."

Ashley's heart sank as the last little bit of hope she had died. She had no one. When she wasn't taking the pills, she felt sick and terrified. The pills helped both. Sometimes it made her feel good. But mostly it made her feel like she was watching a horrible TV show and just couldn't change the channel. What she was seeing was terrible, but it was happening to someone else.

Mike woke up around 9:00 am. They had spent the night in a hotel downtown. Sasha was standing at the window with the curtain open, wearing her usual bedtime attire of underwear and one of Mike's tank tops. She wasn't worried about people seeing her like that; they were twelve stories up.

"Morning," Mike greeted cautiously.

Sasha turned to face him, a coffee mug in her hand and a big smile on her face. "Morning, handsome." She sounded chipper.

"You okay?" Mike asked.

"Great," she answered, not a hint of sarcasm.

"I mean, after yesterday?"

Sasha walked across the room and sat on the edge of the bed.

"I've been up since around 5:00 am," she said. "I had a bit of a restless sleep. I kept replaying the scene in my mind. At first, I was kind of in shock. I've never seen someone like *that*," she emphasized, referring to Orin's head in pieces, his body twisted and slumped.

"So, it was kind of gross, not going to lie," she admitted. "But the more I thought about it, the more I looked at who he was. And the more I read his conversations..." She paused again. "He specifically asked for a young girl. He wanted to have a rape fantasy. He wanted to rape a young girl, and he was willing to pay grown men to set it up. Who knows what he did to that poor girl yesterday? Or how many students he has abused over the years, or how many other young girls in that same position he's done that to?"

She took a sip of her coffee, got up, and walked over to the small kitchenette. She poured Mike a cup of coffee, walked back, and handed it to him while he sat up in bed. She then made her way over to the window. The view showed the city of Victoria and the ocean beyond. Sasha seemed to get lost in her thoughts as she stared outside.

"The more I think about Orin, the more similarities I see with him and Ted."

Mike said nothing. He let her work through the thoughts in her head. She turned back to face him.

"If Orin ever had the chance to do to a young girl what Ted did to me, he'd take it. He'd be all over it. Our courts only do something after the girls are abused. Who knows, maybe by killing him I've saved another girl. Or two, or ten!" She took another sip. "So, yes. I'm okay. I still feel kind of weird that I don't feel bad. Is that wrong?" she asked, genuinely curious.

Mike shrugged. "I can't tell you. The first time for me was an accident. I mean, I wanted to hurt him; I found out later he was dead. I was impartial to it, though." He found himself curious about how she was able to compartmentalize it in her head. Turn off the guilt that comes from killing someone. For years he thought he was an anomaly because of his ability to do that.

"Did you kill all those five men in Niagara Falls?" she asked.

"Yes. It was actually six." Mike admitted very calmly. Sasha looked at him shocked that he finally admitted it.

"We've killed two people together. I mean, we each pulled a trigger, but in the eyes of the law, you're just as guilty of those two homicides as I am. I watched you quadruple tap someone in the head. I think I can trust you now." He smiled before continuing. "Yeah. That was me. I clipped all six; one still hasn't been found, I guess. Seven if you add in your old neighbor. If you're asking how I feel about it, I simply don't. They were all inherently terrible people. The world is a better place without them in it."

"Did you know them?" she asked.

"No. But in tracking that asshole cop, I found they were running a fentanyl ring. Dozens, if not hundreds, of OD's. They were responsible for more deaths in one month than I will ever be responsible for."

He paused, looking at her, and added. "I've never hurt or killed anyone that didn't deserve it. Our justice system has failed the victims in Canada. Most of the sentences handed down are laughable. Even recently I read about a child molester who was sentenced to three years but has served eighteen months waiting for trial. After sentencing he will be released in less than ninety days."

Mike paused and stared out the window. "Imagine being a parent of one of the victims and explaining to the child that their abuser will be out before summer break is over."

He paused again, shaking his head. "Imagine being a victim. Going through the horrors of trial, facing your accuser. And then finding out he'll be home in a few weeks."

Sasha walked back over, sat down again, and took his hand.

"Mike, I need to ask you something. It's very personal. But I've wanted to ask you for a while."

"O-kay," Mike replied, hesitant, feeling a little confused.

"Who is the girl in the picture with you?" Sasha inquired.

"Which girl?" Mike paused, then remembered the picture of himself at the age of seventeen with his then-girlfriend Tamika Sellers. Sasha saw the look of sad realization on his face and gave him time to articulate an answer.

"Her name is Tamika; she was my girlfriend. She was killed on my motorcycle when a reckless driver left his lane. I tried to avoid a head-on collision. He hit us. She died almost instantly. I was laid up for a few months." His eyes averted hers as he looked out the window.

"What happened to the driver?" Sasha asked.

"Nothing. I think he got probation and a suspended license, Mike replied coolly.

She could see that almost twenty years later, his entire demeanour changed when he thought about her. Suddenly everything about him made sense. He wasn't a monster. He wasn't a sociopath that could maim or kill at will. He was one of probably hundreds of thousands of people across the country who had his life torn apart and then watched in horror as the courts let the person responsible walk away.

Mike didn't enjoy killing people, but he had licked his own wounds long enough that he developed a taste for blood. In his eyes, he was performing a public service. He only went after people who, in any decently run system, would be locked away and left to rot, or at least rehabilitated. Not locked away for short timeframes and turned loose to do it again.

"Ted got two years of house arrest," Sasha said quietly. "He could only leave for work, medical appointments, shopping, and his kids' school engagements. It was weird. I sat in court listening as his lawyer tried to blame me. Then I listened to the courts say, 'We don't believe you, Ted, so as punishment you cannot leave your house. Unless, of course, you need to leave.' Pathetic."

Sasha took Mike's hand and forced him to meet her eyes. "You've told me about your Uncle Nick. When did you move in with him?"

"When I was seventeen," Mike replied.

"Before or after Ta—" she paused. "Tamika?"

"Yes, Tamika." He confirmed. "I moved in before the accident. A couple of months before."

"Where were you before that?"

"At Ed's," he answered. Sasha knew Ed was his dad, but Mike hadn't said much about him. "Ed was a monster. He taught me how to fight. Taught me how to throw punches in the gym and how to take them at home."

"And your mom?"

"She left him when I was thirteen. I left with her at first but went back to Ed's a few months later." Mike was staring out the window. "I was already boxing by then. He dangled that in front of me. He was an abusive manipulator who turned me against my mom, made me hate her for leaving us. It's funny, ya know. He could hit her, cheat on her, whatever. But she was the asshole for standing up to him. She told me a few years later she could deal with his abuse when it was directed at her. She could deal with the other women. It was when he started beating her children that she put her foot down. She tried to protect me from him. And I ended up hating her for it." He was still staring out the window, but Sasha figured he was seeing something else.

"Have you spoken with her recently?" Sasha was curious.

"We've tried, but I think a big part of me reminds her of him. She doesn't see her son. She just sees a younger version of him. I'm taller than he was. He was only around five foot nine, but there's no mistaking that I'm his kid. I look just like him. Last I heard, she found herself. Found happiness. I think I'll just remind her of the things she'd like to forget." He paused. Sasha could tell the discussion had caused him pain. He collected himself, and like someone flipping a light switch, he turned it off.

"So, it's only terrible people you go after?" Sasha concluded, changing the subject.

"Yes. Rapists, child molesters, drug dealers. Guys like your old neighbour that threaten the elderly." Mike paused. "People who place larger orders in drive-thrus and those assholes that listen to their music through the speaker on their phones, forcing everyone around them to listen to it too."

Sasha smiled at him and asked. "Okay, so what now?"

"First, we message that ad, then set up a date. Then we kill her pimps." Mike replied without hesitation.

Chapter 13

Tuesday May 23rd, 2023, 11:30 am

Mike and Sasha were sitting in the Wendy's parking lot watching the motel room again. Shortly after parking, they watched as two men and a woman left the room. One man walked around to the back of the motel; the other man and the woman sat in the red Charger. At 11:51 am a silver Hyundai Kona pulled in. An Asian man got out, knocked on the door, and went in.

"Be right back." Sasha called out as she hopped out of the truck before Mike could say anything. She shut the door and walked down to the corner. She looked like she forgot something and came back to the truck. "He's watching the bathroom window," she advised, climbing in the truck. "Message them now. Set up a meeting."

Mike looked at the phone, then at Sasha. "What do I say?"

"Here, let me." she offered, taking the phone. She pulled up the ad, sent a message, and waited a few minutes. "Okay, they replied." She sent another message and waited again. The Asian man left the room. Sasha typed, *"20 minutes,"* and hit send. The response came quickly and included the address as well as the request to, *"Make it 30, baby."* Sasha and Mike watched the two men and one woman go back in the motel room.

Thirty minutes meant it would be a little after 12:30 pm when they were supposed to pull up.

"What's the plan?" Sasha asked.

"Ideally, all three still in the room." Mike replied.

Sasha looked at the clock: 12:12 pm. "Okay, pull up now. One of them will be watching the window."

"Am I dropping you off somewhere first?"

"No. They think they're entertaining a couple." Sasha explained.

"Does that happen?" Mike asked, a little caught off guard.

"Not uncommon."

Mike noticed a change in Sasha. She was staring at the motel room door the entire time. Would not take her eyes off it. It was like bank robbers hyping themselves up in the back of the getaway car before a heist.

Mike put the truck in gear, crossed the street, and pulled up next to the red Charger. Sasha grabbed her phone and sent another message: *"We're early. Is that okay?"* Mike saw the curtains flicker and wondered what was going on. After a couple of minutes, her phone chimed, *"C'mon in.".*

Sasha grabbed the door handle of the truck and then stopped herself, turning to Mike. "There's probably a phone or a camera hidden in the room. If it's a couple coming in, her pimps will want to film it."

"Jesus," Mike cringed.

"Just follow my lead when talking to her, okay?" Sasha requested. Mike nodded.

They walked up and knocked on the door. A young girl opened it. It was not Ashley Brock, but she didn't appear to be much older. She was Indigenous, with long black hair and dark eyes. She looked exhausted, makeup covering new and old bruises on her face, legs, and arms. She was wearing an unwashed pink nighty with matching shorts and a fake smile.

"Hi, come in," she greeted and walked back to the bed.

The room was small and was comprised of one queen bed, a small table with two chairs, two mismatched end tables, and an ancient lamp. A dresser and small flatscreen TV finished off the room. It was a cheap, dirty room. The bedspread was a faded red, and the carpet was green and gritty. Mike couldn't imagine walking on it barefoot. The walls may have been white at one point but were now a dirty shade of beige. The cobwebs in the corners were thick and dark and cast dingey shadows on the walls and ceiling.

Sasha took control of the room, asking the girl what she was into and what was off-limits. The entire ordeal made Mike feel gross. He moved towards the end of the bed opposite the door, where he could see the bathroom door. He saw light coming from under the door and the shadow from a set of feet. Sasha pulled $100 out of her pocket, placed it on the table, and asked, "Can I use the bathroom really quick before we start?"

"Uh," the girl stuttered, "the toilet doesn't work. The manager said he'll get me a new room at one o'clock." A look of terror crossed her face.

Sasha nodded at Mike. The big man took a lunging step and kicked the bathroom door right on the door handle. The door was solid, but the frame was cheap wood and exploded inward. The door swung open violently.

A white guy in his late twenties was sitting on the toilet with the lid down. The door smashed him in the forehead, knocking him out cold. In less than a second, Mike was in the bathroom. The second man, same age as the first and African American, was trying to understand what was happening. Mike swung a right hand into the bridge of the guy's nose, feeling the bones crack and cartilage smoosh under the impact. The man's head slammed into the mirror above the sink, shattering it into pieces. The woman was sitting on the edge of the bathtub, mouth open in shock.

Mike grabbed the woman by the hair and yanked her off the tub. She let out a scream, but it was cut short when he threw her into the main room. She sailed through the air from the doorway of the bathroom until she slammed into the foot of the bed, knocking the wind out of her. As she tried to stand, Sasha kicked her in the side with everything she had. A loud crack was heard as one of the woman's ribs broke.

"Take care of her," Mike directed Sasha, pointing at the young girl.

Sasha was still amazed by what she was seeing. Mike was huge but moved with a fluidity that was surprising. He looked like this was his job and he'd done this exact thing a million times. Sasha focused her attention on the young girl who had backed herself into a corner and was shaking.

"Please don't hurt me." The girl begged, her eyes wide, fear in her voice.

"I'm not going to hurt you," Sasha promised. "We're going to help you get home."

"No, I can't. They'll find me."

Mike had picked the woman off the floor, punched her in the stomach, and grabbed her frail frame. Effortlessly he rammed her into the wall behind the dresser. A loud gasp was heard as the last of the air in her lungs was knocked loose.

"Honey, look at me," Sasha coaxed, bending down but keeping her distance. "Look at me," she repeated.

The girl took her eyes off Mike, who was continuing with the beating of the woman. She looked at Sasha, who stated, "I know what they've done to you. We're going to get you home. They'll never come near you again. I promise."

The young girl started crying.

The woman on the floor was out; she wasn't moving, barely breathing. Mike went back to the bathroom. The man with the broken nose was sitting on the floor, dazed. His face was still pouring blood, as was the deep cut on the back of his head from the broken mirror. His eyes widened when Mike walked in; the realization that something was happening hit him as fast and as hard as one of Mike's punches.

Mike stomped on his chest, grabbed him by the hair, and yanked him off the floor. He walked the man into the main room, slamming his head into the door frame on the way through. The man was staggering like a very drunk frat boy. Mike sent a thunderous left hook to the right side of the man's head, knocking him into a twisted heap on the floor.

Mike grabbed the third guy from behind the door; a tennis ball-sized knot had already started showing on his forehead. Mike tossed him on the floor beside the woman.

"Where did they put the camera?" Mike asked, calmly.

Sasha looked back at him and then at the young girl.

"Did they set up a camera?" Sasha repeated calmly. The girl pointed at the vent above the bathroom door. Mike reached up and pulled the loose vent cover off. There was a small portable camera that ran on Wi-Fi with a 120 GB SD card in it. He took the card out and smashed the camera.

"Money?" he asked.

Sasha redirected his question to the girl. "Which one took the money from you, hon?"

The girl nodded toward the woman. Mike walked over and yanked her up like a rag doll; she groaned in pain. He checked her pockets and found nothing.

"Check the car," Sasha suggested.

Mike checked the other two, found the car keys, and left the room. In the centre console he found a wad of bills. He didn't count it but guessed there was a couple thousand dollars. He also found a baggie with what he guessed was cocaine and two Ziploc bags. One had around forty or fifty small white pills that had *80* on them: Oxys.

Mike himself had had them after a car accident. They made him feel sick, but he understood how people could easily get hooked on them.

In the other bag were around 100 pills, all baby blue with rough-looking edges. Ecstasy, he figured. He brought all the drugs back into the room and flushed them. Sasha was still talking to the young girl. The reality of what had just happened and how quickly she went from being held captive to being freed was finally starting to make sense.

"How often did they use the camera?" Mike asked.

Again, Sasha looked back at the young girl, who seemed to need permission from Sasha to speak.

"Not sure. Every time we went to a new room, he set it up."

Sasha nodded. "What is your name, honey?"

"Elizabeth Green. Lizzy," she sniffled.

"Hi Lizzy. Where are you from?"

"Saddle Lake, Alberta," she answered, wiping tears away.

"And how old are you?"

"Fifteen," the girl replied with a tremble in her voice.

As if on cue, the man with the large goose egg on his head stirred and groaned. Mike looked down at him with disgust at the thought of what had been done to this child.

"Fucker!" Mike growled and soccer kicked the man in the face.

Sasha looked at Mike. "How do we get her home?"

Mike thought for a second before responding. "Ask her where her clothes are."

He was trying to relay through Sasha. Mike was an exceptionally large and very intimidating man. To a young girl that was already terrified, he would only make things worse. He recognized this and used Sasha as a buffer to try to minimize the girl's discomfort.

"My bag is in the car," Lizzy advised.

Without a word, Mike went out and grabbed it. He tossed it to Sasha from the doorway, then jumped in the blue truck and turned it around so the tailgate was near the door. He waited outside for the young girl to get dressed. When he came back in, he pulled Sasha aside.

"Find out who, if anybody, is looking for her. She's still a baby. Someone's got to be worried about her."

Sasha nodded. Mike paused, then added, "We're going to pack this place up. I'll toss them in the truck. You take their car."

He peeled off $500 from the billfold. "Give her this. We're going to drop her off two blocks away from the police station, and we're going to get the fuck out of there while she goes in and gets help. She'll need money for food, travel, whatever." Sasha gave him a quizzical look but eventually nodded again and went over to the girl.

Mike popped the tailgate down and rolled up the tonneau cover. Quickly and efficiently, he went back in, zip-tied all three pimps, gagged and duct-taped them, then one by one, took their cash and phones. He took a look outside to make sure no one was looking and carried each of the pimps out, tossing them into the bed of the truck. He considered throwing them from the door but didn't want to create any more noise or draw unnecessary attention. After he closed the tailgate and the cover, he walked back into the motel room.

"Time to go," he instructed. "We need to drop her off and get the truck out of sight for a bit until it's dark out." Mike wanted to be gone quickly in case anybody else saw him loading the truck. No one had come by, but anyone could have been looking out their window or watching from the street.

Sasha and Lizzy got in the red Charger and followed Mike out of the parking lot.

"Are you okay, hon?" Sasha asked.

"I don't know," Lizzy replied, still trying to come to terms with what had happened. She stared out the window. "Where are we?"

"Vancouver Island," Sasha advised. That seemed to hit the girl hard, and she started crying again.

"I don't remember crossing the water," she admitted.

"I know, honey, I know what you're feeling. These people, they're garbage. They prey on young girls, girls who are scared and lonely. None of this is your fault. Do you hear me?"

"How will I get out of here?" Lizzy asked through tears.

"I'm going to drop you near the police station. You're going to go in. and tell them who you are and that you were kidnapped in Alberta. They'll know what to do." Sasha promised.

"I can't tell people about this," Lizzy sobbed.

They pulled up behind Mike at a stoplight. Sasha turned to face her. "Lizzy, I know it's hard, but you have to. I know you're embarrassed and ashamed. But you did nothing wrong. It wasn't you. It was them. The police will have women that come talk to you. They're very good at helping girls that have been hurt. Please trust them."

Lizzy nodded. The light turned green; they drove on. Mike pulled to the side and turned his four-ways on. It was 1:30 pm on a Tuesday. The sky was dark grey; it was raining. Sasha said, "This is it, Lizzy; you're free." She pointed up the street. "Two blocks up there is the police station."

"Will you come in with me?" Lizzy pleaded, her voice cracking.

"I'm sorry, I can't. We got you out of there, but we broke so many laws doing it." Sasha replied apologetically.

"How will I—What's your name?" Lizzy asked, overwhelmed and realizing she was running out of time for answers to the onslaught of questions that had suddenly filled her head.

"You have a second chance at life," Sasha advised, avoiding the question. "Use it. Get back home. Be safe; finish school. Do something great with yourself."

Lizzy looked at Sasha, her head swimming, not able to articulate what she wanted to say. Sasha sensed this and added, "Get back to Saddle Lake. Once you're there and things calm down, I'll find you."

Lizzy smiled, nodded, and got out of the car. Mike pulled away; Sasha followed, looking at Lizzy in the mirror.

Chapter 14

Tuesday May 23rd, 2023, 9:23 pm

Mike and Sasha had changed into what Sasha referred to as their "work clothes": brown and green thick work pants, dark green and brown hooded sweatshirts, and camouflage ski masks. Sasha had added her own flair with surplus combat boots and a black sheathed K-bar style knife strapped to her left thigh.

The night sky was cloudy but still gave off enough light to see. Mike rolled back the tonneau cover and opened the tailgate of the blue "borrowed" truck. All three pimps were lying in the bed. They had all been knocked out before being placed in there and now had no idea what happened or where they were. The woman had lain awake, silent, but every turn and bump the truck went over felt like someone was stabbing her in the side. The man with the goose egg was awake, his head throbbing. When he regained consciousness, the hum of the truck felt like a jackhammer between his temples. The bumpy road they took made his headache so intense, he wanted to die. The third pimp was awake. He was concussed but able to understand he was tied up and in deep shit.

One by one, Mike grabbed them by the ankles and reefed them out of the bed; the blood they had spilled in the truck allowed them to slide with ease. Mike grabbed the one with the goose egg first. In one hard yank, the man was jerked into the air, sailed what felt like five feet, and slammed into the ground. The second man landed on top of him, both groaning loudly through their gags.

Mike didn't skimp with the woman. He grabbed her ankles and launched her out. She flew a little further and landed a little harder. She screamed with pain through her gag. Sasha's kick earlier had broken a rib and cracked a few others, and the pain was so intense, the woman blacked out for a second when she landed. Mike walked up to them, yanked them up, and had them kneel.

"I'm going to take your gags off," he informed them. "Scream, and I'll kill you. Open your fucking mouths without me asking you a question first, and I'll kill you. You do not need to know who I am. And you all know why you're here, so spare me the bullshit. Nod your heads if you understand."

All three nodded. Mike and Sasha ripped the tape off their mouths. The woman looked at Sasha.

"Please help. They made me do it," she whispered.

Sasha kneeled in front of her and put on the most concerned look she could muster. Then she punched the woman in the same spot she kicked earlier. The women shrieked.

"I know exactly what role you played in this, bitch. Don't play the victim now." Sasha snapped. The women had crumpled over, sobbing. Sasha grabbed her blood-soaked hair and yanked her head up. "On your knees," she ordered through gritted teeth.

Mike stepped forward and looked at the three worthless pieces of garbage in front of him. "I'll spare you guys the drama. I want answers. And I'm going to ask..." he paused, scanning his finger over each one. He pointed at the one with the goose egg. "You first."

The other two looked at the man, terror in their eyes.

Mike warned him. "It doesn't benefit you to tell me you don't know. The only reason you're not dead right now is you might have the information I want. Without answers, you're useless to me." Mike let that hang in the air for a few seconds and then asked, "Who is Lumpz, and how do I find him?" All three looked at each other. They knew who Lumpz was, but like Kevin, they were afraid of him.

"I—I don't know no Lumpz." the guy answered. Mike stepped forward and smashed the man on top of the head with a 36" pipe wrench. A dull metallic *thunk* was heard along with the sounds of his skull cracking.

"What the fuck, man? You just killed him!" The guy with the broken nose had clearly forgotten Mike's warning about speaking out of turn. Mike dropped the wrench, pulled out a large black pistol, and put the barrel against the man's forehead.

"You wanna be next, asshole?" Mike snapped. "I still have that old bitch next to you and a bag full of tools. Believe me, she'll sing like a fucking bird! So, if you want to see tomorrow morning, you tell me what I want to know, or I swear to you on all that is good and holy, I'll kill you right now."

Sasha was almost startled by Mike in this moment. She had witnessed him in action before, but this was a different level of savagery.

"Okay, okay, okay," the guy with the broken nose sputtered. "I don't know his real name. He owns a couple tattoo places and an autobody place on the west end."

"When can I find him there?" Mike asked evenly.

"I honestly don't know. He comes and goes. He has a dark blue Jeep."

"Anything else? There are a lot of blue Jeeps out there," Mike asked, looking for more specific details.

The man thought for a second. "There's boxing gloves hanging off the mirror. Those novelty ones. A Canadian one and a Jamaican one. Look, that's all I know, man, please." The guy begged.

"How does it work? All this. The girls. Lumpz. You guys. How does it piece together?"

"I don't know if it's Lumpz or someone else. But they have all the hotel and motel owners on board. We come in, set up shop. Then we pay them a percentage of what we make while we're there."

Hearing that made Sasha furious. "A percentage of what you make?" she spat. "By forcing young girls to be raped?" She tried to kick him in the face, but Mike stopped her. She looked up at him, confused.

"Not the head," Mike reminded her. "He's talking right now. Kick him in the nuts or something."

A look of panic crossed the man's face, and like a football player kicking a field goal Sasha kicked the man in the nuts while he knelt. He groaned and fell over onto his side. Mike grabbed him by the hair and yanked him back up. The man could feel the gash on his head open more.

"So, you pay for the hotels and motels. What does Lumpz get?" Mike asked. The guy was groaning in pain. "You're running out of time, bud." Mike advised.

Between gasps, the man replied, "We can't operate on the island without Lumpz's approval. We throw him money. He keeps the cops off our backs. If we don't pay him, the cops will raid our rooms. Guaranteed."

"So, does he have the cops on his payroll? Or does he just turn people in?"

The guy paused for a second. The realization hit him. "I don't know."

Sasha stepped in and asked, "How many of you are involved?"

The man gave her a twisted look, a cross between a misogynistic glare and an attempt to play dumb. She kicked him in the nuts a second time. He fell into the dirt again.

"Jesus. That one looked like it hurt." Mike commented.

Sasha ignored him and turned back to the man writhing on the ground. "You assholes roll in packs. You didn't drive to Alberta and pick that girl up. Someone brought her to you. Or you met somewhere and traded her for another girl. How many other people are involved in your group?"

The man rolled, groaning on the ground, but didn't answer her. "Alright, shoot him," she said. Mike stepped forward and pointed his gun.

"About twenty-five," the guy groaned. "There's about twenty-five of us. Mostly groups of two or three."

"How do you stay in touch?" Mike asked.

"WhatsApp," the man replied. "We have a group chat going."

Mike pulled out the three phones. In the dark they were identical. "Two required passwords, the third required a thumbprint. "Yours need a pin or thumbprint?"

"PIN. 1111," the guy said, still lying on the ground.

Mike typed in the PIN and found the app. The conversations went back months. Photos of young girls. Warnings about cops. Times, dates, pick-up locations. A blueprint for their underground network.

Mike picked the guy back up, set him on his knees, and gagged him again. He looked at Sasha. "Well?" he asked, nodding at the woman.

Sasha knelt down in front of the woman and asked, "How many girls have you done this to?" The woman stayed silent except for her light sobbing. Sasha gave her a jab to the ribs again. The woman wailed, "How many?" Sasha asked again.

"I don't know," the woman whimpered.

Without a word, Sasha pulled her knife out and stuck it to the woman's side just below her left armpit, piercing her lung and stabbing into the heart, hitting the left ventricle. She twisted the blade back and forth like she was cranking the throttle on a motorcycle, tearing the muscles, ripping into the left atrium. She yanked the blade out. A stream of blood squirted out then trickled off. The woman's eyes went wide, then rolled back in her head as her body collapsed. Less than eight seconds later, she was dead.

Mike looked down at the remaining guy on the ground. The night was quiet. An owl was heard; small nocturnal animals scampered about. Without a word, he rolled the man onto his stomach, pulled out his own knife, and in a downward stab, stuck it into the back of the man's neck between the base of his skull and the C1 vertebrae. The man jerked and flopped; his muscles spasmed, and he went limp.

Mike pulled the knife out and wiped it on the man's already blood-soaked shirt. He turned to Sasha. "Smash the other two phones. Power that one down, pop the SIM card out." She started doing it. "We need to burn these clothes. Also, lose the guns and knives. Start fresh. If we ever get pinched for one murder, no sense holding the weapons that tie us to a dozen more."

She nodded, then muttered, "Damn.".

"What?" Mike asked, concerned. He knew Sasha had just witnessed more of Mike's vengeance than she ever had before. He hoped it wasn't too much for her.

"I really like this knife," she replied, still holding it and rolling it around in the moonlight. Mike was becoming more impressed with not only her efficiency when it came to killing people but also her ability to stomach it all.

"What do we do next?" Sasha asked.

Mike motioned to the phone in her hand. "We're going to multitask," he replied. "We're going to monitor that group chat. And at the same time, we're going to find out who Lumpz is and how we can shut him down."

Chapter 15

Wednesday May 24th, 2023, 9:00 am.

Gale Robson was in her office with the Nanaimo skyline behind her as she sat at her desk and combed through a stack of paperwork she didn't want to look at. She was burning out. At fifty-three, she was moderately attractive, though she could not claim to be in her physical prime. She was five foot seven and a little bottom heavy. Her shoulder-length, wavy, brown hair that she refused to dye was streaked with grey. Almost thirty years of service had earned her a hardened look on her face and a reduced monthly membership fee at Goodlife Fitness, the latter of which she used to blow off steam rather than to attain the hot-girl-summer body. Consistently putting her career first, she never had time for a man even if she did catch his eye.

She'd been sitting here since 7:00 am viewing and reviewing the same few files. She had Kevin Marin's criminal history in front of her, having read it over so many times she knew it by heart.

Kevin was forty-four years old, born April 11th, 1980, in Airdrie, Alberta. He had his first arrest in 1994 at fourteen years old for stealing a car.

In 1996 he'd been arrested for armed robbery. He and a friend, Charlie Layton, plotted to rob a local convenience store. Charlie walked in, and Kevin ran in behind him, held a knife to his friend's throat, and demanded the money. Unfortunately for them, the store owner had known both boys since they were six years old. He hated Kevin, so he gave him the money, making it a robbery. That was Kevin's first stint in jail. He was sentenced to six months in a youth facility.

In March of 1998, two weeks shy of his eighteenth birthday, Kevin was charged with sexual assault when he raped a very drunk and very passed-out sixteen-year-old girl at a friend's birthday party. He was charged as a young offender and pleaded down. He was given twelve months of house arrest. He was later arrested three more times for breaching his conditions, eventually serving another ninety days.

By his twenties, Kevin had a growing list of offenses. In 2001 he pissed off a group of Hells Angels in Alberta and was handed an intense ass whooping. His tangle with the HA, combined with his dwindling opportunities thanks to his criminal record, resulted in his immediate relocation to Victoria. There he was arrested again and sentenced to two years for what could only be described as the dumbest smuggling operation in history.

Kevin had an extensive list of complaints from former neighbours and family friends about him being inappropriate with their younger daughters but always seemed to skate by.

In June of 2016, Kevin was arrested for assault when the father of a teenage girl in his housing complex confronted Kevin for sending inappropriate text messages. Kevin sucker-punched the man, cracking his cheekbone. Kevin claimed self-defence for the assault and maintained that the texts were consensual. Since the girl was sixteen years old and since Kevin was not in a position of authority over her, the police could do nothing.

Kevin pled the assault charge down and was given a year of probation. Robson stared at the file again. This man knew where Ashley was, or at least what happened to her, but they had no choice but to release him on Friday. He was seen pulling out of his driveway on Saturday evening and had been M.I.A. since. They tried his house but found nothing. When they called his phone, it went to voicemail on the first ring. They checked with the cell provider. He was in Tofino on Saturday night, but that was where the lead went cold. No trace.

At 9:37 am a young up-and-coming constable with the RCMP named Tyson Bent, who had recently transferred to the Major Cases Task Force, walked quickly up to her desk.

"Kevin Marin is dead," he announced, holding up another file.

"What?" Robson almost fell out of her chair.

"Okay, so we know he was in Tofino," Bent explained, "so I started checking things like ATM cameras and gas station security footage. Shortly after 11:20 pm on Saturday night, Kevin entered a gas station on the edge of Tofino. His face was a mess. Someone beat the shit out of him." Bent handed Robson several pictures.

Robson flipped through the still-frame photos of a bloodied Kevin talking to the cashier.

Bent continued, "Next, I talked to the cashier. She said Kevin came in claiming he was attacked. He used the bathroom to clean up and left it a bloody mess."

"Jesus," Robson exclaimed, looking at the battered man in the photo.

HUNTING PREDATORS

Bent handed her another photo of Kevin's blue truck in the still frame and proceeded with his timeline. "At 11:32 pm he drove past a hotel on the edge of town. The next camera that would have caught him was at a small coffee shack a little over a kilometre away. He didn't drive past. That told me he was somewhere between the hotel and the coffee shack. There were three resorts between them. I checked with all three. One reported a guy with a blue pickup truck checking in late Saturday night. Paid for two nights with a visa registered to a 'Richard Harrington.' Records show the transaction at 11:53 pm. The truck was gone in the morning and never returned. She said the cleaning lady reported what appeared to be blood in the bathroom and on the carpet and his clothing beside the bed. I checked the cameras again. At 3:41 am, the blue truck passes the coffee shop." Tyson handed her another picture containing the truck with a very large figure behind the wheel.

"That's not Kevin." Robson commented.

"Correct. So, I check some more." Bent continued. "Took me a bit, but I found out where all the cameras along that stretch of highway are. It's not what the cameras caught; it's what they didn't catch. There are two dozen cameras heading into Ucluelet. Not one of them captured his truck. So, I lost the truck. These things happen; there is a lot of ground to cover between Tofino and Nanaimo, but, he paused, "there's this guy and his girlfriend out camping Saturday night off an old logging road. Converted a school bus into a camper—really cool. It's like a cozy little cabin on wheels..."

"Hey. A.D.D. boy, get back to the case." Robson urged.

"Sorry. Anyways, there's a couple camping. The guy says around 4:30 am he hears a gunshot."

"How did he know it was a gunshot?" Robson asked.

"Ex-military." Bent replied. "I checked into him. His story checks out. So, he hears a single gunshot, but not a rifle or shotgun. He was pretty sure it was a pistol. Figured maybe another camper came across a bear or a wolf. Doesn't pay it any mind, that is until Monday morning. They're still at their campsite. He sees a couple of wolves and then a couple of grizzlies. So, he figures something is attracting them, right?"

"Sure?" Robson says, eager for Bent to make his point.

"Right. So, our camper grabs a shotgun and a camera, and out he goes hoping to get some photos of the wildlife, maybe a dead deer and the predators feasting. Instead, he stumbles across this." He says, handing a photo over.

Robson looked and saw a still frame of Kevin Marin, or what was left of him. Half his head was gone, clothing missing, his left leg was missing below the knee.

"What the fuck?" she mused, breathlessly.

"Autopsy is tomorrow, but preliminary reports indicate someone shot him in the head. The animals did the rest. No casing, but he was zip-tied with his arms behind him around that tree."

"Christ almighty." Robson muttered. "Any idea who did it?"

"Not exactly," Bent replied. "But whoever did it probably did this too." He handed her another photo.

This one showed another man, arms bound behind his back around a tree, slumped over, the tree preventing him from falling. His head was virtually gone.

"Orin Bondy, vice principal at St. Paul's Elementary School. Looks like the same M.O. Tied to a tree, likely beaten, and shot in the head."

Robson looked at the picture. "Turned his fucking head into plant fertilizer. What do we know about him?"

Bent leaned in. "Well, here's where it gets interesting. He was reported missing on Monday evening. His car was found at a Starbucks in Victoria. Keys lying on the ground outside the vehicle with some dropped coffees. Someone snatched his ass up in a parking lot."

"Do we know who?" Robson asked.

"Funny you should ask." Bent was enjoying this. "Nobody saw anything, but" he handed her one more photo. This one was taken from a security camera positioned on top of a light pole; it showed Orin Bondy's SUV with a blue truck beside it. It's Marin's truck." Bent paused for effect. "Same plate number. Whoever killed Kevin Marin also killed Orin Bondy."

"Who found Bondy?" Robson asked.

"Now it gets even stranger," Bent was smiling.

"Cut the fucking theatrics, Bent." Robson snapped.

Bent stopped smiling and regained his composure. "Yesterday afternoon Elizabeth Green, fifteen years old, missing since March 3rd from Saddle Lake, Alberta, waltzes into police headquarters in Victoria and says she'd been kidnapped and was forced into prostitution. The kid was in rough shape, traumatized. Green was interviewed by Detective Lalonde. When Lalonde asked how she got away, Green said a couple rescued her. She described a large man and a smaller woman who posed as clients looking for 'a date.' They came into the motel room and beat the living shit out of her pimp and his friends. They snatched the girl up and dropped her near the police station. Then a couple out hiking yesterday came across Orin's body."

"Did we get the pimp?" Robson asked.

"Nope." Bent advised.

"Of course not." Robson sighed, throwing up her hands.

"Elizabeth Green said the big guy put all three in the bed of a blue pickup. Kevin Marin's blue pickup. Lalonde showed her a photo of Orin's body with his head still intact. She said Orin paid her a visit the day before. He had some sick teacher/student fetish. He was rough with her. I read the statement. He really hurt that little girl."

Robson's eyes went wide. "So, to recap: some guy killed Kevin Marin, stole his truck, beat up a pimp and his friends, kidnapped them, freed an abducted girl, then killed Orin Bondy. And made little effort to hide his body. And possibly had the help of a female accomplice." She paused. "This is what you're telling me?"

"Yes." Bent confirmed, trying to keep the smile from creeping back onto his face. "Except he killed Bondy before freeing the girl."

They both fell quiet for a minute. Bent finally broke the silence. "So, what do we do now?"

"I don't even know where to start," Robson admitted, rubbing her temples in a vain attempt to fend off the impending tension headache. She looked at Tyson Bent, who stood at the edge of her desk smiling.

"Bent?"

"Yes, ma'am," he replied eagerly.

"I want you to go away now, please."

"Yes, ma'am," he said, the smile not fading. He did an about-face and walked away.

"Bent?" Robson called again.

He stopped and turned around, still flashing that goofy smile. "Yes, ma'am?"

"Great job, by the way," she praised.

"Thank you, ma'am."

Tyson Bent was originally from Ottawa, Ontario. He grew up in a family full of cops and firefighters. He was an athlete throughout high school, playing football, soccer, basketball, and of course, hockey. In grades 10 and 11, he tried his hand at lacrosse but quickly realized that the kids from the nearby First Nations territories didn't so much play lacrosse as they used the field as a means to exact revenge on whitey for five hundred years of oppression.

Tyson wasn't a large man. He stood around six foot tall and hovered around a hundred and ninety pound. He was fast and smart, but on the lacrosse field that was like bringing a dentist drill to a demolition site.

HUNTING PREDATORS

After high school he initially thought about a career in medicine and enrolled at McMaster University. He earned a BA in molecular biology but quickly realized he was bored. He was smart, too smart almost, but the thought of another six years of school was too tedious to attempt.

At twenty-seven he talked to his dad and decided he wanted to be a cop. His dad called his uncle, who was a high-ranking RCMP and had worked personal security for several prime ministers. Three weeks later, Tyson was on a plane to Regina, Saskatchewan, to start his 6-month training program at Depot Division.

After Depot, he swore he would make his own name and not rely on the family clout to advance. He was first sent to the small village of McBride, British Columbia, a tiny little speck on a map with a population of around 600 people. He spent three years issuing speeding tickets and responding to traffic accidents, usually travellers hitting moose. Again, boredom set in, and soon he was on the phone with his uncle begging to be transferred.

Six months later, Bent was sitting in a squad car in Nanaimo, reading over internal postings, looking to climb the ladder.

Three weeks ago, he was transferred to a major crime unit. His first two weeks were spent organizing the shelves in the closet. Last week he was pulled in to work on the Ashley Brock case. To call it a baptism of fire would be the understatement of the year. They hit the ground running, and ten days after the girl was reported missing, they had a legit suspect that looked good for the abduction. Then their suspect was found dead. Then another body appeared, this time belonging to a sicko who fantasized about raping young girls. Shortly thereafter an abduction victim is freed, and who the hell knows what happened to her pimps?

11:30 am

Ashley Brock had no idea where she was. It seemed like she'd be in a room for a day or two, then they'd drive her somewhere else. The younger of the two men in the room right now had been with her since the guy picked her up in Nanaimo. She thought his name was Chris but wasn't sure.

The first few days she had spent with him flashed in her memory. She remembered saying something hurt but couldn't remember the pain. He seemed to be the guy in charge most of the time. He told her what to do.

Every day or two, another guy would come around, not a client, but a friend of Chris. They'd set up in a new room. Chris would start posting pictures of her online and answering text messages. There would always be another guy there. He'd use Ashley usually in front of Chris and the woman that travelled with them. That guy would leave, and then the clients started coming. Four, five, sometimes as many as ten in a day. Then it would slow down, and off they went to the next room to start all over.

Ashley was pretty sure they weren't on the island anymore, but she didn't remember crossing on the ferry. One day seemed to bleed into the next. They booked her with clients at all hours, morning, afternoon, and night. She would be falling asleep, and Chris or the woman would wake her up and tell her someone was coming. She didn't protest; she didn't complain. She did what she was told.

They gave her the pills that made her not feel sick and made the whole thing less painful.

Chapter 16

Wednesday May 24th, 2023, 1:30 pm

Mike and Sasha sat in the red Charger across from another dingey motel. This one looked like every other fleabag pay-by-the-hour shack. The night before, they had stripped the blue truck down and wiped it clean of fingerprints. Diligently, they peeled the seat covers off, vacuumed the back seats, and hosed the blood out of the truck bed. Satisfied it was clean, they drove to a deserted logging road, parked the truck in the trees, and walked away.

Mike figured they'd be able to get today and part of tomorrow out of the Charger. After that it wasn't worth the risk. He had the number Tim gave him if they were in a pinch, but between johns and pimps there was no shortage of one-to-two-day vehicles at their disposal.

Sasha had scrolled through the website offering escorts while Mike followed the WhatsApp convo. The two compared notes looking to find anyone that might be in the same loop. So far, they hadn't had any luck, so Mike decided they'd hit another motel room and broaden their search.

As they watched the motel, Sasha stared out the window, unusually quiet. Sensing something was off, Mike gave her some space to process everything that had gone down over the past few days, as well as what they had planned ahead of them. Eventually he asked, "You up for this? We don't have to keep going."

Taking her eyes off the motel, Sasha looked at Mike and took a deep breath.

"It's Lizzy. I can't thank you enough for saving her. For helping me save her. But I have to ask, because something's not sitting quite right with me."

Mike glanced quickly at Sasha, not wanting to miss any activity at the motel. "What's up?"

Sasha took another deep breath. "It's just that—the money. You gave half to Lizzy and took the rest. It feels like we are making money on what she was forced to do."

Mike turned fully to face Sasha, ignoring the motel. "I get what you're saying, but no, we're not profiting from her pain. Truthfully, if I could have given all of it to Lizzy and known she could keep it, I would have. But the cops would have taken it if she had a large amount of cash on her. They'd confiscate it as evidence or some bullshit."

Mike paused, then added, "I know we have money. Some of it is accessible to us, but most of it is stashed between here and Ontario. If we are going to keep going until we find Ashley Brock, until we take down this Lumpz asshole, we're going to need walk-around money. For gas, for cars, for bribes, who knows? The money we kept, every cent, will be used to help these girls and to kill the motherfuckers that have taken them. But we can't do that without cash. You feel me?"

Sasha nodded. "I figured there was a reason. It's just been weighing on me."

"Understandable. We're dealing with people that don't have rules, so we can't either. But there will be no splurging on ourselves with this money..."

Mike was cut off when the pimp's phone dinged.

In reading through the conversation earlier, Mike had determined the phone he had belonged to a guy named James. He had to read it through a few times, trying to dissect any patterns James may have had. The only thing he was able to decipher was that James was borderline illiterate.

"We gud 2morow?" the message read. They were supposed to meet at a motel in Duncan, BC, a small town halfway between Nanaimo and Victoria. Mike understood the plan was to hand over Lizzy Green in exchange for another girl.

"Jesus Christ," Mike muttered, anger burning in his stomach. "They trade these poor kids like they're baseball cards."

"Yup," Sasha agreed. She had been looking at the motel and scrolling through the ads.

"This ones still fresh. Mite hafta make her listen", advised another text, accompanied by a picture of a young girl. She looked to be around seventeen and had tears in her eyes while a man's hand held her face for the photo. The fireball in Mike's stomach grew.

"Oh, right there!" Sasha exclaimed.

Mike looked at the motel and saw two guys leave a room. The first was a Black guy with dreadlocks, about thirty years old, wearing a black and white tracksuit and a lot of gold. The second man was a heavy-set white guy of about the same age. He had close-cropped blond hair and wore baggy jean shorts, a black-and-white paisley-patterned, loose-fitting t-shirt, white high-top sneakers, and a silver chain with a medallion. He lit a cigarette and waddled around the back of the building while the first guy sat in a black Ford Explorer SUV in the parking lot.

"The Black guy will be armed. Fatty thinks he's a fighter," Mike cautioned Sasha.

"How can you tell?"

"Dealt with a million guys like them," Mike replied, then pointed toward the one with dreadlocks.

"This one is a skinny runt. He didn't last in this business by being a pushover. He's either packing or has a weapon nearby. He's not afraid to use it either, so be careful. If you have a gun on him and he moves, plug him. Especially with you being a female. He hates women and will try to test you.

"The manatee over there," Mike pointed at the larger man. "He's big, but he's fat and clumsy. Guys like him are tough when they beat on women or smaller men. He's the type that will kick someone that one of his friends knocked down, then boast about how *he* beat him down. He'll be loud when he talks too. Obnoxious almost. But he's probably a sadist, so they keep him around. He'd be the type of guy that actually enjoys inflicting pain, especially on women."

"Yeah, he's fat with a little dick." Sasha commented.

"If you're covering him, he will try to overtake you." Mike advised.

Sasha nodded and checked the chamber in her small, plastic, 3-D printed pistol.

"We got lucky yesterday. These two are clowns, but they're stupid and dangerous, so we need to be careful. Do not get close enough for them to lunge at you. I'm betting he," Mike gestured again to the one with dreadlocks, "will try to be difficult. I'll try to put them both down quickly. At least face down on the ground, then if they try to move, we can stop them. This isn't Hollywood. If we go in showing guns and tell them to lie face down, odds are they won't. They'll try to be tough guys or honestly be too scared to follow instructions and will try anything to get out of there."

"Well," Sasha pondered. "We only need one of them, right?"

"True."

"Which one is more dangerous?"

"Probably the walrus around back," Mike guessed. "He's more apt to try and fight. The other guy will reach for a gun but won't fight if he's unarmed."

They watched as a white Nissan Sentra pulled up to the room. A slob of a man in his mid-fifties got out and limped to the door.

"Why not take him out now?" Sasha inquired.

Mike pondered her request for a second. "Yeah, okay."

They popped the doors open and made their way across the street.

Sasha looked at Mike. "Follow my lead. I'm mad and storming off; you're trying to stop me." She walked ahead quickly to the edge of the building, rounded the corner, turned back to Mike, and started yelling.

"It wasn't my fault! I'm tired of you!" Sasha started walking behind the building like she was cutting across the property. Mike followed her lead and walked quickly behind her, raising his voice in response.

"I asked you to do one thing! And you couldn't even do that right!"

The back of the motel had a strip of grass and dirt a few feet wide that backed up to a wooded area. Sasha stormed past the fat guy muttering something. The guy looked at her smirking, enjoying watching the white trash argue. Mike walked quickly towards her.

At the last second, Mike threw a four-punch combination into the fat guy's face. The fat guy staggered and bent at the waist to get away from the sudden attack. He turned sideways. Mike raised his foot and kicked the fat guy in the side of the head like he was kicking a door open. Hard. The man's head smashed into the brick wall as he crumpled to the ground, blood pouring out of his nose and mouth. Mike looked at his own right hand; a small cut about an inch long had formed where he'd broken the fat guy's teeth.

"We'll need to clean that." Sasha observed over his shoulder. Then, without being asked, she bent down and emptied the guy's pockets. He had about $1000 in cash and a cell phone. She handed both to Mike.

Mike looked around and saw it was clear. The wooded area behind the motel provided cover. There were no businesses or people. The fat guy stirred and moaned. Mike raised his foot high and stomped on the back of his head, driving his face into the ground; a loud *crack* was heard.

"Okay, let's go." Mike said. They walked back the way they came and paused at the side of the building. Sasha peeked around. The john's white Nissan was still there. The guy with dreadlocks was sitting in his car. A minute later the door opened, and the fat slob of a man walked out; he staggered to his car and got in. The phone in Mike's hand chimed. He checked the message. It was the same two texts over and over.

Incoming said, "*Good?*"

The fat guy's reply was always, " b*et,*" so Mike replied, "*bet*".

The guy with the dreads got out of the Explorer, puffing on a cigarette.

"Wait here," Sasha directed Mike and started walking towards the man, pretending to look at her phone. The man watched her coming.

Sasha was a little on the short side, standing only around five foot four but she worked out regularly, and it showed. She was compact with muscle definition, the type that came from not only the gym but also from fifteen years of construction labor. She worked hard, and being a small female, she had to work twice as hard as the guys on her crew. But at twenty eight, she was in better shape than many girls ten years younger. Add in her crystal blue eyes and her bright smile, and she turned heads everywhere she went. She walked toward the man with dreads as he finished his cigarette.

Standing at the door to his room, he smiled at her and drawled, "Hey, Momma."

"Hey yourself," she smiled back at him. Sasha was usually very reserved and modest. Mike was actually impressed with how easily she turned on her ability to flirt.

"Whatchu doin' here?" the man asked her, reaching his hand out, trying to take hers.

"Just heading back to my room," Sasha replied, holding his gaze. She flashed him another big smile as she added a small bounce in her step.

"Which one's yours?"

"No, no." She said, smiling. "My son's in there. He's napping right now." She paused and tilted her head shyly. "You got any feel-goods?" referring to Percocet or Oxy's

"Yeah, I got you," he grinned.

"Okay, let me check on my boy. I'll come back. This you?" She asked, still flashing that smile.

"I'll be here," he advised.

"Five minutes," she promised and turned to walk away. He turned to head back into the room. As he opened the door, something collided with him from behind. He was shoved forward and crashed into the wall. Sasha had bull charged him and knocked him forward.

Right behind her, Mike was coming in fast. The man quickly reached for his waistband, but Mike was faster and dropped a knee into the guy's chest. Mike reached down, grabbed the guy's wrist with his left hand, and pulled a small semiautomatic pistol out of the guy's waistband with his right. He handed it to Sasha, who took it and then rushed in.

There was a girl sitting on the bed, a shocked expression on her face. She looked a little older than the previous girl, maybe seventeen, but equally tormented and abused.

Mike grabbed the guy by the hair and yanked him up. He was trying to fight back. He hit Mike in the face but didn't know how to punch; it was more like a slap. It was an effective move when you're trying to make a scared teenage girl do what you want, but terrible when a six foot five, two hundred and sixty pound fighter was mad at you.

Mike slammed him into the wall, breaking the drywall and cracking a 2x4 stud. He threw the guy further into the room like a dirty towel. The man tried to scurry on his hands and knees. Mike put his foot on his ass and shoved him forward, slamming the guy's head into the wall. With his pistol drawn, Mike searched the bathroom and found it empty.

Sasha spoke to the young girl. "It's okay, honey. We're not going to hurt you."

The girl was terrified. "I don't know where they keep the money," she cried.

"We don't want their money. We're here to help you," Sasha said calmly.

Mike went to work on the guy on the ground. He zip-tied his hands and feet, then gagged him. He looked at Sasha and asked, "Camera?"

Again, they went through the process. Mike would ask questions that Sasha would relay to the girl. It took a few minutes, but the girl finally understood they weren't there to rob the pimps or to hurt her. They were there to help her. When the realization hit, she began to cry.

Mike loaded the man with the dreads into the back of his Ford Explorer SUV. Again, Sasha followed him, this time in the red Charger. She had the same talk with the girl whose name was Cassie Murray. She was from Prince George in Northern BC. She met a guy from the internet back in late February. She had no idea when they got to Victoria or what the date was. She had been coaxed out to a party one night and had been going through this nightmare since.

Sasha gave her some of the cash they'd taken from her pimps, dropped her two blocks west of police headquarters, and followed Mike out of town.

9:30 pm

Mike opened the back of the Explorer. The man with dreadlocks stared up at him. He was hogtied with heavy-duty zip ties and gagged. Without a word, Mike grabbed two handfuls of hair and pulled the man out, letting him fall on the ground. Mike reached down with a pair of snips and cut the ties on one foot, then the other. He stood the man up, shoved him forward, and ordered, "Walk."

They walked through the woods in the dark. The man, like the others, tripped and stumbled. Again, Mike told Sasha to keep her gun on him and zip-tied his arms around a tree, just like Kevin and Orin.

Mike began with his familiar instructions. "I'm going to remove your gag. Scream and I'll kill ya. Play dumb and say you don't know; I'll kill ya. In fact, the only reason you're alive right now is because I want information. If you don't have it, then I have no reason to let you live. Do you understand me?"

The man glared at him. Mike continued. "Don't play tough. I have a bag full of tools, and I would enjoy dissecting you with them."

As if on cue, Sasha dropped the bag, the tools making several small clanging noises. The man's eyes went wide.

Mike pulled the tape off. The man looked past him and glared at Sasha.

"How do we get to Lumpz?" Sasha asked.

"Fuck you," he spat.

Mike grabbed the man's cheeks and pried open his mouth. Sasha handed him a pair of channel locks. Mike pulled the man's tongue out and down, then held his hand out. Sasha placed a big chrome staple gun in it. With two loud *Ka-thunks*, Mike stapled the man's tongue to his chin. In theory it seemed good, but it didn't work. The man screamed. Mike placed a gloved hand over his mouth to muffle it. When he pulled away, the man's tongue was swollen and bleeding, but it wasn't stuck to his chin.

"Huh, I don't know why I thought that would work," Mike observed.

"Bigger staples next time?" Sasha suggested. "Maybe a nail gun?"

"Noted," Mike said, then turned to the man. "Listen, this is it. You want to see tomorrow morning; you tell me how I can get to Lumpz. Play dumb or act hard; I'll kill you right here and find someone else. Now, last chance, how do I get to Lumpz?"

"His got a body thop. In Ethquimalth," the man mumbled.

"He's got a body shop in Esquimalt?" Mike clarified.

"Yeth," the man replied, gasping for breath. He was bleeding heavily.

"There are a lot of body shops around. Which one?" Mike asked.

"Noth thure the name, ith in Ethqumalth. The thign hath a Jamaican flag on it.

"You're not sure of the name; it's in Esquimalt, and the sign has a Jamaican flag on it?" Mike repeated.

The man nodded. The blood kept pouring out of his mouth. Mike figured he probably nicked the lingual artery, and it wouldn't stop bleeding until the man died. Given the small hole the staple had made, it would take a while.

Mike looked back to Sasha; she nodded, and in a fast motion, Mike shoved a large hunting knife under the man's chin, pushing in and back towards the back of his skull. He twisted the blade around and pulled it out. Blood mixed with cerebrospinal fluid gushed out. There was a gurgle as his body spasmed, and he died instantly.

"Can I ask you something?" Sasha asked as they walked away.

"Shoot," Mike replied.

"I get that he's a piece of shit, but what was the point of this? He didn't tell us anything we didn't already know."

"That's a good question, and you're right," Mike validated. "But he also solidified what the other guys told us. Now we know they weren't making it up."

Chapter 17

Wednesday May 24th, 2023, 10:30 pm.

At the same time, twelve kilometres away, Gale Robson stood in a clearing watching the forensic team with the RCMP major crime unit comb over what could only be described as a slaughter. Three bodies lay about.

"Okay, what do we know?" She asked a Victoria detective named Clara Lalonde.

"Well. It appears the same people that freed Elizabeth Green also freed Cassie Murray. These were Elizabeth Green's pimps. Murray came into the station the same way Green did. Said she'd been abducted, A big man and a small woman burst into the motel room, beat the shit out of her pimp, dragged him off to God knows where, and dropped her off. This case is strange, though. We were tipped off to this location. Knowing what we did about Orin Bondy, we checked it out. And here we are." Lalonde swept her arm towards the scene in case Robson didn't see the carnage behind her.

"Who tipped you off?" Robson asked.

"No fucking clue. Came in from a payphone, if you can believe that. I didn't even know they were still out there!"

"What happened? At least, as far as you know?" Robson inquired.

"Well, we're not exactly sure of the order of events. We have one guy with his head bashed in. Possibly with a ball bat, sledgehammer, who the fuck knows? It was big and heavy, and it was swung hard. Looks like just one hit, and the victim probably died instantly. The other two are stabbings, but very precise. Kind of spooky, to be honest. Most stabbing deaths are done in a fit of rage, where victims die of blood loss from multiple wounds. Both of these victims had pinpoint injuries. The male was found face down and had taken a large blade through the base of his skull, severing the spinal cord. The Wicked Bitch of the West there, she took a blade right to the heart. Up close and personal kills. Whoever clipped them is a heartless bastard. That's for sure. All three had their asses kicked hours earlier too. Bruises are showing. So, it pretty much corroborates Green's statement." Lalonde concluded.

Robson looked at the three corpses. It was a horrific scene, one of the worst she'd ever seen. She felt a tinge of guilt that she felt no sympathy for the three victims, though.

"What about the girl?" Robson asked. "Cassie?"

"Yes, Cassie Murray, age seventeen, disappeared from Prince George a few months ago. Same old song and dance: pimped out, drugged up, passed around. She said a couple she never met blew in the door. We checked her hotel room. There were signs of a fight: busted up wall, blood on the floor. Found her pimp's muscle lying behind the motel. He's alive, but he's probably going to drool when he smiles if he ever wakes up. Someone, likely the big guy, knocked the shit out of him then stomped his head so hard his face dented the ground."

"What do we know about the couple?" Robson asked.

"Nothing," Lalonde replied with a sigh. "Not a goddamn thing. He's big; she isn't. That's about it. I questioned Green, albeit gently, for several hours. She is a smart kid. Remembered very important details, but ask her about the couple, and she clams up. It's not that she doesn't remember; she's protecting them. Murray is similar. She's playing the *'it all happened so fast'* card. But even when we asked for small details about the couple, all she would say is they were white. That's all she gave us. I checked cameras in the area. Saw Green dropped off two blocks east of headquarters in her pimp's red Charger. Kevin Marin's blue truck was in front of them. Saw Murray get dropped off two blocks west in the same Charger, but her pimp's black Ford SUV was in front that time. So, they're switching vehicles consistently."

Robson stared at the three bodies while Lalonde finished with her update.

"Okay, so we have a vigilante couple here. Big guy, small girl, both Caucasian. They're not afraid to kill and seem to be going after pimps and johns alike, then freeing the girls, so this isn't about territory. I don't think these are revenge killings. I'd bet they're extracting information. They're hitting motels, not streetwalkers. We don't know what they're driving because they're switching constantly. We could get the word out for the red Charger, but it's certainly been dumped by now. They may still be in the Ford, but we have no idea, and while we're searching for it, they could have someone else's car because they've just killed another set of pimps. They're moving fast. At my count we have at least five confirmed dead. A sixth is likely dead; we just don't have confirmation, and a seventh is in a coma and will likely never wake up." Robson stared up at the night sky. "Seven bodies in what four days?"

"We could just ignore them," Lalonde suggested, not entirely joking. "I mean, give them a few more weeks, and things might look a lot better around here."

Robson looked at her to see if Lalonde was trying to be funny. Smirking, she added, "I see your point. But we need to get on this. And keep it quiet for right now. The last thing we need is a dozen copycats out doing the same."

"So, what now? Press the girls; see if we can shake some information loose." Lalonde asked.

"No, it won't do any good. Plus, after what they went through, we'd look like assholes grilling them over the people that saved them."

"So we just wait for them to kill more pimps?" inquired Lalonde.

"We may have to follow your suggestion, but not intentionally." Robson mused. "This is the third crime scene they've left, and they're good; they leave nothing behind. Hell, they're only busting up motels they know don't have cameras. And it's useless sending out search parties when we don't even know what we're looking for."

Lalonde nodded and walked away, then muttered under her breath, "I don't really want to look for them yet either."

Clara Lalonde was forty-one years old, although she looked a lot younger. She had light, almost porcelain skin, with dark blue eyes and black, shoulder-length hair, usually worn in a standard ponytail. She was taller than most women, standing around five foot eleven. She had a thick but muscular build that came from lifting free weights at the gym four nights a week and a lifetime of hockey and soccer, both of which she still played weekly.

Lalonde had an incredibly sharp mind and an even sharper tongue. One of the very few homegrown police officers on the Victoria Police Department, Clara was born and raised in Victoria, BC. She moved to Vancouver and attended the British Columbia Institute of Technology for Police Foundations and joined the army the day after receiving her diploma. She immediately applied to the military police program and was sent 5500 km away to Gagetown, New Brunswick, for combat training and later to the Canadian Forces Base Borden near Barrie, Ontario, to complete the military police officer qualification course.

By December she was stationed at a military base in Shilo, Manitoba. She enjoyed her time but wanted to accomplish more and saw a better chance for advancement in the civilian world. After eight years in the Canadian army, she left and was quickly hired as a cadet with the Victoria Police Department, resulting in a move back into her parent's house at thirty-one years old.

Ten years later, she was a detective with VPD and was well respected in the police department. She had worked on several major crime task forces and developed good relationships with other police agencies. During her time with the Canadian Forces, she quickly found she had a strong skill set when it came to interviewing sexual assault victims. She was able to get out all the details and relevant questions, all while ensuring the victims maintained their dignity.

Admittedly, the job horrified her at times. She supported the victims right through the entire trial, and when she gave them her card and said, "Call anytime," she meant it. She had an opportunity for the advancement she always wanted when a supervisory position in the Street Crime and Auto Theft Division opened up, but the more she thought about it, the more she realized her calling was right where she was: helping the people she felt needed her the most.

Clara Lalonde looked at the three bodies: hands bound behind their backs, forced onto their knees. Maybe at first, they thought they'd survive, but once the first one was killed, Lalonde guessed it was the one with his head bashed in; the other two must have felt terrified, trapped, helpless. Scared that any second could be their last. They knew they weren't coming out of this alive. The exact same way they made dozens of young girls feel.

"Good, fuck 'em," she concluded as she walked back towards her car.

Chapter 18

Thursday May 25th, 2023, 11:00 am.

Mike had been monitoring the WhatsApp conversation while they sat in the parking lot across from a three-story hotel in Duncan, BC. It was a large, wide building, recently updated with grey panels, giving it a new modern look. This time it wasn't a drive-up room. This was a three-story hotel, and Mike and Sasha had no clue which room the pimps were hiding out in.

At noon the pimp with the dreadlocks (whose name was Wesley, according to the WhatsApp conversations) was supposed to drop his girl off in exchange for another one. The girl in the picture was a redhead and appeared to be a teenager. At least Mike guessed she was in her teens, but it was clear she'd been abused and looked a lot older.

"What's the plan?" Sasha asked.

"Thinking," Mike replied, staring at the building. "We need to find out what room they're in without getting their backs up."

"Tell him the cops were out front." Sasha said. Mike gave her an inquisitive look. "Not that the cops are here for them, but just that there are two unmarked cars in the parking lot, this Wesley guy wouldn't check in with a girl if cops were around. He'd go right to their room and drop her off. Smoke a joint, then either go down by himself or send one of the other guys down."

Mike pulled up the conversation and typed. *"Yo, 5-0 in the lot. Wut room u in"*

He watched the checkmarks appear. Fifteen seconds later, came the reply, "211." Mike put the phone away.

They went to the back of the black SUV and popped the hatch. Mike grabbed Sasha a small 3-D-printed pistol.

"This is a 0.40 calibre. It's a heavier round. This one will kick a lot more than the last one, but it's the smallest one I have right now. Be prepared."

Sasha nodded, testing the weight of the gun in her hand.

Mike grabbed a similar pistol for himself, checked the chamber, and stuck the gun in his waistband, keeping his shirt untucked over it. He grabbed what looked like an overnight bag with tape, gags, zip ties, and a few other essentials, and they made their way inside.

Mike and Sasha were both wearing black ball caps with sunglasses. Their clothing was unremarkable; dull, faded colours with no logos. The easiest way to hide was in plain sight.

Heads down, they walked into the hotel. It was clear the place had been renovated within the last few years; there was lots of brass and beige in the lobby that doubled as the breakfast area, trying to add the modern amenities but forced to use the limited space from the original build.

They walked past the front desk to the elevators. Mike hit the button. Under his breath he muttered, "Cameras in the elevator."

Sasha let out a quiet "Mmmhmm.".

The door opened, they entered, Mike hit the "2" and they waited. When the door closed, Mike instructed, "If they're in the hallway, we rush them. Follow my lead. If not, we figure out the floor's layout and head to the stairwell to come up with a better plan. We don't know how many there are. This is dangerous, so when we take them, be hypervigilant. Keep them in front of you at all times. If there are several of them, one may try something while I'm tying them up. Don't worry about who I'm tying; I'll deal with them. You keep an eye on the others."

The door slid open. There were two brass plates directly across the hallway; one showed an arrow pointing right that had *"201–224"* engraved on it, and the other said *"225–250."*. They turned right and made their way down the hallway. The numbers went downward: 224 on the left, 223 on the right; each subsequent room dropped by two, putting 211 somewhere near the middle.

Mike focused his attention on the even-sided numbers, just in case someone was looking at them. As they neared 211, they could hear voices, loud voices. It sounded like a party. The smell of weed got stronger. They got in line with the door for 211, and Mike stopped. He heard what sounded like two guys talking loudly with an occasional bout of laughter. Only two voices, though. The door was ajar. Whoever Mike was texting with must have popped it open, thinking Wesley would let in himself and his girl.

Mike looked at Sasha. "On three, ready?"

She nodded and took her small gun out.

"One, two, three." Mike slammed his weight into the door, and it flung open.

Mike burst through at full speed. The bathroom was on the left. He flew past it, hoping Sasha knew enough to check it. Mike needed to keep moving because inside the room, perched on the dresser, was a man in his early twenties, Black with lighter skin. The man was wearing baggy black jeans, a black and white paisley patterned tank top, and a thick gold chain around his skinny neck. He was smiling as he looked over at Mike. The smile quickly dropped. Confusion set in for a second, then realization hit, and he attempted to get up.

That second of hesitation was all Mike needed as he ran into the room at full speed. With a pistol in his left hand, Mike crashed a solid right hook into the side of the man's head, knocking him out cold. Mike spun to his left and saw a second man of similar age smoking a joint. This man was white and wore black shorts and a white tank top. Mike pointed the gun at his stunned face and yelled, "Get on the ground now!"

The guy stood with his hands up. "I want a lawyer."

Mike smashed the butt of his pistol into the bridge of the guy's nose. The guy put his hands over his face as blood squirted out between his fingers, and he dropped to his knees. Mike's attention shifted to a young redheaded girl wearing next to nothing, sitting on the bed. Her eyes were wide open, fear spread across her face.

Sasha came in right behind Mike. "Bathrooms clear." She kept her gun trained on the guy that had been sitting on the dresser.

"If he moves, shoot him in the face." Mike directed. He dropped the small black bag on the bed, pulled out zip ties, and tied the white kid's arms together. He pulled out a small rag and some tape, gagged him, searched him, then went to the other guy and started doing the same.

Sasha looked at the girl and soothed, "It's okay, honey, we're getting you out of here." The girl looked terrified, completely lost, and incoherent all at the same time.

"Did they have a camera in here?" Sasha asked her. A blank stare was her response. "Hey, sweetie. Over here?" Sasha gently nudged her.

Snapping back to reality, the girl looked at Sasha with confusion. "I go home now?" The obvious drawl of a speech impediment was in her voice.

"Christ," Mike exclaimed, realizing the girl was mentally challenged and had the mind of a child. His level of rage and disgust with her pimps hit a new level. He finished gagging, binding, and searching the second guy before hefting him like a sack of potatoes and tossing him on the bed.

At that moment, the door opened, and a third guy, a little older, in his early thirties, also Black, and dressed in similar colours, walked into the room with a large Burger King bag and a tray with three drinks. He stopped dead in his tracks and looked at Mike and Sasha with a confused expression on his face, like he'd stumbled into the wrong room.

As the realization of what was going on hit him, he dropped everything and ran back out the door. Mike and Sasha both took off after him. He tried to make it to the elevator but didn't have time. He kept running down the hall towards the stairs. He crashed through the stairwell door. The ascending stairs were directly in front of him, so he went up the stairs two at a time. Sasha, although small, was fast and went through the door right behind him. She stopped and levelled her pistol. "Stop!"

The guy wasn't stopping. Sasha cocked the gun.

Mike caught up and yelled, "No!" trying to stop her. He smacked her hand down just as she fired two shots in rapid succession. She only heard the first one. The sound echoing in the cement stairwell was tremendous. Sasha's eardrums felt like they blew up. The concussion was so loud, she dropped the gun and grabbed her ears.

Mike flew past her. The guy they were chasing had it even worse as the sound came directly at him. His ears were bleeding. He had stopped at the base of the landing, hands on the side of his head, staggering. Mike ran at him at full speed, grabbed his head, and slammed it into the cement wall. The man crumpled in a heap on the ground. Blood streamed from his ears, and a large cut opened on the back of his head. Mike emptied the man's pockets, then turned to Sasha; the ringing in his ears was blistering.

He thought he yelled, "We need to go," but couldn't hear his own words. He made eye contact with Sasha and pointed down. She mouthed a reply, a look of fear crossing her face as she realized she couldn't hear her voice either. Mike jumped the half flight of stairs to her, picked up her pistol, took her by the hand, and made his way down the stairs to the first floor, out the stairwell emergency exit, and back to the SUV.

As they rushed towards the vehicle, Mike pointed at the door. Sasha's balance was off, and she fell. She got up and jumped in the SUV. Mike drove off. The ringing in both their ears was torture. Mike kept an eye on the mirror. He couldn't hear anything, just the nonstop, ear-splitting, unending high-pitched tone. Sasha tapped his arm; he looked at her, and she pointed at her ears and shook her head. Mike pointed at the clock, then with his fingers showed a two and a zero. *"Twenty minutes."* In twenty minutes, the ringing should die down, at least enough that they could speak to each other.

12:30 pm

Tyson Bent rushed into Gale Robson's office with a big smile on his face.

"We got something!" he announced.

"What's that?"

"Cops in Duncan just called. At 11:15 am they responded to a call about shots fired. When they got there, they found two .40 calibre shell casings in the stairwell."

"Bent, if you play this game again, I'll pistol whip you to death right here," Robson warned, not wanting him to continue with another one of his drawn-out reveals.

"Yes, ma'am," he replied dutifully. "I'll try to keep it brief. In the stairwell was Edmond Waters. He's a minor dirtbag, with a couple of assaults and a couple of pimping charges. Edmond is out cold. Someone smashed his head into the wall. He had blood coming out of his ears. He's going for a CT scan to make sure his brain isn't bleeding.

HUNTING PREDATORS

"Down at the other end of the building was Edmond's room. Two more scumbags in there. Both hogtied with the same zip ties we found around Marin's body, on Orin Bondy, and on all three of last night's victims. They also had an eighteen-year-old girl in the room. She'd been put through the wringer, bad. When asked where she lived, she gave her address, right down to the postal code. It's like her parents had her rehearse it in case she ever wandered off and got lost." Bent advised, putting an inflection on the end of his sentence explaining the young girl was developmentally challenged.

He continued, "So it looks like the mystery couple went after these guys. Through my awesome powers of deduction. I figured it out: the couple got into the room and were working the goons over when Edmond walked in. They chased him down and caught him in the stairwell."

Robson stared at him. ".40 cal in the stairwell? Jesus. That would have been deafening."

"Right, which explains why the pimp and goons were left behind. The shots went off; they all went deaf. Bonnie and Clyde got the hell out of there." Bent concluded.

"Okay, so cameras?" Robson inquired.

Bent handed her a grainy black-and-white photo. Heads down, sunglasses, long-sleeve shirts—they looked like a couple that had gone hiking earlier that day. "This is… This is shit, Bent."

"Yes, ma'am. Best picture we could find. They were in a black SUV. We were able to track them to the edge of Duncan; after that, they disappeared. None of the cameras caught their faces."

"I thought you said we had something?" Robson was exasperated, her annoyance coming through.

"We do, ma'am. Matthew Edworthy. One of the goons. Swears he'll tell us everything. He was told that he faces kidnapping and human trafficking charges. Scared him shitless! And he'll give us everything. I asked him about the couple that came in. He only saw the male. Said the guy was huge, said the guy smashed his face in with a gun, but not before he got a good look at him. He's with a sketch artist now."

"And what about the pimps and the girls?" Robson asked.

Bent didn't reply.

"So, we're going to give a pimp a free pass because he'll tell us who is killing pimps? And what exactly happens after that? He's going to go right back into the streets and start doing it again."

"Ma'am, I don't understand. We have five dead bodies, another in intensive care. Edmon's head was cracked open; his skull is fractured. We have another person missing and presumed dead. Shouldn't we focus on catching this couple?"

"Listen, Dudley fuckin Doo-rite," Robson snapped. "I don't really give a good goddamn how these pimps get shut down, be it us or this fucking mystery couple. This entire country is overrun with parasites like..." she paused. "What the hell is his name?"

"Matthew Edworthy," Bent offered.

"Matthew Edworthy and his friends. There's no deal!" Robson insisted. Bent stared at her blankly until she barked, "Stop looking at me like that."

Chapter 19

Thursday May 25th, 2023, 12:35 pm

Mike had smashed the phone he had been using to monitor the WhatsApp conversation. Considering they had dropped two girls with the police, he didn't want to risk carrying a phone that belonged to a dead pimp, especially after the fiasco that morning. He and Sasha sat off the highway on another logging road. Sasha had her head tilted back. The ringing had subsided, and what was left was a nasty headache.

"Jesus Christ," she uttered.

"What did we learn?" Mike asked, sounding like an annoyed first-grade teacher.

"Fuck, that was loud." Sasha remarked, ignoring his snarky tone. "You see full gunfights in movies. They shoot, then talk like nothing happened."

"Yup. Welcome to the real world. Guns are loud. Deafening, even with a silencer. Fire it in a hallway or stairwell, and you'll wish you hadn't." Mike agreed. The ringing was still buzzing in his ears, but at least they could hear each other now.

"We didn't save that girl." Sasha lamented.

"Cops would have swarmed that place within seconds. The two in the room weren't moving. I don't know if the guy in the stairwell lived; I rammed the back of his head into the wall pretty hard. I'm sure the cops have the girl by now." Mike assured her. He paused for a few seconds and added, "That girl had the mind of a four-year-old." A sickening feeling crept over him.

Sasha sat up and looked at him. "They're predators. They prey on the weak and the broken. To them, that girl was nothing more than a source of income. Until she can't earn anymore, then they'll throw her out in the cold."

"But the johns, they'd have to know she wasn't cognizant. As soon as she opened her mouth, they'd have to know something wasn't right with her." Mike said, shaking his head.

"I'm sure they did." Sasha agreed. "Some of them come and go in a matter of minutes. Others love the weak, the feeble. They're monsters. The more the girl cries, the meaner the johns get." Sasha's voice trailed off as she looked out the window. She took a deep breath, bringing her mind back to the present. "So what now?"

Mike sat looking forward. "We need to keep moving. I'll drive; you scroll through those phones to see if there's anything useful. We're heading back to Victoria. Time to start focusing more on Lumpz. Seems like all roads lead back to him."

Sasha checked the first phone. "Needs a fingerprint."

"Pull the SIM and toss it." Mike instructed.

The other two required PINs. She pulled the SIM cards on those as well and flung all three phones out the window when they crossed over a bridge. The sky was getting dark. Rain was coming.

1:00 pm

Lumpz was driving around Victoria. Something was wrong; he knew it. First Kevin Marin disappeared. He had two separate guys that were supposed to contact him, one yesterday and one today. Both were supposed to drop him off some cash; neither one showed up.

He wasn't sure what happened in Duncan, but rumour was cops raided the hotel where Edmond was staying and there was a shootout. That didn't sit well with Lumpz. Edmond was a piece of shit and a coward. Even if he had a gun on him, he would be too chicken shit to use it.

Then there was that random dude. A schoolteacher found tied to a tree and murdered. Normally Lumpz wouldn't give it a second thought, but the picture in the newspaper showed that ball-busting bitch, Clara Lalonde. She was still working sex crimes, not murders, so what the fuck was she doing there? Something wasn't right. His phone rang.

"Yeah?" he answered.

"Cops are all over the hotel in Duncan. I talked to some dude staying on the same floor. He said a young girl was escorted out. Two guys left on stretchers. A third was led to a squad car in cuffs. Guy said his face was busted up." The phone crackled as Lumpz was given the rundown.

"Were they raided?" Lumpz asked.

"Doesn't sound like it. This guy I talked to said he heard the shots. The coppers rolled in with lights and sirens a few minutes after the shots. Maybe a sting gone wrong?" the voice offered.

"Maybe," Lumpz agreed, unconvinced. "Hang back; keep me posted." He rung off and dialled another number. This one belonged to Jose, one of his enforcers.

"Yeah," Jose answered.

"You make it by Wesley's room?" Lumpz inquired.

"Just pulling in now. Hold on." There was silence for a few seconds. "There's police tape over the door." Jose was quiet for another couple seconds before adding, "5-0 in the parking lot too."

"Huh," Lumpz said, trying to keep his frustration from boiling over. "Check them other dudes from Calgary. They were supposed to bring me something yesterday."

"On my way," Jose promised and rung off.

This wasn't good, Lumpz thought. Kevin, Wesley, and Edmond, a raid, the other room with police tape on the door. This wasn't good. Eight minutes later his phone rang; it was Jose.

"Yeah," Lumpz said with more than a little irritability in his voice.

"Same deal here." Jose informed. "Police tape on the door, cop in the parking lot."

"Fuck!" Lumpz cursed. "Okay, meet me at the garage in twenty minutes. Bring your crew with you."

"Coming." Jose rang off again.

Chapter 20

Thursday May 25th, 2023, 1:30 pm.

Lumpz was standing in the office section of his autobody shop. He had bought the place a few years ago, and it acted as nothing more than a front for his other dealings. He used the business to employ friends recently let out of prison. It was a functional shop, known throughout the Victoria underworld as the place to go if you were involved in a hit and run. Smoked a kid in a school zone and wanted your car fixed for cash, no questions asked? This was the place to go. A sign out front boasted about easy cash payment plans that helped explain the high cash volume he reported.

At 1:35 pm, Jose walked in out of the rain. He had seven guys behind him of various heights, builds, and ethnic backgrounds.

"What's up?" he greeted, meeting Lumpz eyes.

Lumpz nodded at him and motioned for him to follow. He walked back to the shop area, then out the backdoor to the alley. It was pouring rain, the usual noise from the several other shops and factories drowned out by the drops cascading over the aluminium awning.

"Something ain't right," Lumpz confided, barely loud enough for Jose to hear him. Jose said nothing, just waited. "Kevin went missing, then the raid in Duncan, then the other two rooms. This isn't good. Someone is taking us apart, but they're doing it quietly." Jose nodded; Lumpz continued. "I don't know if they've been arrested or what.

But it seems odd the cops would seal up the rooms for busting a couple low-level pimps. Plus, I ain't heard nothing. No calls for lawyers, nothing. These motherfuckers just vanished."

Jose took a deep breath. "So, what are you thinking?"

"I dunno. But here," Lumpz handed Jose a list. "I got people set up in these rooms. Send your guys to each one. Report back; see if any are busted up too. If not, have them sit tight and keep an eye on the rooms for a bit. See if anything happens."

Jose took a quick look at the list. "Anything else?"

"Yeah," Lumpz replied. "You keep an eye on the other two spots too. Soon as the cops leave, go talk to the owners. See what the fuck happened." Jose nodded, and Lumpz added, "Ask them hard if you need to." They bumped fists, and Jose left through the garage.

1:30 pm

Clara Lalonde walked into an interview room and dropped a file on the table. Matthew Edworthy was sitting handcuffed to the table. A bandage lay across the cut on his nose, placed by an EMT. The swelling and bruising had started to form under his eyes. The blood that soaked his shirt was bright red in some spots and turning crimson in others.

"Matthew Edworthy?" Lalonde began as she sat down across the table. "You're in deep shit right now, buddy."

Matthew sat quietly, and she continued. "That young girl you guys were with, she went missing as a minor, and she's developmentally challenged. That's a kidnapping charge, transporting, aggravated sexual assault. There's a minimum five-year sentence right there. Hell, with your record, fuck-o, they're going to push for a life sentence. And I hope they get it." Lalonde's eyes flashed with hatred. "You may as well have raped a child, you piece of shit!"

"I told that other guy everything I know," Matthew replied defensively.

"I don't give two fists up a fat rat's ass what you said to anybody, you scroungy little fuck!" Lalone spat as she slammed her hands on the table. "You kidnapped a mentally disabled girl. Her birth certificate says eighteen, but she has the mental capacity of a six-year-old. Is that what you need? Someone who can't understand what a short, dick little worm you really are?"

"Hey, fuck you!" Matthew snapped.

"Go ahead! Stand up, tough guy," Lalonde dared as she shot up out of her chair. "Give me just one reason to knock your fat ass back down."

Lalonde was seething. She had encountered some real low-lives in her career, but these three were definitely in the running for first place. She counted to ten in her head to cool her temper before speaking again.

"So, here's the thing. I'm supposed to come in here and strike up a deal with you. I really don't want to, though. I want to send you down to the holding cells right now, tell everyone why you're there, and slam the door shut."

She held his eye contact and added, "I'd like to record your screams and use them to help me sleep at night, but since I can't do that, here's the deal. And this is the only deal you're being offered. You give me everything. Every single lowlife scumbag you deal with. All of it. And with that I'll tell the crown you were cooperative. Cooperate, and you'll stay in this room until you're arraigned. But if you give me even a shred of a reason to think you're not being honest or that you're holding out on me, or if you try to lawyer up, I swear to God almighty Himself, you'll find yourself 'accidentally' placed in the bullpen. And I'll make sure we raid the homes of every 1% biker and every hardened criminal on the island tonight and hold them on suspicion so that bullpen will be nice and packed with angry men looking to blow off steam. Angry men that would love nothing more than getting their hands on a piece of shit that kidnapped a mentally challenged girl and raped her for months on end." Finished with her offer, Lalonde smiled at him.

"You're being charged to the full extent. Nothing is going to change that. But it's really up to you whether or not you live long enough to make it to trial. I'm fine letting them rip you apart down there."

Matthew heard her words. He'd sat in similar interview rooms before. He'd been threatened and even beaten by the police before. But this was different; this lady wasn't tossing out idle threats. She wasn't lying or exaggerating. She meant every word she was saying. "What do you want to know?"

"Everything!" Lalonde replied, emphasizing each syllable. "Names, dates, locations, who you run with, where they are now, how you get the girls. I want you to write me a goddamn *'How to'* screenplay on pimping out young girls, and I want the full cast."

Chapter 21

Thursday May 25th, 2023, 2:35 pm

Mike and Sasha found another motel and sat parked across the street. Mike took a deep breath. He needed to be upfront. "This is only going to get harder."

Sasha sat watching the parking lot from her side mirror.

"How so?"

"We've used the 'set up a date' strategy already. We blindsided one group of pimps and played the others via text. If word is out, especially after this morning, the people in that whole network are going to be extra cautious. We need to assume we won't be able to rush them like before or surprise them in bathrooms. They'll be on guard. We don't know what they know. We don't know if they have our descriptions. We don't know anything. So, we'll need to assume the worst, that they have everything and they're waiting for us. If it gets too hot, we back off."

Sasha looked away from her mirror to face Mike.

Mike continued. "I want to help. I want to shut them down completely, but not if we get killed in the process. We're no good to anybody if we're dead."

Sasha nodded and stared back at the mirror. "So, what do we do?"

Watching his mirror, Mike answered, "We wait and see what's going on. How many there are in there. If only two come out, we have to assume they placed a third in the bathroom, and it wouldn't hurt to assume they're armed and ready to come out shooting."

He paused before continuing. "Look at me." Sasha looked. "I hate to keep saying this, but this isn't the movies. People don't always fall if you shoot them. It's not laser tag or paintball. They don't put their hands up and walk off the field. People can get shot even in vital organs and still shoot back. There's an old cliché that says a deer will run faster and further on three legs than it will on four. People are the same. There's also a reason police aim centre mass and keep shooting till they're empty. So, if it starts, get down low. Never stand when you can crouch; never crouch if you can lay down. And don't assume because you shot them that they're out of the fight. People can live and function for several minutes with a bullet in them."

"Okay," Sasha promised.

"I don't really want to, but we'll need to take at least one of them with us. We need a phone with a PIN if possible. I don't want to keep these assholes around to change their security settings from a thumbprint to a PIN, but the phone is crucial. We also need to make sure the girl stays quiet."

Sasha nodded again and suddenly sat up a little straighter. "Something happening."

A white man around forty, dressed in clothing marketed to people twenty years younger, stepped out of a room. A woman that could have been twenty-five or sixty, rail thin with bright red hair and the telltale signs of opiate and meth abuse, followed. They sat in a silver

Nissan Pathfinder and waited. As if timed perfectly, a blue Toyota Corolla pulled up. A fat man with a bald head in his late fifties or early sixties got out and walked to the motel room door.

Seventeen minutes later he left. Mike and Sasha watched the couple exit the vehicle and go back into the room.

"So?" Sasha asked.

Mike thought for a second. "Okay, who is more likely to have the phone, him or her?"

"Hard to say. It'll depend on who they think the girl belongs to." Sasha replied.

"Fuck." Mike paused. "Okay, we'll do a fast sweep. Keep situational awareness. It's a small room; assume there's someone in the bathroom. I'll boot the door in, we'll rush them, take 'em both, and deal with them later. Leave the girl; have her call the police after we're gone."

"Shouldn't we drop her off?" Sasha asked.

"No. Not anymore. After this morning and the last two we dropped off, they'll know it's all connected. They could be watching the streets near the cop shop." Mike advised. He put the car in gear and drove across the street. They parked next to the Pathfinder.

"Ready?" Mike asked.

Sasha checked the chamber on the 0.40 calibre pistol. Seeing the brass casing, she looked at Mike and nodded.

"Fast and hard. Don't give them a chance to react. Keep them both in front of you. I'll check the bathroom. As soon as we're clear, we bind them, toss them in their own car, and we get the fuck outta there." Mike instructed.

"Got it," Sasha affirmed.

Wasting no time, they flung the car doors open. In three steps Mike was at the motel room door. He raised his foot and, in a violent thrust, kicked the door below the handle. The door and frame both splintered and exploded inward. Mike flew into the room, Sasha right behind him.

Inside they found a man sitting at a small table smoking a cigarette, the red-haired woman sitting on the bed smoking meth in a glass pipe. Both looked shocked. Sasha trained her pistol on the man.

"Lay down!" Sasha yelled.

Mike didn't slow down. He went straight to the bathroom; the door was open, the shower running. He looked in; nobody but the young girl in the shower. He quickly rushed back toward the couple.

"Watch her. If she moves, shoot her," he directed Sasha. Mike bound and gagged the man, then the woman. The water in the shower turned off. A young girl stepped out wearing a towel, her head dry except for the bottom inch of her shoulder-length brown hair. She had bruises on her arms, face, and shoulders.

Sasha looked at her and explained, "We're taking them away. Get dressed, wait ten minutes, and call the police." Shock registered on the girl's face. "Hey!" Sasha called out a little more firmly. "Look at me." The girl looked, and Sasha asked, "What did I say?"

Confusion showed, then the girl repeated Sasha's instructions. "Wait ten minutes, call the police?" It was more a question than a statement.

Mike searched the man and found his keys. Again, not talking directly to the girl, he spoke to Sasha. "Tell her to say their car was a blue Toyota." He grabbed the man by the belt and the hair on the back of his head and lifted him up; then he did the same with the woman. "Back of your car, go. Now." The man took a step and stopped. Mike grabbed the zip ties at his wrist and hoisted the man's arms back and straight up, folding him forward. The man screeched with pain.

"Don't get tough with me; I'll kill you right here," Mike warned and started walking. Sasha grabbed the red-haired woman the same way.

Less than 1 minute after kicking the door in, they walked out, put both the man and the woman in the cargo hold of the Pathfinder, and pulled out of the parking lot.

A man in a black Honda Accord sat watching a fleabag motel.

"This is stupid. The fuck am I doing this for?" he asked himself out loud. The time passed slowly; he was bored out of his mind. He watched a new black Ford Explorer roll up in front of the unit. He thought it looked like a cop car. He watched as two people, a large man and a small woman, got out and hustled towards the door.

"Oh, shit!" he exclaimed as he grabbed his phone, scrolled down to "Jose," and sent a text: *"5-0. Raid."*.

After a few seconds he saw a response. *"Wait."*.

He sat waiting. Less than a minute later he saw the large man and small woman walk out with two people cuffed; at least he thought that's what he saw. He couldn't figure out why they were being put in the back of their own car, though. And was even more confused when the cops jumped in and drove away.

He started to follow and called Jose.

"Yeah?" Jose answered on the first ring.

"Eh, listen. Something is fucked up. The cops, they took them people out of the room, put them in their own car and drove off. Left the cop car there."

"What?" Jose asked, trying to understand.

"Yeah, man. I'm following them right now. They put them people in their own car and drove away."

"Stay on them." Jose instructed.

Chapter 22

Thursday May 25th, 2023, 2:40 pm.

Lumpz was driving around Victoria. He didn't have a destination in mind; he just knew he needed to keep moving. He was worried the cops were onto him and figured it would be harder to arrest him if he wasn't stationary. It was a fight-or-flight situation, and he was choosing flight. Despite his reaction, Lumpz wasn't a coward; he'd grown up fighting. The boxing gloves on the mirror weren't for show. But he knew better than to come to a fight unprepared, and he was anything but prepared.

Lumpz came from an abusive household. His dad, Leon, was a drunk and a sadist. Lumpz had watched his dad beat his mother unconscious more than once and had suffered the same fate several times. That's where the nickname came from; his dad had battered him so badly at eleven years old that he had several permanent knots left on his head.

When Lumpz was twelve, Leon, in a particularly nasty mood one night, turned his rage on Lumpz' mom again. Lumpz tried to stop him but was shoved and sent tumbling down a flight of stairs. He could hear his mother's screams, pleading for the beating to stop. In an act of desperation, he called 9-1-1. It took them four minutes to arrive; those were the longest four minutes of his life. He'd heard his mother's cries stop, but the blows kept landing.

What happened next changed Lumpz' life forever. The front door flew open, and a short, squat, fire hydrant of a man in a police uniform flew into the house, past the young boy, and up the stairs. There was a loud commotion with banging and crashing, and then Lumpz saw his drunken father come flying down to the bottom of the stairs without touching a single step.

The short cop came barreling down after him like an overprotective pit bull, his teeth bared, snarling. He ripped the radio off his uniform because it was in the way. Leon tried to get up, but the cop stomped on his hand, then the back of his head. He kicked Leon in the face, then bent down and started pummelling him with both hands. Lumpz could hear the cop cursing as he gave Leon a beating far worse than Leon had ever given his wife. Lumpz sat in the corner and covered his head with his hands.

More police started rushing in, two of them grabbing the small, squat man.

"Stop, you're gonna kill him," Lumpz heard one cop yell. Two more rushed up the stairs. There was chaos all around them. A female cop grabbed Lumpz and ushered him outside.

Lumpz stayed with his mother's friend for the next six weeks while she recovered in the hospital. He hated it there. He had to clean the house for them and had to go to bed at 8:00 pm, even on Saturdays. The food was gross; it had no flavor. He missed his mom, and when the kids at school found out what happened, they started teasing him.

One kid made jokes saying his mom had it coming. Lumpz hit him and was given detention. He was ordered to help the janitor clean out the classroom garbage pails on the recess break. While cleaning out the third-grade classroom, he saw Mrs. Richards had left her purse on her desk. Lumpz took a $10 bill out of her wallet. She was always a fucking bitch to him anyway, and he wanted it for food. The people he was staying with gave him peanut butter and jelly on white bread; it was gross, and he wanted something else. As he slipped the $10 into his pocket, he was startled by a voice from behind.

"Oh, am I ever glad you did that!" The voice was loud, and he jumped. Lumpz turned around and saw his principal, Mr. Baker, standing in the doorway. "Come with me; let's go." Mr. Baker ushered the young boy to the office. "Call the police, please," he instructed the school administrator. "We have a little thief here."

Lumpz was made to sit on a chair outside the office. He was terrified. *Am I going to a group home now?* he wondered, *Or worse, jail?* Leon was in jail. *Will I have to see him again?* He watched the clock tick by. He wanted to run, but he had nowhere to go. He looked out the window and saw a white police car pull up. His stomach felt like it was on fire; a jolt of fear and adrenaline hit him. He sat terrified. He heard the door open but couldn't stand the thought of looking over.

He could hear murmurs of a conversation between the secretary and another person with a deep voice. Out of the corner of his eye, Lumpz saw the light blue shirt come around the corner. His heart dropped; it was the same cop that busted his door down and beat up Leon. This cop was scary. The cop looked at him with a mean sneer on his face. The secretary, Miss Harris, escorted the cop past Lumpz into Mr. Baker's office, closing the door behind them. Lumpz sat there, terrified.

A few minutes later the door opened.

"Let's go. Get in here," Mr. Baker ordered.

Lumpz tried to get up, but his legs felt like they were going to give out under him. He slowly walked towards the office door.

"Come on, hurry up!" Mr. Baker snapped.

Lumpz stood in the doorway, eyes fixated on the ground. The cop sat in a chair.

"Give us a minute, please," the cop requested in a deep, gruff voice. Mr. Baker left the office and closed the door behind him. Lumpz stood frozen.

"Sit down," the cop instructed. His voice seemed less scary now, almost friendly.

Lumpz, still unable to take his eyes off the floor, sat down in the other chair. He looked at the wearing on the floor tiles.

"Do you remember me?" the cop asked. Lumpz couldn't look up.

"Hey, look at me." The cop's voice was calm. Lumpz slowly looked up and met his eyes. He initially thought he was going to see the monster under the bed. But it turned out the man's face was friendly, almost smiling. "Do you remember me?" he asked again.

Lumpz nodded.

"What's going on? Talk to me." The cop's demeanour had changed from when he first walked in, but Lumpz couldn't forget the memory of his dad lying in a heap at the bottom of the stairs. Lumpz sat silent. The cop continued to question him.

"They called us. Said you're fighting and stealing. Is that true?" Lumpz couldn't reconcile the two versions of this cop in his head. A few weeks ago, he had seen this person, more monster than human, smash into his home and beat Leon within an inch of his life. He looked like a beast doing it. But now he was sitting there, friendly.

"They," Lumpz croaked out, barely audible. "They make fun of my momma. Said she's retarded now." He could barely be heard.

"Is that why you're fighting? Because they're teasing you?" the cop asked. Lumpz nodded, his head still looking down.

"What about the stealing?" asked the cop.

Lumpz shrugged his shoulders in reply.

"That's not an answer. buddy. I know you took the money. You're not in trouble. Just tell me why."

"H-hungry." Lumpz replied.

"Are you not being fed?"

"Yeah. But it's gross. It's all peanut butter and jam and Kraft Dinner." He sat quietly for a second trying to hold back tears. "I miss my momma. I miss her food," he squeaked out. "I wanted to go to the store she brings me to."

The cop sat quietly for a second; the silence was loud. Eventually he leaned forward and said, "My name is Ed. I'm a policeman, but I teach boxing too. Would you like to start coming to the club with me?"

Lumpz couldn't believe his ears. He was certain he was going to jail today. But this cop wasn't being mean at all. "We have everything you'll need. There are other boys there. Boys like you. Good boys that have had a hard time and just need the right friends. Does that sound like something you'd like?"

Lumpz sat quietly as he considered the offer. His gaze slowly travelled from the officer's black boots up over the black tactical pants. His eyes paused slightly on the shiny leather gun belt. Lumpz suppressed a smirk, thinking that with all the attachments, it reminded him of Batman's utility belt.

His scrutiny continued up over the light blue uniform shirt, pausing once again, this time on the chrome Windsor Police Department badge and the name tag underneath that read, "WOLLY." Finally meeting the officer's gaze, Lumpz nodded.

"Good," replied Officer Wolly. "Very good, Wallace. I'll talk to Miss Harris and get your address. I'll pick you up tonight; is that okay?" Lumpz nodded again. "Okay. Go back to class." Lumpz left the office.

Mr. Baker was standing at the door, a look of confusion on his face. Lumpz walked past him and heard the cop's mean, gruff voice again. This time he was yelling at Mr. Baker. "Do you have any fucking idea what that kid has been through?"

"Well, I just..." Mr. Baker fumbled for words.

"You just what? Thought you'd bully a traumatized kid?"

Lumpz could hear the cop yelling as he ran down the hall and headed back to class.

5:00 pm

Mike and Sasha pulled down another logging road. They drove on for what felt like miles, overgrown tree branches encroaching more and more on the path, now scratching the side of the Pathfinder almost steadily.

They stopped at a small clearing and hopped out. Mike popped the back window up and dropped the latch. He grabbed the man by the head and yanked him out, letting him fall to the ground, then did the same with the red-haired woman. He pulled out a black cell phone. "Whose phone is this?"

The man and woman looked at each other and said nothing. Mike looked at Sasha. "Slice his ear off," he instructed. Sasha stepped forward with her knife out.

"Wait, wait, wait, wait," The man sputtered. "It's mine."

Mike tapped the screen. It needed a PIN. "What's the code?"

"1111," the man replied. Mike shook his head and sighed. He tapped in the PIN and scrolled through the apps. Finding WhatsApp, he opened it and flipped through the conversations. He had a brief bout of relief when he saw the previous conversation he'd been monitoring. He scrolled a bit more and froze on one message. *"LUMPZ"* was the name of the other person in the conversation. "Bingo!" Mike exclaimed.

He opened the conversation and skimmed its contents.

After about twenty seconds Mike nodded at Sasha. With her knife still out, she stepped up behind the woman and cut her throat. The woman gurgled loudly for a few seconds, then went quiet.

The man looked at the red-haired woman with panic in his eyes. He shifted his gaze back to Mike, who was coming downward with his knife. Mike drove the blade into the top of the man's skull, burying it to the handle. He twisted and wrenched it around, then pulled it out, wiped the blood on the man's shirt, and put the knife back in its sheath.

"We good?" Sasha asked.

"Yes. We're back into the conversation. He has Lumpz in his contacts too." Mike added as they hopped back into the Pathfinder. They made their way back down the path in silence. Mike was used to the brutality, but part of him was curious about how Sasha was coping. It had been a crazy few days, even by his former standards. This would be a lot for someone that wasn't familiar with this type of brutality.

"How are you doing?" he asked her.

"Fine," Sasha replied, staring forward.

"Really?"

"No, not really." Sasha sighed. "We've been killing pimps for four days and still have no clue where Ashley Brock is."

"I get that." Mike empathized. "You may need to come to terms with the fact that we may not find her, but we've rescued four other girls. That's got to count for something. But how are you doing with all the killing?"

"I'm fine with it. Like you said, the world is better off without these people in it." Sasha gave him a sad smile.

They bumped down the pathway. Sasha flipped the radio on, scrolled through the stations, then flipped it off again.

"I want to find her." Sasha was insistent.

"I know. We'll try." Mike promised. Sasha looked at him and smiled a little more warmly. She was caught off guard when he slammed on the brakes and slid along the gravel.

"What the fuck?" she shouted. Mike had locked up the brakes and skidded to a stop. In front of them, twenty yards away, was a large group of men. Mike didn't get a head count, but there had to be at least fifteen. He slammed the Pathfinder in reverse, then grabbed her head, shoving it down.

"Get down!" Mike yelled. "Stay below the dash!" As soon as the words were out of his mouth, Sasha could hear the *pop pop pop* of multiple guns being fired at them. Small holes opened up in the windshield.

Mike had slumped down and was driving backwards, trying to use the mirrors to see. The Pathfinder slammed upward, then down hard, as the rear passenger tire hit a large rock, Mike continued driving. The passenger taillight hit a tree, the front end of the SUV whipped around, and they came to a stop with the passenger side door now broadside to the group of men. They had only put another ten yards between them. Mike popped his door and jumped out. He reached in and grabbed Sasha and yanked her out as the window above her shattered. He threw her to the side.

"Are you okay? Are you hit?" he asked as bullets continued to riddle the silver SUV.

Sasha looked at herself and patted her body. "No, no, I'm okay."

"Stay behind the rear axle!" Mike yelled as he rolled to the front wheel. The pops continued. The tires on the passenger side deflated first the rear, then the front. It sounded like a string of firecrackers being set off; a never-ending line of pops punctuated by the occasional "*BOOM* of a shotgun.

Mike was behind the front axle, the engine block shielding him. He had his. 45 out. They were seriously outnumbered and outgunned. He peeked under the SUV, trying to get a head count. There had to be at least fifteen men, with varying firearms, including pistols, shotguns, and at least two assault rifles that Mike could see. The only advantage they had was the SUV. Mike was able to lie on the ground. From under the Pathfinder, he could fire up at the group from a position of cover, whereas they were trying to fire downward towards him.

He aimed at the crowd of men and fired off three shots *Pop Pop Pop*, a small cloud of dirt kicking up with each shot. He watched as two men fell. He ducked back behind the axle.

"Fuck," he cursed. He looked at Sasha, who was in a battle-ready position, her. .40 calibre pistol in her hand.

"I'm going to cover you; when I start shooting, you get into those trees," Mike directed.

"What about you?" Sasha asked as bullets ripped through the sheet metal door.

"Just do it!" Mike ordered. "Get safe and get to your brother's. Stay off main roads."

The bullets kept coming. Mike took a deep breath, counted to three, and rolled back under the SUV. *Pop pop pop pop pop pop pop pop.* He fired until the slide stayed back; he was out of ammo. Three more guys went down. Mike ducked behind the axle again.

He looked and saw that Sasha was gone. He rolled to her spot at the rear axle, wrenched the door open, and grabbed the black bag. He released the magazine of his pistol and slid another one in, then filled his pockets with four more mags. Bullets were still coming, but they seemed to have slowed down. Mike chanced a quick peek under the SUV; two guys were twenty feet away, creeping up towards the front end. They were trying to flank him and must not have seen him jump sides.

Mike peeked a second time from under the Pathfinder and fired off a total of five rounds. The first struck the closest guy just below the left knee. He went down groaning. Mike shot him again, this time in the face. The second guy didn't have time to react as Mike fired three shots, hitting him twice in the right thigh, first directly above the knee, the second higher up. The bullet ripped through his femoral artery. The man yelped and limped back towards the group, collapsing ten feet away. Two more roars from the shotgun were heard as slugs ripped through the door of the SUV. A piece of shrapnel flew off, slicing Mike's right cheek open.

"Other side, other side." Mike heard someone yell. More fire was concentrated on the rear of the SUV, cutting off his exit behind Sasha. He rolled back to the front axle, reached his hand over the hood, and fired off three shots at the group before diving into the bushes.

Mike moved in a few yards, but the brush was thick, and he couldn't see what was in front of him. As he stepped forward, he lost his footing and dropped down a seven-foot cliff. He rolled down the hill and through the rocks. Coming to a stop, he caught his breath. This was bad. There was a goddamn army waiting for them, he thought. He collected his thoughts for a second, and like a wave, the realization that he was separated from Sasha hit him.

"Fuck," he muttered to himself. He was about to climb back up when he saw the bushes move. He fired off two more shots and heard a man yell in pain.

"Over here!" Mike heard someone else yell.

Mike moved out of the clearing and dropped the magazine. He'd lost track of the number of rounds he'd fired. He jacked a fresh one in. He heard a crack, then a *pop*. Someone shot at him again. He dropped down low and crawled to a large rock. He heard two more shots come his way. He was hiding in the woods. They couldn't see him, but it was just a matter of time before they made their way down. He had to get out of there.

"Fuck," he cursed to himself again. There was a blood trail from the cut on his cheek. If any of these guys were hunters, they'd track and find him. He had to move.

He stayed low and worked his way deep into the woods. The yelling faded out behind him.

Sasha dove off to the side when Mike told her to. She had her pistol on her as she moved deeper into the woods, hoping he would follow. Everything was happening so quickly she didn't realize she was near a ledge. The rocks below her gave way as she lost the ground under her and went tumbling down a small rock hill, smacking her head off a rock. It didn't knock her out, but she saw a white flash.

She shook her head to get her bearings and heard a few more shots from Mike, followed by some yelling. The shooting stopped and was replaced by some more indistinct yelling. The sounds continued to alternate. Sasha looked around and couldn't see her gun; she must have dropped it when the ground gave out.

"Shit," she hissed.

She crawled along the rock ledge, staying close. She didn't realize when it happened, but she was suddenly aware that the shooting had stopped; it was quiet. She became aware of her own breathing. Her heart slammed in her chest; she could feel it in her ears. No other sounds except the faint sound of the loose rocks rolling away as she crawled close to the ledge.

She hugged the edge, moving quickly. She figured she must have gone at least a couple hundred yards when she found a small path that brought her back up to the trail. Carefully, she scaled back up and waited. She couldn't see anyone. The trail looked empty in both directions. The only sound was the wind in the trees and the chatter of a nearby squirrel. She hopped onto the trail and started running back towards the highway.

      Her ears were still ringing. She paused for a second, trying to listen, but she could only hear the sounds of the forest. She set off running again, rounded a bend, and came to a dead stop. Three men stood at a blue Jeep right in front of her, guns drawn. She turned to run back the other way to find two more behind her now. All five rushed her. She tried fighting them off, but they overtook her quickly.

Chapter 23

Thursday May 25th, 2023, 6:57 pm

Rick and Angela had just finished dinner and were working together with the efficiency you'd expect from a military couple when it came to cleaning up. They both seemed to float through the kitchen around each other, always knowing where their partner was at all times, packing up leftovers, scrapping off the crumbs, rinsing the dishes, and placing them in the dishwasher.

"Tea, love?" Rick asked, filling the kettle and placing it on the stovetop.

"Yes, please." Angela closed the dishwasher door and started the cycle.

Rick prepped the teapot. This was their nightly ritual: dinner, tea, discussing the day, and watching Jeopardy. Afterwards Angela would focus on one of her many hobbies for an hour, playing her guitar, painting, or (depending on what they'd had for dinner) going for a run. Rick was ex-British army and had started working as a consultant. After Jeopardy he would usually spend an hour or two reading over a report or buttoning up an upcoming presentation.

Both were startled when they heard a rap on the patio door. Rick, always extremely cautious, stopped and looked. A large figure loomed through the glass.

"Who the bloody hell is that?" It was more of a statement than a question.

Angela looked, and her heart sank. She opened the door. Mike walked in without being invited, clothing torn, dried blood on his face and shirt. He walked to the kitchen sink, turned on the water, and started washing his face. Angela grabbed an ice pack, placed it on the counter, then went to the bedroom, returning with one of Rick's shirts. Mike and Rick were close to the same height, although Mike weighed an additional 40 lbs. or so. Angela placed a black t-shirt on the counter without a word. She took Rick by the hand; he'd been watching this unfold with confusion.

"What's all this?" Rick asked, wanting answers.

"Just," she paused, "give him a minute." She calmly led Rick into the living room.

Ten minutes later, Mike walked into the living room with the ice pack on his left elbow, wearing Rick's plain black t-shirt that was stretching at the seams. He stood quietly in the doorway. Angela, in her usual calm demeanour, asked, "What's going on?"

Mike held her stare for three heartbeats, then filled her in on everything: the pimps, the girls, Kevin Marin, Orin Bondy, and finally the ambush and being split up from Sasha. He didn't give graphic details, but he also didn't sugarcoat anything. When he finished, the three of them were quiet. The ticking of an old clock in the kitchen was the only sound.

Finally, Rick spoke. "I must say, you certainly live up to your legacy."

Mike wasn't sure how to take the comment. He'd invaded their home. Once again, he'd made his problems Angela's, only this time they weren't children, and it wasn't his drunk father. Even telling them what happened put them in a bad position. Knowing what they knew and not turning him in could land them in prison. Mike realized that simply by being there, he could very well cost her everything she's worked her entire life for.

"I—I'm sorry. I shouldn't have come here." Mike apologized, turning to leave.

"Mikey, stop!" Angela jumped up from her seat. "Where is Sasha?"

"I don't know. In the chaos I lost her. I told her to get to her brother's." Mike explained. "I tried to follow her, but there were bullets everywhere." The guilt on his face broke Angela's heart.

"How would she reach you if she made it to her brother's?" Angela asked, already thinking of strategies.

Mike considered the question for a minute. They didn't have their phones, which eliminated the obvious method of contact. Months before, when Mike was stashing cash on their way out west, they had talked about what to do if they ever got separated and lost phone contact. Email was the next best thing because they could access email from just about anywhere.

"Email," Mike replied, a glimmer of hope returning to his eyes.

Angela grabbed her tablet and handed it to him. Mike logged in. Nothing from Sasha.

"I should leave," Mike said, handing the tablet back.

"You're not going anywhere, pal," Rick corrected, standing up. "I don't know ya, but Angela's told me a lot about you. You're her family, and we're going to help."

Mike was about to reply when he heard the pimp's phone ding. He looked at the notification. It was WhatsApp, and the sender was Lumpz. Mike opened the message.

"Big Man. I have your girl."

"Fuck," Mike cursed. "They have Sasha."

7:45 pm

Tyson Bent and Gale Robson sat in Gale's office. They were waiting for the others to join an online meeting. A chime came in over the speakers, and the icon showing "CL" appeared in the corner. Three seconds later, Clara Lalonde's face filled the screen.

"Detective Lalonde, nice to see you," Robson greeted.

"What's all this about?" Clara asked impatiently, not accusing Robson but annoyed at the situation.

"Apparently we're getting more help." Robson advised.

This wasn't the first time Gale Robson and Clara Lalonde had worked together. They had a good relationship. Lalonde usually worked sex crimes for the city, and Robson worked major crimes at the federal level, and unfortunately the two were not always mutually exclusive. But this case was different. What started as a missing minor had turned into something they had never encountered before. It felt like every time the phone rang, they were being told about more young girls being rescued and more dead bodies left behind.

The three engaged in small talk, with Bent telling them a story of a man in a pickup truck hitting a moose during his time in McBride, BC. The EMTs had been amazed that the man walked away without a scratch. Bent was describing the way the moose had walked off, seemingly unscathed, when Robson's laptop speaker chimed again. The word "Chief" displayed on the screen, followed by a video link of a man in is late fifties: Victoria Police Chief Robert Hamil. Seconds later there was another chime with RCMP written on the screen. A middle-aged woman with a stern, no-nonsense look popped up: Chief Superintendent Sara Walton.

Gale Robson took a gulping breath; if Chief Superintendent Walton was on this call with the chief of police from Victoria, then this would be bigger than just big.

"Hello Chief Hamil, thank you for your time today." Walton began, as if they were not just on the phone together right before logging on.

"Superintendent Walton, thank you for the invite," Hamil responded, the fake politeness almost nauseating to the other three.

"Okay, let's jump into it." Walton said. "We all know why we're here. Detective Robson, can you please brief us all?

Gale was caught off guard but quickly snapped back online.

HUNTING PREDATORS

"Yes, okay. On May 12th, we received a report from Nanaimo Detachment about a missing minor, Ashley Brock. Fifteen years old. Missing since Friday, May 10th."

She flipped through her notes. "I'll skip over the non-relevant items. But on May 16th, Victoria Police detective Harland Grant, working off a list of late-model North Sky Blue Chevy Silverado extended cab pickups, noted there were four registered on the island, with three here in Victoria, He eliminated two. One was on the ferry to the mainland at the time of the abduction. Another, the owner contacted VPD when the front-page photo ran, said he had a similar truck, and brought it to police headquarters to eliminate himself as a suspect. The third belonged to Kevin Marin."

"The first murder victim," interrupted Walton.

"Yes, the first murder victim," Robson continued. "Detective Grant noted an oily residue on Marin's plates and a distinctive sticker in the bottom corner of the windshield consistent with one from the suspected vehicle. Marin agreed to let Grant search the truck. Some brown hairs with blonde tips similar to Ashley Brock's current hair colour were found. Marin was brought in for questioning. He lawyered up right away and was subsequently released. He disappeared the next day."

Robson turned to Tyson Bent. "Constable Bent can fill you in on the incident in Tofino."

Bent ran through the gas station, the blood at the resort, and the campers finding Marin's body. When he finished, Clara Lalond chimed in.

"The timeline initially wasn't known. The autopsy later determined that sometime after Kevin Marin was executed, his truck was used to kidnap Orin Bondy. Bondy was tied to a tree, same as Marin, only Bondy was left attached. He was shot several times in the head. The following morning, fifteen-year-old Elizabeth Green, missing since March from Saddle Lake, Alberta, walked into police headquarters. She claimed a large man and a small woman rescued her. Details are vague; she's not very cooperative when it comes to the couple."

"Understandable," Walton commented without a hint of sarcasm in her voice.

Lalonde resumed. "We showed her a picture of Orin Bondy; she stated Bondy paid her a visit the day before and was very rough with her." She cleared her throat, then continued. "Green stated the couple freed her, dropped her off, and took her pimps. The following day we received an anonymous tip, likely from a hiker that didn't want to involve themselves. James Carson, Bruce Evert, and Wendy McMillan were found dead in a small clearing in a wooded area about fifteen kilometres southwest of Victoria. James Carson had his head bashed in with what we believe was a pipe wrench. Bruce Evert and Wendy McMillan were stabbed to death. Based on the descriptions Green gave us, we believe these are the pimps that held her captive."

Clara paused and took a sip of water before continuing. "The following day, Cassie Murray, missing since February 13th from Prince George, BC, walked into police headquarters. She claims a large man and a small woman rushed her pimp, dropped her off, and drove away with her pimp in the back of his own car. We searched the room and surrounding area. Her pimp's muscle, a David Bastien, originally from Calgary, was found lying in a pool of his own blood behind the motel. Someone, likely the large man, did a hell of a number on him. The back of Bastien's head had been stomped on, driving his face into the ground. He's currently in a medically induced coma due to swelling on the brain. Murray stated her pimp's name was Wesley. We've identified him as Wesley St. Pierre from Surrey. Wesley comes with a long rap sheet, including pimping, drugs, and theft. The guy's a tier one loser."

Lalonde paused while Walton scribbled. A few seconds later Walton encouraged, "Go on."

Robson took over. "Then came the report from Duncan this morning. Shots fired. Police arrive to find two pimps hogtied in a hotel room. A third was found at the end of the hall in the stairwell, head cracked open, unresponsive. The three were pimping out an eighteen-year-old named Rebecca Edworthy. Miss Edworthy is developmentally challenged and was reported missing in June from Fernie, BC. She has the mind of a six-year-old. The three pimps were Edmond Waters, Carl Mead, and lastly, Matthew Edworthy, Rebecca's cousin." She paused as Walton, Lalonde, and Chief Hamil digested the last detail with shock on their faces.

"Her own cousin was involved in her abduction." Robson repeated. "At 2:42 pm today, a 911 call came in from All Star Inn, a dirty little pay-by-the-minute motel. The caller identified herself as Christine Eldridge, a sixteen-year-old missing from Brandon, Manitoba, since April 4th. She had the same story: large man, small woman. Grabbed her pimps and told her to call the police. Initially she said they left in a blue Toyota, then twice slipped up and eventually admitted they told her to say that, and they actually left in the pimp's silver Pathfinder.

"And that's where we are as of now. Five dead bodies, another three now presumed dead, two in comas, and two more in custody. Four human trafficking victims rescued." Robson let a moment of silence hang in the air after her summary.

Without any segue, Walton began her briefing. "At 5:21 pm today, a 9-1-1 call came in saying there were shots fired west of Sooke on a logging road. RCMP responded. Said they came upon the aftermath of a warzone. A silver Pathfinder was riddled with bullet holes. They're still combing through the scene, but preliminary reports indicate that hundreds of rounds were fired. There are eight more dead, all with gunshot wounds. Five were found in the mass of spent casings, two were closer to the Range Rover, and another in the bushes. We're working on identifying them now. Looks like the vigilante couple was ambushed. Whether they survived or not is unclear."

"If I may?" Bent interjected.

"Go ahead." Walton allowed.

"Since eight bodies were left behind, I have to assume the targets lived and maybe got away. Those who attacked them would be more likely to pick up their own dead and leave the target. The fact that they left their own behind tells me when the targets got out of there. The attackers did too, and quickly."

"I'm inclined to agree," Hamil affirmed, finally speaking. "They could be wounded, lying in the woods now, but it looks like they got away from the initial assault."

"There was blood found at the Range Rover," Walton advised. "But not much. Search will continue throughout the night." She paused and then asked, "Do we know anything about this couple?"

Lalonde, Bent, and Robson sat silently. After a few seconds, Lalonde offered, "They're white, he's large, she isn't. That's about it."

"That's not very helpful." Walton admitted.

"Sorry, ma'am, but we can't give information we don't have." Lalonde replied. "We have the statements from the three girls they rescued. He is large. One of the rescued girls said seven feet tall, but that may be an exaggeration. We did see a grainy still frame of them. There is a significant height difference. We don't know how tall she is, though. If she's five feet tall, he'll look huge by comparison; if he's six foot seven, she'll look small by comparison, so we really don't know. Cassie Murray is a taller girl, around five foot nine. She said standing next to him, she barely came up to his shoulder. The photos we saw show he's a bigger guy, though. Wide shoulders. Thick chest. From Elizabeth Green's statement, he tossed all three pimps around the room like rag dolls. So, let's say between six foot four and six foot seven and somewhere in the 250-270 lb. range. He's a big guy, and he's strong." Lalonde finished.

"And mean." Bent added.

"I'm sorry?" Walton raised an eyebrow.

"And he's mean. They both are." Bent elaborated. "They smashed Kevin Marin's knee to pieces. The animals didn't have a hard time making off with his left leg; there was only soft tissue holding it on. He took a large calibre round point-blank to the side of the head. Orin Bondy's head was mutilated with multiple gunshots. James Carson had his head bashed in with a pipe wrench. Whether they did that first or killed the other two first, it's still pretty barbaric, and either way, all three were killed in a gruesome manner. Whoever did that shit has ice in their veins."

Bent looked at Robson, who nodded. Bent continued. "David Bastien was battered and stomped. That wasn't accidental; the attacker tried to snap the man's neck with the heel of his boot."

Walton's attention shifted off camera; someone handed her something. She read it. And said, "Two more confirmed dead. Sounds like Christine Eldridge's pimps. Forty-six-year-old David Armstrong. He was found with a big fuckin hole in the top of his head. Thirty-two-year-old Melissa Carter has also been found with her throat slashed. Both were discovered about a kilometre up the road from the shootout." She slammed the paper down. "Jesus Christ, what the hell is going on out there?" she asked rhetorically.

"Someone is taking the trash out." Lalonde replied, forgetting that they could hear her.

Walton's eyes shot up to her screen. "I beg your pardon?" she asked sternly.

Lalonde doubled down. "I said what we're all thinking. Someone is taking out the trash. Look at who they're going after: rapists, pimps, and a guy that kidnapped his own disabled cousin. I get it. They're breaking the law, but the trash is taking itself out."

"Detective Lalonde, I've heard very good things about you, but I'll caution you against comments like that." Walton warned.

Hamil interjected, "Detective Lalonde is one of our finest. She understands."

"I hope so!" Walton retorted angrily. "Because starting immediately, she and Detective Robson are spearheading this investigation. We need to find out who this couple is and put a stop to this mayhem as soon as possible."

Chapter 24

Thursday May 25th 2023, 8:00 pm.

Sasha was being kept in a closet in a small apartment somewhere. The geographical location didn't really matter to her; she didn't know the city that well anyway. When Lumpz and his goons grabbed her, she tried to fight back. She took a small beating, but she'd suffered worse. She tried to fight the whole time they were driving. She knew she was in shit, and given what she'd dealt with when she was eighteen, she made the decision right there that she would fight till her last breath. They may kill her, but she was going down fighting.

One man wrapped his arms around her and made a comment about "taking her pussy." When they got back to his apartment, she headbutted him in the nose with the back of her head. When they dragged her into the apartment building, she fought tooth and nail; the four men ended up carrying her by her arms and legs. One stuck a gun in her face and told her to keep quiet. She spit at him and called his mother a whore as loud as she could.

They struggled to get her up the two flights of stairs to the third floor, then struggled to drag her down the hallway. She would occasionally get an arm or a leg free and kick or claw at whoever was closest. They struggled to get her into the apartment.

At first, they threw her in a bedroom. She kicked the door repeatedly, breaking the wood. Then the four men rushed in when they heard the window smash out. They pulled her back inside before she was able to jump from the third story. She swung a piece of broken glass, slicing one on the arm and cutting her own palm in the process.

From there she was tied up and thrown in a closet, but not before kicking one of her abductors in the nuts and biting another on the hand bad enough to draw blood. They punched at her and kicked at her, but she wouldn't stop fighting. Once she was tied up, the leader of their group, a Latino man with a slight accent, grabbed her face with his left hand and punched her in the mouth, busting her bottom lip open.

"You hit like a bitch!" she snapped as she spat blood at him. They tossed her in the closet and slammed the door shut.

The four men went back into the small living area. A seventeen-by-seventeen room, it was dingey and unkempt. The walls were once painted white but were now grimy with years of filth from smoking, cooking with grease, and the overall buildup that came from living in a shithole apartment and never cleaning up.

Against the wall directly outside the bedroom door sat a black leather sofa with a matching recliner. Both faced a large wall-mounted TV. The kitchen shared the space and was really nothing more than a countertop with a sink, fridge, and stove. The bathroom was tiny and filthy.

"So, you still want to fuck her?" Jose joked to Bill, the one she'd kicked in the nuts.

"No, I'm good," Bill declined, limping back to the couch. "Though she'd be a wild little romp. That crazy bitch would bite your nose off your face if you got too close to her."

Danny, the third man of the group, was at the kitchen sink washing the blood off his arm.

"Need stitches?" Jose asked.

"I don't think so." Danny replied, not sounding certain. "Fuck me, what a woman. I think I'm in love," he joked.

"Yeah, you'd wake up with her plunging a knife in your heart while you sleep." Jose laughed. Turning to Brooks, the fourth guy, who had made his way to the tiny bathroom, Jose asked, "She get ya?"

Brooks was washing his hands. Sasha had bitten him on the side of it where the pinky meets the palm. Brooks had punched her twice in the forehead to try to get her to let go, eventually yanking his hand out of her mouth, causing the skin to tear.

"Think I need stitches." Brooks admitted.

"Can't sew up human bites," Jose advised. "Too many bacteria in the mouth. Gotta leave it open, clean in constantly, and watch for infection."

"Fuck," Brooks hissed, watching a steady stream of pink water go down the drain.

The four men went silent, and, like a dark shadow creeping over all of them, the day's events caught up. Less than three hours had passed since they ambushed this couple on a logging road. Somehow, both the man and woman not only lived but had managed to kill eight of their sixteen men. the odds of ambushing someone, outnumbering them eight to one, and having them not only live. But killing 50% of the attacking force had to be astronomical. Jose stood looking out the window. Of the eight killed, Jose had been good friends with three.

Jose had watched unbelieving as the men on his left and then his right dropped, one after the other. Both died almost instantly. Seconds later, three more fell dead. Another few minutes went by, then Carlos Rodrigues, a guy Jose had known since childhood, was shot in the knee, then in the face. Christian Mendoza, Carlos' cousin, was shot in the leg. He ran back towards Jose and dropped dead a few feet away as the bullet tore through his thigh, shredding the femoral artery and tearing a large chunk of flesh off at the same time. Shortly after that, Travis Whitehead, a lifelong friend of Jose's, was shot twice in the chest and died gasping for air in a tree line. The entire ordeal felt like it lasted hours but somehow also felt like it was over in seconds.

When the shooting stopped and the smoke cleared, Jose had lost three close friends. Now all he had to show for it was a psychotic little fucker tied up in the closet.

Lumpz had told them all to stay off their phones. The group had no idea who they were dealing with or what they knew, and Lumpz was working on a way to bait the big guy in.

At 9:00 pm, Jose headed out to meet Lumpz at the garage and figure things out.

"I'm heading out. Keep an eye on that crazy bitch in there. If you need anything, tell me now. Phones stay off."

"Beer!" Billy yelled.

"Hit up a drugstore. I need a first aid kit for this arm. Rubbing alcohol, gauze, all that shit." Jose wrote down Danny's request.

"Food too," Brooks added.

Jose nodded and headed out the door.

8:28 pm

Ashley Brock had officially been missing for two weeks. She tried more than once to ask for help from the men that visited her. The last one agreed to help her, but then he told Sadie on her when he was leaving. Sadie held Ashley face down in a pillow while Chris punched her repeatedly in the side and kidneys. Three days later there was still blood when she peed, but now it was darker instead of the bright red of the first night.

The day before, it seemed like everything went crazy. Chris burst into the room saying they had to pack everything and leave right away. Once they set up in another room, Chris was constantly looking out the window. There were no visitors, no friends, and nothing posted online. Something was happening.

9:00 pm

Jose walked into Lumpz Garage. There were eight men sitting in various seats, all keeping an eye on everyone coming and going up and down the street. Jose knocked on the office door.

"Yeah," Lumpz yelled.

Jose let himself in. "So?" he asked expectantly.

"Nothing, man. Told that cat we have his girl. No reply." Concern creased Lumpz's brow.

"Strange," Jose commented. "Think he's plotting something?"

"I dunno. He has to be. But he should've moved by now. I mean, we got his woman. How is she anyway?" Lumpz asked, a smirk crossing his face. He wasn't asking about her well-being. He was asking if the four men had raped her.

"She's fucking crazy, bro. No shit. In the car, Billy said he wanted to throw a fuck into her, and she headbutted him in the nose. Had to fight that bitch all the way inside. I stuck a gun in her face and told her to shut up. She just screamed louder, called my momma a ho. Bitch got no fear. We whooped her ass; it only pissed her off more. She kicked Bill in the nuts, smashed a window, and slashed Danny's arm with the broken glass. Then she bit Brooksy on the hand. I busted her in the mouth; she spit blood on me, called me a bitch." Jose recounted.

Lumpz couldn't help laughing at the situation. "You four, and the little chick is fucking you guys up?"

"No joke, bro. She's got no fear in her. Straight up. Put a gun in her face, told her to shut up; she got louder. Whopped her ass; she just keeps fighting. We got her tied up in the closet so she don't escape." Jose chuckled. "So, what's the plan? What do you need from me?"

"Have to wait and see. I got everyone out looking for her man. You go back. Keep the phones off. If I need you, I'll send someone by. Keep her alive until I say so." Lumpz instructed.

Jose nodded. "Give me a half hour to get back. I gotta grab some food and first aid stuff."

"Watch your back, bro. He's still out there." Lumpz cautioned.

9:05 pm

Mike was perched on the roof of a small commercial plaza across the street from an autobody garage in Esquimalt on Victoria's west side. He could see several guys, mostly thugs, walking around. If they were on lookout, they were terrible at it: playing on their phones, opening the door, looking up and down the street, standing in the windows with the blinds open. It was amateur hour. Mike wasn't positive, but he was pretty sure he saw a couple of these guys at the shootout earlier. He had watched a black Dodge Ram pull up. A short Latino man had jumped out and went inside. Five minutes later he left. Mike followed him.

Jose left the garage. He stopped at a drugstore, grabbed some gauze, disinfectant, bandages, and a 12-pack of Coke. Next, he picked up some pizza, then some beer and a bottle of whiskey. If they were babysitting this psycho bitch all night, they might as well enjoy themselves.

He pulled up in front of Billy's building, a three-story red brick structure built sometime in the early 1920s. The units were small. The neighbourhood had turned industrial sometime in the early 1950s, and only a few residential spots survived. Billy stayed because it was quiet. The place was a shithole, but everyone minded their own business, and there was no way the police could converge on him without him seeing them coming from a mile away. The growing number of drug addicts that lined the streets daily was a small price to pay.

Jose parked, got out of his black Dodge Ram pickup, and made his way up the front steps. He fumbled to hit the buzzer, waited, and heard "Yo" crackle over the speaker.

"I'm back." Jose announced.

"Bring food?" the voice asked.

"Open the fuckin door, man." Jose demanded, his patience wearing thin. The door buzzed; he fumbled to open it, his arms already busy with bags and pizza boxes. He stepped inside and made his way to the stairwell. As he went through the door at the end of the hall, he was shoved forward, hard. Dropping everything, he tried to catch his balance. He fell onto the stairs. What felt like a boulder landed on his back.

Mike had been stalking him. When Jose stepped into the stairwell, Mike rushed forward and kicked him between the shoulders. Jose lurched forward, dropping everything he was holding, and fell onto the stairs. Mike didn't give him an inch. He jumped on Jose's back, grabbed his hair with his right hand, and clamped a set of vice grips on Jose's nose with his left.

"Scream and I'll kill you," Mike warned.

Jose grunted.

"Where is the girl?" demanded Mike. Jose said nothing. "Tell me, or I swear to you right now, I'll rip your fucking nose right off your face. Your eyelids are next. Where is she?" He started to twist.

"Upstairs." Jose said through gritted teeth. The pain was like nothing he'd ever experienced. His eyes filled with tears.

"How many people are up there?" Mike asked, applying more torque.

"Two more." Jose groaned.

"What unit?"

"304. Please stop," Jose whimpered.

Mike hogtied Jose with zip ties and dragged him under the steps. "I'm going up there. If there's any more than two people up there, I'll kill them all. Then I'll come back down here, and I'll rip off your nose, ears, lips, and eyelids with those pliers. Are you sure it's only two?"

Jose couldn't think straight. The man was so calm he was terrifying.

Mike continued. "If you want to live to see tomorrow morning with your facial appendages intact, tell me the truth right now."

"There's three." Jose admitted, his gaze and his shoulders slumping simultaneously in defeat.

"Whose place is it?" Mike asked, patting Jose down. He found his wallet and looked at the ID. *Jose Hudalgo*

"Billy's," Jose replied, still looking down.

Mike lifted Jose's chin and stared him in the eyes. "Listen closely. If you want to live and not look like a freak, you shut up and lay here quietly. I'm going for the girl. Your friends are dead; that's not changing. But I'll let you live. Do you understand me?"

"Yes." Jose had been threatened before. Been in shitty spots before. This was different. This guy wasn't playing. Mike gagged him, tapped his mouth shut, and in a flash, he was gone.

Mike stepped out onto the third floor. The hallway was filled with the smells of a kitchen that had been used to constantly cook with old grease, accumulating garbage, dirty diapers, and weed. The hallway was around eighty feet long with three units on each side. Billy's unit was in the middle of the hallway and faced the street.

Billy was sitting on the couch while Brooks and Danny were playing PS5, taking turns on the latest Call of Duty. The three of them had been smoking weed since Jose left. Billy had thought about dragging the girl out of the closet and having his way with her. He'd had his way with feisty women before, but this one was on another level. Even undoing her restraints to get her clothing off would be dangerous, so he decided against it. There were two loud bangs on the door. Like someone kicking it because their hands were full.

"Whozat?" Billy yelled.

"Jose!"

Billy got up off the couch, walked over, and unbolted the door. He started to open it and saw a white flash.

Mike was holding the pizza boxes, an empty case of beer, an empty Coke case, and a bag that had held a bottle of whisky stacked on top. If someone looked out of the peephole, they wouldn't see anything but someone with an armload of stuff. He kicked at the door.

"Whozat?"

"Jose!" Mike replied. He heard what sounded like a couple of guys laughing and the sound of the deadbolt unlatching. As the door started opening, he dropped what he was holding, lunged forward, and kicked the door with everything he had, smashing it into Billy's face, knocking him out.

One down, two to go, or so Mike hoped. He rushed in and found one guy on the couch and another sitting in a recliner. Both were high. Both were trying to figure out what was happening. Mike barreled in, running almost full speed.

Brooks tried to scramble out of the recliner, but Mike smashed him on the side of the head with a gloved hand. A loud crack was heard as Brooks toppled over the arm of the chair.

Mike didn't slow down. Danny had sprung up from the couch, but Mike kicked him, knocking him back down. Mike drove his knee into Danny's chest. He pulled a large black knife out and held the tip against his right eye.

"Where is she?" he snarled.

"Whoa, whoa, whoa! Bro, relax!" Danny stammered.

Mike pushed the tip, applying pressure to Danny's eyelid.

"Where... is... she?" He repeated, venom dripping from his words.

"Bed—bedroom. In the closet," Danny whimpered.

Mike got up, grabbed Danny, and yanked him off the couch. "Move. Now."

Danny stood with his hands up. Mike pushed the tip of the blade into the base of Danny's skull, the other hand on his shoulder, ready to shove the blade in. Mike steered him towards the bedroom door, then to the closet. With a shaky hand, Danny opened the door.

Sasha was lying on her side, wrists and ankles bound together in front of her. There was bruising, swelling, and dried blood on her face, but through it all she still had fire in her eyes.

"Hi, honey. I thought I heard you come in," she said nonchalantly, smiling up at Mike.

Mike looked at her and his heart dropped. She looked bad. Beaten up. He pushed Danny against the wall with the blade at the back of his neck, holding him out at arm's length. "Did they hurt you?" Mike asked steadily.

"Only what you can see," she answered.

Mike felt a tinge of relief. They roughed her up, but they didn't rape her. His relief quickly turned to rage. He put the knife away, grabbed Danny by both shoulders, spun him wide, and rushed him. Without slowing down, Mike threw him out the broken window headfirst. He didn't check to see if he died or not. He rushed back to Sasha and cut her restraints.

"Baby, I'm sorry," he began as he sliced through the rope. "I'm so sorry; I tried to follow you, but I couldn't."

"It's okay. I knew you'd come get me." Sasha soothed.

Mike cut her free and hugged her. "Are you okay? You sure?" He was looking her over, almost panicked, not waiting for answers.

"Baby. I'm fine." Sasha insisted. "I'm sorer from lying on the floor than I am from them hitting me."

Hearing that should have calmed him down, but it didn't. Hearing her say they'd hit her made his chest burn.

"C'mon," he beckoned, helping her up. They walked back into the living room. Brooks was on the ground starting to stir. Mike looked at Sasha. In the light, her face was bruised and swollen. Mike looked down at Brooks.

"Did he hurt you?" Mike asked.

Sasha pointed at the dark bruises forming on her forehead from where Brooks had punched her earlier. Mike grabbed him by the back of his head and rushed into the bathroom. The small, cramped area could barely fit them both.

The room looked like it hadn't been cleaned in years. The toilet was a disgusting mess of dried urine and fecal matter that had been left for months, if not years. Mike shoved Brooks' face into the toilet. Brooks flailed, trying to get free. He couldn't. He reached for the lever to flush. Mike grabbed his hand and shoved his head further into the bowl. Splashing and gurgling, Brooks fought and fought, but eventually he went limp. Mike held him there for another two minutes.

HUNTING PREDATORS

After dealing with Brooks, Mike walked toward the door. He grabbed Bill by the hair on top of his head and dragged him down the hallway towards the stairs.

Jose was struggling, unsuccessfully, to get free when he heard a door above him open, then the sound of something heavy, like a big garbage bag, being thrown down the stairs; it took him a second to realize it was a person. He heard footsteps come down to the first landing, then go back upstairs, followed by the sounds of someone being thrown down the stairs again. Then the process started again. He heard the door to the hallway open and someone being dragged away. Three minutes later the footsteps returned. Mike was standing over him. He was still calm, but his face was angry. He grabbed Jose by the hair and yanked him outside.

Chapter 25

Thursday May 25th, 2023, 11:30 pm

Lumpz was getting antsy. The waiting was driving him insane. It had been over four hours since he messaged the big guy and told him they had his girl. He knew the guy saw the message, but he didn't reply. He paced the garage for a while. Feeling like he was climbing the walls, he eventually left to drive around. Not his brightest move. There was someone out there killing off his pimps and henchmen, but he couldn't sit by and wait. He decided to drive along the coast. It was usually busy, but easy enough to spot a tail if he was being followed.

One night when he was a teenager, Ed, his old boxing coach and retired cop, had taught him how to see if he was being followed. Ed had been in a drunken state at the time and had slurred out, "I shouldn't tell you this, but if you're ever running from the cops and they lose sight of you, turn left. Most people instinctively turn right. The cops will too, so if they can't see you, turn left."

Lumpz cruised along trying to formulate a plan when his phone dinged. He looked at the screen and saw it was a WhatsApp notification. He opened it while driving; the message was from "Shaggy." That was the name he had given David Armstrong, one of the pimps that had been taken out by the big guy. It was the phone he was using to leverage him. "Shit!" Lumpz cursed as he pulled over quickly and opened the message.

He could see his previous message.

HUNTING PREDATORS

"Big man. I have your girl."

The reply was short and sweet: *"No, you don't."*

Lumpz stared at the phone for a second, tossed it down onto the passenger seat, and took off for Billy's apartment.

Mike powered the phone down and put it in his pocket after he sent the message to Lumpz. He turned to face the two men. Both were gagged and zip-tied to trees.

"Boy, did you guys fuck up," Mike commented with a bit too much enthusiasm. Jose and Billy looked at each other. Mike continued, "We're going to play a game. Whoever tells me what I need to know gets to live. The other will welcome death like a warm handshake from an old friend when it finally does arrive. But that's a few hours away."

There was a hiss and a loud *click*. The blue flame of a small propane torch lit up the area. Mike held the torch in one hand and rolled a pair of vice grips in the flame with the other, turning them a dull orange in the darkness.

"Who should I ask first?" Mike asked Sasha.

"Not sure," she replied.

"Okay, who should we hurt first?" Mike clarified.

Sasha's eyes targeted Bill. "You couldn't wait to get me back to your apartment so you could *'take'* my pussy, huh?" She looked back to Mike. "Start with that one."

Mike stepped forward; Billy was trying to scream under his gag.

"Shut up!" Mike hissed, holding the glowing vice grips near Billy's cheek. Billy squinted and tried to turn his face away. "I'm going to ask you a question. The only thing stopping me from using these is whether you have the answers or not." Mike reached for the tape and paused. "Remember, *'I don't know'* is going to hurt." Mike ripped the tape off.

"Please, please, I'm sorry." Billy was concussed, so Mike didn't expect he'd have a lot of information. Given how hard the door hit him, he probably didn't even know why he was in this position.

Mike pressed the glowing tips to Billy's cheek. There was a slight hissing noise from the burning flesh but no scream. Billy was trying to scream, but between the pain and the fear, no sound came out.

Mike pulled the vice grips back. "Shut up! Open your mouth for any reason other than answering my questions, and I'll rip your tongue out. Now, how did you know where we were to ambush us?"

Billy tried to steady his breath. He was practically hyperventilating. "I—I don't know. I swear I don't know. I don't remember anything. I woke up tied up in the back of a truck with a really bad headache. Please, I'm begging you."

"Think he's telling the truth?" Mike asked Sasha.

"Yeah. When you asked him, he looked terrified; he couldn't answer."

"I saw that too."

"Hurt him anyway." Sasha said evenly. "He was bragging about how he wanted to rape me."

Mike nodded and put the tape back over Billy's mouth. Billy was trying to shake his head in protest. Mike clamped the vice grips on his nose. There was a sizzling noise. Billy finally managed a scream under his gag. Mike walked over to Jose.

"Same deal. 'The I *don't knows*' are going to hurt. Bad." Mike reminded as he ripped the tape off Jose's mouth. The raw torn skin on his nose from the vice grips earlier was visible in the moonlight. "How did you know where we were.?" Mike asked.

"Dan." Jose answered. Sasha stepped forward and swung a baseball bat, smashing Jose's ribs on the right side. He groaned loudly, then wailed as he tried to take his next breath.

"The more we have to ask, the more it'll hurt. Dan Who? Was Dan at the apartment?" Mike asked.

Jose coughed, then groaned. "Yes, he was. She cut his arm with the broken window." Jose said, nodding toward Sasha.

Mike looked back at Sasha, who clarified, "The asshole you threw out the window.".

Mike nodded. "How did Dan find us?"

"A few people that owed Lumpz money vanished. He sent some guys around the rooms looking for them. Kept hearing the rooms were sealed off by cops. Sent more guys out to check other rooms where we had people set up. Dan was watching Shaggy's room when you grabbed him. He called me." Jose said between gasps, struggling to breathe.

Mike considered the information then moved on to his next question. "What's Lumpz's real name?"

Jose froze for a split second, trying to decide between the pain of saying he didn't know or the potential backlash if he gave up Lumpz' name. He appeared to steady himself. He'd made a decision. "Wilson."

Mike placed the tape over his mouth. Sasha took three more swings with the bat, each one echoing a *thunk* in his core. Jose screamed under his gag. He coughed and retched. Mike pulled his gag off. Jose coughed out dark blood; it looked black in the darkness.

"Lie to me again, and the tape stays on. We haven't begun to hurt you yet." Mike threatened. "What's his real name?"

"Walter, I think," Jose puffed. He was having trouble breathing. "I swear I don't know his last name. Walter, Walt, Wallace, something like that. I heard his mom say it at the garage one day. He got mad when she said it."

Mike stopped and stared at him. "Did you say 'Wallace'?"

"Yeah, Wallace. That's it. That's his real name, I swear."

"His name is Wallace? You're sure?" Mike asked again.

Jose was scared. "Yes. It's Wallace. I heard his mom say his name."

"Wallace, and he was a boxer?" Mike clarified. Sasha couldn't understand why Mike was acting the way he was.

"Yes," Jose replied with terror in his voice, worried that any answer would hurt.

"Tell me about his mom." Mike demanded. "Tell me something that stands out about her." Sasha was staring back and forth between them, confused.

"What do you mean?" Jose asked. Mike grabbed the bat from Sasha. Jose panicked. "She has a limp!" he shouted quickly. "She walks with a limp. She has a stutter when she talks too. Lumpz babies her. Always taking her arm when she walks, pulling out her chair, shit like that. Doesn't like it if any of us talk to her."

Mike stared at him, almost in disbelief, for a few seconds. "Where does he live?"

"He has a condo downtown. I don't know the address; there's a Thai food place on the main level. It's the only Thai place in the area. But he wouldn't be there. With everything going on, he'll be at a safe house. He has a couple of apartments around town. I don't know where they are. Nobody does." Jose flinched when he answered.

"Where would I find him?" Mike asked quietly.

"I really don't know. He stays out of trouble because he's paranoid." Jose's breath was getting shallow. "Not like paranoid that people are out to get him, but he's guarded. No one really knows a lot about him. He's very private and doesn't trust anybody. No one knows his real name. very few people know where he lives. I know the building but not the unit. He has a couple of places he can hide, but nobody knows where they are. When he gets a feeling or even a hint of trouble, or if he thinks there's any heat on him, he shuts everything down and goes M.I.A. until the dust settles."

Mike looked back at Sasha. "I think we've gotten all the information we're going to get." She nodded.

"Please." Jose was gasping for air. "Let me go."

"Would you have let me go if I begged you?" Sasha asked, stepping forward. "How many young girls begged you and your friends to stop, and you didn't?"

Jose hung his head and closed his eyes. The last thing he saw was his sweat-soaked shirt and urine-stained pants.

Chapter 26

Friday May 26th, 2023, 3:34 am

Clara Lalonde stood in the rain. The red and blue flashing lights reflected in the droplets as they fell. She was tired, wet, and cold.

"What do we have?" she asked Detective Grant.

Harland Grant blew out a sigh. "Well. That's Dan Riley, a lifelong loser. He took a headfirst swan dive from up there," Grant pointed up at the third floor. One window had a bedsheet half hanging out, snagged on broken glass. Clara looked back at the body on the ground. The man had fallen from the third floor and landed headfirst. A large pool of blood had accumulated around him. Bits of broken glass scattered the sidewalk.

"Guessing it's not suicide?" she asked, her voice loaded with sarcasm.

"Not likely," Grant agreed. "You should see inside," he nodded towards the main doors.

"What's it look like inside?"

Grant looked back at the building. "A fucking mess," he summarized in his usual monotone voice. "There is blood in the stairwell, all over the place. Drag marks too. Looks like someone was thrown down each flight of stairs while they were bleeding. At ground level there's a case of pop and a case of beer dumped out, a pizza, and some first aid stuff thrown about in the stairwell. Boxes for all of them were found in the hallway outside the unit's door.

The apartment door was kicked open. There was blood on the floor inside with drag marks; it looked like someone was opening the door, and it was booted hard. Steven Brooks, another low-level piece of shit, was drowned in the goddamn toilet. There's blood in the kitchen and blood in the bedroom."

He sighed as he spoke, "Found some restraints; a nylon rope cut in the closet. There's some blood on the floor in there as well. Boot prints all over the inside of the bedroom door. I have no fucking clue what was going on in there. But whatever happened, it was ugly."

"Okay, two dead, possibly a third missing?" Lalonde asked. "Signs of forced entry and a struggle. Would it be unreasonable to suggest that someone was being held there? And someone else came in and freed them?"

Grant's face lit up. Then he got an inquisitive look. "What do you know that I don't?"

Lalonde filled him in on everything. Kevin Marin's death, the girls being freed, the dead and missing pimps, and the multiple shootings. When she finished, Grant stood looking at her with the same stern look he always carried.

"Sounds like someone is making our job a lot easier."

"Well, they were. Now I'm charged with finding out who the hell they are." Lalonde replied, walking towards the front steps of the building.

"Think this is related?" Grant asked, following behind, slowing his speed to not rush up on her.

Grant had worked with Lalonde multiple times over the years. He was old school. At fifty-two years old, he was large and gruff. Grant knew his way around a boxing ring and a back-alley slugfest. He came from a small First Nations village in Northern BC near Kitimat, a town known for an aluminium smelter and ridiculously high cancer rates. He grew up playing hockey, lacrosse, and fighting the locals every Saturday night.

Grant was tough, but he was also very smart. He had what seemed like an uncanny ability to tell when people were lying. It was said he had a photographic memory growing up. In his early twenties he investigated and found out there was no such thing, but there was an eidetic memory. He didn't fit the bill for that; he didn't remember details like *'how many spots are on this picture,' b*ut he did remember people, places, and events with a clarity rarely seen. He would find authors he enjoyed and binge-read their novels. He couldn't tell you what page a specific paragraph was on, but after reading 26 novels by the same author back-to-back, he could tell you which story a scene happened in even after several years had passed.

What set Grant apart from others with strong memory recall was his unmatched problem-solving abilities. At first glance, he looked like a blockhead. He was big, physically strong, and intimidating, but he was far more dangerous with his brain than he was with his hands. He was also the man that many of the female cops in Victoria looked up to the most. He treated them no differently than he treated the men, good or bad. He never cracked inappropriate jokes; he didn't use terms like 'sweetheart' or 'darling' when referring to his female colleagues, choosing instead to refer to them by their last name or rank.

He gave credit where it was due and called people out on their mistakes. Harland Grant recognized good police work. To him there were two classes of people in the world, police and civilian. Race, religion, and gender— none of it mattered to Grant. If you were a cop and you did your job, then you earned Harland Grant's respect.

"Has to be related," Lalonde replied. "I don't believe in coincidences. I have a hard time believing we've uncovered multiple murders in the last week, but somehow these aren't involved."

Lalonde walked through the main entrance of the building. She made her way to the end of the hallway where the stairwell door was propped open. A man and a woman both worked expensive cameras, photographing everything from different angles. Small yellow plastic evidence tags marked different items. Lalonde noted the discarded contents of the boxes and made her way up the stairs. Grant followed.

"So, what do you have to work with now?" he asked.

"Not a goddamn thing," Lalonde confessed. "I mean sweet fuck-all. No name, no ideas. He's big; she isn't. Don't know how big or how little. We know they're white. We've asked witnesses to guess their ages. We got nothing. *'Between 20 and 60'* is what one girl told us. The others wouldn't even confirm that!"

They made their way down the third-floor hallways to the unit. The empty pizza, pop, and beer boxes lay in the hallway.

"Do we know who lives here?" Lalonde asked.

"Yeah. William Barich." Grant advised. "Like the other two, he's a piece of shit."

Lalonde bent down and looked at the spot on the floor, then the door. "Footprint on the door where it was kicked," she observed. Looking at the inside, she added, "This clear dent right here," she pointed to a depression in the centre of the door, "fits our guy's M.O. He's kicked a couple doors, using them to knock people out."

Grant nodded. Lalonde walked into the small unit and made her way to the bathroom. Steven Brooks' face was still in the toilet, waiting for the coroner. The room was disgustingly filthy. "Jesus," was all she said. She took a closer look at the body. "Make sure they check his hand," she added, looking at the gash on it.

They made their way into the bedroom. "Windows broken from the inside, but—" Grant paused, pointing at a piece of glass on the floor with blood on it. "If I had to guess. That's the cut on Dan Riley's arm."

They looked in the closet and found a few splotches of blood and some cut ropes. "Someone was being kept in here," Grant guessed. Clara stood in the room looking around. "Think they freed another girl?" Grant asked.

"I don't know," Clara said. "This feels different." She kept scanning the room, then the bathroom. "This isn't the type of thing we saw earlier. I mean, the brutality is the same, but something is different here." She kept scrutinizing her surroundings. She looked at the window, the floor in the closet, then the bathroom again. She looked at Steven Brooks, half lying on the floor, his face in a filthy toilet. "This feels personal," she finally concluded.

Lumpz was sitting in a black Chevy Malibu with the windshield wipers off, a block away from Billy's apartment. There were police and firefighters all over the street. He could see one figure on the ground covered with a sheet and a steady stream of people going in and out of the building.

What the fuck is going on here? he thought to himself. He needed to get inside to take a look, but he couldn't. His whole network was unravelling, and the individual events weren't as nerve-wracking as the moments of uncertainty in between. They'd been involved in a brutal shootout earlier that day. They'd had the guy right in front of them, opened fire, and the fucking guy not only lived but he killed eight of Lumpz' men in the process.

They had the big guy's woman. She was supposed to be upstairs, but the text had come in, *"No, you don't."* And now this. It stood to reason that the guy had rescued the girl, but how? Lumpz had placed four of his men up there, assuming Jose made it back. And he must have. If he had come back and seen this scene, he'd have let Lumpz know right away. So, who the fuck was this guy? And why was he targeting Lumpz's girl operation? He didn't touch any of the dope dealers. Didn't go after anything but the girls. It made no sense.

10:00 am

Clara Lalonde was at the crime scene at Bill Barich's apartment until 4:30 am. She got home at 5:00 am only to be rudely awoken at 9:30 am with a request to get to headquarters as soon as possible.

She stopped for a coffee and was still wearing her sunglasses when she walked into Chief Hamil's office. Harland Grant was already there looking equally tired.

"Sir," she greeted, the fatigue not hidden.

"Thank you for coming. Grab a seat. We have a conference call coming in," Hamil instructed. He clicked around on his keyboard, then turned on the large TV on the wall. It showed his desktop screen: a picture of himself with a child standing on a dock, holding a large fish. Clara guessed the child was his grandson.

"Nice catch," she commented.

Hamil smiled. "Taken at my son's place last summer. He's a cop in Northern Ontario."

The MS Teams app was opened, and they joined a meeting already in progress. Lalonde, Grant, and Hamil were in one office, and Bent and Robson were in another. Another screen showed a woman in her early sixties. Her hair was so grey it looked like white silver; it was worn short but styled. She had a very unpleasant attitude but immediately addressed Lalonde and Grant.

"Thank you for joining. We understand you were both out until sunrise this morning. I know it's not easy to wake up and run back in. We appreciate you coming." Lalonde and Grant nodded, and she continued, "I'm Inspector Sue Blenkhorn with the RCMP. I spoke to Chief Superintendent Sara Walton, who will be joining us shortly, as will Inspector Sergeant Karl Sampson from the Ontario Provincial Police."

As she finished her sentence, the screen chimed twice. The first icon read "RCMP," as the face of Sara

HUNTING PREDATORS

Walton appeared on the screen. Seconds later, a man in his fifties with a thick head of grey hair and a barrel chest appeared on the screen. Beside him was a man in his mid-forties who clearly did not want to be there. He had a scruffy beard with shaggy hair and had a face that resembled a boxer who had no idea how to block. He looked tired and miserable. While everyone else on the call was in office attire or uniform, this man was wearing a faded Social Distortion t-shirt that had been washed so many times it was paper thin.

Walton began the meeting. "Okay, thank you everybody for coming in on short notice. Let's get right to it. Inspector Blenkhorn and I have been discussing the case; we all know which one. She feels she may have some valuable information. Blenkhorn, if you will?"

Blenkhorn cleared her throat. "Yes, thank you. I'd like to start by introducing the two gentlemen that just joined us: Inspector Sergeant Karl Sampson and Constable Steven Parent, both with the OPP." Both men nodded a curt greeting. "Some of you may have heard of the case Operation Shooting Star from January of 2019. Constable Parent was working undercover on our joint task force. He was our boots on the ground."

"He's the one that got taken hostage," Grant chimed in quietly.

"Please don't interrupt," Blenkhorn snapped. "But yes, that was Constable Parent. Late December 2018 a buy was set up and subsequently robbed. Parent was injured in the ordeal. A few weeks later, our suspects were tipped off, and Constable Parent was taken hostage. The following morning there were five people found dead in and around Niagara Falls, Ontario. The death toll included Constable

Parent's kidnappers as well as our target. Yes, Detective Lalonde?"

Blenkhorn paused in her report as Lalonde had put her hand up.

"We were led to believe that was an internal cleansing, wasn't it? His abductors realized he was undercover and killed off the small fish in the operation. Lalonde questioned.

"That's the official story," Karl Sampson replied, "but unofficially—and this doesn't leave this meeting—we believe the man that robbed the buy in late December is the same man that rescued Constable Parent."

Lalonde, Grant, and Hamil looked at each other with confusion. Gale Robson and Tyson Bent did the same.

"Look, it's not that hard to figure out," Parent finally spoke up. "I know hearing it sounds pretty fucked up, but I was tracking the guy that robbed us. I believe I got too close without realizing it, and to get me to back off, he blew my cover. It not only impacted my work on Operation Shooting Star but also other deals I was working on as well. Maybe he figured if my cover was blown, they'd pull me out. Instead, the goons grabbed me. We think he realized he may be an accomplice to killing a cop, so he stepped in and rescued me."

"Think?" Grant asked.

"Not sure. They beat the shit out of me pretty good. I don't really remember anything." Parent admitted.

"Well, glad you're okay, but how does this tie in with us?" Lalonde asked.

Parent suppressed a smirk. "Big guy? Killing shitbags? Kills seem barbaric at first, until you look closely, and you realize this motherfucker knows what he's doing. Kills with knives in one stroke, crossbow bolts, or bullets with one shot. We think it's the same guy."

The meeting fell silent for a few seconds. Parent continued, "The massacre in the Falls wasn't his first time. It just took us a while to connect the dots. He's good. He's very good. And very smart. He doesn't follow patterns per se: knives, guns, bare hands, a fucking crossbow. The only pattern we saw was notoriously shitty people kept turning up missing or dead. Some looked like accidents, some like suicides, and some were put down like dogs in the street. The only thing connecting them was they were all shitbags. He's a mean son of a bitch. Big too. I stood face to face with him. He's probably about six foot five, over two hundred and fifty pounds. He's fast. He moves quickly, like someone a hundred pounds lighter, and he hits hard. I've been in more than one scuffle in my day, but he hits different. This dude was squared up to me, and I didn't see him move when he hit me. He has fast hands, a lot of weight, and a bad fucking attitude behind them. There's definitely some extensive training there."

"Thank you, Constable Parent, for that colourful explanation." Blenkhorn interrupted coolly. "We believe he is ex-military. According to our count, he looks good for over a dozen homicides in Ontario alone."

"Five in one night," Parent interjected.

"Okay, but the guy we're looking for has a female partner. Could this be the same guy? Lalonde asked.

"Yes," Parent confirmed without hesitation. "It's him." Karl Sampson turned his attention to Steve with a curious look.

"How can we be sure?" Lalonde asked.

"Because it is." Steve replied impatiently. "Look, whether he has a girl with him or not, it's him. How many dead shitbags do you have in this investigation right now?

"Not enough." Gale Robson muttered just loud enough to be heard as she flipped through her notes.

"Thirteen dead, counting last night," Tyson Bent confirmed. "Thirteen dead, two in the hospital, one of whom will likely be taken off life support today, and two more are missing and presumed dead. But let's face it; they're dead or as good as dead. So, by the end of today, let's call it what it is. We have sixteen dead human traffickers and one more with a fractured skull."

Hearing the numbers out loud, everybody sat silent for a few seconds. Bent, the youngest in the group, repeated himself.

"We have sixteen casualties. In less than a week, this guy and his girlfriend have killed or eliminated sixteen people that we know of. Kevin Marin was their first victim; his time of death was early Sunday morning. They've been on a rampage through multiple cities. They've been involved in multiple shootings in public. *'Shitbags'* or not, there are sixteen bodies that we know of!" Bent was staring directly at Gale Robson.

"I'm reminded of Thomas More and William Roper in A Man for All Seasons," Bent continued. "And when the last law was down, and the Devil turned 'round on you, where would you hide, Roper, the laws all being flat? This country is planted thick with laws, from coast to coast—man's laws, not God's! And if you cut them down, and you're just the man to do it, do you really think you could stand upright in the winds that would blow then? Yes, I'd give the Devil the benefit of law for my own safety's sake!" Tyson quoted. "These two are killing people at will in broad daylight. Who they are killing is irrelevant. We don't get to turn a blind eye to what's happening because of who it's happening to." Tyson held his stare with Robson. "I'm no Dudley Fucking Doo-rite, but murder is murder."

Robson understood why Bent was upset. Tyson Bent was a good cop, one of very few good cops. He believed in the laws that governed society. He didn't believe in the blue wall of silence; he believed the police needed to be held to a higher standard and lived his life according to that principle.

Bent believed everyone was innocent until proven guilty and believed that everyone deserved a day in court. He believed someone should be allowed to drink a beer in a park, but since it wasn't legal, he issued the ticket, regardless of how he felt about it.

"Okay," Robson redirected the conversation back to Parent. "What can you tell us about him?"

"Nothing more than I've already said. He's big, well trained."

"Ex-military," Blenkhorn added again.

Steve's face showed annoyance. "I know it's not much, but think of this as an information session. This guy is not going to be easy to catch. He's very smart. When I was tracking him, he seemed to always be two steps ahead of me."

"How close did you get to him?" Bent asked. "Name? Address? Anything?"

"I have no idea," Parent responded. "I spun my wheels in the sand. That's part of his skill set; he's very good at manipulating from a distance. In my search I thought I was on to him, but he was steering me where he wanted me the whole time. I thought I had him at work. I went in to arrest him; it turns out he'd fed us just enough info to fool us. If you find evidence or even clues pointing at a suspect, there's a good chance he planted it to throw you off his trail."

Gale and Bent's eyes met. "Marin's truck.?" Gale suggested.

"Please elaborate." Walton requested.

"We were actively searching for Kevin Marin." Bent explained. "It was purely accidental that he was found. But whoever grabbed up Orin Bondy used Kevin Marin's truck to do it."

"That's what I'm referring to," quipped Parent. "He's very good at misdirection. When I was tracking him, I thought for sure I had him. We went to where he was working and walked up to the top of a thirty-story blast furnace. We were sure the guy at the top was our man, but he ended up being a five-foot-ten ex-con named Curtis Walters. And if not for the fact that I've seen with my own eyes how big our guy is, we easily could have locked up Walters; we had enough evidence pointing at him.

This guy knew there was no way we could confuse him with Walters, though. He was laughing at us the whole time. It's also safe to say that he knows you're on to him. There is a very good chance he knows who each of you are and possibly where you live as well. When the massacre in the Falls happened, we found three dead in a small office. Our guy is responsible, but we only found the place because he broke into my home and left the information on my fridge."

Grant's attention piqued. "I'm sorry, what?"

"I was released from the hospital and went home to rest. When I woke up, our guy had been in my home. He left a photo of our target from Shooting Star on my fridge, identifying the man by name and listing the address where he could be found on the back. He entered my home in broad daylight and did it without the security system catching him. I was very good at covering my tracks, so this guy is skilled in counter surveillance."

Parent paused a moment, then added, "Ladies and gentlemen, this man you're looking for is not to be taken lightly. He's heartless and will not hesitate to hurt or kill police if you get too close. He knew where I lived and broke in while I slept. As I have already stated, he is incredibly smart. You may think you have him dead to rights in your scope, locked in. Don't be surprised if you find out you've been chasing the wrong person the whole time. You may think you're after a vigilante who got lucky. That's not the case. This man is cold, calculating, and, in my experience, always seems to be two steps ahead."

Everyone sat in silence trying to figure out what to do now. Finally, Walton spoke. "Thank you, Constable Parent, for your insight."

The meeting ended shortly afterwards. Lalonde, Grant, and Hamil sat in the office. Grant was the first to speak up.

"He knows more than he's saying."

"I caught that too." Lalonde affirmed. "I think he knows who the guy is. But why isn't he telling us?"

"I don't think he's dirty," Grant paused, staring out the window, "but something isn't right there. He either knows who the killer is, or he's choosing not to find out."

Hamil sat quietly looking at both detectives. Eventually he chimed in. "Maybe when he was rescued, they struck a deal? I'll let you go if you let me go."

"Could be," Grant agreed without enthusiasm, staring out the window. "But five dead afterwards. And we just told them we have sixteen here. That would be enough to say something, wouldn't it?"

"Parent said the guy broke into his house while he was sleeping?" Lalonde asked rhetorically. "Maybe he's afraid. He said the guy won't hesitate to kill police. Maybe Parent is afraid this guy will kill him."

"Plausible." Grant said, nodding. "Kidnapped, beaten, then your attackers are slaughtered. The guy responsible threatens you. I could see him clamming up. I think he was about 85% truthful. Everything except identity. I think he got close enough to find out who it was, but then his cover was blown."

"That's the 15% we need, though." Hamil protested.

Lalonde thought quietly for a moment. "Still, that far undercover. How did the guy make him in order to blow his cover?"

"It would explain the fear," Hamil explained. "I don't think he was lying about who we're dealing with. Parent said the guy was smart, always two steps ahead. I don't think he was exaggerating there. I have to agree with you both. He likely knows at least a name. But given what he went through, he isn't saying anything, whether it's fear, or holding up his end of some sort of deal. We're shit out of luck."

"So, what do we do now?" Lalonde asked.

"We play it smart and stay safe." Hamil stated matter-of-factly. "The main point I took from that meeting is we're dealing with a very dangerous individual."

"We already knew that." Grant added dryly.

"Yes, I'm aware. But most people would have a cognitive dissonance about killing police. To a vigilante, there's a difference between killing a shitbag that pimps out kids and killing a cop. I don't think our suspect sees a difference. So be careful."

The three of them ended the meeting. Both Grant and Lalonde walked out together.

"Think we should contact Parent privately?" Lalonde asked as they stepped onto the elevator.

"Won't do any good." Grant replied; his usual gruff expression seemed to be exaggerated by the lack of sleep. "He didn't want to be in the meeting. Didn't want to be talking to us."

Lalonde nodded. "Buy me a coffee?" she asked with a hint of a smirk.

"No," he answered, suppressing a grin of his own. "You buy me one. I have an image to uphold."

Chapter 27

Friday May 26th, 2023, 2:30 pm.

Sasha woke up in her own bed. Domino, her mean little bulldog, was snoring loudly beside her. At thirty-four lbs., Domino managed to snore like a three hundred pound man. Oscar the Trash Dog was lying on the floor, facing the door in protection mode. He wasn't sure what happened, but his momma came home hurt. Since then, he'd been perched facing the doorway, ready to fight anybody that came near her.

She carefully got out of bed, her whole-body aching, and slowly made her way down the stairs. She was wearing the usual white tank top and underwear. Blue bruises that would soon turn purple were starting to show on her legs and arms.

Mike was sitting on the couch; his black duffle bag, usually full of weapons, had been emptied out onto the large coffee table in front of him. He was in the midst of cleaning a black 12-gauge shotgun when Sasha stepped into view. Scanning the aftermath of the assault she endured, he instantly felt guilt wash over him.

"I'm okay," she repeated, reading his face. He said nothing, but his face remained unchanged. "Baby, look at me." Sasha stepped directly in front of him.

His eyes met hers. Her bottom lip had a bad cut and was swollen. There were dark black markings under her eyes and a bump on her forehead. Mike couldn't hold her gaze.

"I'm sorry," he apologized, his gaze downwards. "I'm so sorry. I tried to follow you, but—"

"Hey," she interrupted him. "You didn't get distracted or run away on me. There were bullets flying. You'd have been killed if you followed me right away. We both would have." She winced as she sat down and took his hand. "I wasn't scared. I knew you'd move heaven and hell to come get me. And you did."

He looked at her hand, a thick bandage on the palm, then up at her bruised face. His eyes welled with tears. "I'm sorry they hurt you."

"Meh. I was asking for it." She smiled.

Mike coughed out a laugh. "Jesus."

"No, really. Once they had me, I fought them every step of the way. They talked about raping me. I headbutted, kicked, scratched, and bit them back; I even broke the window and slashed one with the glass."

She told him about Jose sticking a gun in her face and how she screamed louder.

"One of two things was going to happen: you were going to save me, or they were going to kill me. But there was no way they were going to hurt me." She smiled as she spoke.

"But they did hurt you," Mike protested.

"No, they didn't," she insisted, making him look at her. "I fought them. I fought all four of them. I earned these cuts and bruises."

Sasha took a breath, closing her eyes as she exhaled. She opened them again. "I'll look in the mirror every day till they're gone, and I'll be proud of them. I'll look at the scar on my hand, and my mouth knowing that they didn't take anything from me. They had their disgusting plans, and I fought them off. They didn't win. I did."

She slowly stood up; dark blue bruising showed on her back through the baggy armholes of her tank top.

"A lot of women who have been victims of sexual assault get assaulted again and again," Sasha explained, looking out the window. She turned back to face him. "I swore I would never be a victim again. And I wasn't. They didn't rape me. And not because you busted in before they could. I was in that closet for what felt like hours. They didn't rape me because they couldn't. I didn't let them. I'd have killed them or died myself. But it wasn't happening."

Mike noticed she was standing taller when she spoke. She wasn't telling him this to convince herself; she'd never been surer of anything in her life. And she meant every word.

"I just wish we found that poor girl," Sasha added.

"It's not over yet." Mike said. "I'm going back."

"I need to recover."

"You're not coming." Mike insisted sternly. Sasha looked almost hurt at the notion. "I've been doing this a long time," Mike explained. "I move faster, and I'm more efficient if I'm alone."

"What if you need help?" she asked.

"I won't," he promised. "It's easier for one person to disappear into the shadows. It's easier for one person to escape an ambush. I know you want to help, but I can't risk you getting hurt again."

Sasha held his stare. She didn't like the thought of not being there.

"I'll be a nervous wreck, though. I don't think I can sit here waiting to hear, or worse, never hearing anything."

Mike stood up and walked to her. "My uncle taught me how to move without being seen or heard. How to get in, hit hard, and leave before anybody realizes what's happening. But he taught me how to do these things alone. Slip in and out before they know it. An extra body, no matter who it is, makes things harder."

Sasha wanted to protest, but she'd seen him in action. She knew he was right.

"Can I come to the city and wait at Adem's?" She requested, the thought of sitting and waiting alone was almost unbearable.

"Not looking like that. He'll think I beat you. Stay here, keep the dogs happy, and let your body heal. I got this." He wrapped his arms around her small frame.

"What are you going to do?" she asked, burying her head in his chest.

"I'm going to draw Lumpz out. Find out where Ashley is, or at least who has her. Then I'm going to kill him." Mike replied.

"Do you know where he is?" Sasha asked.

"I will. But better than that, I know *who* he is." Mike answered.

"When are you leaving?"

"Right now." He kissed her on the forehead and started gathering his things.

3:38 pm

Harland Grant was woken up to the sound of someone pounding on his door. He first looked at his clock, then his phone. Six missed calls and seven text messages from Clara Lalonde.

POUNDING

"Enough, goddammit," he yelled. "I'm coming."

He got out of bed, threw on a pair of black jogging pants and a plain black t-shirt, then staggered to the door where the pounding continued.

"I said I'm coming, goddammit!" He checked the small monitor by the door showing the doorbell cam: Clara Lalonde was standing in the hallway of his condo. He opened the door a crack. "What in the blue fucking Christmas do you want?" he growled.

"Let me in," she said redundantly as she pushed past him, handing him a coffee with a McDonald's logo on the cup. "You're right. He's lying."

"Who?" Grant asked.

"Parent, from the OPP. He's lying." Lalonde exclaimed, almost excitedly.

"Explain," Grant grumbled, sniffing his coffee.

Clara sat on the couch without being invited. It dawned on her that this was the first time she had ever seen Harland Grant outside of work and not wearing a suit. She was almost shocked at the size of him in street clothes. He wasn't just a large man; he was in incredible shape. The seams on the biceps of his t-shirt strained above equally large forearms that looked like skin over steel cables instead of muscles. She paused, taking it in, then continued.

"It was something he said. Two things, actually. A rather rookie slip-up at that." Lalonde began. Grant looked at her, expressionless. She continued. "First, he said, *'We think he realized he may be an accomplice to killing a cop, so he stepped in and rescued me.'* That was real. He meant that," Lalonde gave Grant a moment to absorb what she was saying.

"Okay."

"But not a minute later, he said. 'Ladies and gentlemen. This man you're looking for is not to be taken lightly. He's heartless and will not hesitate to hurt or kill police if you get too close.' That was a rehearsed line. Why would the guy rescue Parent to avoid a cop-killing beef, but then Parent warns us the guy's a cop killer? It's not adding up."

Grant's face showed a twitch of emotion. "Yeah, I get it," he admitted begrudgingly. "Missed that at the time."

"We were tired," she added. "It took me some time too. So, what do you think?"

Grant stared out the large bay window for a few seconds before replying. "Call Hamil. I want to get the RCMP back in on this. If Parent is covering for a murderer, they need to know. And we need to know why."

Lalonde pulled out her phone and started messaging.

"We're going to need to go confront him." Grant said.

Chapter 28

Saturday May 27th, 2023, 1:08 am

Lumpz had been pacing the inside of the garage for hours. He hadn't slept since Thursday morning and was coming up on thirty-nine hours awake. He was exhausted, both physically and mentally. He had run by his condo and grabbed a duffle bag with some clothing, $200,000 USD and the keys to a 2017 GMC Terrain with Michigan plates that was securely stashed in the small town of Port Angeles, WA.

On a clear day he could see the harbour. He had planned his escape route years ago. Ray Wheeler, one of his goons had the keys to his father's 2019 Ranger R-27 Tug. If the area got too hot, he could be at the marina, across the water, dropped off, and drive away in minutes. Less than an hour after Lumpz decided it was time to go, he could be heading south down Highway 101. A few short hours later he could be lost in the US.

The car was registered to his cousin Ricky in Detroit, as was the driver's license and passport in Lumpz's duffle bag. Ricky narrowly survived a shooting as a teenager. His two friends that were with him were not so lucky. All three were innocent bystanders. As a result, Ricky suffered from agoraphobia and PTSD and rarely left his mom's basement. Once every five years he'd swallow a handful of anti-anxiety meds, smoke a big fat joint, and have his mom drive him to get his driver's license and passport renewed. He would then promptly mail the updated documents to his cousin for $5,000 USD.

HUNTING PREDATORS

Ricky was an inch shorter and skinnier than Lumpz, but to a highway patrolman in the US, it wouldn't send up any red flags. Plus, Lumpz was a firm believer in only breaking one law at a time; if he was driving through the US with a fake driver's license and $200,000 in cash, it didn't make much sense to speed and draw attention to himself.

His legs were starting to ache from pacing the cement floor, but he knew he was too agitated to sit. He was debating going for another drive when his phone chimed. He looked at the screen and saw the name *Hugo*, his code for Jose. He opened the message and saw the text.

Heat gone?

He stared at the screen, confused, then replied, *Who dis?* He watched the screen. The check marks appeared, then the three bouncing dots underneath.

The reply came in: *Who do you think? 5-0 was everywhere I been hiding. Can I drop in quick? *

Lumpz felt pure relief; Jose was alive. He must have gone back to Billy's, saw the chaos, and went into hiding. Lumpz started typing. *Where u at*

*Just down the street. Look out the window.

Lumpz ran to the front window of the garage. About a block away up the street, he saw the high beams of a large black Dodge Ram flash. He replied, *Get down here*.

Lumpz felt relieved. Jose was still alive. Things weren't as bad as he thought. He watched from the window as the truck pulled away from the curb, high

HUNTING PREDATORS

beams still on. He watched as it started speeding up. He kept watching, shielding his eyes from the bright halogen headlights as the truck seemed to continue to gain speed, racing towards the front of his garage.

The truck blew through the intersection, up into the parking lot, and raced towards the window. At the last second, Lumpz heard the brakes screech as they locked up. Because of the high beams, he hadn't noticed something large lying across the hood. Jose's dead body came flying towards him, crashing through the large tempered glass window, shattering it into a million pieces. Jose's lifeless body slowed but didn't stop until it hit one of Lumpz' henchmen, knocking them both into the large brown desk.

Lumpz was trying to understand what had just happened. He heard the tires screech again as the truck flew backwards out of the parking lot, the front end whipping around ninety degrees. The transmission crunched as it was thrown into drive. The tires squealed again as the truck took off down the road.

Tyson Bent was parked on Cave Street, staring ahead at the T-intersection with Devonshire Road. He had spent the last five hours staring at the front of an autobody garage. He figured he must have seriously pissed Gale Robson off to draw watch duty. Matthew Edworthy had given them a list of places worth watching, and Bent got the garage. He wasn't entirely upset. There was activity at the garage: people walking around, opening the doors, looking out the windows. He had counted six people so far. Not exactly action-packed, but better than watching an empty building. He occupied his time by listening to a Marc Maron podcast and playing Texas Hold 'Em on his phone.

HUNTING PREDATORS

He wasn't thrilled about having to watch the building until 5:00 am, but between the podcast, poker, and the banter with the other surveillance units, the time was passing reasonably well. He was halfway through the May 17th podcast episode with Eric Bana when he saw a truck in his mirror flash its high beams once, then flick them on again and leave them on. He placed his phone on the console and muted the radio. A few seconds later, he saw the vehicle start moving.

The black Dodge Ram raced past him, picking up speed. Bent watched as it blew through a stop sign at the T-intersection and headed straight for the garage. He heard the brakes screech and watched as something flew off the hood and smashed through the large window. The truck backed up fast, its front end whipping around to the right, then sped off down the road. Tyson fired up the SUV and took off after the truck. He fishtailed around the corner and keyed his mic.

"E-12-Bravo-2, All Units Code 3. Suspect vehicle westbound Devonshire Road, in pursuit of a late-model black four-door Dodge Ram pickup. Plate unknown, Request immediate back up and air support. Suspect is high risk possibly armed." Bent stomped on the accelerator. He was trying to close the distance, but the truck had a big V-8 and was already moving fast when he started chasing it. He could hear the dispatcher relaying his position and other units replying that they were en route.

Bent watched the truck fly through an intersection without taking his foot off the gas. Bent narrowly avoided a collision himself as he followed. It dawned on him he hadn't switched on the lights and sirens. He watched the truck turn left onto Porter Street.

HUNTING PREDATORS

"Vehicle now southbound on Porter Road. Maintaining code 3, requesting backup units to intercept." Bent made the turn. Porter Road was only one block long and ended on Shearwater. If the driver turned right, it was a dead end. A left turn onto Shearwater would take them down one block before opening up onto Adlebury. If the truck made it to Adlebury, Bent could easily lose sight of him. He watched the truck turn left. Bent stomped on the gas.

"Eastbound on Shearwater, heading towards Adelbury. Maintaining Code 3" Bent hoped there was another unit close enough to block the intersection. He made it to the turn and had to lock his brakes. The truck was stopped, door open, and a large man was walking away from it.

Mike sped down the road in Jose's black pickup. He had just launched Jose's corpse through the front window. He had no idea how many people Lumpz had in there with him, but one surefire way to get them out without burning the place down was to hurl his dead friend through the window. He backed out fast, cranking the wheel hard. The front of the truck whipped around as he flipped the dial and put the truck in drive, already stomping on the gas. The truck sped off.

Mike blew through the first intersection without slowing down and turned left at the next street in a small residential area. He floored the big truck. The street was only one city block long. He turned left at the end of the street and hopped out of the truck. He had stashed a blue 2002 Ford Mustang on the block earlier that night. Like a lot of the cars he'd used over the years, the body was rough, but the engine had a lot of power, and it ran smoothly. He unlocked the door with the fob, walking quickly as he reached for the handle. He heard tires screech, and a voice yelled.

"Don't move, asshole! Hands up. Now!"

Mike thought about jumping over the hood. He was armed and wearing dark clothing; he could be over the hood shooting at them before they realized he'd even moved. But this wasn't a henchman. A goon wouldn't have yelled; they'd have pulled up shooting. This was a cop. He'd probably been watching the garage, which would explain how he was on Mike so fast. Mike raised his hands and started walking backwards.

"Hold it!" The voice was loud, the tone amped up but not panicked. Mike kept backing up.

"I said stop!"

Mike backed up two more steps. The cop was starting to get angry.

"One more step, and I'll blow your fucking brains out," the cop warned, then he touched the back of Mike's head with his gun and tried to push him forward.

And that's what Mike was waiting for. As soon as he felt the gun, he knew the cop was close. Mike spun to his left at the waist and, in a fast motion, used his left forearm to knock the gun away. Following the momentum, he continued with a thunderous right hand to the cop's temple, followed with a hard left uppercut. As the cop staggered, Mike clasped both hands around the back of the cop's neck, keeping his elbows tight in a Muay Thai clinch. He wrenched the cop's head to the left, then right, keeping him off balance. In a vicious motion, he pulled the cop's head downward while simultaneously driving his left knee under the cop's chin.

Mike let go, and the cop collapsed on the asphalt, knees and forehead colliding with the ground at the same time. The cop slumped to his right, motionless. Mike checked him over. Finding his handcuffs, he cuffed the cop's hands behind his back and laid him in the recovery position. Mike took his gun and left.

Once behind the wheel of the Mustang, Mike hauled ass back to Cave Street. Several Victoria Police cars and a few RCMP SUVs flew past him with the lights on. Mike parked half a block away, facing away from the garage, and waited. Less than five minutes had passed since Jose's body was hurled through the window, but Mike figured any second now, Lumpz and his guys would be leaving. He watched as two guys ran from the back of the shop with some plywood. Together they lifted one sheet and screwed it over half the open window, then did the same with the other. The busted window was completely covered.

The first car to leave was a black Chevy Malibu, heading east down Devonshire. If not for the tan interior, Mike wouldn't have realized Lumpz was driving. He threw the Mustang into drive, hurried to the end of Cave Street, turned right onto Ellery, and floored it. Ellery ended at Dominion Road. Devonshire crossed Dominion, veered slightly left, and became Pine. Mike had to move quickly. He fishtailed onto Dominion and eased off the accelerator when he saw the Malibu fifty meters ahead at the corner on Devonshire and Dominion.

The Malibu continued through the intersection, then immediately turned right onto Hereward Road. Mike followed at a safe distance, never taking his eyes off the black car.

The Malibu wound its way through the city, eventually leaving the urban landscape and travelling down Munro Street. Mike was hanging back almost a half a kilometre and watched as the Malibu turned left into a parking lot. Mike sped up, stopped a block away, and did the rest of the trek on foot.

Chapter 29

Saturday May 27th, 2023, 1:57 am

Lumpz parked and made his way down to the water. There was a boating dock with a blue Ranger tug R27 bobbing softly on the waves. He hopped aboard while Ray completed a small circle check, looking for any issues that might make the boat unseaworthy. The stocky looking watercraft was deceivingly agile. And could reach 65km/h roughly 35 knots if they pushed it. He tried the ignition; it fired up right away. There was nothing to do now but wait.

Leaving at 2:00 am was risky. The coast guard tended to notice things like boats crossing international waters in the middle of the night. Better to wait until 5:30 am when the sun was coming up and the narrow Juan De Fuca Straight between Victoria, BC, and Port Angeles, Washington, would be packed with early morning fishermen and recreational boaters from both sides of the border. Ray's task was simple, drop Lumpz on the US side and bring the boat back before anybody noticed it was gone.

"Got any weed?" Lumpz asked Ray

"Naw. I can get some, though," came the reply.

"How long?" Lumpz inquired.

"I live about five minutes away," Ray advised. "I'll grab some beers too."

"Go. Make it quick, though. I don't wanna be sitting here waiting." Lumpz said redundantly. He would be waiting either way.

Ray hopped out of the boat and made his way up the dock. Lumpz realized he'd been awake now for close to forty hours and hadn't eaten in almost as long. He ran up the dock towards the Malibu and saw Ray reaching for the door handle.

"Hey," Lumpz yelled, "Bring back fo—."

His sentence was cut short by a white-hot light and a loud roar with a blast of heat that he could feel almost forty yards away. When the Ray lifted the door handle, the Malibu exploded. Lumpz, initially blinded by the light, saw the chassis for the Malibu fly five feet in the air before crashing back down to the asphalt in a flaming twisted mess.

Ray was nowhere to be seen. Lumpz, having been knocked to the ground, got up and ran down the dock to his boat. He jumped in, untied the ropes, and started it up. He slowly pulled away from the dock and started heading for open water. He figured he could at least hide in another inlet for a few hours. As the boat coasted out to open water, he startled when someone appeared behind him quickly. The large figure put Lumpz into a chokehold.

Mike had used the diversion of the exploding Malibu to jump in the boat. He hunkered low as Lumpz ran down the dock, jumped in, and started the motor. Mike sat silently watching as Lumpz slowly coasted out of the small inlet to open water, glancing back over his shoulder. Once clear of the inlet, Mike stood in the dark, and in three long strides, closed the distance between them.

He wrapped his right arm around Lumpz's neck. He stepped in close, and using his left arm behind Lumpz's neck, he clasped his own right bicep. By pulling Lumpz' neck into the bend of Mike's elbow, he effectively cut off Lumpz' breathing and blood flow: a rear naked choke. It was a fairly basic, almost primitive move in martial arts, but a highly effective one.

Mike locked on to Lumpz, applying heavy pressure. Lumpz immediately reached for the trunk-like forearm across his throat and fought to break the hold. It didn't work. Mike squeezed harder, keeping his chest and head close to Lumpz's back, preventing any escape. Within ten seconds, Lumpz went limp.

Mike let his body fall to the floor. He didn't have long; usually people getting put down with blood chokes were only out for anywhere from twenty to sixty seconds. Mike zip-tied Lumpz's ankles together and then did the same with his hands behind his back. He hefted the man up and sat him on the bench seat on the left or port side of the boat.

As Lumpz started to regain consciousness, Mike threw a black canvas bag over his head and returned to the steering wheel. He opened the throttle halfway and headed west. Ucluelet was 91 nautical miles, or around 170 km, straight west. With this boat he'd burn a little more than half a tank of gas if he opened the throttle all the way. It would take three to four hours, but that was fine. They still had another three hours of darkness.

The boat bounced along. The water wasn't too choppy, but the mist that came up was ice cold. Mike kept a watchful eye, scanning every direction looking for other boats or lights. He had caused a large explosion in Victoria. If anyone noticed the boat leaving right after and notified the coast guard, they may be looking for him.

After forty-five minutes there was nothing but blackness to his left and the faint scattered lights from Vancouver Island on his right. He pulled the throttle back slowly. The boat dropped speed as the motors stopped working. The boat bobbed slightly in the water.

Pulling the black bag off Lumpz's head, Mike casually asked, "Hey Wallace. How ya been?"

"What the fuck? Mike?" Lumpz asked, dumbfounded.

"It's been a while." Mike's voice was even.

"What? How?" Lumpz stammered, looking like he'd seen a ghost. "What the fuck are you doing here?" he finally managed.

"Taking you apart," Mike answered calmly. "What happened to you? Pimping out kids?" Mike asked, disgust and disappointment in his voice.

"This was you!" Lumpz yelled, shock and accusation both registering across his face. "You killed my guys?"

Mike snapped out a fast right hand, punching Lumpz square in the nose. "And those animals put their hands on my woman Wallace. Guess what I'm more concerned with?" Mike growled.

"You're lucky they didn't hurt her, Wallace." Mike continued, pulling a large black blade out of a sheath. "If they had, we wouldn't be talking. I'd be carving you apart by each muscle group and feeding it to the sea life."

"You have any idea how much money you cost me?" Lumpz said through a trickle of blood that was dripping from his nose.

Mike answered him with another fast right hand in the same spot. "Money?" Mike snarled, grabbing Lumpz by the throat. "You're worried about money? You're raping kids." He let go of Lumpz's throat.

Lumpz coughed, hacked, then laughed. "Still with them fast hands, eh?" He spit blood that had been running from his nose into his mouth.

"So what now, huh? I'm supposed to believe you're gonna kill me? Is that it? C'mon, Mikey. We both know you ain't got it in you to kill me. Them other fools maybe. But me?"

"Where is Ashley Brock?" Mike asked.

"Who?" Lumpz asked, genuinely unsure.

In one lightning-fast motion, Mike grabbed the handle of the large knife and stabbed Lumpz just above the left knee. He twisted the blade, the tip of it digging into the femur. Lumpz screamed in agony.

"You were saying?" Mike asked calmly. "I don't have it in me?" He twisted the blade again. "Ashley Brock. The young girl taken from Nanaimo. The one your buddy in the blue truck picked up." With a jerking motion, he pulled the blade out.

Lumpz was panting. He couldn't breathe through his nose. It was broken again. His leg felt like nothing he'd ever experienced. The pain was so intense he thought he was going to faint, or puke, or both. "I—I don't know wh—"

His sentence was cut short. Mike rammed the blade down into the same spot on the right leg and twisted again. Lumpz screamed loudly. "Keep screaming, buddy. Nobody can hear ya. Where is she? I have two hours before the sun comes up. I can keep this up longer than you can." He pulled the blade out again.

Lumpz was sobbing. "Okay, please stop. Jesus Mike, we're family," he pleaded.

"Where is she?" Mike repeated.

"I really don't know. Most of the street and guys went quiet when you started killing them. She was with a couple, Chris and Sadie. Last I heard, they were heading for the mainland," Lumpz explained, referring to Vancouver.

"Where's your phone?"

"Why?" Lumpz asked. Without another word, Mike buried the knife in his left thigh about six inches higher. "Jesus Christ," Lumpz screamed. "Stop. Please just stop."

"Phone." Mike demanded again.

"It's in my bag." Lumpz nodded toward the black bag next to the steering wheel. Mike slowly walked over. He dug the phone out. Took note of the cash.

"Planning your departure?" Mike guessed.

Lumpz was panting heavily. "Listen, just let me go, okay? I'll leave. Down into the States. I'll disappear. Come on Mike, you know me, man."

"Do I?" Mike growled again as he flew back towards Lumpz, grabbing his face and pushing his upper body over the low-sitting backrest. "Do I know you? The guy I knew wouldn't pimp out kids. Wouldn't kidnap my woman and encourage his boys to rape her. No, Wallace. I knew you. I don't know you anymore." He pushed Lumpz's head back and looked at the phone. "How do I unlock this? Passcode or fingerprint?"

"Passcode: 1111," Lumpz replied.

"Jesus fucking Christ," Mike mumbled to himself. "Chris and/or Sadie when are they in your phone under?"

"C&S."

"Oh, for Christ's sake," Mike said exasperated as he scrolled through the phone's WhatsApp. "When did you get so goddamn sloppy?" He found the C&S text conversation and put the phone away.

"Mike, please, bro. Just let me go."

"Ya know, I'm not much for theatrics. Over the years I've had a lot of people in your position. Usually before I put them there, I ask myself, 'Do they need to be here?' The answer is always yes." Mike explained as he sat back down in front of Lumpz. "But lately, there's been another question that I've heard being asked, and I think it's fitting."

"What's that?" Lumpz asked, still panting heavily, dizzy from pain but trying to buy time.

"How many girls have begged you or your boys for their freedom and been ignored?" Mike replied, staring directly at Lumpz.

"I—I don—"

Mike reached down, grabbed the zip ties on Lumpz' ankles, and lifted quickly. Lumpz was thrown backwards overboard and splashed into the water. He bobbed up once and shouted.

"Mike, please?"

Mike walked back to the steering wheel. Pushed the throttle forward and set off for Ucluelet.

Chapter 30

Saturday May 27th, 2023, 1:08 am, 7:45 am, Toronto.

Clara Lalonde and Harland Grant walked through Pearson International Airport with purpose. They were both tired, jetlagged, and hungry. Although catching an 11:00 pm flight out of Victoria, BC, to Pearson and landing first thing in the morning had initially seemed like a great idea, it had quickly turned into a nightmare.

Neither detective was able to sleep on the plane. There was a screaming baby behind their seat that didn't stop for the entire flight. The parents seemed to be that new-age type that figured their baby was important enough to cry it out with zero regard for the other 107 people on the flight. Somewhere over Manitoba, Grant voiced his disapproval with having to leave his firearm behind. Lalonde agreed.

Lalonde waited till she had a coffee and then turned on her cell phone and was instantly bombarded with multiple text messages from Chief Hamil and Gale Robson. She called Hamil first. He answered on the first ring.

"Have you landed?" he asked. His voice seemed panicked.

"Yes. A couple of minutes ago."

"Do what you need to and get back here ASAP," he ordered, adding, "Tyson Bent attempted to make an arrest last night. He was badly beaten."

"What?" Clara said in disbelief, stopping in her tracks. Grant waited for her. "What happened?" Her voice strained with concern.

"It's unclear. He had been watching an autobody garage when he radioed in saying someone smashed the window. He gave chase. A minute later there was no response. He was found shortly after, beaten and handcuffed."

"How bad?" Lalonde inquired.

"Pretty bad. Jaw is broken in three places; he's missing some teeth. He's got a broken orbital bone and a bad concussion. He's out of commission for a couple of months at least."

"Do we know anything?" Lalonde asked.

"Not really. Bent is waiting for surgery. Also worth noting, there was a car that exploded on a side street off Munro Street in Esquimalt. Charred remains were found. Looks like a bomb." Hamil added.

Clara sighed. "It's related, isn't it?"

"Likely, so make it quick. We're having your return flights booked right away."

Lalonde rang off and called Gale Robson, who answered on the third ring. Lalonde had to remind herself of the three-hour time difference. It was 4:45 am in BC.

"Robson." The voice came through, cracking.

"It's Clara. What happened?"

There was a pause as Robson sniffled. She was clearly in tears. "Stupid boy," she lamented. "Stupid, stupid boy. He called in. Didn't specify, but he saw something and said he was in pursuit. Made it about three blocks away from the garage. Looks like he tried to apprehend someone, and they beat the crap out of him." Her voice cracked again as fresh tears started rolling.

"Any idea who it was?" Lalonde inquired.

"No. No idea. This wasn't a swarming. It looks like one person. Tyson has a kind heart, but he's tough. Always was a scrappy kid. If someone put him down easy, they'd have to be really good." Robson paused. Lalonde could hear her wiping her nose and sniffling.

"His gun?" Lalonde questioned, almost afraid to hear the answer.

Robson let out a deep sigh. "Gone."

"Shit," Lalonde cursed. Nothing worse than a cop's gun being stolen. "Chief Hamil said he's waiting for surgery?"

Robson's voice broke again. "Yes. For his jaw." She paused to compose herself. "Broken in three places. He'll require reconstructive surgery. They're worried about him losing the use of his left eye as well." Robson was trying to remain professional but was on the verge of a total meltdown.

"I swore to his mother I'd keep him safe," she finally said.

"His mother?" Lalonde asked, surprised.

"My sister." Robson explained. "Tyson Bent is my sister's only son."

Lalonde understood why Robson was so upset. She was a good leader; she'd be upset if anybody on her team got hurt. But Tyson Bent was family. Lalonde thought back to the different interactions they'd had. Bent always seemed to get his cues from Robson. Moreover, Robson seemed to communicate with him without speaking. Bent could pick up on her demeanour and body language. It made sense to her now that Tyson Bent and Gale Robson had the type of relationship that went back years. It also explained why Robson was always so hard on Bent and why she felt like garbage right now.

"Where is his mother?" Lalonde asked.

"She lives just outside Toronto," Robson replied.

"Want us to go see her in person?"

"God, no!" Robson blurted. "Thank you, but no. If you knock on the door, she'll think he's dead. I'll call her shortly. Thank you."

"We'll get back as soon as we can," Clara promised and rung off. She filled Grant in on what happened. His face showed little emotion.

They made their way outside, where they were met by a young female OPP officer. She was standing in full uniform, holding a sign with the name "Lalonde" on it.

Twenty minutes later, they were led into a conference room. Sue Blenkhorn, Karl Sampson, and Steven Parent were already sitting down.

"Detectives Lalonde and Grant, nice to see you," Blenkhorn greeted, pretending to be surprised to see them in the office 3000 miles from home on a Saturday morning.

Grant nodded and sat down without waiting for the offer. Lalonde nodded and grabbed another chair.

"Excuse us for being curt, but let's skip the formalities," began Lalonde. She turned her gaze to Parent. "You lied to us the other day. We need to know why."

"The fuck I did!" Steve replied, immediately defensive.

"In one breath you told us that your suspect rescued you because he didn't want to be an accomplice to killing a cop. The next breath you said he won't hesitate to hurt or kill police. You can't have it both ways." Lalonde snapped. "There is no third side on this coin, heads or tails. Will he kill police, or will he risk everything to save one?" She stared at him.

Steve looked trapped. He looked back and forth between Karl Sampson and Clara Lalonde.

"This is ridiculous," he retorted dismissively.

Lalonde switched her attention to Sue Blenkhorn. "Are you in on this?"

"I beg your pardon!" Blenkhorn replied indignantly.

"His story has holes so big you can park a goddamn Greyhound in them. You guys didn't pick up on that?" Lalonde asked with an accusatory tone in her voice. "You have five dead, ties to at least another dozen that you stated. We have sixteen dead and a growing body count. And as of three hours ago, an RCMP is in critical condition after getting his ass handed to him trying to make an arrest."

She switched her attention back to Steve Parent. "You know more than you're saying. You know it; I know it. Everyone in this goddamn room knows it. Are you protecting him?" she yelled.

"No!" Steve snarled back. "Look, bitch, I'm not some dirtbag junkie you can shake down or scare in Victoria, and I don't appreciate you coming into my backyard and calling me a liar. I've shovelled more shit in more ovens than you can imagine, so I suggest you get your fucking attitude in check. Your name and rank mean exactly jack shit here, got it?"

Steve sat upright and held her stare as he continued. "I told you and everyone else everything I know. In my first interaction with him, he damn near killed the mark I was buying from with a single blow and broke my nose bad enough that I haven't had a decent night's sleep since because I can't breathe lying down. We *suspect* he was the one who rescued me. I'm not sure. It was a large man wearing similar dark clothing. We didn't talk. If you'd done your homework before flying across the country thinking you cracked some secret code that everyone else overlooked, you'd know I was in a targeted car accident, beaten—on camera, I might add—and kidnapped. I was punched, kicked, and stomped over the course of a few hours after the accident. So, if—and big IF—I did have any type of conversation with our suspect, I don't remember it, thanks to the head trauma I sustained.

"I do vaguely remember Thomas Paterson walking towards me, ready to shoot me in the goddamn face, closing my eyes and waiting for the bang. Next thing I know, I'm getting showered with his blood when a crossbow bolt tore the front half of his neck open. But the rest of the details that night are a little fuzzy!"

"Okay." Karl Sampson interjected, trying to diffuse the room. "Everybody calm down. Detective Lalonde, I appreciate your frustration here. I'll be the first to admit that Constable Parent is more than a little rough around the edges. But what he lacks in bedside manner, he makes up for in the field. We have interviewed and debriefed him multiple times about that incident, and I'm inclined to believe him. I saw the vehicle collision and the beating he sustained on camera that night with my own eyes. I was also in the emergency room with him immediately after his rescue."

Lalonde held Parent's stare and replied, "I'm not doubting any of that; I'm questioning whether or not Constable Parent knows the identity of our suspect."

"I don't," Parent said flatly.

"You know an awful lot about someone you don't know." Grant piped in quietly.

Before Parent could respond, Grant continued more loudly. "You sat in that meeting trying to tell us he's a criminal mastermind, but you know nothing about him. It doesn't add up." Grant adjusted in his seat and continued.

"You said you must have gotten close without realizing it, and that he blew your cover, so you must have crossed paths with him, whether you realize it or not. But my partner is right; you can't have it both ways. Are you covering for him? Or are you so incompetent that he was right under your nose, and you didn't realize it?"

"What did you call me?" Steve shouted, glaring at Grant.

"I didn't call you anything. I asked you a question. Would you like me to ask it again?" Grant held Parent's stare. "I asked if you're covering for a murderer, or are you too fucking stupid to realize he was right in front of you?"

"Hey, fuck you, pal." Steve snapped.

"No, fuck you." Grant said calmly. "I didn't fly across the country all goddamn night to sit in Toronto and be lied to."

Grant turned his attention to Sue Blenkhorn. "One of yours is in the hospital. I'm guessing you have about," he looked at his watch and saw it was 8:48 am, "twelve minutes before Gale Robson speaks to Sarah Walton. After another thirty minutes you'll get a phone call from the commissioner Duffy of the RCMP in Ottawa." He turned his attention back to Parent. "Tyson Bent is Gale Robson's nephew. He's the one that got hurt last night." He let that hang in the air.

Parent seemed unbothered until he looked at Sue Blenkhorn. Her face was bedsheet white. "Who is Gale Robson?" he asked.

"Gale is Commissioner Duffy's daughter." Sue replied, shoulders dropping.

"That's correct," Lalonde affirmed. "And Commissioner Duffy's grandson is on an operating table with potentially career-ending injuries right now."

"Stephen, if you know anything that you haven't told us, I suggest you tell us now," Blenkhorn urged.

"This is bullshit," Steve spat as he stood up and stormed out.

"Parent. Parent! Get back here." Karl Sampson yelled after him.

Without waiting, Clara Lalonde jumped from her seat and rushed after him. She caught him at the elevator as he pushed the down button.

"Okay, you're not covering for him because you know him. Even if you had worked out some type of deal in the Falls where he saves you and you leave him alone. That would have gone out the window when he started killing again," she began.

Steve ignored her and continued staring at the red digital display, watching the numbers climb.

"You're scared of him," she concluded. He glanced at her, but otherwise gave no indication of whether she'd hit a nerve.

"That's it. He found you before you found him. He blew your cover and broke into your house. You were face to face with your own bogeyman."

The elevator dinged and the door started sliding open.

Clara tried to block him from stepping into the elevator. "You're worried if he finds out you turned us on to him, he'll come back and kill you." Steve ducked under her arm and walked into the elevator. He pushed a button, backed up to the wall, and waited.

"So, that's it? You're going to live the rest of your life in fear of this man?"

Steve's eyes met hers. "Living in fear is better than not living." The door slid closed.

Chapter 31

Saturday May 27th, 2023, 12:10 pm.

Clara Lalonde and Harland Grant made their way back to Pearson Airport. So far, the trip had been nothing but a frustrating waste of time. Steve Parent had all but admitted he knew more than he was saying at the elevator, but Lalonde was the only one who heard him.

Chief Hamil had their return flights booked, but whoever did it was new. They were booked on a WestJet flight, which meant they would have a three-hour layover in Calgary. They made their way through the airport departures.

"Can you grab coffee? I need a pit stop." Lalonde asked.

"Double Cream?"

She nodded and made her way to the closest restroom. The restroom was standard, apart from not having a door to enter. Instead, the entrance was an S-shaped corridor that prevented anybody outside from looking in but afforded the luxury of walking in without fumbling with a door while carrying your bags. On her way out she was stopped midway through the S as a man made his way in.

"Ladies room, pal," she directed, not realizing who was standing in front of her.

Steve Parent had followed her and stopped her from leaving at one of the blind corners. He was wearing a hooded sweatshirt, with a black Blue Jays ball cap and sunglasses. He looked like he didn't want to be noticed while simultaneously flashing a sign that said, *Look at the suspicious guy.*.

"Listen closely, because I'm only going to say this once. If you tell anybody about this conversation, I'll deny everything." Steve advised in a hushed tone. "The people you're looking for are a couple. His name is Mike; her name is Sasha. He's about six foot five 250-260 lbs. I've never seen his face; he had a mask on both times I dealt with him. She's smaller, five foot four, with a muscular build. She's got tattoos all over her biceps and chest. She had short blonde hair when I saw her working at a small hole-in-the wall bar in Hamilton a few years ago. What really stood out was her eyes; the bluest eyes I've ever seen. She's got a big smile..." He paused. "She's very pretty but has a sharp edge to her."

Clara was trying to take it all in.

"I didn't exactly lie," he continued quietly as an older woman made her way out, glaring at him.

"I saw him in a bar one night, but I didn't see his face. I did, however, see him when he robbed our buy, and I watched him a few days later as he thumped out two brothers in the blink of an eye. I also watched him murder someone with a crossbow; I don't think his heart rate went above eighty-five beats per minute during any of those events. He was so calm it was almost scary. Prior to killing a man with a crossbow, he fucking nearly decapitated the guy's partner. I saw the aftermath and the rest of the victims that night. I wasn't exaggerating. The guy is a vicious son of a bitch. He killed three in a small room. Two quickly, with gunshots, execution style. The third one he really worked over. I've never seen anything like it. What I can tell you is this: I think he set me up in order to rescue me."

Clara blinked hard and shook her head. "I'm sorry, what?"

Another woman made her way in. She glared at Steve, who snapped, "Can I help you?" She rolled her eyes and kept walking.

Parent continued. "I don't know how he figured out who I was, but he outed me. I think the initial plan was to blow my cover and get me off his back. When they snatched me up, he saw an opportunity and took it. By rescuing me, he was able to wipe them out. The thing is, with all the bodies, it's not what we found; it's what we didn't find."

"What didn't you find?" Lalonde asked, transfixed.

"Money." Steve replied. "Our target, his goons, all of them. There should have been hundreds of thousands at least. We didn't find one fucking red cent. The office where we found the three bodies had a safe. It was opened, same as the houses that belonged to the goons that grabbed me. They were all cleaned out. We don't even know how much your guy got away with. Given the money our target was raking in, it could have been millions."

Clara nodded. This made things worse. "And with millions in cash, they could be living off the grid. Don't need to work. Landlords won't think twice about cash-in-hand payments. And there's nothing stopping them from getting up and walking away," she muttered, more to herself. "Why didn't you tell us?"

"Couple reasons," Parent replied. "Yes, he struck a deal with me. If I let him go, he would let me live. Detective, I was kidnapped, beaten, and tied to a chair. Thomas Paterson was walking towards me, gun drawn, ready to shoot me in the face. This guy saved my life; that means something to me. He could have let them kill me and still gotten away with what he did."

Clara nodded. She didn't agree with Steve, but she understood.

"The other reason... look at who he's killing," Steve pointed out.

"Well, yes, but—"

"But nothing!" Steve snapped. "Listen, I spearheaded taking down a human trafficking ring right before Shooting Star. The RCMP left me in a fire watching kids get abused and tied my hands, preventing me from putting a stop to it, just so they could build a stronger case. I've witnessed with my own two eyes what some of these kids are suffering through. I think Mike and Sasha deserve a medal for what they're doing. I'm telling you this as a courtesy and nothing more. Look deeper into who they're killing; I promise you, these are targeted attacks, and there's a lot more going on than you realize. Follow the victims, and you'll likely crack a much bigger case. And if I were you, I'd back off of them. He may not kill police, but he'll definitely fuck you up if you get too close. He's already hurt one of you." He pointed at his broken and misshapen nose. "I'm speaking from experience."

"You think he's ex-military?" asked Lalonde.

A Toronto Metro police officer walked in at that moment. He looked at Steve. "Okay buddy, let's go." The older woman from a few minutes ago stood smirking behind the cop. Both Steve and Clara pulled out their badges.

"Take a walk, asshole." Steve directed. The cop glared at him and walked away.

"They think he is." Parent continued, referring to Karl Sampson and Sue Blenkhorn. "I don't. But they're both adamant about that and refuse to let it go. I think they're gunning the engine in neutral going down that road. He doesn't feel military. He's trained, definitely a fighter. I'd guess weapons training with knives, clubs, shit like that. He can shoot too. He could be a hunter that knows how to fight. But he's thorough. He'll shake out his victims, grab their wallets, cash, and phones."

"Yeah. He's used their cars after they're killed." Clara confirmed.

"He'll be using their phones too." Steve advised. "These pimps, they're all in networks. I'll bet anything he'll whack someone and then use their phone to set up his next move. But this guy is different. Don't be surprised if you find out he's monitoring police channels. Like I said, he outed me. He knew where I was and when I was there, and he got into my home without my home security system picking him up."

"Do you think he was a cop?" Clara asked.

Steve knew he wasn't. "No, but I've wondered if he's related to one," he fibbed. "He thinks like a cop. More to the point, he seems to know our tradecraft, how we operate. If you set up to do surveillance, he'll know where you'll be. It's hard to explain. I think he baited me into revealing myself. Everything else I said was true. He's smart, very smart. And cold-blooded. You've seen it yourselves. He's a pro at misdirection."

"Anything else?" Clara asked.

"No." Steve shook his head. "I'm telling you this because I was in a bad spot in both Shooting Star and Project Nichols."

"Nichols?" Clara looked confused.

"Human trafficking case. I was deep undercover and started using pretty heavily. It helped numb me to what I was seeing. I can't have the RCMP opening an investigation where either of those cases gets looked at. My conduct in some areas could have dozens of pedophiles walk free and cost me my job. I've told you everything I know, so don't fuck me here. You don't have to like me. I don't expect you to care about my job. Truth be told, I don't much care about it anymore either. But think of the victims in Nichols. If you ring this bell, they'll be the ones that suffer." Parent spun on his heels and briskly walked away. Lalonde tried to watch him, but he quickly vanished into the sea of people and disappeared.

HUNTING PREDATORS

Steve hustled out of the departures, across the busy drop-off area, and into the parking garage. Given that Tyson Bent had been injured, likely when the poor bastard tried to arrest Mike, Steve couldn't let them go away empty-handed. He hoped the little bit of info he fed them could be enough for Clara Lalonde to convince everyone that Steve Parent was a dead end. The last thing Steve wanted was the RCMP going over Operation Shooting Star with a fine-tooth comb. It wasn't just the drug use and the number of unethical things he'd done. Steve didn't want them discovering that he knew exactly who Mike Wolly was. Steve knew his name, date of birth, and what he looked like. He knew Mike's dad was a retired and now deceased Windsor Police Sergeant. He knew Mike was an accomplished boxer and had been an ironworker. He knew that life for Mike was a chess match, and he always had his next two or three moves planned.

He knew Sasha had been forcibly held against her will as a teenager and escaped twice, once through sheer willpower and the other by scalding her captor with boiling water. He had seen the fight in her firsthand when he tried to intimidate her and narrowly avoided her bashing in his skull with a baseball bat. He knew everything there was to know about Mike Wolly and Sasha Hovart, including the fact that the cops would never catch them. Mike always planned for the worst and had an escape plan, and Sasha wouldn't hesitate to pull a trigger. They made an extremely dangerous duo. Not only did Steve firmly believe they couldn't be caught, but he also believed that Mike would make good on his promise and kill Steve in his own home if he found out Steve named him.

Clara made it back to Harland Grant, who had been standing at the bottom edge of the security checkpoint waiting for her.

"That was weird," she commented, taking the coffee from him.

"What's that?" Grant inquired.

"Steve Parent just met me coming out of the bathroom."

Grant raised an eyebrow, waiting for her to elaborate.

"He said he wasn't lying but admits he left a few pieces of info out. Turns out we were all correct; he's terrified of the killer and grateful at the same time. Told me they struck a deal. Parent lives; the killer flees. But Parent is still scared shitless of the guy."

"Huh," Grant mused. Anything else?"

"Yeah, he said their first names are Mike and Sasha. Mike is big, which we already knew. Sasha's short, muscular, and very pretty with blonde hair and really blue eyes. Her arms and chest are covered in ink. He said he doesn't think the guy's ex-military, but his bosses do. Parent agrees there's likely some law enforcement, though."

"He's a cop?" Grant was shocked.

"No. I asked that. Parent said he doesn't think the guy is or was a cop, but he knows the tricks of the trade. Maybe has or had cops in the family."

"So, we're looking for a big guy named Mike who has family members that are cops?" Grant summarized, a hint of sarcasm in his voice. "Shouldn't be too hard."

"And a girl named Sasha," Lalonde added, "with blue eyes."

"Have you ever met a Sasha that didn't have blue eyes?" Grant questioned rhetorically. Lalonde smirked to herself.

They cleared security, grabbed their seats in the lounge, and waited to start the nine-hour trip home.

9:40 am, Ucluelet, B.C.

Mike had made it back to Ucluelet. He had a little less than half a tank of fuel. The sun was up, so he slowly puttered down the Pacific Rim coastline. He was using the digital GPS on the dash and saw a small inlet called Halfmoon Bay. He cleared the rock edge and saw the empty beach. He turned sharp. gave the boat some speed and braced for impact.

The boat moving quickly scraped the sand and rocks underneath and came to a staggering, sudden stop about twenty yards from shore. Mike grabbed Lumpz' small black bag, stuffed it inside his bigger black weapons bag, and jumped over the side. He quickly trudged his way up to shore and darted for the woods off the beach. The last thing he wanted was to be seen near a boat that had recently been the scene of a homicide before being run ashore. He made it to the woods and changed quickly.

HUNTING PREDATORS

Halfmoon Bay had a small path that connected to the Willowbrea Trail. Sixteen minutes later, Mike was standing at the edge of the visitor's center. He called the number for Sasha's burner phone from memory. She answered on the second ring.

"Are you okay?" she asked as a means of answering the call.

"Yes, I'm fine. Want to come get me?"

"Where?" She answered quickly.

Mike told her where he was and where to meet. Thirty-three minutes later, Sasha sped into the parking lot of the Ucluelet visitor center. Mike had been hunkered down outside of the security camera's view. As she pulled in, he stayed low. He opened the trunk, tossed in the black bag, then hopped into the front seat. Sasha was trying to get to him but forgot to take her seat belt off, and it stopped her with a jolt. She clawed at the release, then jumped over to the passenger side and kissed him.

"I was so worried," she breathed, planting kisses on his lips and cheeks.

"I'm fine, babe," he assured, trying to hold her back.

"How did you get back here so fast? Is it done? Are you hurt?" She started patting his body, looking for injuries.

"Baby, baby. Stop. I'm fine. It's done," he promised.

Sasha sat back in her seat and looked at him. "I was so scared you wouldn't make it back." Her eyes welled up. "Please don't ever leave me like that again."

Mike looked at her; the bruising from her assault a few days before had turned dark black in some areas, the swelling still showing.

"Jesus, you look terrible."

"Hey, fuck you, buddy!" She laughed.

"Not what I meant." He still felt horrible and guilty that she had been hurt.

"I'm fine. It's okay. Did you find her?"

"No. But I know who has her," Mike advised. "Let's go home. I need sleep."

Sasha put the Range Rover in gear and headed for the highway. On the way home, Mike told her about flinging Jose's corpse through the window. He told her about having to knock a cop out and rigging the car to blow up.

"How did you know they'd go back to the car?" she asked.

"I didn't," Mike admitted. "When they got on the boat, they didn't move. I figured he was going to try and cross to the States. He'd have to wait till sunrise; otherwise, he risked getting stopped. I was going to blow it to cause a distraction. Just dumb luck he sent the other guy back."

"Where's Lumpz now?" Sasha inquired.

"Ocean floor, 'bout halfway between here and Victoria." Mike guessed. He stared off into space. She'd seen him after he'd killed people, several times now. He seemed different.

"You okay?"

"I've known him since we were kids." Mike confessed.

"Lumpz?" she asked, shocked.

"Yeah. His real name is Wallace. Was Wallace. We grew up fighting together. Ed was his boxing coach. We lost touch after I moved into Nick's, but we were like brothers when we were growing up."

"I'm sorry," Sasha offered, realizing Mike had just killed a childhood friend.

"Don't be. I killed Lumpz. Wallace died the second he took money for hurting a child. The world is a better place without him."

He took her hand as she drove. The rest of the trip was silent.

Chapter 32

Saturday May 27th, 2023, 8:00 pm, Victoria, BC.

Clara Lalonde and Harland Grant walked off the airplane in Victoria. They were both exhausted and spent. They had flown from Victoria to Toronto, Toronto to Calgary, and Calgary to Victoria, all in the last eighteen hours.

"I need a shower." Grant commented.

"Me too," Clara agreed wistfully, then looked at Harland and added, "Shower together, conserve water?" as a joke.

"Not appropriate," he scolded.

"Oh relax, big guy, I'm kidding." She teasingly bumped into him as they walked.

Harland stopped and addressed her; his usually stern tone had an extra edge to it. "Listen, you're a pretty woman in a male-dominated industry. You need to work three times as hard for half the recognition given to your male counterparts. I make a conscious effort to show you respect based on your police work and nothing more. We don't need any rumours about us."

A little taken aback, Clara thought maybe he was overtired and frustrated and taking it out on her. She understood what he was saying, and even though he'd barked at her, she felt her respect for him grow.

"I got it. Thank you," she conceded, and they started walking again. "You really think I'm pretty though?" she jabbed at him.

"Compared to my last partner, yes," he replied with a slight smirk.

Clara laughed. His last partner was a tall, overweight former NHL player who had the scars to prove it.

The two walked to the parking lot and into the unmarked Victoria Police SUV they had driven in the night before. Harland drove. Clara leaned her seat back and closed her eyes. It felt like she blinked, but the next thing she knew, Grant was nudging her.

"Hey," he said, and nudged her again. "Hey, your phone's ringing."

Clara opened her eyes and realized she must have been out for a while; they were nowhere near the airport. She answered, "Lalonde," her voice sounding like gravel.

"Good, you're back." She heard Hamil's voice. "Can you guys come to headquarters?"

The thought of not going home and sleeping made Clara's stomach lurch. "Ugh. Fine." She rang off. "Hamil wants to see us."

Grant didn't so much as reply as he grunted.

At 4:40 pm they walked into Chief Hamil's office.

Both Lalonde and Grant plopped down in chairs. Hamil looked up from his desk, equally dishevelled and tired.

"So? What did we find out?" Hamil inquired.

"Not a goddamn thing," Lalonde admitted. "First names, maybe. Not even sure if it's their real first names. Mike and Sasha might be their names."

"You flew all the way there for that?" Hamil asked sarcastically. Grant's upper lip snarled in response. "Why didn't he say that during our conference call?"

"Because he isn't sure." Lalonde explained. "Look, Steve Parent is a certifiable grade A-asshole, no doubt there. But I looked into him more. The Mounties hung him out to dry. He was the guy in the field on that big child porn and human trafficking ring a couple of years ago too. He saw some dark shit, and they left him in the oven too long, so he's a little reluctant to deal with the Mounties right now. He went through hell during one case, then almost got killed in the next. That explains his hostility and being apprehensive, but he's not dirty."

Hamil looked at Grant for his opinion. "She did most of the talking. But yeah, she's right. He's hostile, but he's upfront." Grant agreed.

"He didn't tell me about the names until after he stormed out of the meeting." Lalonde added. "I caught him at the elevator and confronted him. The only thing he told me that was in the debriefs but not in the Teams meeting was the potential first names: they might be called Mike and Sasha, but he's not sure. He didn't mention it in Teams because, like the other hundred dead ends, there's nothing supporting it. He said they talked to a bartender that thinks she might have known them, but she wasn't sure. There's nothing to back it up."

Hamil looked up at the ceiling and tapped his pen on his desk, blowing out a loud sigh. "Okay, changing gears. Last night Bent was monitoring a garage in Esquimalt. We've listened to the recording. He sounded excited, but we're not sure what he saw. We know that a window was smashed, and he gave chase."

"He didn't say?" Grant probed.

"He did. But he had the mic too close to his mouth, so it was all garbled. He gave chase to a black Dodge Ram pickup. It was found a couple blocks away in the street, door open, engine running, as was Bent's car. Bent was on the ground handcuffed. By the time backup got over to the garage, the window was already boarded up and the place was empty."

"And the car?" Lalonde asked.

"Think it was a Malibu. Nothing left of it. Still trying to find out what explosive was used." Hamil advised.

"Victim?" Lalonde inquired.

Hamil coughed out a laugh. "Don't even know if it was human at this point. We're assuming it was; it had something that resembled a shoe with something that resembled what might have been a foot at one time. But they were picking bits of whatever it was up forty yards away. It'd probably be a hundred yards away, but those pieces are in the water."

"Anything else?" Grant asked tightly, trying to hide his disgust, not for the grisly scenario, but for the way Hamil was disrespecting the victim.

"Yeah, Halfmoon Bay, down near Ucluelet. A boat ran ashore. Blood all over the back. Registered to Alfred Wheeler. Talked to him, He said, as far as he knew, the boat should have been docked in Victoria," Hamil informed.

Lalonde sighed again. "It's related, isn't it?"

"He's in Tofino." Grant said calmly. The other two looked at him. "Kevin Marin was assaulted in Tofino, taken from a resort, and killed not far away. The kid went missing from Nanaimo; Kevin went to Tofino to lay low. He was plastered all over the paper. This is what started the ball rolling: when he was spotted in Tofino. Whoever killed everyone in Victoria took a boat and used it to get back to Tofino."

Lalonde gave it some thought. "That makes sense. Parent mentioned to me that this guy, whoever he is, will use the victim's cell phones. We've seen him use their vehicles. If this vigilante couple crossed paths with him in Tofino, say at the resort..."

"Wasn't the resort." Grant interrupted. "He was attacked in town and checked into the resort after. I'll bet next week's paycheck that whoever kicked his ass in Tofino is the one we're after."

"We're going to Tofino, aren't we?" Lalonde asked.

"Yes. But not till tomorrow. I need to contact Robson and Sarah Walton. We're going to focus everything on Tofino for now." Hamil advised.

"Is that smart?" Lalonde questioned, doubting that they had enough evidence to focus all their resources.

"We literally have nothing else to go on right now," Hamil replied. "Go home. Get some sleep. You leave in the morning."

Sunday, May 28th, 2023, 12:10 pm, Tofino, BC.

After Tyson Bent's assault, the RCMP tripled the manpower available for the case. Earlier that morning, Detectives Grant and Lalonde arrived in Tofino. The RCMP barracks was a tiny brown structure on the corner of Campbell and Third Streets. Immediately after Grant and Lalonde walked in, the decision to move to a larger location was made. The small structure could barely accommodate more than four people. With the now twenty-four-person task force, it was standing room only.

By noon they were set up in the banquet hall of a local hotel. Round tables had been set up, four seats at each table, with manila envelopes containing the case information at each seat. At the head table sat Clara Lalonde, Harland Grant, Gale Robson, and Sara Walton.

Walton checked her watch and began. "Okay, thank you everybody for coming."

The room was a mashup of both plainclothes and uniformed RCMP members. The low murmurs of their voices faded out as Walton continued.

"As many of you know, there has been a sharp increase in the number of dead pimps found around Victoria. During the course of this investigation, Constable Tyson Bent was injured when he attempted to arrest a suspect—"

"What happened?" came a voice from the crowd.

"Details are unclear at the moment," Walton replied. "We only know that he was doing surveillance, called for backup, and sometime between calling and arrival he was assaulted."

"Sounds like he fucked up," chimed another voice.

Lalonde could see the anger on Robson's face and interjected. "If I may?"

Walton nodded.

"We found out after the fact that we're actually searching for two suspects," Lalonde advised. "So, it's not unreasonable to assume he confronted one and the other blindsided him." There were a few nods from the group.

Lalonde continued. "I'm Detective Clara Lalonde, Victoria Police Department. If you open your packages in front of you, we can get you all caught up."

HUNTING PREDATORS

Lalonde walked them through everything from Kevin Marin's disappearance to the boat run ashore at Halfmoon Bay. When finished, she asked, "Any questions?" The group was silent.

Grant stood up and introduced himself before adding, "For now, most of you are on standby. Detective Lalonde and I, as well as six RCMP officers, will conduct ground interviews. We're focusing on any bars, restaurants, or pubs that would have been busy on the night of Saturday, May 20th. It was the holiday weekend, so it would have been busy. We're looking specifically for any physical altercations around 11:00 pm. Our first victim was caught on camera at the Co-op gas bar on the edge of town shortly after 11:20 pm with a freshly kicked ass. We need to find the boot that kicked it. Marin wasn't local. The stores were all closed, so our best bet is the bars."

"What if a tourist kicked his ass?" someone asked.

"We thought about that." Grant said. "In fact, we figured that for a while. It's the boat in Halfmoon Bay. Our assessment is someone whooped Marin's ass, went on a rampage in Victoria, and made their way back here."

The group started murmuring, and Grant continued. "It's a shot in the dark, we know. We've been chasing ghosts for weeks, but right now it's quite literally the only lead we have to go on. If they're not here, then we have zero clue where to even start looking. What we have figured out is if we find them, we need to be able to pounce immediately. Calling for backup and waiting hours for it to arrive won't work. These people have eluded us like experts; anytime we've gotten close, they've vanished."

Lalonde stood up with a clipboard. "David Clark and Robert Pelerin?" Two hands went up. "Heading out of town on Sharp Road is the Dolphin Motel. Each of you takes an unmarked car and heads there. Keep your phones on. When the call comes in, block the highway. Nobody in or out."

The two men got up and made their way out, envelopes in hand.

"Detectives Samir and Duncan?" Lalonde continued. Two more hands went up. "You'll be canvassing the local establishments." They nodded. She called out two more sets of names and gave similar instructions. By 2:30 pm, everyone had their assignments. The eight detectives all set out in different directions. Tofino was a small town with a lot of tourists, but still a small town. With four groups, it shouldn't take more than a few hours.

Chapter 33

Sunday May 28th, 2023, 3:30 pm, Tofino BC

Mike and Sasha made their way to Tim's shop. Sasha was still showing the effects of the beating she had taken, and they decided it would be best to go camping somewhere secluded for a few days. Out of sight, out of mind, with two purposes: the first was to let her heal, and the second was to let things calm down. They pulled up in the yard and made their way to the silver camper van. Mike backed the Range Rover in beside it.

"Shit," he muttered, looking up.

Sasha followed his gaze and saw Tim and Hailey walking towards them.

"Oh, no." Sasha exclaimed, flipping the visor down and looking at her bruised and cut face in the mirror.

"Car accident," Mike said quickly. "You were T-boned in Adem's car." Sasha nodded, and they jumped out.

"Hey hun, how are y—" Hailey's voice cut off when she saw Sasha. "What happened?" she asked, panicked.

Tim looked at Sasha, then an unpleasant look crossed his face when he looked back at Mike.

"We got T-boned in Victoria." Sasha said. "My brother was driving." Hailey immediately helped her to the van.

Turning to Tim, Mike asked, "Got a sec?"

Tim nodded. "A quick one. Taking Hailey to work." The two walked over to the shop.

"What the fuck did you do to her?" Tim asked the second they walked in the door.

"Wasn't me. The fuckers that did it are dealt with." Mike replied. "Listen. We gotta go for a bit. I got some heat."

Tim said nothing, just nodded. "Check in with you in a week or two. When I call, I'll say I'm looking to store my RV. If it's safe, tell me you have room. If not, you're full."

"That shit in the cities. That you?" Tim asked, a bit wide-eyed.

Mike looked at him but didn't say a word. After a minute, Tim nodded. "When are you leaving?"

"Gotta run by the house, load up the last of my things. We'll be on the road in fifteen minutes.

"Damn," Tim mumbled softly. "Sort your business out. Always room for you here." He stuck his hand out. Mike shook it.

"Call you within the week." Mike promised.

5:00 pm

Ahmed Samir and Steve Duncan walked into the last of the bars on their list. It was a small beachfront-style place on the main drag. At 5:00 pm, it was already busy. The barmaid was a short, curvy girl with long black hair and a bright smile that dropped the second she saw them.

"Think she knows we're cops?" Duncan joked.

They walked to the bar and watched as the girl did everything she could to avoid talking to them. Finally, Samir caught her attention.

"Look, the sooner you talk to us, the sooner we'll leave," he proposed.

"What do yas want?" Hailey's voice was equal parts irritation and impatience.

"A few weeks back, on Victoria Day weekend, were you working?" questioned Samir.

"I work every weekend," Hailey replied dryly.

"Was there a fight here around 11:00 pm?" Samir continued.

"There's fights here every weekend," Hailey quipped.

"Think hard. Around 11:00 pm." Samir instructed, his frustration showing.

"Listen, bud," Hailey said, clearly ready for the conversation to be over. "I've worked every day for the last twelve without a break. Most nights I'm here by myself. I don't know what day it is today, let alone what happened a few weeks ago. On long weekends there's always at least two or three dustups. Every goddamn tourist that comes here thinks he's the one guy on the planet that can kick everyone's ass. Add in a long weekend fueled with liquor and who knows what else they're snorting outside, and we have fights pop off all the time. It's a bar." She concluded, her frustration matching Samir's.

Duncan stepped in. "Sorry, ma'am, it's been a long day. A few Saturdays ago, a guy ran into the Co-op gas station beat to shit. The next morning, he was found dead. We have to ask."

The wheels in Hailey's head were turning. She clearly remembers the fight. It was Sasha that attacked the guy. Tim had joined in. But she was with Tim all night; he definitely didn't kill anybody.

"Ma'am?" Duncan's voice snapped her back to the conversation.

"No. I don't remember." She said quickly and hurried away.

Samir and Duncan stood at the bar looking at each other.

"She saw it," Samir commented.

"Yup." Duncan agreed. He followed Hailey to the back area where the pool tables were kept. Hailey was talking to Tim when Duncan confronted her.

"Listen, this wasn't a small dustup, lady. That victim that night was killed, and whoever did it beat him up earlier in this bar."

"Who the fuck are you?" Tim stepped between them, chest out, chin high.

"Detective Steve Duncan, RCMP. Who the fuck are you?"

"I'm her fiancé. What do you want, Dick?"

"To talk to her." The annoyance was not hidden in Duncan's voice.

"She doesn't want to talk to you. More importantly, she doesn't HAVE to talk to you." He turned to Hailey. "You don't have to talk to them. At all." He turned back to Duncan. "You have questions for either of us; you can talk to my lawyer."

"You do all her thinking for her?" Samir asked, joining the group after hearing the escalation.

Tim held his stare, neither one backing down.

"Were you here Saturday of the long weekend?" Duncan asked Tim.

"I'm here every night she works."

HUNTING PREDATORS

"You involved in a fight?" Duncan inquired.

"Been involved in a lot of fights," Tim replied vaguely.

"Look, asshole," Samir's patience was all but gone. He nudged Tim with the back of his hand. "Someone got beat up here then killed shortly after."

Tim, like Hailey, relived the scene in his mind. He knew exactly what night these cops were talking about. And that meant he knew exactly who killed the guy they were talking about.

Tim looked down at the cop's hand that was touching him. Although short, squat, and over fifty, Tim could still move, even if only for a couple seconds. In a quick motion he lunged forward and smashed his right fist into Duncan's nose. Samir reacted right away, but not before Tim landed a second punch, this time on the side of Samir's head. Both cops recovered quickly and tackled Tim to the ground. The scuffle was over as quickly as it started. Tim looked up at Hailey. She already had her phone out and was filming the altercation.

"Film my face," Tim instructed. "I don't have a mark on me. If I'm beat up in court, they did it after I was cuffed!" he yelled, facing the phone.

"I got it all, baby." Hailey advised. "Security cams caught it all too."

By 9:00 pm, Mike and Sasha were set up at Montague Creek Recreational Site. It was really nothing more than a small opening in the woods with a fire pit, but it was well off the main road and quiet. They had initially driven northeast towards Parksville on #4A Highway. Mike had Sasha pull the batteries out of all the electronics, pulled a U-turn, and headed west; they stopped in Campbell River and bought a map.

An hour later, they were set up on the small campsite. Mike got the fire going while Sasha let the dogs splash in the water until the sun went down. She put the pups in the van, then crawled into the folded-down bench that doubled as a bed where Mike was waiting. She crawled closer, and he edged back.

"What's wrong? You're trying to get away from me," she said, trying to sound playful, but there was a tinge of concern in her voice.

"No, not at all. I don't want to hurt you."

The lighting was dim, but Sasha could see his eyes scanning the dark bruising all over her face and body.

"It's fine. I'm pretty tough, ya know," she assured, smiling at him. Even with dark bruising under her eyes and a cut on her lip, her smile was still beautiful.

"I know that." Mike reached out and gently caressed the side of her face with his thumb. "I still feel horrible that happened to you. I didn't want you getting hurt."

"I told you I'm fine. They didn't hurt me," she insisted.

She lay down and curled into him. As he wrapped his arm around her, she asked, "What now?"

Mike sighed. "We stay low for a bit, until the bruising goes down. Then we see Adem."

"Why?" she asked, surprised.

"To say goodbye. We have to leave the island." Mike advised.

Sasha pressed herself back into him. "Bummer," she said wistfully. "I really like it here."

"I know, babe. But they tend to not stop looking for mass murderers. It's better if we keep moving."

"Is that what we are? Mass murderers? I thought we were serial killers." Sasha joked.

"A mass murderer is someone that kills three or more people at one time, in one location," explained Mike.

"I thought that was a serial killer." Sasha mused.

"No. A serial killer is someone who kills three or more people within thirty days, with a cooling-off period in between murders."

"Are you sure?"

"Ummm, yeah. Trust me, I've read up on this." Mike replied. "Technically speaking, you're a mass murderer. I'm a serial killer."

"My god, you silver-tongued bastard. You know how to get a woman's motor running."

"Shut up." He laughed while nudging her away. "Get some sleep. Your body needs it."

9:35 pm

Tim was standing at the doors of the small six-by-eight holding cell. Hailey had called a few of his club brothers, and within four hours, a short man with a long grey ponytail, round gold-rimmed spectacles, and a silver suit blew through the door of the RCMP barracks.

Sara Walton was standing inside the office when she saw him slam his briefcase down on the counter.

"Oh, fuck me," she muttered under her breath. Gathering her composure, she greeted him. "Hello, Greg. Nice to see you."

"Cut the shit, Walton. I'm here for Tim Ciarolo. Turn him loose."

"Have you lost your fucking mind?" Walton barked out a laugh. "He swung on two cops."

"Bullshit he did," the lawyer corrected. "Those two assholes harassed my client and his fiancée, refused to stop questioning when my clients asked for a lawyer, assaulted him, and then arrested him for defending himself."

The man tossed a small black USB stick on the counter. "It's all right there, Walton. Another case of your overzealous assholes making up the rules as they go."

Walton looked at Samir. "Did he ask for a lawyer?"

Samir looked frozen, like a deer in the headlights.

"Yes, he did. It's all on video," the small lawyer said. "You turn him loose, right now. If you're lucky, he'll let bygones be bygones. If I have my way, I'll have him nail your asses to a fucking cross in the town square."

"Who the fuck is this guy?" Samir questioned a little too loudly.

"Shut up." Walton hissed back at him. She cleared her throat. "Release Mr. Ciarolo immediately."

"Are you ki—" Samir's sentence was cut short.

"Now!" Walton snapped.

Detective Samir nodded to a uniformed RCMP behind the counter, who walked to the cell door and opened it.

"The ad online said this was a five-star resort. I definitely won't be returning," Tim joked sarcastically as he walked out. He shook hands with the lawyer and smiled at Detective Samir. "Thanks for your hospitality." He winked and stepped outside.

Hailey was waiting on the sidewalk. She ran to Tim and hugged him. "What the hell was that all about?" she asked Tim, referring to the altercation in the bar.

Tim took her hand, and they started walking. "Gave Mike and Sasha a chance to get out of town."

"Babe," concern flooded Hailey's face. "What's going on?"

"They needed a distraction," Tim explained. "They're gone. And that bought them a few hours."

Hailey had a tinge of sadness on her face. "Damn. I really liked them."

HUNTING PREDATORS

"Me too, babe." Tim agreed.

"Think they'll ever come back?" she asked hopefully.

"Doubtful," replied Tim. "He'll check in with me in a week or so. We have a code set up."

"That's why all those cops are around here? Looking for them?" Hailey guessed. Tim shrugged in response. "I wonder what they did," she added.

"No, you don't." Tim's reply was firm. He was not a stupid man; he'd put two and two together in his shop earlier that day. He also knew some of the lowlifes that were killed in Victoria, and he had to admit. part of him admired Mike for doing it.

"Whatever they did, they had their reasons for it. If anybody ever asks us about them, tell them what you know. She was friendly and worked hard at the bar. He did installations for me. And they were polite and seemed happy."

Hailey nodded. "Hungry?"

"I could eat," he admitted as they made their way back to the bar, having been removed from it by police only a few hours earlier.

Chapter 34

Sunday June 4th, 2023, 2:25 pm.

Clara Lalonde sat in an uncomfortable wrought-iron chair at a matching table that wobbled every time she touched it. She was enjoying the start of summer by having drinks on a patio with friends from high school. She tuned in and out of the conversation, listening to bits and pieces of her friends talking about their kids, husbands, divorces, and families in general.

"You okay?" her friend Kristen asked, noticing Clara's faraway look. The two had been friends since high school.

Clara snapped back to the present. "Yeah, yeah, sorry. Just daydreaming."

"About what?" Kristen inquired.

"Work," Clara admitted, guiltily. Over the years, she had adapted to the fact that her life wasn't on the same track as her friends'. She'd been close with the three girls at the table since they were teenagers, but she had learned that offering up too many details about her work often made them uncomfortable. When asked, she would discuss what she was allowed to, but she had also learned to keep the gory details out of conversation.

"Is it good?" Kristen prodded with a mischievous grin.

"It's something," Clara replied. The other two women stopped talking and gave her their full attention.

HUNTING PREDATORS

"Well?" Kristen said with one eyebrow raised. "Spill it."

Without compromising her investigation, Clara gave the three women a summarized version of the case, starting with Kevin Marin and ending with the boat running ashore.

"Wow!" Kristen exclaimed, wide-eyed. "So where are they now?"

"No. Fucking. Clue." Clara admitted, holding her half-empty pint of beer, rolling it in the sunlight. "They just vanished without a trace."

"I know you can't tell us any details, but you legitimately have no idea who or where they are?" asked Kristin as she leaned forward in her seat.

"Nothing," Clara confirmed. The killings had been front-page news for the first few days, especially after the RCMP released a statement asking if anybody had witnessed a physical altercation in Tofino around 11:00 pm on the Saturday of the long weekend. What followed was over 1,600 phone calls. They'd all seen fights at bars, on the beach, and in parking lots, but all 1,600 callers were drinking at the time, and the fights ranged from 9:00 pm to 4:00 am. None of the sources gave them any new information.

"So, what do you guys do now?" Stephanie, another friend at the table, asked.

"Nothing we can do." Clara sighed. "It's frustrating. We think they may be tied to crimes in other cities, but realistically there is no physical evidence and no witnesses.

Whoever they are, they're very good at what they're doing."

"So, you just sit and wait for them to kill someone else?" Kristen asked incredulously.

Clara shrugged. "It's like nail clippers. When you're looking, you can never find them. Then one day. You move the couch and bam... there they are."

"That's a strange analogy," grinned Kristin.

"That's how this works; we chase our tails for weeks, sometimes months. Then one day the answer falls in your lap." Clara explained. "This one is different though. There's nothing, nothing left behind. We have a few video clips of who we think we're looking for, but they always manage to keep their faces out of the frame. It's bizarre, like they're ghosts."

"Is it true that they were killing pimps?" Kristen could have been a journalist in another lifetime.

"Not just pimps," Clara clarified. "But they were all lowlifes. They were all tied together, one way or another: drug dealers, pimps, hired muscle."

"No innocent victims?"

"Just the girls that were rescued." Clara answered.

Kristen stirred her drink with her straw. "Sounds like they did you a favour."

"Yeah, sure, until they're involved in a shootout at a pharmacy and a father of three takes a bullet in the chest because he was in the wrong place at the wrong time. It's easy to say we want to turn a blind eye to what they're doing, but when an innocent victim does get clipped, it's our fault for not putting a stop to it sooner. It's about what they're doing, not who they're doing it to. They can't be allowed to play judge, jury, and executioner. No matter what I think of their crimes, they're still victims, and this couple is robbing them of due process." Clara stopped, realizing she was a bit agitated. The attack on Tyson Bent had resonated inside her.

"I understand, hon." Kristen replied gently, slurping the last sip of her vodka cranberry through the straw. "But even still, you gotta admit, just a little bit. It's about time."

Clara snorted a laugh and waved at the waitress for another round.

Mike and Sasha had spent the week driving around the western coast of Vancouver Island, mostly avoiding the bigger towns and cities. Mike usually filled up the van, bought food, and handled any dealings with people. They would find small motels or lodges, pay for a night, shower, then hit the road right away and not return. They slept in the van, usually down old logging roads. They lived off the grid with nothing but the stereo in the van and newspapers for updates. The story was starting to fizzle out. Say what you wanted about today's distracted society, but if the cops were looking for you, people tended to forget about it after three or four days.

Mike had decided to check in with Tim to see how things were looking. He stopped in at a Walmart in Campbell River and bought two new burner phones. His first call was to Tim.

Tim answered on the third ring. "T.C. Welding."

"Hey, how are ya. I'm looking for a place to store my RV. A friend said you might be able to help." Mike said, as promised.

"Sorry friend, all booked up." Tim replied without missing a beat.

"Oh really? Completely booked? Can you squeeze me in anywhere?" Mike followed up, testing the waters.

"No can do, amigo. I am at full capacity. Had a few people leave early last week, but it's still packed with more people showing up every day," Tim relayed, hoping Mike would read between the lines.

Mike understood the message. The police presence had died down, but there were still more than the usual few RCMP officers kicking around.

"I was told to mention my friend's name. He's the guy you bought the black Range Rover off of; the one with the busted glove compartment."

Tim was quiet for a second, then said, "Doesn't change things. We're still packed."

"Can you recommend anywhere else?" Mike inquired.

"Only if you want to commute from Victoria." Tim retorted.

"Alright, thanks anyway." Mike conceded. "I'll check in maybe next week to see if there's any openings."

"Do that. Let me know if I can do anything else for you." Tim added and rung off. He was a little confused about the Range Rover comment. He went out to look at the newer SUV. He opened the gas cap and found the keys, clicked the unlock button, and looked through the interior. As he opened the glove box, he found an envelope with T & H scribbled on it. He opened it up and found a signed copy of the ownership with a bill of sale saying Tim bought the Range Rover for $14,000. Also inside was a small, folded piece of paper scrawled with Sasha's pretty handwriting and a small wad of hundred-dollar bills.

Looks like we can't make the wedding. Please transfer this into your name. Consider it a wedding present. M&S

Tim looked at the black SUV and the note and smiled.

Mike rung off with Tim and looked at Sasha. "Tofino is out of the question. Cops everywhere. Tim suggested his friend in Victoria might be able to help us get off the island."

Mike handed the other phone to Sasha.

"If the cops were by Adem's or he saw you on TV, would he tell you?"

"Oh, definitely," she replied. "He might not come out and say it, but I'd know. If he's joking or happy like he normally is on the phone, we're okay. If he's serious, then something is up."

Mike nodded, and she dialed. Adem answered right away.

"Hey," Sasha greeted. "We were thinking of coming for a visit. You guys busy?"

"Cool! When can I expect you?" Adem's voice sounded chipper.

"Maybe, 7:00 pm tonight? Not staying long." Sasha advised.

"Sounds rad. See you then."

Sasha rang off and put the phone in her pocket. She looked up at Mike. "What's the plan?"

"We'll stop over at his place. I may need tomorrow to set up our exit. We'll need someone to get the van and the pups back on the mainland." He put his arm around Sasha as they walked back to the van.

"Once we're off the island, the heat will die down. If they knew who we were or what we were driving, they would have released it by now, even if they were trying to keep it hush-hush. After a week they'd have released it."

"So, we're okay?" Sasha asked.

"Not at all," Mike cautioned her. "The reason I've been able to do what I do is I've learned to nail people when they don't expect it. From now until we're driving out of the city of Vancouver, we stay on guard 24/7. Lazy people get caught, and at this stage, getting caught and thrown in prison is probably the best outcome."

"Gotcha," Sasha replied, flipping her sunglasses open and sliding them on dramatically.

Mike couldn't help but chuckle. "You're a dork."

7:08 pm

They pulled up in front of Adem's to find him standing on the small front porch with the door wide open, the same way he always did when waiting for them. A look of confusion crossed his face when he saw the van. His confusion quickly turned to concern when he saw his sister get out. Most of the bruising had subsided, but she was still showing the marks from the attack.

"What happened?" Adem asked, a hint of panic in his voice.

Sasha gave him a reassuring hug. "Got in an accident last week."

Adem returned her hug, then pushed her away so he could get another look at her. "Why didn't you call me?"

"I texted you on Monday," Sasha lied. "You didn't get it?"

"N-No." Confusion returned to Adem's face. He looked at Mike. "Why didn't you call?"

Mike nodded towards Sasha. "I asked her if she wanted me to. She said she messaged you. After that I was a little busy taking care of her."

"I'm fine!" Sasha interjected forcefully. "Some asshole from California blew through a stop sign and hit me. I'm okay. The Range Rover is toast, though," she added as she limped up the stairs.

"Car shopping then?" Adem guessed.

"No. Coming for a visit, then we're hitting the road for a bit." Sasha advised, leaning against the kitchen island. "We're going north for a while. Hit the Arctic Circle. Drive across Canada. I love Tofino, but it's getting too busy. I prefer it before summer or in the fall."

"You're coming back though, right?" Adem did his best to hide his disappointment, but Sasha could hear it in his voice.

"Probably in the fall," Mike reassured. "Need a favour though?"

"What's that?" Adem asked, eager to assist.

"Gotta spend a few days in Vancouver. She has a follow-up with two specialists," Mike nodded towards Sasha. "Then we're setting out. Having a hard time finding somewhere we can bring the dogs. Would you mind bringing them across on the ferry for us? We're leaving the day after tomorrow. If you could meet us Friday night or Saturday morning, that'd be a huge help."

Adem, not needing much of a reason to take the ninety-five-minute ferry ride to Vancouver, agreed.

Chapter 35

Monday June 5th, 2023, 8:00 am.

Mike woke up early and went through the morning routine of feeding the dogs and taking Oscar the Trash Dog for his early morning run. When he returned, Sasha was awake, sitting at the island in the kitchen. Oscar headed right for her, tail wagging so hard his whole hind end swung with it.

"Breakfast?" she offered, walking over to the fridge to see what options they might have.

"No, I'm good." Mike answered. "I need to take the day to set up our way out. If all goes well, we'll be leaving tomorrow morning."

"What do you need from me?" She moved from the fridge to the coffee maker. Breakfast or no breakfast, she knew Mike would want a coffee.

"Nothing. Hang out with the pups. Relax. The only thing we have to worry about now is whether or not the cops know who we are. And at this point, if they did, they'd have busted down the door at 4:00 am."

Mike showered, kissed Sasha, and started to head out. He turned to her just before he stepped out the door. "Keep an eye on the news; it's been over a week, so I'm sure they'll be talking about some idiotic hockey player's TikTok account by now, but if you see anything related, let me know right away."

Mike's first stop was to visit Angela. They met for coffee at a small local cafe. Angela was already there when Mike arrived.

"Morning," she greeted him with a big hug. She touched his chin and turned his face, looking at the almost-healed cut on his cheek from the week before. "Looks better. Gonna leave a nice scar, though."

"I'll add it to the pile." He winked as he sat down.

"How's Sasha?" Angela asked.

"Good. They roughed her up a bit, but she fought tooth and nail. Looks like she was in a rollover accident, though." Mike answered, taking the coffee cup Angela had placed in front of him.

"So? What now?

"We're leaving." Mike said bluntly. "Things got out of control. We gotta put some distance between us and the area."

Angela had anticipated this, but it still stung. She reached across the table and took his hand. "Damn," she sighed. "I just got you back, and you're leaving again."

"I'm not much for social media." Mike explained, handing her a piece of paper. "That's a fake Facebook profile. I made it last night. Send it a friend request. At least this way we can stay in touch."

Angela took the paper and saw the name John Smith. "Jesus, Mikey, there's gotta be a million John Smiths on Facebook."

"This account has a black-and-white picture of you and me from when we were 12. We were on a boat on the Detroit River. Hometown is listed as Regina, Saskatchewan."

Angela nodded. "Anything else?"

"The plan is to be gone by tomorrow evening. You can watch my back 'til then." He smiled and stood up.

Angela hugged him tightly. "Please take better care of yourself, Mikey. You look like shit."

Mike squeezed her back but didn't say anything. He let go, walked to the door, and looked back in time to see Angela's welcoming smile drop at the sides as her eyes welled with tears. Mike paused and tried to take everything in as he looked at her one last time. He gave an awkward half smile as he tried to hide his sadness. He turned and left.

Mike's next stop was at the same scrapyard that he had acquired the Mustang from less than a month ago. He pulled the big silver van into the lot and was met by the owner.

"How'd 'em wheels work for ya?" Asked a short man with half his teeth missing, dressed in oily coveralls.

"Real good," Mike praised appreciatively. "I've got an ask. Pays well."

"Oh?" The man's eyes widened at the offer. "What's that?"

"I need this beauty taken from Nanaimo to Vancouver on the ferry." Mike explained, patting the side of the van.

"That's it?" The man asked, surprised. "How much it pay?"

"A thousand bucks," Mike offered. "There's a catch though." The man said nothing, just waited. "There will be a locked suitcase in the back under the bench."

"Do I want to know what's in it?" the man asked.

"No. You definitely don't." Mike's tone wasn't threatening, but the man got the point. "One thousand dollars, cash money, but the trailer's gotta be on the ferry from Nanaimo and in Vancouver by tomorrow morning."

"$1,500. I'll drive it myself." The owner countered.

"$2,000, and you give me a set of wheels for today." Mike shot back.

"Deal." They shook hands, and the man in the oily coveralls set Mike up with a black 2004 Chevy Impala.

Mike was surprised with the car. The body was in decent shape. The engine ran smoothly. It was showing 311,000 km, but he'd only need it for maybe thirty-six hours.

Mike's third stop was at a pharmacy with a post office. He shipped a box to his friend Dave, who owned property in Nelson, B.C. Mike had worked with Dave years ago in Northern Alberta. Mike and Sasha had stopped at his place on their drive out west the year before. Mike had stashed $25,000 in cash there just in case. Mike and Dave had worked out a deal; if Dave ever received a package from Vancouver Island, he was to receive it but not open it. In return, when Mike rolled through town a few days later, $10,000 of the $25,000 would be his. They knew each other well. Mike trusted him, and Dave knew better than to ask what was in the box.

Mike walked out of the pharmacy, keeping his eyes open for anybody trying to rush up on him, police or otherwise. He saw neither. With that he let out a slow breath. His bases were covered. Most of his weapons were in the van on their way to Nanaimo, then Vancouver. The cash they had was being shipped to Nelson. Mike had $7,000 on him, and Adem was going to bring the dogs to Vancouver on Saturday. He made his way back to the black Impala.

He made it back to Adem's early. Sasha had been pacing the house. The dogs, having kept pace with her for the first hour, had given up and were napping on the couch near the door where they could lazily keep an eye on her. Mike was used to the planning, the hiding, the waiting. Sasha wasn't. Her anxiety was through the roof.

"Can we do something?" Sasha pleaded.

"We really shouldn't go out, babe." Mike replied regretfully.

"I know, it's just..." Sasha paced and looked out the window. "I can't just sit here."

Mike sighed. "Okay, want to walk through Beacon Hill?" referring to a nearby park, one of Sasha's favourite places to visit in Victoria.

Her face lit up. "Yes, please." Sasha grabbed a lightweight jacket, scratched the dogs behind their ears, and followed Mike to the Impala.

Chapter 36

Monday June 5th, 2023, 10:00 am.

Clara Lalonde and Harland Grant were both feeling like they'd dropped the ball. It had been over a week since they were in Tofino, and they still had no leads. Two RCMP detectives thought checking out a small bar's security footage would be worth a look, which initially seemed promising. They had questioned the bartender and fought with her boyfriend. They contacted the owner and found out the security footage was stored on a 128 GB SD card, but it was set up to record over itself every four days. Another dead end.

After the explosion and the boat running ashore, there had been nothing else. It was like the suspect (or suspects) had just vanished into thin air. Both Lalonde and Grant had worked and cracked tough cases before, but this was different. They needed a lead.

On Monday, Chief Hamill had suggested revisiting the motel rooms and William Barich's apartment. Maybe a fresh look would jar something. Both Lalonde and Grant figured he was giving them 'make work' projects until the next case came along, but with pimps and scumbags being slaughtered a week before, the Victoria underworld had gotten pretty quiet.

They spent the morning visiting the motel rooms. Crime techs and forensics had gone over each room multiple times. They revisited William's apartment. Again, techs and forensics had dissected the place. The only thing they came up with was that type AB negative blood drops in the closet matched the blood on the broken glass, but they had no one to compare it to.

At 11:30 am they broke for lunch at a small pub near Beacon Hill Park. They sat at a small bistro table and each ordered sandwiches and coffees. Clara excused herself to go to the washroom. She didn't need the facilities; she just wanted to wash her hands after being in William Barich's apartment again, and there wasn't enough Purell on the island to make her feel clean.

She was scrubbing her hands when the stall door opened, and a shorter, muscular girl stepped out. She had short hair almost completely hidden by a black military-style cap. Her face had some bruising; a cut running vertically down from her bottom lip was visible. Clara didn't think much of it at first. She'd been a cop for almost two decades; she'd seen battered women but also crossed paths with women who had taken soccer balls or hockey pucks in the face, been in car accidents, and gotten drunk and tripped over dogs. Seeing a well-built girl in her mid-twenties with bruises and scars didn't send up any red flags.

It wasn't until the girl bent down at the sink to wash her hands that Clara could see a little bit down the front of her loose-fitting shirt. She immediately noticed the large, colourful tattoo across the woman's chest. Clara's eyes flickered to the girl's face in the mirror. The girl returned her gaze with a bright smile. She was a very pretty girl, if not for the bruises, and she had the most piercing blue eyes Clara had ever seen. Her heart skipped.

"Car accident," Sasha explained, seeing the woman's face.

"Oh, I wasn't..." Clara stuttered.

"It's fine, love. The last week and a half I've been getting a lot of stares and advice to 'leave him.'"

"You're okay though?" Clara said, snapping back to the present.

"Yes. A little sore for a bit, but it could have been a lot worse." Sasha pushed the button on the air blower, let it dry her hands, and left.

Clara stood almost in shock. This couldn't be real. They'd been chasing ghosts for weeks, and suddenly, in a bathroom at a pub at lunchtime. There she was. *Nail clippers*, thought Clara. Surely it couldn't be that easy.

She dried her hands and rushed back to the table, almost tripping over another chair.

"I think I just saw her!" she whispered loudly.

"Her, who?" Grant barely looked up from his phone.

"Sasha! She was in the bathroom." Her eyes scanned the pub, but there was no sign of her. Lalonde looked across the street and saw the woman reach the other sidewalk. A large man was waiting for her, and they walked towards the park hand in hand.

"There!" she directed, pointing.

Skeptical and unamused, Grant followed Lalonde's gaze and saw the couple: a short woman and a large man. He felt a spike of adrenaline. "Shit," he snapped as he jumped out of his seat. The two set off after them.

Mike and Sasha walked the two blocks down Oliphant Road towards Heywood and the park entrance.

"You okay?" Sasha asked, concerned. "You're quiet."

"We're being followed." Mike replied calmly. "Two people, a man and a woman, about thirty yards back."

"How do you..." Sasha stopped herself. She knew better than to ask if he was sure. "What do we do?"

"When we get into the park, we split. You go right; I'll go left. Don't just bolt, though; they'll give chase. Act like we're separating for a few minutes. Just behave like I'm running over to the restroom, and I'm going to meet you after. As soon as you're out of their sight, run. Go about twenty yards and wait. You'll see them cross into the park. You'll have to be quick, but head back towards the pub. Find a taxi, a bus, anything—get on it and get back to the small beachfront motel near Adem's and wait for me."

"What are you gonn—" Her sentence was cut short.

"Just trust me. Don't get stopped. Take three or four taxis if you need to. You'll have to be quick." Mike said sternly. They entered the park together. Mike pointed left. Sasha pointed right, and they walked in separate directions.

"Shit, they're splitting up," Lalonde observed.

"I'll follow him; you stick with her," Grant instructed. They continued at the same pace, fighting the urge to run in. They crossed Heywood and walked into the park. Clara looked to her right; she couldn't see Sasha. There was a trail visible that veered to the left. She gave

Grant a quick nod and set off walking quickly, hoping to close the distance.

Sasha had been hiding in a tree line. She watched the two people cross the street and come towards her; definitely cops. As they walked into the park, Sasha bolted back across Heywood Street through an apartment complex. She came out onto Vancouver Street and ran down Sutlej Street back to Cook. She came out in front of the pub where the cop had first seen her. Sasha was ecstatic to see a taxi dropping off a fare. She waved; the driver waved back, and she jumped in.

Mike split to his left and walked faster, eventually running. He knew from a previous visit there were washrooms not far away, so he made his way towards them. As he passed a set of shrubs, he chanced a look back. The male cop was jogging; he slowed when Mike did, trying not to be seen. Mike walked around the side of the bushes, ducked into them, and waited.

Harland Grant jogged to the restroom. He figured the big guy had gone in. He drew his service pistol and crept inside. Looking low, he didn't see any feet in the stalls. He walked down the line, checking all three by gently nudging the doors. Nobody there. Aside from Grant, the restroom was empty. "Shit," he grunted, putting his weapon back in the holster.

He figured the big guy must have kept going. He was thinking about what else was in this area of the park that would cause the big guy to separate from the girl. Walking back out the door, he caught a glimpse of movement and was knocked back inside.

HUNTING PREDATORS

Mike watched the cop jog by, watched him pull his weapon, and then head into the bathroom. He waited outside and listened. He didn't hear anything; no talking, no panicked voices from someone taking a leak who was suddenly startled by a man running in holding a gun. Just as Mike had concluded that the cop was alone, he heard a voice mumble, "Shit," then heard footsteps coming back. As the cop walked into the doorway, Mike threw a clean left hand that landed square on the man's forehead and knocked him back into the wall, but to Mike's surprise, he didn't go down.

Mike stepped in and fired off two more power shots, first a right then a left. The cop staggered and stumbled deeper into the bathroom but continued to stay on his feet. *Fuck me*, Mike thought; *dude can take a punch*.

In the split second it took for Mike to process that thought, Harland Grant was able to recover enough to realize he was in a fight now. He smirked a little as he stepped towards Mike.

Mike snapped out a jab with his right hand. Harland slipped to the outside, torqued at the waist, and hit Mike with a solid blow to his ribs on the right side. Harland followed with an overhand right that barely missed its mark, grazing the side of Mike's head. Both men took a fraction of a second to reset.

Their eyes met; in that moment they both knew this wasn't just a fight. If Mike lost, he was going to prison for the rest of his life. If Harland lost, he fully believed this guy would kill him. Harland reached for his gun. Mike stepped forward and kicked him in the chest. Harland was knocked back into the divider between two stall doors, the air escaping his lungs on impact.

Mike threw a four-punch combination, landing two. Harland somehow managed to slip the last two and countered with his own combo. Again, he reached for his gun. Mike responded with a straight left between the eyes and a right uppercut. Blood flew from Harland's mouth.

Harland reached out with both hands and grabbed Mike by the shoulders. The old-school hockey player in him grabbed Mike's collar with his left hand and started punching with the right. Mike, having boxed his entire life, was happy to let him fight one-handed. Both men started throwing heavy power shots. After taking two, Mike began deflecting Harland's punches with his left hand while striking with his right and following with his own left.

Harland would swing, get hit, have his punch blocked, and get hit again with the hand that blocked it. This exchange didn't last long, maybe ten seconds, but it felt like the longest ten seconds either man had ever lived through.

Harland realized he was getting nowhere. He stepped in and drove a knee into Mike's ribs. Mike let out a loud "oof." The ribs didn't break, but it felt like they did. Mike pushed Harland back, swung twice, landing both hits clean. Harland took them both and kept coming forward.

Mike knew how to punch. Seldom did he ever have to throw more than one or two punches to knock someone out. But every now and then, when he was boxing, he would face someone that could eat his best shots all day long and wouldn't slow down. Harland Grant was one of those people.

Mike decided right there that trading punches wasn't going to work. This wasn't a battle for a girl's

HUNTING PREDATORS

honour outside a bar; this wasn't a heated argument that turned physical between friends where they'd shake hands afterwards. This was literally life and death. Mike threw a short left hook that landed square and grabbed ahold of Harland, forcing his head down. Mike had trained in MMA a few years prior and had learned one of the core principles of any grappling sport: when you control the head, you can control the body.

Mike pushed Harland's head lower and spun around him, taking his back. He tried a rear naked choke but couldn't lock it in. Harland put his foot on the sink and pushed back, slamming Mike through a stall door. The toilet hit him in the back of his legs, forcing him into a sitting position. Mike lost his grip.

Harland stepped forward and turned to face him again. Mike shot forward and grabbed Harland in a double-leg takedown, forcing his way forward. He knocked Harland off balance, causing him to land on his back. Mike kept his body tight to Harland's and slid his legs off to Harland's right side. Mike now had side control and smashed his left elbow down twice onto Harland's face. Harland tried to block, but Mike shot up, putting his knee on Harland's stomach.

He hammer-fisted downward again. As Harland raised his hand to block it, Mike grabbed his wrist, sat back, and threw his left leg over Harland's face and his right leg across Harland's chest in a textbook armbar. But this wasn't the gym floor on the mats; there would be no tap out. Mike wrenched back and raised his hips. An audible snap was heard as Mike broke Harland's right forearm. Harland roared with pain.

Mike let go and hopped up. Harland followed. Mike couldn't believe what he was seeing: Harland was back up on his feet and challenging Mike, who wasted no time.

He reached out and grabbed Harland's left arm near the back of the triceps. Mike dropped to his ass, sticking his left foot into Harland's stomach, causing Harland to bend at the waist. Extending his left arm, Mike wrapped his right leg around Harland's shoulder and rolled up into a sitting position, forcing Harland's head onto the floor in an *omoplata*, not the easiest submission to secure, but a very dangerous position for Harland to be in. Mike cranked his hips and heard another snap as Harland's left shoulder was ripped from the socket.

Mike released the hold. Harland was on his knees trying to stand.

"Stay down, goddammit," Mike said, short of breath. "I don't want to kill you, but I will if I have to."

Harland, with a separated shoulder and broken forearm, tried to reach for his gun again. Mike took a leaping step forward and soccer kicked him under the chin, finally knocking him out. He reached in and took Harland's pistol before cuffing his hands behind his back and laying him in the recovery position. Mike checked himself in the mirror. He had some bruising, but it wasn't too bad. Mike checked outside. No one was there. He set off to find Sasha.

Clara Lalonde was kicking herself. She had somehow lost the girl. She backtracked to the entrance and kept going down the pathway Grant had taken. She made it past a set of bushes near the public bathroom when a young Asian man in his mid-twenties came rushing out in a hurry.

"Call the police!" He shouted to her, panic in his voice.

"I am the police," she replied, her stomach dropping. She knew something had happened to Grant. She shoved past the man into the restroom and saw Harland Grant, beaten and bloodied, his hands behind his back.

"He was like that when I came in," the young man explained.

Lalonde dropped to his side and checked his vitals. He was breathing, just knocked out. She fumbled for her handcuff key, undid the cuffs, and heard him groan when she did it.

"Keep an eye on him," she said to the young man, then stepped outside and dialled 9-1-1.

1:04 pm

Clara was sitting in the hallway outside the emergency room at Royal Jubilee Hospital. Harland Grant had been rushed in via ambulance and moved to the top of the wait list in the emergency room. Gale Robson made her way in, walking with purpose.

"What the hell happened?" Robson asked, rushing in and hugging Clara.

"We saw our suspects," Clara advised. Her face was void of emotions. "Followed them into Beacon Hill Park. They must have spotted us. As soon as they entered, they split up. I followed her; Grant went after the male. Not sure how, but she slipped me right away. I mean, in the time it took me to walk twenty-five yards through the entrance, she was gone. No trace. Grant followed the male. Must have tried to confront him in the restroom."

"Is Harland okay?" Worry lines creased Robson's forehead.

"He'll live, but he's far from okay. They're still triaging him. Both the radius and ulna are busted in the right arm. The left shoulder is a mess, ripped out of the socket, and the clavicle is broken. His face..." She paused, composed herself, and continued. "They must have scrapped it out. Harland was badly beaten. He has a bad concussion and a broken nose. He's a mess."

Robson said nothing. She sat beside Lalond and held her hand. "Harland is a tough, tough, durable man. He'll be fine."

"We shouldn't have separated," Clara sighed. "We both should have stayed with the male. He's the more dangerous of the two. We knew better, especially after Tyson. We shouldn't have separated." Clara was going to blame herself. And no amount of reassurance would change her mind. "How is Bent, by the way?"

"He was released the day before yesterday." Robson advised with a small smile. "He'll be off another month or so. We'll try to reintroduce him with modified duties. They saved his eye, thank God. But he's..." Gale paused. "Different. He's not the same."

"How so?" Clara asked, looking concerned.

"His whole attitude, his demeanor. He's not the same. Took a really bad concussion. Still can't be around bright lights. I checked on him yesterday. His apartment was completely darkened out. I think getting hurt messed with his head, though. He seemed nervous, scared almost. I don't know if he'll ever fully recover."

Clara didn't bother with the clichés like *"I'm sure he'll be fine."* Both women had been in law enforcement long enough to know sometimes people didn't come back. Tyson wasn't the type to milk the system, but the mental and emotional ramifications of what he'd suffered could be enough to end his career, never mind the lasting physical damage. Vertigo, migraine headaches, and anxiety attacks were all not only possible but also common.

"Detective Lalonde?" A man's voice broke through Clara's reverie.

Clara looked up and saw a doctor standing in front of her. "Yes?"

"We're prepping Detective Grant for surgery. We need to reset his right forearm, as well as repair his left shoulder. He'll be in surgery for approximately eight hours. If you'd like to leave, we can have someone contact you when he's moved to recovery."

Clara said nothing, just nodded.

"Does he have family?" Robson asked when the doctor left.

"His mother. She's on the Haisla Territory up near Kitimat. We're booking her a flight out of Terrace. She'll be in tonight."

"What can I do?" Robson offered.

"Nothing, thank you. I'm going to go home and wait for them to call." Clara replied, referring to the hospital staff. "I need to think."

Gale squeezed her hand. "Phone's on if you need me." She didn't wait for a response as she got up and left.

Clara walked outside shortly thereafter. Two Victoria Police cruisers were parked outside the ER doors. She recognized one of the uniformed officers.

"Hey, Craig."

"Detective," he nodded. "How's Detective Grant?"

"In surgery. Mind giving me a lift back to Cook Street? Our ride is still there."

"Sure thing, ma'am." He nodded to the other uniformed officer, who took the cue to leave.

She hopped in the front seat of the Dodge Charger, which had been retrofitted with the Victoria Police insignia.

"There are a lot of rumours floating around about this case, Clara," Craig commented, backing out of his parking spot.

"Well, there's never any shortage of those. Anything juicy?"

"Just that the suspects are a couple, and they keep vanishing then popping back up."

"That's not a rumor. It's pretty accurate." Clara confirmed, staring out the window.

"Is it true they killed a shit-ton of people back east?" Craig asked.

"It's suspected. Nothing concrete. But given the way these two have been out here, it's a safe bet."

Clara had known Craig for a while. He was from Alberta originally. He'd been on the Victoria PD almost as long as Clara and was married to a friend of hers from high school.

"Cops back east have nothing?"

"Not really," she said absently, but that got her wheels turning. She dug her phone out and made a phone call.

"Robson." Gale answered right away.

"Can you get me a phone number for Steve Parent with the OPP?" Clara asked, her voice hurried.

"Wait one," Robson said. Clara sat patiently; her phone buzzed next to her ear when Robson came back on the line. "Just sent it via text; you should have it."

"Got it, thanks." She rung off.

Craig dropped Clara off at her car outside the pub. She pulled up Steve Parent's contact card from Robson and called him.

"Detective Lalonde," Parent answered, sounding overly happy. "To what do I owe the pleasure?"

"You were right," she began, unamused.

"I'm always right; be more specific."

As much as she detested this man, she couldn't help but smile at his comment. "We crossed paths with who we believe were Mike and Sasha. Tailed them to a park. They split up; we followed. I lost Sasha—"

"And Mike knocked the shit out of Grant," Steve finished on her behalf.

"Correct." Lalonde said bracing for the inevitable *told ya so*, but it didn't come.

"What do you need from me?" Parent asked with genuine concern in his voice.

"Advice, an opinion, anything. I don't really know." Lalonde admitted. "You've dealt with him; what should I do here?"

Steve was silent for a few seconds. Clara was surprised. She thought she was going to have to swallow her pride and take at least some shit from him, maybe a little gloating on his end. But there was none. He was completely professional.

"Again, my contact with him was limited." Steve reminded her. "But I'd hazard a guess that they're fleeing if they haven't left already. They have an alarmingly high body count, plus two seriously injured cops. He's not stupid; he's either left the island already or he's working on it now and will be gone within a few hours. I doubt he's flying; that requires ID. But then again, he may think you suspect that, and he'll walk right out the front door. How many people at your disposal?"

"The whole goddamn department right now." Lalonde advised.

"Give me a hard number," requested Steve.

Clara thought for a few seconds. "Upwards of fifty. I have VPD and RCMP ready to go."

"Fifty." Steve repeated. "I'd suggest sending ten to the airport. Keep an eye out for Mike and Sasha, together and individually. He's smart; he may put her on a ferry and fly out himself or vice versa. Delegate the rest to the ferry terminals. My money is on them leaving the island as soon as possible."

"Do you have anything on him? Appearance, tattoos, anything?" she pleaded.

"Detective, if I had it, I'd tell you. The only thing I was told came from someone that saw him in a bar fight, and it was weeks after the fact. She said he looked like a boxer. When I pressed it, she said her uncle used to box and had the same look. Flattened nose, some scars. Look for a big boxer and a small, jacked, tattooed woman."

"Given what happened to Grant, I'm about 99% sure I was face-to-face with Sasha this afternoon. I'll recognize her. It's hard to just stop a big guy with a battered face when we have nothing else to go on." Clara added.

"If I had any info, I'd share it," Steve promised. "I'd put money on them leaving the island, though. Exactly how they're leaving, I don't know."

"If you think of anything, please let me know." Clara requested.

"I have some vacation coming up. I could come out to the island. Buy you dinner?" Steve offered.

Clara didn't hide her laughter as she hung up.

HUNTING PREDATORS

Clara first called Chief Hamil, then Gale Robson. She explained her conversation to both. She asked Gale to man the Nanaimo ferry depots. Robson delegated fifteen RCMP at each, plus another twelve for the Victoria Airport. Chief Hamil sent twenty to the Seaspan Ferry at Swartz Bay, north of Victoria.

Lalonde rung off, hopped in the unmarked SUV, and headed for the Swartz Bay ferry terminal.

Chapter 37

Tuesday June 6th, 2023, 1:10 pm.

Sasha had taken three different taxis, the first to Hillside Shopping Center. She entered via the main door, walked to the first clothing store she saw, and bought a new shirt. She put it on in the changing room, then went out another door to a cab stand. She hopped into another taxi. This time she was dropped off in the core of the downtown corridor of Victoria at Yates and Government.

She walked two blocks, flagged another taxi, and took it back to Royal Beach Park, which was within walking distance of both Adem's and the small seaside hotel where Mike had asked her to meet him. She stopped at a convenience store, bought a bottle of water, and casually set off walking towards the hotel. A block before she reached it, a black Chevy Impala rolled up beside her. The passenger window rolled down to reveal Mike smiling at her.

"Hey sailor! Need a ride into town?" Mike asked with his eyebrow raised.

Sasha's big, bright smile crossed her face. She jumped into the passenger seat. "Hey babe!" She fastened her seat belt. "Any trouble?"

"Some," Mike understated. Sasha looked at him and saw the early signs of swelling and bruising on his face.

"Oooh, are you okay?" she asked, panic in her voice.

"Fine. Had a pretty intense scuffle with that cop. He's a tough, tough man." Mike said with a hint of admiration in his voice.

Sasha had reached over, both trying to examine him and comfort him at the same time. "I'm fine." Mike assured her again. "I'll be sore for a couple of days. I've been through a lot worse. But we need to assume they know who we are. They were tailing us."

"I bumped into her in the bathroom," Sasha commented.

"Where?"

"At the pub where we ate lunch. I came out of the stall, and she was washing her hands. She looked at me in the mirror. She kept looking at me like she'd seen a ghost. I thought she was looking at the bruising..."

Mike thought for a second. The pub had been empty when they were there. They ate, he paid, and Sasha ran to the bathroom while he waited outside. He remembered the other couple; they were just sitting down when Mike stepped outside. "Well, I'll be dipped in shit," Mike said, smiling. "That was a completely coincidental encounter."

Sasha looked at the fresh battle scars on Mike's face. "I'm so sorry. I know you said we should stay out of sight; I just..."

"It's fine," Mike interrupted. "You were a nervous wreck. I thought a walk would do you some good. It's over now, but we have to leave. Now. Next ferry to Vancouver, we need to be on it. That was way too close a call. And..." Mike paused.

"And?" she asked.

"And I really hurt that cop," he admitted.

Mike had to hand it to Harland Grant. He was one of the toughest men Mike had ever locked horns with. Mike did what he had to do in the bathroom, but he had no shame in admitting that Harland Grant deserved respect for the fight he put up. A small part of Mike felt some guilt for the recovery Grant had ahead of him.

"That's the second cop I've sent to the hospital," Mike continued. "They're going to pull out all the stops now. We either leave the island now or we go back into hiding for the next month. But all our gear, money, the pups, everything—we leave it all behind."

Sasha understood what he was saying. Mike wasn't overly dramatic. If he was saying they needed to leave, then they needed to leave. She called Adem.

"Y'ello!" he answered, sounding chipper.

"Hey. My doctor just called. They asked if I could go for the follow-up tomorrow morning. So, we're going to head over today. Are you still good to bring the pups on Saturday?"

"Roger Roger." Adem replied.

"Thanks. I'll call you Friday evening." She promised and rung off. "Okay, let's make like a tree and get out of here." She dramatically flipped her shades on again, staring straight ahead and trying not to smile. Mike shook his head and started for the Swartz Bay ferry terminal.

Clara Lalonde was parked at the Swarts Bay terminal. She'd been watching the unmarked police cars roll in. She watched as a large tactical armoured personnel carrier drove in. She grabbed her phone and called Hamil.

"Sir, get that tank out of here!" she said through gritted teeth, not attempting to hide her anger. "If they see that thing, they'll turn around and leave."

"We have a full SWAT team in there. We need it. I'll make sure they stay out of sight." Hamil promised.

Clara got out of her car and walked to the terminal. The ferry ran eight times a day and could carry up to 310 cars and over 1500 passengers. This time of year, the terminal was packed.

"Detective," Clara heard as she walked by. She looked back and saw another plainclothes officer leaning on a vending machine.

"Hi Dale," she greeted, smiling.

"What are we looking for?" Dale asked.

"Large man, shorter woman, may be travelling alone or together. He looks like a fighter. She has tattoos."

Dale stared at her with a blank expression on his face. "This is a joke, right? A short, tattooed woman leaving Vancouver Island? There's fifteen of them in my line of sight right now!"

"Just keep an eye out for anybody fitting that description looking like they don't want to be seen." Clara instructed.

HUNTING PREDATORS

"Jesus, we're looking for a needle in a stack of other needles." Dale muttered as Clara walked away.

Clara returned to her car and was running through possibilities in her mind as she sat. Would she recognize someone fitting the male's description? Would she recognize the girl again? What if they were separate? What if they were driving and bought tickets online? She had no idea what kind of vehicle to look for. What if she flew out? What if she was leaving from Nanaimo?

Clara's spiral came to a complete standstill when she looked outside and saw the short, tattooed woman, now wearing a red t-shirt, standing with a big guy. Her immediate thought was she was hallucinating. When she realized it was real, she watched them for a few more seconds. She noted how they constantly avoided cameras. It was like they knew where the lenses were at all times and managed to hide their faces.

She keyed the mic on her wrist. "Suspects in sight. Female, red t-shirt, black jeans, black cap. Male, Black t-shirt, blue jeans, black ball cap. Walking into the Land's End Café."

She heard several responses of, "Copy" and "En route.".

Mike and Sasha parked the Impala in the big lot and walked into the small café. They had an hour before the next ferry left and figured a coffee and a snack would help the time pass. Sasha ordered while Mike used the washroom.

When he came out, he noticed the roadway way out front seemed busier. He chalked it up to a rush of people trying to catch the ferry. They were planning on leaving the Impala there. Eventually it would get towed; it wasn't tied to anything they had done, but they gave it a good wipe down anyway. Sasha handed Mike his coffee, and they walked out through the main door.

"FREEZE!" A woman's voice yelled. It seemed like twenty people just appeared out of nowhere. They were hunkered down behind flowerpots, vehicles, and parking barriers. They just appeared with guns drawn.

"Don't fucking move!" the woman's voice yelled.

"Babe?" Sasha asked, fear in her voice.

Mike, slowly raising his hands, quietly whispered. "Just wait. When I say run. We run. You follow me."

"Both of you, on your knees. Right now." The woman's voice ordered. Neither of them moved. "NOW!" She yelled.

Clara Lalonde had the couple in her sights. They had left the café too soon, before anybody could be positioned behind it. That didn't matter, though; there wasn't much behind the café, just a parking lot full of tractor trailers.

"I'm not going to ask again!" Clara yelled. "On your knees, now!" There was a loud snap, like a bullwhip cracking over her head, and the empty car beside her exploded. A loud roar, with intense heat. Clara was thrown a few feet and slammed down into the blacktop. She didn't lose consciousness; she was just confused for a second. She shook her head and got back to her feet. Police were running towards her. She looked at the café; the couple was gone.

HUNTING PREDATORS

"Are you okay?" A uniformed Victoria cop checked in on her.

"Where'd they go?" Clara asked, panicking. She took a step towards the café, but her knee gave out.

She heard a fire extinguisher spraying. There were people everywhere, some shouting, some asking her questions. "Where'd they go?" she demanded. Everyone looked back at the café again. There was nothing of significance to see, just people in the window looking on with curiosity, a few cell phones out filming.

"They're gone," a middle-aged, uniformed cop confirmed.

Mike and Sasha ran behind the café, both in a full sprint. Mike was in front with Sasha only a couple feet behind. They ran through a maze of parked trailers. Mike chanced a look back: nobody was chasing them yet. They cleared a hedge and ran through another small gravel parking lot to a small dock.

Sasha was still right behind Mike. They saw a shirtless man about their age on a red and white cigarette boat. He was tall, very muscular, and had tattoos covering his entire back, up onto his neck. Without a word, Mike jumped on.

"What the fuck?" the man asked.

"I got five grand! Cash. It's yours. Go now. Vancouver." Mike said, helping Sasha on board.

The owner didn't say a word; he chanced a quick peek back towards shore and saw a plume of black smoke. He figured they had something to do with it. He hit the ignition and started towards open water. Mike and Sasha ducked into the small sleeping compartment, out of sight. The man cut hard starboard, putting along slowly until he hit open water, where he opened the throttle.

Fifteen minutes later, he kicked the small door twice. "We're clear."

Mike came out and thanked him before handing the man a stack of mostly $50s and $20s.

"Saw a couple cops at the entrance to the dock right before I hit open water. They didn't really look at us. More like they were trying to figure out what happened," he said. Mike nodded in reply. The guy added without making eye contact, "I know a place in White Rock. I'll drop you there."

"Appreciate it," Mike said and ducked back through the small door.

Angela and Rick stepped out of a tree line where their truck was parked on Neptune Road, west of the woods that butted up to the Swartz Bay ferry depot. They quickly tossed two military-issued C15A2, .50 cal sniper rifles in the back seat. Rick had fired the first shot, puncturing the gas tank of an unmarked police car. A half second later Angela fired the second, an incendiary round. The spark caused the unmarked police car's gas tank to explode, giving Mike and Sasha the distraction they needed.

Driving away, they pulled off their camouflage balaclavas.

"Right, love. We're good now?" Rick asked.

Angela had come home that morning after coffee with Mike and explained that she was going to be watching

HUNTING PREDATORS

his back until he got off the island. It didn't take a lot for Rick to offer his services. They agreed this would be the only time Angela would help Mike escape.

In her mind, this act would make amends for her leaving him behind in their youth. When Mike left the coffee shop the morning before, he'd asked Angela to watch his back. He'd said it jokingly, but he could tell from the look on her face that she would, and that no amount of arguing with her would change her mind. Now Mike was gone again. She knew that. But at least she was there when he needed her most.

"We're good." She echoed, looking in the mirror, seeing no one following them. She took Rick's hand. "Thank you."

"No, thank you," he replied with his thick accent. "Always wanted to blow up a police car. Now I can cross it off my bucket list."

Angela snorted a laugh and asked, "Hungry?"

Clara Lalonde was being examined by a young, pretty EMT in the back of an open ambulance when Chief Hamil walked up.

"Are you okay?" he asked.

"Yes. I'm fine." Clara answered as the EMT took the blood pressure cuff off.

"Okay, good. So, what the hell happened?" Hamil demanded.

"No idea." Clara admitted. "We had them. They were in the café. When they came out, they were virtually surrounded. I gave them instructions, and the next thing I know, the goddamn car next to me fucking blew up!" she exclaimed, seeming more frustrated than upset. "It just blew up. No warning. I was knocked over. When I got up, they were gone."

"Cameras pick anything up?" Hamil inquired.

"We checked the videos in the café. Our suspects ordered but had their heads down, faces hidden. A cam in the parking lot behind the café caught them running, but once they cleared the lot, they vanished. We checked cameras catching all the boats coming and going. Nothing suspicious. There were four boats that left the inlet. We're looking into them now, but on camera there's jack shit." Lalonde stared ahead, lost in thought.

"Parent wasn't lying then, was he?" Hamil mused, sitting down beside her. "Always a couple moves ahead."

Clara leaned her head on his shoulder. Tears of frustration streamed down her face.

"I don't understand," she lamented. "How did they pull this off?"

"You'll drive yourself crazy asking questions with no answers," Hamill warned. "We were cautioned; we knew this guy planned ahead. You're not a mind reader, Clara; nobody could have anticipated this."

"All that work for nothing," she sighed.

Hamil didn't reply; there was nothing to say. He knew how she felt. There were no words to comfort her. He sat quietly for another couple of minutes and finally spoke.

"Go home, Clara, and get some rest. Check on Harland in the morning and come see me after." He squeezed her hand and got up. He took a few steps, surveying the damage around them, then shook his head and walked away.

Chapter 38

Friday June 9th, 2023, 4:05 pm.

Clara Lalonde walked into Harland Grant's hospital room. Harland was awake and sitting up. His right arm was heavily bandaged and hanging at his side. His left arm was heavily bandaged at the shoulder and in a sling. His face was swollen and bruised; he looked terrible, but for the first time in Clara's memory, he was smiling when he saw her.

"You look happy," she observed, placing a brown bag with a red barn logo in front of him.

"It's the morphine," his mother explained drily. Clara had met her the day before and thought she couldn't have been any more than fourteen or fifteen when she gave birth to Harland. She was in her mid-sixties and looked the same age as her son, if not younger. They shared the same serious tone and expressionless face.

Clara smiled at her and handed her a coffee and another bag.

"Doctors said I'm going home tomorrow," Harland advised. Clara opened the blinds, washed her hands thoroughly, and pulled a chair up beside Harland's bed. She unwrapped his sandwich and helped him eat.

"Anything new?" he asked between bites.

"Not a thing. We went over hours of video. Nothing of use. They figure someone shot the car's gas tank with an incendiary round. Who fired it, we don't know. Gunshots

HUNTING PREDATORS

were masked by the explosion, but a couple of the tactical guys heard at least one shot right before it blew up. A few other guys swear it was two."

She held his sandwich while he took another bite. She continued, "We lost them when they left the parking lot. We looked at the video of the boats leaving; we can't see them on any. Nothing reported stolen. The boats we did see leave the inlet are all accounted for. One guy that was docked there said he saw what looked like a small woman run from the parking lot to the woods on the other side, but he didn't remember the details. He has a record a mile long, though. They could still be on the island laying low."

"Could be," Harland mused.

"So, what's happening with you?" Clara asked. "How long till you get use of at least one arm?"

"I'll lose the sling in about two to three weeks, depending on how it heals. In the meantime, Mom's going to stay with me, and I'll have a nurse coming by four times a day."

Clara looked to his mother. "If you need a break, please call me. You can tag me in," she offered.

"Start tomorrow then?" his mother joked.

Clara's phone rang. She looked at the call I.D. and explained, "It's Robson. Excuse me." She went to the hall and answered.

"Hi, Gale."

"Are you sitting down?" Robson asked.

"No, should I?"

"At 12:38 pm today, Ashley Brock walked into the RCMP barracks in Kelowna." Robson advised.

Clara sat down. "Do I want to hear the rest?"

"She said a large man and a short woman burst into her motel room, clobbered her pimp and his friends, and dropped her off down the road from the barracks." Robson seemed almost excited.

"Same couple?"

"One hundred percent. Ask me how I know. Go on, ask." Robson urged.

"Gee, Gale, how can we be so sure?" Clara asked with an exaggerated tone.

"Because the RCMP and Kelowna Police checked out the motel. The pimps, Chris Legge, Sandra Thompkins, and Marcel Landry, were all found in the room. Dead. Landry had his throat cut ear to ear; Legge and Thompkins were both beaten to death. When questioned, Ashley almost completely clammed up. Says she can't remember any details and that she was taken outside when the beating started. She was dropped off with a message, though."

"Message?" Clara prodded.

"Yeah, a message. For Harland Grant." Gale seemed almost giddy. "The message is: 'Sorry things went down how they did. For what it's worth, you're the toughest man I ever fought.' Can you fucking believe that? Gale shouted.

Clara lowered the phone. Her face was half smiling. "Nothing surprises me anymore. Anything else?"

"Nope. But we know they're off the island. From Kelowna, they could be anywhere by now. Lord knows they didn't stick around."

"How's Tyson?" Clara inquired.

"Getting better. He's been put in touch with a trauma counselor. Gale answered. "When I told him what happened to Harland, he was obviously concerned, but I think in a weird way it helped him come to terms with what happened. Tyson has a great deal of respect for Harland."

"Kinda like getting knocked out of the playoffs in the first round by the team that goes on to win the championship?" Clara suggested.

Gale barked out a laugh, then composed herself. "That's one way of putting it." She paused. "How is Harland?"

"He's got a long recovery ahead of him, but I think he'll be just fine." Clara added, "I'm at the hospital now; I brought dinner for him and his mother."

"I'll let you get back to it then," Gale cut in. "Chat soon."

Clara rung off. She walked back into the semi-private room. Harland's mom was helping him eat. Clara offered to take over.

"That was Gale. The suspects are off the island," she declared. "Ashley Brock just walked into the RCMP barracks in Kelowna. Her pimps were all killed."

Harland stopped mid-bite.

"That's what they were after," he said, looking at Lalonde. "Or at least who they were after."

Clara held his stare, and he continued.

"This all started with Kevin Marin, when Ashley was abducted. Everyone they clipped was in the same circle. They were trying to get Ashley back."

Clara had to admit, not only did it seem plausible, but it also made a lot of sense. "Steve Parent, he told me to take a closer look at who they were killing. He was adamant that they were targeted hits, and if we looked at the victims, we'd see there was more going on than we realized."

"Son of a bitch," Harland exclaimed softly.

"Ashley's rescuer, he had a message for you." Clara said, feeling an odd mixture of anxiety and nausea telling him.

Harland had a look of skepticism on his face. Clara relayed the message. His face looked angry at first, then softened into a smile. Clara did not understand the male fighter mentality.

She finished feeding Harland, visited for another twenty minutes, and she let herself out.

The following morning, Lalonde sat at her desk in a small cubicle in a busy office. She turned on her computer and waited for it to boot up. Chief Hamil appeared in front of her.

"Morning, Detective. Any news?"

She informed him of the Ashley Brock update and filled him in on Harland's condition, but suspected he was aware of both already.

Chief Hamil listened intently. When she finished, he spoke. "Off the record, Clara, that whole case was a nightmare, start to finish. We put you on it with Harland because if anybody could have cracked it, it would have been the two of you. And you were close too. A couple of times. Don't think we didn't recognize that." He smiled. "There's still an opening for the Detective Sergeant position in Street Crime and Auto Theft. It's yours if you want it. You can put your own team together."

Without needing to think about it, Clara replied, "Thank you, sir, but I'm right where I need to be." She smiled. He nodded in understanding and started back for his office.

"Lalonde, you busy?" another man's voice called over.

"What do you need?" she answered.

"You're up. Seventeen-year-old S.A. victim at Victoria General. The man advised, handing her a report with the information. Clara had just caught her next case.

Epilogue

Saturday July 8th, 2023, 6:30 pm, Saddle Lake, Alberta

Saddle Lake was a small native community of about four thousand people, two hours northeast of Edmonton, Alberta. There wasn't a lot to do there. It was rural. And quiet.

The temperature earlier in the day had reached the low 30s, humidity was low, but the sunlight was blistering. By 6:30 pm it had dropped to 25 degrees Celsius; still hot, but manageable. Lizzy Green had been making progress reassimilating since her abduction.

She had detoxed; that was hard. She had also been put in touch with a counsellor that specialized in sexual assault victims. They met in person once a week in Edmonton and had virtual meetings two to three times a week, depending on Lizzy. She was starting to understand that what happened to her wasn't her fault. She had been taken advantage of by people who specialize in taking advantage of young, impressionable girls. Predators like them sought out young girls like Lizzy, girls from broken homes and rural areas where boredom set in and the allure of big city excitement made them easy to manipulate.

Lizzy had a virtual meeting that afternoon. She'd stayed in the house most of the day to avoid the heat, but also because she was growing increasingly tired of the stares and whispers when she did go out.

HUNTING PREDATORS

She had finally stepped outside, but only to sit on the front porch of her grandmother's small house. She watched as a large silver camper van drove by slowly, then stopped. Having been recently diagnosed with PTSD, her anxiety skyrocketed. She tried to calm herself down, but when the taillights lit up and the van stopped, she started to panic.

"Grandma?" she called over her shoulder. The passenger door of the silver van opened. "Grandma!" Lizzy yelled, fear in her voice.

Lizzy's grandmother and her uncle, a large First Nations man with a history of working on oil rigs and logging camps, rushed to the door.

"What is it?" her grandmother asked, first looking at the van, then the terrified child frozen on the porch.

Lizzy's uncle pushed through, walking fast towards the van.

"What do you want?" he demanded, slowing when he saw a pretty woman in a black tank top with tattoos on both arms and across her chest. A large man walked slowly from the driver's side, palms out, showing he wasn't a threat. The man leaned on the back of the van, keeping his distance.

Her uncle couldn't put his finger on it. He'd never seen these people before. But their descriptions were familiar.

"I'm looking for Lizzy Green." Sasha called out.

"Who are you?" the uncle demanded again.

I'm—" Sasha's sentence was cut short.

"It's okay, Uncle," Lizzy said, walking off the porch. The fear on her face gone, replaced with disbelief.

"Lizzy, who are they?" he asked her gently, a comforting tone in his voice.

Lizzy walked slowly towards Sasha, not believing what she was seeing at first. She picked up her speed, eventually running into Sasha's arms. Her grandmother stepped off the porch and joined the uncle, the two of them looking at Mike. Mike didn't move. He knew he was big and intimidating. He was trying to remain as non-threatening as possible.

Lizzy could be heard sobbing. Sasha said nothing, just hugged her until she was ready. After what felt like an eternity, Lizzy let go. She looked back at her grandmother and her uncle. Big tears rolled down her face. She took another few seconds to compose herself and finally spoke.

"These are the people that saved me."

Her grandmother walked to Sasha. Mike finally stepped away from the van to join her. He was met by the uncle, who hugged him. The grandmother hugged Sasha, then focused on Mike.

"I thought I'd never see you again." Lizzy exclaimed, wiping away tears.

Sasha smiled her big, beautiful smile. "I told you when things calmed down, I'd find you."

"Please, come inside." The grandmother insisted.

"We really can't stay." Mike said calmly, "We just wanted to make sure Lizzy was home safe."

HUNTING PREDATORS

The uncle leaned in close to Mike. "I know why you can't stay," The massacres on Vancouver Island had made national headlines. "But you're safe here. Please. Come inside."

Mike nodded, and they entered the house. The grandmother wanted to call the rest of the family and have a short notice party. Mike politely explained to the uncle why that wasn't a great idea. The uncle agreed.

Sasha sat at the table. It was difficult, but she told Lizzy her story, what she had gone through. Lizzy listened intently. Sasha explained how she had lived through similar horrors but managed to fight her way back.

Mike's phone rang. He saw *Claude* on the caller ID and let it ring.

The phone rang again. He ignored it a second time. This time a voicemail was left.

Sasha spoke to Lizzy for a few more minutes before it was time for Mike and Sasha to go. Lizzy hugged her at the door. Mike heard Sasha say.

"You have a second chance, Lizzy. Do something great with yourself." Lizzy promised she would. Lizzy looked at Mike, hesitant. Although she was grateful, she still kept her distance from Mike; her only interaction with him had been watching him beat and stomp her pimps. Even though it saved her, the ferocity she had witnessed still terrified her.

Lizzy's uncle walked Mike and Sasha back to the van. He thanked them again.

"We were never here. I know there's a bounty on us right now. So, the fewer that know, the better." Mike requested calmly.

"You're safe with us," the uncle promised. "We're so grateful for what you did for our family. Travel safe." They shook hands, and Mike jumped in the van.

"You good?" he asked Sasha.

She was staring at Lizzy, who was standing on the porch. Lizzy's grandmother stood behind her with her arms wrapped around the young girl.

"Yeah. Yeah, I'm good. She turned and faced Mike. "It's okay that I don't regret any of it, isn't it?" She paused. "The killing. I'd do it all over again if given the choice."

"I don't know if it's okay, but I'm on the same page." Mike admitted, starting the van. "Maybe we're both broken," he shrugged.

He pulled away from the side of the road when his phone rang for a third time. Claude again.

"Hey, ole timer." Mike said into the speakerphone.

"Mike, honey? It's Tammy." Mike took his foot off the gas, and the van coasted to a stop on the shoulder.

"What happened?" Mike asked calmly.

"Claude suffered a heart attack sometime last night," Tammy explained with sadness in her voice. "Chris found him this evening." Mike stared straight ahead. "I'm so sorry, Mike, but it was too late. Claude's gone."

Mike continued to sit silently, staring ahead. Finally, he spoke. "I'm in Alberta right now. I'll be back in a couple of days."

"Okay, hon. I'll let Chris know." She was quiet for a few seconds, then added. "I'm sorry."

Mike thanked her and rung off. Claude was the closest thing to family that Mike had left, and now he was gone.

Sasha was quiet. Looking at Mike, she put her hand on his shoulder. "Want me to drive?"

After a few seconds, he cleared his throat and replied, "No, no, I'm alright."

"Okay, babe." Her hand dropped a little, and she squeezed his arm. "C'mon. Let's go home."

Mike pulled the van back onto the road. They were driving again.

AUTHORS NOTES

When I sat down to write this second novel in the series, my intention was clear: to draw attention to what I, and many others, see as a grave injustice toward the Indigenous communities across Canada. The crisis of Missing and Murdered Indigenous Women (MMIW) has been grossly ignored and swept under the rug for far too long.

This novel touches on that crisis, particularly in one scene where a character questions; *"How long would they look for a missing native girl, he rationalized? A couple of days tops, then something else would happen and he'd be fine"* Let me be unequivocal: this sentiment does not reflect my personal beliefs. Rather, it is intended to expose the lack of urgency and involvement many Indigenous families face when searching for a missing loved one.

In Western Canada, there is a highway known as the Highway of Tears, named for the devastating number of Indigenous women who have gone missing or been murdered along its stretch. Being a Caucasian man myself, I cannot help but recognize the disparity: if it were a single *"pretty white girl"* who went missing, the RCMP would likely move heaven and earth to find her. Yet, the collective response to closer to 1,800 missing Indigenous women, who are six times more likely to be victims of murder in Canada has been appalling, and this inaction should disgust and enrage every Canadian.

In this story, I also delve into Sasha's backstory, shedding light on the dark reality of human trafficking. During my research, I read accounts from 16 survivors, and the similarities in their stories were both striking and harrowing. Writing this chapter was one of the most difficult tasks I've ever undertaken. It may be triggering, upsetting, and even terrible for some readers to experience. But it is a reality for many. I faced the challenge of keeping this section authentic and unflinching without crossing into exploitation or sensationalism. My goal was to honor the victims and portray their stories with the gravity they deserve, without sugarcoating the horrors they endured.

Some of the language and violence in this novel is unpleasant. That is intentional. These atrocities are horrific. But they are real. During the drafting process, I engaged in numerous discussions with beta readers, my agent, and my editor. Some hinted, while others outright suggested, that I tone down certain parts or make them less shocking. However, I felt strongly that these truths needed to be portrayed as realistically as possible to do justice to the victims and their experiences.

The people and events in this story are fictional. Any similarities are entirely coincidental. However, the themes and scenarios draw heavily on real-life examples and, in some instances, on my own experiences. My aim is not to write the feel-good story of the year. I wanted to write something that will stay with readers long after they have finished, and something that acknowledges or informs readers of what is really going on out there. I wanted to craft something raw and honest that shines a light on the darkest corners of our world. These horrors happen every day, right here in Canada.

If even one person reading this book takes action—whether by contacting their local MP or MPP, or by demanding that the RCMP, provincial, and local law enforcement agencies take the disappearances of Indigenous women and the scourge of human trafficking more seriously—then I will have accomplished what I set out to do.

Thank you for taking this journey with me.

Manufactured by Amazon.ca
Bolton, ON

43781310R00221